Altered State 1
The Berlin Principle

J. G. Jenkinson

PRESS

Copyright © J. G. Jenkinson 2022

Published by Vulpine Press in the United Kingdom in 2022

ISBN: 978-1-83919-478-8

www.vulpine-press.com

The Berlin Principle

For my daughters, your potential knows no bounds, and for every kid who failed English but loved to read.

Prologue - Berlin, 1945

She was not dead, but right now, that was all she knew. The searing pain in her chest masked all other senses.

Even the orchestra of bombs, bombers, sirens, and screams were little more than a faint echo, to the point that she could have dismissed it as her imagination. One thought did penetrate, however. It wasn't clear at first, but it grew; a blurred mental image of two people, two children, *her* children, Carla, and Rudi, but where were they?

She screwed her eyes up against the pain, desperate to clear her mind and think. Little Rudi, her bright, intelligent boy was on duty with the Hitler Youth and Carla, sweet, uncomplaining Carla, was at Zoo Tower.

She pictured them both now, Rudi in his new *Feldgrau* uniform, complete with coal scuttle helmet. He was far too young at twelve to be fighting for the Fatherland, but being the product of years of indoctrination, he would die happily for his Führer, and she couldn't help but feel at least partly responsible for that. She imagined Carla in her *Luftwaffe* uniform, black with soot from a night on the anti-aircraft guns, still smiling from under her over-sized helmet, her face drawn with hunger, like all Berliners.

Emma was alone in their Prenzlauer Berg apartment, sleeping off a double shift when the Allied bomb had scored a direct hit and removed one side of the building, leaving her exposed to the elements on the fourth floor, with hot shrapnel sending waves of intense pain outwards from her chest.

Without their mother, Rudi and Carla fended for themselves in the open-sided apartment for days while Emma recovered in hospital, eating the rations that they both brought home after their shifts on the guns each night. Huddled together around an oil lamp in the only room that still had four walls, they consoled themselves with the old saying about lightning and its propensity to leave alone those it had already harmed.

On the third day, Rudi rode his bicycle to K Battery of the *HJ-Abteilung* "Herbert Norkus", the patch of waste ground that had once been home to three four-inch Howitzers, was now a crater. He stared at the rubble-filled hole, the guns lying on their sides damaged beyond repair, and he had not known what to do. Desperate to contribute to the defence of Berlin and half drowning in his oversized uniform, he cycled through the streets in search of a way to avoid accusations of idleness or worse, desertion. The sound of distant artillery fire that had become commonplace in Berlin seemed to be louder today and every so often when Rudi would hear the rattle of gunfire or the sound of a building collapsing, he had to remind himself to be brave. He caught a glimpse of his reflection in a shop window; he wore the uniform of a soldier, and he must act like one.

As Rudi rounded the corner of Bergmann and Heim, he found bodies swinging from lampposts, swaying gently in the breeze, signs hanging from the neck of each man which read: "I deserted my post, and I paid the price."

Two soldiers stood talking with an officer in the crumpled uniform of an *oberleutnant* of the *Wehrmacht*. They were questioning a man in a dark suit. Rudi tried to cycle past, but the man caught his eye, causing the oberleutnant to turn.

"You," the officer said, "come here, *Junge*." He used a riding crop to beckon Rudi.

"Where are you going, little *Rottenführer*," he asked, using Rudi's Hitler Youth rank.

"When I reported for duty this morning, Herr Oberleutnant, my gun battery was gone, destroyed by a bomb or a shell," he said nervously. "I am looking for another unit to join."

Canvas-topped trucks rumbled past, the men in the back looking gaunt and anxious, some barely older than Rudi.

"You can join us, *Junge*," one of the soldiers said, smiling grotesquely and jerking his head towards the bodies swaying in the wind.

"What is your name?" The oberleutnant seemed kind in that moment, like he genuinely wanted to know him.

"Rudi. Rudolph Kessler," he said eagerly.

"And where's your rifle?" the oberleutnant asked, still kindly, almost paternally.

"There weren't enough, Herr Oberleutnant, and they said that because my job is to load the shells into the gun, I don't need one."

"Well, I'll tell you what, little *Rottenführer*, we've run out of rope," and he turned to smile at his men.

"I will fetch you rope, Herr Oberleutnant," Rudi said eagerly.

"No, no, I have a far more expedient plan. See that rifle?" He pointed with his riding crop at a weather-beaten *Gewehr* leaning against the wall. "Go and get it."

Rudi carefully laid his bike down and ran over to the weapon. He had coveted one of these for as long as he could remember, and now he held one in his hands.

"Do you want it?" the oberleutnant asked.

Rudi nodded apprehensively.

"This man is a deserter." He pointed at the dark-suited man. "He left his post and tried to run away from defending the Fatherland. You know happens to deserters, don't you, *Junge*?"

Rudi nodded again.

"My men are tired, it's been a long war, and if you help us out by shooting this man, I'll let you keep the rifle."

A wave of anxiety washed over Rudi; suddenly the rifle felt heavy, his uniform felt far too big. A burning sensation that began at his neck spread to his ears until he could hear his pulse throbbing.

But this was his chance. If he had a gun, he could fight the Russians when they came, and he would be able to help defend the Fatherland. To protect his mother and sister. This man would die anyway, he reassured himself, and he deserved it because he was a coward and a traitor. He looked at the oberleutnant for a moment while he drew himself up, filling his lungs and setting his jaw.

"Okay," he said with far more confidence than he felt and stepped forward, straining to remember his training. He forced the butt into his shoulder, losing his balance slightly, and drew

4

back the bolt. A spent casing spun out and landed on the cobbles, but he could see that there were four more rounds, so he awkwardly pushed forward the bolt, chambering another.

"Stand back, boys, this one is a steely-eyed killer," one of the soldiers called, laughing at his own joke.

When Rudi looked up, they had blindfolded the man. He was old, maybe fifty and overweight. What was more, it was obvious he had been sleeping rough by the state of his clothes, and his face bore the marks of a recent beating. The oberleutnant called him to attention.

"In the name of the Führer and of the Reich!" He sounded bored, like he had said these words so many times in the last six years, they had lost all meaning to him. "You have been found guilty of deserting your post. Rolf Schilling, you are hereby sentenced to death by firing squad, may Gott have mercy on your soul."

"Detail!" He paused, still sounding distracted, "take aim… *Fire!*"

The rifle danced around in Rudi's trembling hands, and all he could focus on was the condemned man's quivering lip, as he willed himself to calm down, trying to breathe deeply.

Just do it, the man will be shot the second you cycle around the corner anyway, you're not saving him by not doing it. Rudi, you are just making yourself look weak, just do it.

He closed both eyes tight and snatched at the trigger. Opening them to see that he had missed. The sound of mirthless laughter reached his ears, as the men mocked the ability of a child to commit murder.

He was angry now, his adrenaline pumping as fear became embarrassment, so he fired again, and a third time, but still he missed. He forced himself to concentrate, to control his breathing and to relax before this time squeezing the trigger. There was no familiar sound of the bullet on brick, more of a wet *thwomp*. Rudi watched in horror as a patch of red spread across the man's white shirted stomach before he slumped to the ground. The oberleutnant held his Luger by the muzzle and offered it to Rudi.

"You want to finish him off?"

Rudi shook his head and turned away to hide his tears, putting the rifle down and wiping his eyes on his sleeve as the pistol's report echoed around the square.

"Listen, little *Rottenführer*, I know I said you could have the rifle but you're a terrible shot and it would be irresponsible of me to give it to you, you might kill more Germans than Russians."

The group all burst out laughing again, and Rudi picked up his bicycle to flee the scene with hot tears streaming down his face.

Several days passed and Rudi buried the incident deep down in a seldom used part of his mind, refusing to acknowledge that it had even happened, but he never shook the image of that man's quivering lip.

Rolf Schilling. The man's name haunted him.

When Emma Kessler was finally discharged from hospital and discovered that her children had been living in the ruin of their old apartment, she was horrified, blaming the block warden, the hospital, the police and their *Gauleiter*. She decided that they should leave immediately for her sister's place in Aldershof.

Unfortunately, as they set out for the only place of safety and comfort Emma knew in the world, the Red Army finally broke through 'into the lair of the fascist beast,' and Ivan was encouraged to show his anger. Posters from the Soviet propagandists urged, "Soldier: You are now on German soil. The hour of revenge has struck!"

Emma concluded that quiet side streets would offer a greater chance of avoiding the fighting, but the nature of side streets meant that, at some point, one had to cross a main thoroughfare. The three of them pushed their hand cart, laden with what little they owned eastwards through Berlin.

As the familiar whistle grew ominously louder, mother and children ran for cover. The shell landed, the cart was overturned, and Rudi went with it to be thrown several feet through the air.

He woke up on the ground, covered in rubble and other detritus, unsure of how he had come to be there. He lay still, blinking the dust from his eyes and trying to take in his surroundings. They had turned on to Sonnenallee in order to cross the Neukölln Ship Canal, which was all he could remember, but where were his mother and sister? He turned his head, causing the dust and rubble to shift – to blind him again – and when he opened his eyes, he realised blood from a cut above his eye was making the dust stick to his skin.

In the street he saw a large group of Russian soldiers standing in a circle. They were watching something on the ground, cheering encouragement and jostling for position. The men were filthy, unshaven, and barely in uniform; most had only one or two items of clothing that marked them out as Red Army men.

Rudi could tell that they were not of this place, that they were different to him. A kind of beast, a rougher, harder being, forged in the frozen hell of the Ost front, half-starved and barely human.

Sickening realisation struck Rudi as he watched his sister's bear, 'Kuschelbär', fly through the air and land on the ground a metre or so from where he lay. Without thinking, Rudi scrambled from his hiding place to run screaming towards the crowd. A quick-thinking Yefreytor, who had turned away from the entertainment to light up a cigarette, casually levelled the butt of his rifle, so that Rudi ran straight into it, the weapon knocking him out a second time and breaking his nose. The young soldier turned back to the crowd, unaware that he had just saved the boy's life.

It was dark when he woke again to find his mother and sister sitting in the road sobbing and holding one another, as a solitary Russian soldier stood over them fumbling with his trousers and slurred something in his native language.

Carla had Kuschelbär back in her arms and was clutching him tightly as she wept. Rudi had been dragged to the side of the road and left for dead. He fingered his father's iron ring and found that it was gone. He stood, slowly drawing his Hitler

Youth knife as he read the inscription: *Blut und Ehre*; Blood and Honour. He looked at the women in his protection and knew what he must do.

Rudi had failed them. If only he still had the rifle, if only he was not such a coward...

He could not know that their story was far from unique, that when this dark period in German history was over, Russian soldiers would have raped over two million women and girls.

He walked up calmly and quietly behind the stumbling soldier, encountering no moral dilemma this time because this man *had* to die. Holding the eight-inch knife at his side, Rudi thrust it hard and fast into the rapist's kidneys, withdrawing it with difficulty and losing his balance as he fought against the suction. He recovered quickly, and as Iván turned, he pushed the blade in again, up below the ribs and into the heart.

Rudi did not cry out, nor did he feel any particularly strong emotion as the unwashed creature looked into his eyes and put his hands on Rudi's shoulders, coughing blood into his face before finally collapsing.

The smell of blood mingled with that of the unwashed soldier and the vodka on his breath, the piercing eyes and the gaunt face, the grotesque gurgling as blood from his lungs began to froth at his mouth, every image from this experience would haunt his dreams for the rest of his life. Rudi wiped the blade on the soldier's sleeve and turned his attention to his mother and sister.

He silently helped them onto the handcart with what possessions they could find. Tears of shame ran down his face, mixing with the blood of his victim, as he tried to process what had happened, beginning a cycle of lifelong self-torture, wondering what he might have done differently.

Die Zukunft, London, 2034

The future

Olga awoke to the sound of the coffee grinder and the smell of fresh arabica. She stretched and yawned as she swung her feet to the floor, sitting upright on the edge of her bed. She looked about the room at her familiar surroundings, her lovely things, and the safety they represented, the pile carpet luxurious on her bare feet.

She stepped into the bathroom and inspected her face in the mirror. People told her that she had the look of a classic beauty, but all she saw was a tall girl with a band of freckles that ran across a broad nose and a wide smile that revealed a mouth crowded with chunky white teeth. When she had washed and plaited her blonde hair, the clock showed that it was nearly six, so she headed downstairs dressed in a simple brown dirndl–The dress was the uniform of a senior guide in the Germanic Maidens League. In the kitchen she would help her mother prepare breakfast and a midday plate for her father and brothers.

Olga found her mother dressed for the day in her dirndl, fully made up and standing over a menagerie of pots and pans that before long would be five laden breakfast plates and three hearty lunches. Nadine Felsen was a sturdy yet feminine woman with broad shoulders, broad hips, and pleasing features. She was always impeccably dressed, her hair in its flawless crown plait and her makeup were never out of place.

11

Olga began her own duties; it would be an hour before her father and brothers came down to eat before work. She swept and mopped all the floors downstairs and dusted the reception rooms of their suburban home. She collected eggs from their chickens and sorted through the recycling. Other families with more prominent positions in society had the use of *Ostarbeiter* or "workers from the east" who came from the Slavic states, and Olga's father often mentioned that with his next promotion at the ministry, he would be entitled to one, and Nadine would be able to put her feet up.

Olga collected their copy of Graf von Rothermere's *Daily Mail* from the doorstep and placed it on the kitchen table just as her father walked in. Franck Felsen was a huge man of forty-three, athletic and handsome but for a livid scar that ran from his left eye to the corner of his mouth; the result of shrapnel in a war he had fought in before Olga was born.

He moved around the kitchen with the grace of a much smaller and younger man, and as he reached the stove, Nadine turned from her work to receive her routine morning kiss. He placed his hand on the small of her back and drew her to him as he kissed her passionately on the mouth, smearing her lipstick and causing her to make the same feminine noise of delighted surprise she had made every morning for the last twenty-two years.

As they drew apart, she straightened the collar of his grey uniform tunic and centred the Knights Cross of the Iron Cross with oak leaves that hung around his neck; the reward for the scar.

Shortly after this much-repeated scene, Paul and Theo came bounding into the kitchen. Although almost as large as their father, his sons were clumsy and graceless, like a pair of adolescent hounds, too loud, and only polite when they thought they were being watched.

As the sons of a warrant officer about to commission after twenty-five years of distinguished service, they had both received the finest education courtesy of the state, and were now completing the four-year degree program at the Imperial Military Academy at Sandhurst.

They wore tracksuits today as they were on leave, and there was a stark contrast between their modern clothing and the décor of the kitchen, a room which, apart from the surveillance cameras, the smart fridge and the chrome-finished tap that dispensed hot water for tea and a range of cold drinks, looked much the same as it would have in the 1920s.

The same could have been said of Olga's parents, had her father not been holding a newspaper depicting a *Reichskriegsflagge* flying from a pole on the surface of the moon and wearing a smartwatch that peeked out from under the cuff of his tunic. Nadine was now planning today's grocery delivery on the smart fridge's touch-screen interface, her nails impeccably manicured, though short, and practical.

Olga's eyes fell on a perfectly rectangular patch of slightly darker wallpaper beside the huge modern appliance, where once had hung a framed embroidery protecting the wall behind it from the sun. She had brought it home with her on the final day of maidens education and deportment school, where she had learned to be the ideal housewife and mother. She had also

13

learned German as it was the language of the ruling class. It was at school that she was shown the dangers of feminism and of the over-education of women, the wickedness of lust and the importance of her role in populating the Reich.

She was twelve when she presented the gift to her mother and father. It showed an elongated Cross pattée in blue and white with a gold border. The cross rested on a golden starburst and in the centre was a painstakingly stitched imperial eagle surrounded by the words *Kinder, Küche, Kirche*, or "children, kitchen, church." Some joked, in the privacy of their own home and with the radio turned up, that certain women, namely the idle wives of high-ranking officials, enjoyed an altogether different meaning to the three Ks, *Kaffee, Kuchen, Kolben*, or "coffee, cake, cock." But the likes of Olga would be horrified to hear such talk after the piety of the schoolroom.

The cross in Olga's embroidery was the Cross of Honour of the Germanic Mother, presented to Germanic women of good standing who had borne four or more children for the Reich. Olga had been sworn to secrecy by her teacher during the weeks leading up to her graduation and, along with six or seven other girls had been allowed to complete her work away from the rest of the class to be sure of the surprise.

One of the girls had been moved back into the main group and forced to start again on an embroidery without the cross when her mother had been branded a promiscuous whore, after she was found in flagrante with her husband's driver. Later, after a trial, the wretched woman had been deemed unfit for motherhood and sent to work for a wealthy family in sub-Saharan Africa, now known as German South Afrika, much like the *Ostarbeiter* she had enjoyed in her own home.

The light patch on the wall reminded Olga of Klaus, her younger brother, who had died after a lengthy battle with leukaemia. Shortly after his death, Nadine received a letter from the ministry of moral affairs which informed Nadine that she was under formal investigation for failing to care for her child, and should expect further communication regarding this most serious of matters.

Children had become the most precious commodity the Greater Reich possessed since the 1970s when mass infertility became the globe's number one problem. The irony that the Reich had spent most of the fifties and sixties sterilising the lesser races or *die geringen Rassen,* was lost on the stuffed shirts in Berlin. The population of the Great British Reich was just twenty million, in Europe it was two hundred and fifty million and the global population was less than two billion.

The whole community turned out for Klaus' funeral, a sea of black apparel and drab uniforms contrasting against gleaming medals, pale faces and glistening eyes. The mourner's collective breath formed a cloud of mist that hung above them in the cold February air. The ceremony stood out in Olga's memory as one of the most traumatic days in her young life. They sang dirge-like hymns, drowning out the sobbing of those in attendance. Nadine read Matthew chapter 18 verses 1-5 and 10-14. When she had finished, the pastor said the committal while the family threw handfuls of earth onto Klaus' casket.

As the congregation began to leave, a well-dressed man from the ministry approached Nadine as she stood over the open grave of her son and explained that she was no longer eligible to wear her Cross of Honour of the Germanic Mother. He pulled the cross from her neck, breaking the clasp, and tossed it into the tiny grave where it hit the casket with a sound like thunder in the still winter morning. Franck was held by three comrades as the man smiled at the scene.

"So desperate to be seen as Germanic, so eager to please your betters," he sneered in an educated Berlin accent. "Perhaps if you are good little subjects and make another baby for the Kaiser, we may return this honour to you one day."

Nadine stood rooted to the spot as tears ran silently down her cheeks, her eyes following the man to his chauffeur-driven Mercedes. The design had not changed much since the 1940s and the beautiful black and chrome machine seemed to glide silently from the cemetery, tyres on gravel the only sound above the muted hum of the electric motor. A church bell tolled, and Olga snapped out of her reverie.

Nadine never got over the shame it brought upon the family, but she pushed it all down, continuing to play her role for Franck and her remaining children. Sometimes, when Nadine thought that she was alone she would take out a box of memories and cry silently for the loss of her youngest child.

After breakfast when Franck rose to leave, the rest of the family stood in deference and he kissed his wife and daughter goodbye, clapping both young men on the back. Olga was now eighteen and soon she would be required to complete her one-year service to another household. These households generally had many children and required girls with suitable values to help raise them. She hoped for a family of girls, as the memory of her little brother came back painfully whenever she saw a boy of about his age.

After this she would be expected to join the Faith and Beauty Society while she looked for a husband of similar social standing, and this was a source of anxiety for her because, with her father's impending promotion to captain, the whole family's social status would be raised. When she was born, her father had been a mere Corporal, but by the time she would marry he could be a Major. The daughters of officers had completed a far more sophisticated course of education and were versed in literature and music, capable of polite conversation in German while her own grasp of that language was rudimentary at best, they would also know how to conduct themselves at social gatherings.

Franck received his commission in time to wear his new sword at Theo's commissioning parade. Paul still had a year until his course was completed and the whole family looked splendid; Olga and Nadine in beautifully cut dresses while the three men in their tailored uniforms and Sam Browne belts cut a marvellous figure. The photo taken that day was hung over the stain on the kitchen wall. Olga noticed that when her mother was watching the parade, her hand went subconsciously to her neck, where her medal certainly would have hung on such an auspicious day.

A solution was found to Olga's anxieties through a near-perfect domestic placement; the family were all girls and the eldest agreed to help Olga learn to meet the demands of her new position in society. The patriarch was something important in the Reich security services Communication Headquarters in Gloucestershire, and the family had a picturesque country house in the Cotswolds.

Olga took the train from Paddington to Bristol. Her father, who now had his own chauffeur-driven Mercedes – a slightly less imposing model in military grey and built at the Dagenham plant – had walked her to the Trans rapid mag-train terminal. He placed a hand on each of her shoulders; she was as tall as her brothers – nearly as tall as he was, and athletic too.

"Let me look at you," he said, tears threatening to escape his eyes. "You are a young woman now and I couldn't be prouder. Make the most of this opportunity, learn all you can about our new world, and remember," here he lent his eye a cautionary aspect, "Josef Altstötter is a powerful man. His opinion matters, and my masters listen to him, so please bear that in mind before you act or speak in a way that might be regrettable."

Then his face lost all severity and he smiled fondly at his only daughter. "But most of all, remember that your mother and I love you." He pulled her close for a bone-crushing hug and whispered, "Learn German," in her ear before releasing her, kissing her on the cheek.

Olga smiled her wide, overcrowded smile and placed a hand gently on her father's face.

"I love you too, Dad," she said quietly.

Franck followed her onto the train with her small bag and placed it in the rack for her.

"Goodbye then, Schatzi," Franck said as he turned to leave, looking ridiculous in his outdated grey uniform beside the ultramodern train. This man had been a constant in her short life, steadfast and kind, but now everything she knew, everything in which she found comfort, seemed to have been left on the platform with him.

The panoramic roof provided natural light and made the already spacious compartment feel even more so. The seats reminded Olga of a dentist chair and she was disappointed to find that they did not in fact recline. But this train was specially designed for the one-hundred-and-seventy-kilometre journey to Bristol, so passengers would have no need to recline during the twenty-five minute journey.

"Did you know," announced a man with the nasal accent of the *Ostentor*; the new name for east London. "That this train will reach speeds of six hundred kilometres an hour? London to Edinburgh in less time than it takes to cross the Channel bridge! Hell, London to Berlin in one and a half hours!" then he murmured something inaudible about Berlin.

Olga smiled politely, but she rarely spoke with men outside of her family and this one made her uncomfortable. She glanced up to pair the irritating voice to a fussy looking man with fingers of wet black hair scraped across his bald pate.

"Well?" he demanded. "Are you mute, girl?"

"No, mein Herr," she answered meekly as she stared at the floor of the cabin.

"*Mein Herr*, is it?" the man said haughtily. "You won't catch me bowing and scraping like that, they know that I'm far too important to be bothering with any of that *Yar mein Herr, nein mein Herr, three bags full* mein Herr!" The man uncrossed his legs and recrossed them the other way as he turned towards the window and away from Olga as a chime sounded from the speakers.

"The service to Bristol Temple Meads will leave now. *Der Service nach Bristol Temple Meads wird jetzt abfahren*," came over the announcer.

Olga felt a gentle but increasing pressure to lean back into her seat as the train picked up speed. The only sound apart from a barely audible electric hum was that of the wheels retracting as it left the station sidings and gained further speed. Around Slough, the train entered the vacuum tube and increased its speed to six hundred kilometres per hour, but Olga felt little more than a curious sense of weightlessness. Fifteen minutes later, the train emerged into the sunlit suburbs of Bristol where the air resistance outside the vacuum slowed the train to three hundred kilometres per hour.

The impressive gothic structure of Brunel's Temple Meads railway station reminded Olga of the older parts of Paddington, as well they should, since Isambard Kingdom Brunel built them both. His long obsolete tracks had been melted down and turned into tanks in the 1960s and blown up in Afghanistan in the 1970s.

Locomotives were on display throughout the concourse, turning the whole station into some kind of shrine to Brunel and to engineering as a sort of artform. Olga might have acknowledged this concept when she saw Brunel's statue, but she knew nothing of science, history, or engineering, because how was that relevant to motherhood or housekeeping?

Fortunately, her ignorance did not stop her from soaking up the atmosphere and appreciating the magnificence of both the old and the new technology around her.

Olga boarded a similar, slightly more crowded, and considerably slower regional service, and in fact, the sixty-kilometre journey to Cheltenham took about the same time as her first leg from London. As she took her seat, she looked out of the window and saw the nasal man from her compartment being frog-marched off the concourse by uniformed SB men.

The brilliant white train pulled away from the station and followed the river Avon to the harbour, where Olga saw gargantuan, multicoloured container ships with their enormous, wing-like sails casting long shadows across the water. The stevedores and crane operators worked tirelessly to unload and reload before the ship missed her tide and was forced to wait hours for the next. A wizened old lady watched Olga as she stared at the behemoth.

"You know, my dear," she said, making a sucking noise to re-seat her teeth, "when I was a little girl, the ships had enormous engines, with funnels that pumped clouds of thick black smoke into the air. The great Magnus von Braun saw the damage that we were doing with our coal and our diesel, and he told us we were killing our beautiful planet. So he petitioned the Kaiser, and we all did our bit to use less plastic, while Magnus the Magnificent led a team of the Reich's best and brightest to find a solution, and you are looking at the two finest examples of their work." The old lady smiled at Olga serenely and continued.

"You show me a verdammt schwarzer or a Jew that could do that, and I'll show you a *schmutzig* liar."

She said this so casually but with the malice and conviction that came from generations of indoctrination.

"Forgive me, Damn, I thought there were no more Schwarzer or Jews?" Olga used the Anglo-German word derived from Madam and Damen, a term of deference to one's elders.

The old woman smiled and patted Olga's hand affectionately.

"Well, my dear, there are none in Europe. The Jews were driven back to Israel where they cannot subvert the good people of the Reich, and the Schwarzer are kept by some of the Americans as Sklavenarbeiter. There are also some in remote areas of Afrika and South America." She smiled again, as though she were giving words of comfort to a scared child.

They chatted banally for the rest of the journey and Olga, who was little more than a child, *was* comforted by the heinous rhetoric of her parents and teachers from the mouth of this sweet old lady and she felt much calmer when she arrived in Cheltenham.

This station was a far more utilitarian affair, modern in design and decor but for the neglected statue of nineteenth century composer, Gustav Holst, another figure from history that Olga's narrow path of education had not deigned to visit.

His orchestral suite, The Planets, was a piece she was probably destined never to hear, because the class of people predisposed to seek out recordings of such music also tended to be the type of toadying sycophant that would only ever play German composers, and Olga's family did not belong to that stratum of society. Indeed, teachers of such music did not dare to expose their pupils to anything else in those kinds of schools.

Oberst Altstötter SB was waiting outside the station for her in a car identical to that of the deplorable government man from Klaus' funeral.

She had not enjoyed riding in her father's car that morning and this even more vivid reminder of that day made her feel like running back to London, to the arms of her father, and to the warmth of the only home she had ever known.

Altstötter was tall like her father, but where her father was large and imposing, Altstötter was sparse, his hair was thinning, and his face was gaunt with a beak-like aquiline nose. As if acknowledging the sunshine, Altstötter wore a lightweight linen suit and a Panama hat. He stubbed out a cigarette as he caught sight of Olga and gave a nonchalant wave from the elbow.

"Olga?" he did not wait for a reply as he took her hand in his, placing his other under her forearm and speaking in the clipped accent of the Prussian aristocracy, but his words still made Olga's skin crawl. "My name is Josef, a name which you may use all the time except when we are hosting official parties. It is a pleasure to meet you." He seemed to take her in for a moment before saying, "My, you *are* exquisite, aren't you?"

Olga blushed. She did not find this man in the least bit attractive, but she saw so few men outside of her family and received even fewer compliments.

He picked up her wheeled bag with ease and placed it in the boot of the car, while she stood staring at the road lest she blush further.

"Come, let's get you to Grunewald," he said with a conspiratorial grin as he opened the car door and helped her in.

Formerly Whitelands, Altstötter had renamed the farm Grunewald after his family's estate in Prussia. The eighteenth-century house overlooked immense limestone uplands bordered by the majestic River Severn to the west and the Sussex Downs to the east. The circular drive stood in the shadow of an ancient oak, its branches reaching out like wizened fingers to touch the yellow sandstone of the house. When Olga and Josef pulled up, a servant appeared to greet them and show Olga inside, while Altstötter removed the car to some other part of the grounds, no doubt where a forlorn looking chauffeur waited for his eccentric employer to return his livelihood to him; dusty and drained of power.

Kaiser Reich – Berlin, 1912

The name given to the German Empire after the unification of Germany in 1871.

It was nearly dark when Ludendorff, feeling clumsy in a plain grey suit and bowler hat, sat in the rundown café on Freisinger Straße. He looked around with contempt at the grubby poets, artists, and writers, all communists no doubt. He knew there would not be one among them who would know his face. Ludendorff's tea had arrived by the time von Falkenhayn joined him looking equally forlorn in a brown suit with a heavy woollen overcoat. His bushy moustaches were waxed into points, and he displayed a full head of hair that stood stiff like a brush on his head.

"What's it all about, Ludendorff?" he asked, after ordering a tea and Schnaps for himself and looking around disapprovingly.

"I…" he paused and cleared his throat, "that is to say… you are to be the next Minister for War."

"Yes, it is fairly certain that is what will happen. Is that why you brought me here, to congratulate me?" Falkenhayn asked genially.

Ludendorff was famed for being devoid of any humour and lived up to his reputation now.

"No, Herr General, I have some very interesting information, but it is from an irregular source, and I cannot share it with von Moltke."

Falkenhayn stiffened. "I cannot be involved in anything *irregular* as you put it, certainly not now."

"It is not like that, Herr General, it is only the source, which I do not have to reveal if you are not willing to trust me?" Ludendorff made this sound like a question as he leaned back in his chair and fixed his interlocutor with a cold stare.

"Now see here, Ludendorff, I do not know you. Of course, I have heard of your work, but we were never comrades." Falkenhayn responded.

"We are brother officers, sworn to the same cause, and I am talking of the future of the Fatherland here."

"Very well, what do you have?" Falkenhayn said, more interested in the lint on one of epaulettes than this junker.

"Documents, Herr General," Ludendorff clarified as he slid a near-empty folder across the table.

Falkenhayn flicked the folder open without picking it up, as if it were something unclean that he didn't want to handle any more than necessary, his face registering a brief change as he looked up at Ludendorff.

"Where did you get this, is it some sort of communist propaganda?"

"As far as I can determine, this is bona fide."

"How can it be?" Falkenhayn hissed in disbelief. "It's dated 1918."

"It seems…" Ludendorff hesitated before continuing and leant back, straightening his arms against the edge of the table, "it seems at some point in the future that they have developed some sort of *Zeittelegraph*." He said the last word, translating as time telegraph, with a slight inflection as if it were another question.

"*Zeittelegraph*?" Falkenhayn nearly choked on his Schnaps.

"Ja, surely, if we can send messages around the world, it is only a matter of time until…" he trailed off and made a vague gesture with his glass.

"Assuming that I decide to humour you, what else do you have that can help us avoid this tragedy?"

This was the moment of greatest danger. Ludendorff had to reveal just enough to entice the influential General without overplaying his hand and losing the potential power it could bring him. He sipped his tea while he weighed up the situation. He had already sorted the material into two categories: documents intended to convince the recipient of the need for action, and tools with which to take the action.

"There are several highly interesting documents," he said as he reached for the file from Falkenhayn and passed him another folder containing an explanation of the MP40 sub-machine gun, with illustrations, rates of fire and production requirements.

"This is an example that you will, I hope, find very interesting."

Falkenhayn, now sitting with one leg crossed over the other, leant forward to take the proffered material. He let the folder fall open onto his lap, his only perceptible reaction a widening of the eyes.

"Is it all like this?" he sighed.

It was Ludendorff's turn to be aloof.

"Some of it is. There are a few more files like that, some about airships, medical advances and so on. Also, there is to be a successful invasion of France about thirty years from now. I have the battle plan for that, and some very interesting doctrinal and tactical literature that would change the very concept of warfare as we know it."

Falkenhayn could see that this fat, humourless loner wanted something, and he was building himself up to ask for it.

"Just tell me what you want," he demanded.

"I simply want your patronage, for you to bring me onto your staff, promote me to General Major and when the war begins, give me the Western Front." Ludendorff sighed inwardly, he had said it, the hardest part was over.

A ghost of a smile appeared on Falkenhayn's face.

"You do not ask for much, Oberst," he said sarcastically, "but these things could be in my gift," he added pensively. "I would need you to turn over everything you have to me, immediately."

Rather than argue with his new patron, Ludendorff had already decided that all the evidential material from category one and a small selection of material from two would be handed over; just enough to give Falkenhayn the kind of power that would grant him want he wanted, and then he would use the rest to surpass him and eventually usurp his position.

"Ja, Herr General," he agreed deferentially. "I will report to you tomorrow, at your office on Bendlerstraβe, with everything."

Falkenhayn knew that this man was no fool, he would keep some gems back, but as long as he had enough to prevent the tragic scenes depicted on those pages, he could wheedle the rest from him later. Besides, he was a capable staff officer with an exemplary record, and Falkenhayn could use such a man.

Both men lay awake that night, listening to their respective Hausfrau's snoring, while their heads spun with the possibilities and improbability of the *Zeittelegraph*. With pictures of the Royal Palace taken over by mutinous sailors and draped with red communist banners. When they did finally find sleep, it was the deep and restful sleep of a man who had a bright future and the means to realise it.

~

Ludendorff sat in a comfortable chair and stared out of the window of his office near to the Bendlerblock, the huge Prussian War Ministry near the Tiergarten. He picked up the file on his desk with its strange paper and foreign-looking typeface, and he fingered the pages until he found the handwritten note at the back of the file.

Of all the treasure that this mysterious package had provided him with, he had given this note the most attention and, since discovering it on Marshall von Moltke's desk, he had shown it only to Falkenhayn during their meeting the previous evening.

The most shocking document by far, however, was the copy of the treaty of Versailles, reinforced by pictures of Herman Müller with the other world leaders as they signed. The demands made upon Germany in this document were egregious and Ludendorff had to force himself to finish reading it. If they complied, the Great German Empire would be reduced to a shell, starving, defenceless and bankrupt.

Initially, Ludendorff had dismissed the whole thing as some sort of disinformation ploy by the British or the Serbs and he had set his own agents to work, carefully infiltrating the various industries where this material could be best used and establishing its legitimacy. The overarching message, Ludendorff surmised, was that marching through Belgium in the first days of the war would bring the British to France, and this meant four million additional enemy troops as well as naval blockades which would lead to the German people starving while they slowly lost a war of attrition.

Ludendorff soon came to realise that the contents of this file in the right hands could make him the most powerful man in the Empire, and in turn give the kind of power to the Empire to rival that of Great Britain.

He began to plan how he might rise to power; Ludendorff, a mere colonel knew that he was not in the running for any prestigious appointments in time to have any effect on the outcome of the war, and this information was obviously meant for von Moltke.

His meeting with Falkenhayn had gone well and now it was time to follow up the clandestine rendezvous with more a conspicuous meeting in the Bendlerblock. He summoned his batman for a brief *Putze*, a spruce-up, before walking briskly along Bendlerstraβe to Falkenhayn's office in the War Ministry.

"I think you need a command, Oberst Ludendorff, and I plan to give you the Kaiser's tactical demonstration battalion. There you can test out the modern tactics from the…" he looked at his notes, "yes, the Manstein Plan." Noticing a detail on the page, Falkenhayn's face broke into a wide grin. "Manstein, his name is also Erich, the three Erichs will win the war," he said in a mock officious tone.

"Vielen Dank, Herr General," Ludendorff said, blinking as the joke passed him by.

Worried that he was being conveniently side-lined, he added, "perhaps the job description should include some liaison and consultancy duties, regular meetings with the general staff, consultations with weapons manufacturers? In addition, I would like to be introduced to the Kaiser and receive some of the credit for the new doctrine, in his presence."

"That can be arranged, Oberst Ludendorff," Falkenhayn said impatiently, understanding that this man was going to milk his lucky find for everything it was worth.

"Can I have this in writing, Herr General? Also, I would like post-dated orders for my appointment as your chief of staff for when you are confirmed as Prussian Minister of War next year."

"You are beginning to anger me, Oberst," Falkenhayn said icily. He opened the silver cigarette box on his large Biedermeier desk and gestured for Ludendorff to help himself as he lit one and held out the gold lighter for his subordinate. Ludendorff had to lean awkwardly over the desk, in a move that reasserted some of Falkenhayn's authority.

"What would stop me from posting you to some colonial backwater once I have all of your precious material?" he hissed in Ludendorff's face as he lit the cigarette.

"I have made contingency plans for this," Ludendorff said stiffly as he straightened, "so you cannot imagine that you would receive even close to half of what I have."

Falkenhayn just smiled and drew on his hand-made cigarette until Ludendorff continued.

"I have the rest with my man of business who has instructed a solicitor to destroy it if I miss one of our scheduled meetings or if he receives a coded message from me. I have not been told the name of the law firm, nor does anyone there understand the significance of what they are safeguarding."

"Very well, Ludendorff, I will play your game, I certainly have as much to gain as you from this and I can see that you are an intelligent, capable officer and I want you in my corner. Come back on Friday morning with the plans for that sub-machine gun and the Manstein plan, and I will have your orders all typed up and signed by von Moltke."

Quantenphysik Berlin, 1960

Quantenphysik is the German term describing the study of matter and energy at its most fundamental level.

Doktor Rudolph Kessler hated hospitals. The smell of disinfectant and antiseptic, the brisk manner of the nurses, the institutional environment all irked him, but most of all he loathed the hopeless atmosphere of death and disease.

Rudi held his mother's hand as she slept, the skin that covered it translucent, her breath rasping and weak, he could see that her sleep was not restful. Frau Emma Kessler's life had been one of unending hardship, but this was not abnormal. The same could be said for many of the Berliners born during the second decade of the twentieth century.

She had known only fear, hunger, and pain for most of her short life and, like many women her age, she was a widow. The reason she lay here dying in her late forties was, as she saw it, a testament to her extraordinary Glück. Luck that she and her children were all still alive after their home was all but destroyed.

Over the last ten years the tiny scrap of metal that entered her chest that day in 1945 had migrated towards her heart, and now death hung over her like the sword of Damocles.

Rudi was experiencing it all again now, the taste of metal, the smell of burning flesh. He remembered the eyes of the Red Army man as he coughed blood into his face, but by far the most vivid memory was the feeling of shame, shame that he had allowed his mother and sister to be raped, while he lay metres away, cowed, and senseless, dead to the world around him.

"Herr Doktor?" Rudi was jerked from his reverie by the nurse, who seemed to mock him with these words. He *was* a doctor, albeit a Doctor of Physics and not medicine, and he felt the distinction acutely, particularly when speaking with medical people.

"Herr Doktor, visiting hours have finished, you must leave now."

"Of course," Rudi said as he kissed his mother's forehead and straightened her blanket. She looked so wretched, her life had been so unimaginably awful, and only the early days of the Third Reich had been bearable. The guilt she carried with her after discovering the price others had paid for this time of peace, prosperity, and joy marred her once cherished memories.

"I will take good care of your mother," the nurse said. She was smiling at Rudi now, and he noticed that she could have been quite pretty if she had not been so malnourished. Perhaps he had imagined the derisive tone before?

"Thank you, Schwester," he answered, smiling nervously while she helped him into his pathetically thin winter coat. He was not a conventionally attractive man, but women did seem to like him. He had been described as a perfect Aryan by his schoolteachers and *Hitler-Jugend* leaders. He remembered the pride he had felt when his long face, prominent chin, narrow nose and dolichocephalic skull had been measured by a Nazi doctor specialising in phrenology.

He was told he was Herren-mensch and would one day be allowed to serve in the Führer's most prestigious regiments. Now at the age of twenty-eight, he wore wire-rimmed spectacles and his once celebrated blonde hair was thinning; to complete the transformation, a cut above his right eye had left him with no eyebrow and a livid scar.

A bitter wind cut through Rudi's inadequate clothing and made him shiver as he stepped into the night. The Charité hospital and its sprawling campus was in Berlin's Mitte district.

When Berlin was taken over by the Red Army, the hospital fell on the Soviet side of an imaginary line, a line which separated the worker's paradise in the east from the decadent capitalist west.

Rudi was ever aware of the drab oppression of the German Democratic Republic, a Soviet puppet state and poster child for communism. He felt it now, an unrelenting sensation that he was being surveilled. He paused and looked West, where even the streetlights seemed brighter. This was probably true; the Russians had dismantled many of East Germany's power stations after the war and shipped them home to be reassembled to power the homes of the Motherland.

Ossies, or East Berliners, were malnourished, poorly clothed and had little to spend their meagre wages on. These hardships, along with the constant threat of torture in the basements of Normannenstraße for minor infractions like demonstrating western imperialist views or being unemployed, led to a mass exodus. East German citizens fled the worker's paradise every day, in the hope of a better life in the West.

The arbitrary lines drawn by the Allies left West berlin essentially an island, a shining beacon of hope in a sea of grey, totalitarian misery. Beset on all sides and split into zones, West Berlin was home to representatives from the other victorious allied nations and all their spies. Since 1958 both sides of the border had been locked in a diplomatic stalemate desperate not to be the proponent of World War Three.

Rudi walked through a fog of paranoia and oppression to the U-Bahn station. He could afford a car on his salary, but the waiting list to purchase one was a decade long. It was a short ride to his apartment near the East German Academy of Science, but the gloomy carriage did nothing to assuage his dark mood as he rattled along in the half-light.

He occupied the basement apartment in a hastily erected block. These flats had been thrown up to house the influx of farm workers who were desperately needed to fuel the ever-expanding Berlin of the early twentieth century. It was plain, utilitarian, and stood out in concrete defiance against the affluent villas that one usually associated with Aldershof, although since the devastation of World War Two, it seemed more and more to fit in with the changing skyline.

He arrived home to find his colleague Doctor Torsten Schweighöfer waiting for him in their basement laboratory, otherwise known as Rudi's combined kitchen and living room.

Torsten was nearly ten centimetres shorter than Rudi, with dark hair and thick-rimmed, black glasses. He had full lips and barely any chin, and he spoke with the comical accent of Lower Saxony.

36

"How is your mother?" Torsten asked absentmindedly and without turning to look at his friend. He was hunched over at the workbench in a pool of yellow light from a desk lamp.

"She is much the same," Rudi sighed. "What do you have there?" he asked as a minute spark of excitement dared to dance at the edge of his conscious thought.

"It came." Torsten, still not turning from his work, held up a sheaf of pages that made up the half of the article he had already consumed. The cover sheet confirmed Rudi's excitement: "Electron Diffraction at Multiple Slits," by Claus Jönsson.

"Oh, mein Gott!" Rudi snatched up the papers, rushed to the other workstation and turned on the light. The silence that followed was only punctuated by the sound of pages being turned.

In 1956 the pair had learned of a brilliant young physicist called Hugh Everett and his paper on the multi-worlds theory. It blew their substantial minds. They had been trying to piece together what this all meant for the last four years, and they both hoped that Jönsson's paper would be the key.

By day they both worked as GDR-sponsored physicists, but by night they used their combined knowledge and intellect to develop something that could change not only the future, but the world as they knew it.

Despite his traumatic wartime experience and the hardship of the Berlin blockade during his formative years, Rudi had performed well at school and had matriculated with ease. The worker's state had taken care of his sick mother and broken sister, allowing him to concentrate on his studies and pursue a career in science.

His sister Carla married a minor government official and seemed to have found happiness on some level. Although she was unable to have children, sexual equity in the GDR was decades ahead of the West, and she made a career for herself as a cog in the endless bureaucracy of the party machine.

The GDR refused to acknowledge the orgy of depravity that followed the battle of Berlin, meaning she could not discuss her horrific past with her party-faithful husband. Rudi did not like or trust Lothar Smidt. He was ten years Carla's senior and just as he now carried his Communist Party card with pride and espoused party rhetoric at every opportunity, he had once shown the same zeal for national socialism and had hero-worshipped Hitler and his cronies. In Rudi's opinion, Lothar had seen Carla as an easy target, luring her in with promises of safety and security.

Rudi was sure that Lothar mistreated his sister and felt sick about how powerless he was to help. Though he could never leave them behind, he also knew he could not move them. So, for now, he was trapped.

When Rudi finally finished reading, Torsten was ready to explode. "Have you finished?" he demanded excitedly.

"Yes, it was very interesting, but I still can't get on board with this concept of 'many worlds'. I understand the theory, and how on some level the behaviour of the particles demonstrates how this might be possible—"

"Just imagine though! Multiple realities, multiple Torsten's and Rudi's, there is a world where you are the Chancellor, and I am the janitor!" Torsten interrupted. This had been a point of contention between the physicists since they had first read Everett's "Wave Mechanics Without Probability."

"That is just it, it is so fantastic that I can't see a practical application for it, not for us anyway. I still favour the Copenhagen interpretation," Rudi argued.

"That is where you are wrong, my friend, the many worlds theory disproves the paradox loop theory, don't you see? If there are many multiple realities, then instead of changing the reality we live in now, we create a new one every time we travel through time."

"Not necessarily, it is only a theory, and surely, if that is the case, then—"

There was a noise from beyond the door, the screech of brakes, the slam of van doors, boots on the stairs, harsh voices in the hall, and a door smashed to splinters.

More boots, muffled screams in the foyer, the building doors closing, and a van door slamming shut. An engine roared to life, and they were gone, one of Rudi's neighbours was also gone, and it was unlikely that they would ever be seen again.

Rudi looked at his partner. They both knew it was wrong, but Rudi also knew that Torsten's mind would be in overdrive trying to justify this oppression somehow. He would be accusing them of disloyalty or dissent or espousing seditious capitalist views.

He had once tried to tell Torsten the painful story of that day in May fifteen years before, but he quickly realised that his reaction would ruin their friendship forever, and perhaps result in a trip to Normannenstraße to explain what he was doing in his basement apartment with all that literature every evening.

"I have to be in early tomorrow," he said. They both knew this was a lie, but Torsten simply nodded curtly and made for the door.

Torsten Schweighöfer was the only son of Winfried and Charlotte, both unwavering communists, and members of the Internationales Sozialistisches Kampfbund or ISK, a hard-line group of socialists who abstained from almost everything that could be considered fun.

They evaded Nazi persecution by fleeing to Zurich in 1938 and were still in hiding when the Red Army swept through Berlin and wrought their horrifying revenge on its citizens.

As a result, the Schweighöfers were able to toe the party line, pretend that it didn't happen and continue to love the GDR, genuinely believing in the socialist utopia they were helping to build. Torsten was in this for pleasure; time travel was a fascinating subject, but he never really thought it would come to more than some interesting new theories that might help with his tenure application someday.

Jönsson's paper was going to fill in the gaps in Rudi and Torsten's knowledge. They hoped first to build a teleportation machine using quantum entanglement. Then, when they were able to move through space, they would try to tackle the time evolution equations for density states in the presence of closed timelike curves.

This should enable them to travel in both space and time. For Torsten this was all theory, but for Rudi, this was *all*.

Rudi had a plan.

He would prevent Germany from becoming the broken puppet state of a despotic lie machine, hated and pitied in equal measure the world over.

Rudi believed that if Germany had not lost World War One and suffered the indignities inflicted by the treaty of Versailles and the years that followed, the weak Weimar Republic would not have led Germany into economic ruin. The Jewish population would not have been blamed for causing both socialism and capitalism, for losing the war and ruining the economy all at the same time, managing all of this whilst somehow being racially inferior.

Adolf Hitler would not have been able to trick the German Volk into believing that national socialism was the answer, bringing about some of the darkest days of humankind. The holocaust could be prevented, as could the atrocious Nazi programs like *Aktion T4* whereby anyone "deemed incurably sick" was euthanised or *Gnadentod* as the programme was called, resulting in the murders of three hundred thousand vulnerable adults and children.

Rudi believed that the Great War was inevitable.

Natürlich, he could stop Princip and save the Archduke, but Europe in 1914 was a tinderbox and he reasoned that some other event would spark the war, and he would no longer have the advantage of hindsight.

Instead, he thought, if Germany could be made to win the war early enough, then all those young men's lives would be spared. The Russian revolution might be avoided, and Stalin's reign of terror would not claim over twenty million innocent lives.

He had once calculated, using western figures as the GDR and Nazi history books he had available to him left much to be desired, that he could save the lives of over one hundred million people if he could just figure out how to turn back the clock. Sometimes, however, he would doubt himself.

What if my actions lead to food shortages from overpopulation? What happens if I prevent myself inventing time travel because I inadvertently stop Einstein, Gödel, Heisenberg, or Schrodinger from paving the way? What if I kill Schrödinger's cat? What if I don't kill Schrödinger's cat?

Along with his illicit research papers, Rudi had acquired a trove of western geopolitical and historical literature. These would help him to pinpoint the precise moment to change the world, and ultimately, though he would never admit it even to himself, prevent the sanctioned, public rape of his mother, sister and, two million other German women in the spring of 1945 all encouraged by Moscow.

He kept all this literature in a hole painstakingly excavated under the concrete floor of his basement on Hackenbergstraße. He knew that Stasi informants worked at the university and probably even lived in his building, so he covered the hole with a board and a motheaten rug that had come all the way from Prenzlauer Berg on the hand cart that day in 1945.

Say what you like about communism, but in East Germany the homes of the proletariat were always warm and crime levels were low. Unfortunately, while he was snug in his bed, Rudi never slept easily.

Grunewald – Cheltenham, 2035

Despite the bright August sunshine the entrance hall to Grunewald was dark, receiving very little natural light. Art adorned the walls – art that had once been in museums – art that Olga would know from a picture postcard. A custom adopted and much loved by the German presence in England was afternoon tea, although almost always coffee and rarely ever scones, but it did happen at four o'clock and it was an opportunity for parents to see their children. This was how Olga found her hostess; in the opulently appointed drawing room, enjoying *Kaffee* und *Kuchen* with her seven children.

Josef's wife, Ava, was a slender woman of once striking beauty, the remains of which had her still turning heads at fifty. The girls or *Die Mädchen*, as they were always called, seemed to be carbon copies of their mother, varying only in height and eye colour, from green-eyed Lisle, a lilliputian in pink tulle, to grey-eyed Cara, a pre-teen in purple suede.

"*Mädchen, seht, hier ist ein weiterer zahmer, unkultivierter Inselaffe.*" Ava turned to a forlorn looking Olga, "Sorry, *Liebling*, do you speak German?"

When Olga did not answer immediately, the eldest of the *Die Mädchen* said loudly, "*Sprichst du Deutsch, Inselaffe?*"

"*Ja, ich spreche Deutsch,*" Olga said hesitantly in a questionable accent, to the girl.

The congregation of girls roared with laughter at her attempt, while Ava looked at her new charge with disdain.

"You will remain out of my sight until you can *sprechen Deutsch* correctly," she said these last words in a mocking imitation of Olga's accent. "Frieda, take her to her room, you will teach her to speak German, or you will not return to school next month." This she said in English so that Olga would understand. The instruction was directed at the eldest girl, a tall teenager with pursed lips and a small, pointed nose.

"*Mama, das ist nicht fair, ich will den Rest meines Urlaubs nicht mit diesem stinkenden Inselaffen verbringen!*" Frieda protested with a stamp of her foot, her withering gaze appraising the interloper.

"*Was ist Inselaffen?*" asked Olga.

Another roar of laughter came from the room as Olga blushed, and her audience laughed even harder. She understood that Frieda had said she smelled bad and did not want to waste her holiday teaching her German, but the term *Inselaffe* was alien to her.

"Island Monkey!" howled Anna, a ten-year-old creature in calico. She danced and made noises like a monkey to the evident delight of her siblings.

"*Warum bin ich ein Inselaffe?*" Olga demanded indignantly.

"Frieda, I have grown tired of this, take the girl to her room, she can eat her meals below stairs until she is fluent." Ava said this in a such a distracted, uninterested way that it pushed Olga over the edge and tears began to form at the corners of her eyes. She felt her neck become hot and her pulse throbbed in her ears. She did not want this, she wanted to appear strong and mature and not cry like a child. Desperate, she ran from the room when Frieda finally showed her which way they would go.

They ascended the grand staircase in silence as Olga stared around her at the richness of the furnishings and the many beautiful paintings. There were at least two Turners and a Constable among what were mostly landscapes, but some were battle scenes or animals. Olga felt certain one of the hunting scenes was a Herring. Art history had been taught to her, as one of her teachers had managed to convince the board of governors that a knowledge of art might enrich the breeding stock.

"This is where we live," Frieda said with a limp arm movement as they reached the second floor. "Here is the schoolroom, you will meet me here at seven every morning." She spoke in slow, deliberate German, "verstehen?" She paused while Olga nodded to confirm that she did in fact understand.

"Sieben heir Rhein," Olga said resignedly, pointing to the open door of the school room.

"Good, and that is a better accent. From now on we will converse only in German. Listen, it will seem like I am being nice to you but, do not mistake my eagerness to leave this dump for anything but that, we are not friends, you are here to…" Frieda stopped abruptly and looked out of the window. Up to this point she had made positive eye contact when she spoke to Olga, but now she could not hold Olga's gaze.

"What, what am I here to do?" pleaded Olga, who was suddenly feeling nauseous, her mind racing, because what could be so bad that Frieda could not say.

"German only," Freida said firmly.

Olga racked her brain for the correct vocabulary and how to order it correctly. "*Warum bin ich hier?*" she attempted.

Freida spoke German to her so fast now that she could only make out every third or fourth word but, she manged to get enough to realise she was being admonished and not told what she wanted to know. So, she shut out the torrent of German and tried to imagine what she could have been about to say.

"*Verstehen, hallo, Olga?*" Freida said impatiently. "Are you deaf?" until she finally got her attention by waving a hand in front of Olga's face. Olga stared at her, dumbfounded for a moment.

"Sorry," she replied in German, "I was a million kilometres away, what did you say?"

"I said that asking too many questions round here will get you and your family in trouble."

She pronounced the word for trouble, *Schwierigkeiten* with particular gravity, and the word danced around in Olga's mind, often returning to her later on, especially in moments of high stress. She nodded assent.

Freida led her along a wide, carpeted corridor, down which they passed the comfortable looking children's rooms, a colourful, well-equipped playroom, and a beautifully decorated nursery, apparently fully stocked and ready for a new arrival.

Sunlight shone through the window in rays that seemed to land exclusively on the crib at the centre of the room. Olga was about to ask if Frau Altstötter was expecting but she checked herself, remembering the word *Schwierigkeiten*.

Now she thought about it, Frau Altstötter was at least fifty even if she might pass for much younger, and her svelte physique did not suggest even the early stages of pregnancy. The young maidens' school had taken great care in perinatal instruction and ensured, without being vulgar, that the girls fully understood how to get pregnant and the early signs of pregnancy. Olga had spent a week in the maternity ward of her local hospital and assisted the delivery of five babies, more than any other girl in her class.

She thought she might like to train as a midwife, but that was a decision for later, as it was the duty of all Germanic women to marry and then try to become pregnant as soon as possible. Female professions such as teaching, midwifery, and caring for the sick and elderly were for barren women. For women who could not fulfil their primary role in the Reich.

At the end of the corridor they stepped through a concealed door into a sparse, windowless, stairwell, which contrasted immeasurably with the rest of the house. Olga and Frieda climbed the steep, narrow stairs until they reached a cheap wooden door. The door was stiff; swollen by the damp that often plagued the attics of old English houses.

The corridor was narrow with bare wooden floors, patched in places with a more modern wood-like material. Each door had a small whiteboard hanging on the outside, the board showing the name of the occupant, their role in the house and what hours they were on duty.

Frieda showed Olga to a room with her name on the whiteboard and stepped inside, where Olga followed her into a small garret room with a tiny window and just space enough for a bed, a side table, a small desk and chair, and a narrow wardrobe. There was a plain mat on the floor by the bed and nothing else.

To add to Olga's dismay, the yellowing walls were bare and there were clear signs that mice had been in the room.

"Sign this." Frieda handed her a clipboard, listing the items in the room, right down to the coat hangers in the tiny wardrobe. Olga complied, offended that they imaged her capable of stealing.

"You will probably be moved to a room in the guest wing once you have mother and father's approval," Frieda said in an unapologetic and casual way, like she had not just brought this young girl to a rodent-infested prison cell in the damp attic of her country mansion.

"I hope I win their approval soon," she said, fighting back tears for the third time that day.

"You seem like a smart girl. I hope you can figure out what's expected of you before they get bored," Frieda said, closing the door.

Olga's suitcase had been left on her bed, presumably by a servant, and this was some consolation because it reminded her that, although she was living amongst them, she was to be treated as a guest by the staff, at least. She pulled it onto the floor and kicked it under the bed, which she now fell onto in despair. This was not at all like her bed at home, the only bed until now that she had fallen into in this way. It hurt, the mattress was thin, lumpy, and was in no way sprung. Now she let herself cry and the tears came, gushing down her cheeks, but she made no sound for she did not want anyone to know her weakness.

Some hours later, though the sun had not quite disappeared behind the faint band of silver that was the Severn, Olga made her way down the servant's stairwell to the cellar in search of food. She found the kitchens a hive of activity, where uniformed maids and cooks bustled through the maze of corridors paying little attention to Olga. When she reached the servants' dining room she found a simple plate of bread, cheese and fruit, and a folded scrap of paper with her name on it sat propped up in front of the plate on the scrubbed oak table.

She ate mechanically, dutifully, and without relish. When finished, she took the plate into the kitchen and washed it up amid the chaos. No one spoke to her, they all seemed too busy, so she trudged back up the three flights of steep, narrow stairs to her tiny room and too exhausted even to undress, she cried herself to sleep.

Olga woke early to the sound of the servants at five o'clock the next morning. The thin, lumpy mattress had provided a poor night's repose. The light shone in thick, dusty beams through the tiny garret window of her east-facing room, and she decided she would have to cover it, or she would always wake at this time. She set about cleaning her room, finding what she needed in a cupboard in the dark corridor. She located and blocked up the mouse entry points and disinfected the surfaces, unpacked her belongings and tried to make the space feel less like a prison cell. By half past six, the room no longer smelled of damp and mice, and the small table, with the addition of some flowers and writing materials, detracted from the general sense of oppression the room had given her before.

At two minutes to seven Olga was waiting at the door to the schoolroom and by seven, she and Frieda were sitting together conjugating verbs. By lunchtime Olga felt the two had genuinely bonded, and Freida thought her prospects of returning to the sanctuary of her boarding school in Essen were high.

Freida was good at this; she instinctively knew how to get people to like her and how to the make them do what she wanted them to. She was beautiful, charming, and manipulative, and her greatest disappointment was that none of her charm worked on her mother. She had her father, her sisters, and all of the staff in the palm of her manicured hand, but her mother remained obstinately immune. At school she ran the place, but Ava Altstötter knew this without having to see it, and she wielded her own power like a sword to withhold Frieda's access to her empire. It was the only weapon Ava needed, and when Freida was at home, the mother ran the house through her daughter, partly to train her for the day she would marry a high-ranking German aristocrat, and partly because she could.

Each day the pair walked through the grounds during a self-ordained lunchbreak. Today, Freida had organised a picnic for them, and they took a hamper to the brow of a high hill where she pointed out the gothic spires of Cheltenham and Gloucester set against the backdrop of the shining River Severn.

Frieda kept the conversation going effortlessly, noting that Olga possessed a strong foundation of German from school, and a month or so of immersive learning would be all she would need to bring her up to the standard her mother required of her.

After the first insistence that the two would not be friends, Freida made no further reference to it and Olga found herself talking with ease to her new companion, and as days became weeks Olga began to reveal increasingly personal aspects of her life.

She had no real secrets, but there were things she did not like to tell just anyone, such as boys she had kissed, the death of her brother Klaus, her mother's medal, her anxiety about her father's new rank and the new social rules. Freida was inherently cruel, and this kind of sentimental drivel turned her stomach. She found the idea of London society laughable, like the island monkeys were attempting a weak parody of Berlin society. She nearly laughed aloud when Olga told her of Klaus' funeral and her mother's humiliation, but she knew how she was expected to react to these kinds of things, so she dutifully patted Olga's arm, showering her with reassuring platitudes while abject contempt bubbled away just beneath the surface.

Olga was in awe of her new friend, feeling so close to her that she trusted her implicitly. They had developed a habit of spending all afternoon wandering the grounds and walking back to the house, just in time for tea. Olga was often reminded of the first day they had done this and her attempt to walk through Grunewald's grand entrance.

"Where do you think you are going?" Frieda said, her voice devoid of any warmth she had shown that day.

"You said we would go for tea?" Olga protested.

"Go and wait in the playroom, mother does not wish to see you. I will make us a plate and bring up," Freida said directing

Olga to the back door of the house, an entrance Ava would never use.

"Can't you have a servant do it?"

"No," Freida sighed, rolling her eyes. "At tea, the family serve themselves. So I would have to go to the drawing room *anyway* to make a plate up, then find a servant to bring it up for me." She tutted, leaving Olga to walk around to the rear on her own.

Her accent had vastly improved in the few weeks she had been at Grunewald, and she was eager to show it off, but Freida said that her mother was only interested in the finished article and never the work in progress. Olga longed for Ava's approval, she felt as though gaining it would change everything. She thought about the many ways her life would be different as she danced up the staircase and down the empty corridors.

Aufsteigen – Berlin, 1913

To Ascend

Oberst Erich Ludendorff, Officer Commanding 39th (Lower Rhine) Fusiliers, surveyed his command. A crack battalion of infantry soldiers, handpicked for demonstration duties, masters of the state-of-the-art warfare that Ludendorff and Falkenhayn had developed over the last eighteen months.

Falkenhayn, true to his word, had introduced his new protégé to the Kaiser and given him joint credit for much of the new military doctrine and stratagem the German Imperial Army now used. During this period of unending success, Ludendorff's heart seemed to lighten. He found that he could laugh and be witty, surprising himself that he made friends with ease and looked forward to dining in the mess each night.

From the balcony of his office, he looked down at the parading troops, stock still in perfectly squared ranks. His close friend and regimental adjutant, Wilhelm Breucker, stood front and centre, waiting to conduct Ludendorff's farewell parade before dining out banquet with his fellow officers.

Officer's swords and soldier's bayonets gleamed in the August sun and Ludendorff basked in the glory of his toil, because this battalion was the finest in the army and the credit lay squarely at his feet. He and his staff had drilled the men hard for over a year to master the new tactics, weapons, and equipment, first with notional wooden MP40s then later the prototype.

More recently they had toured the fatherland demonstrating their new way of waging war.

Stuffy Prussian colonels scoffed at the appearance of these crack stormtroops with their *Stahlhelm*, the new coalscuttle helmets, the more comfortable uniforms with leather patches at the elbows and knees, and the scruffy looking bags of tater-masher grenades slung at every man's neck. Ludendorff watched with satisfaction as they saw the efficacy of the methods and equipment, he saw the greed on their faces as they thought of the glory this type of fighting might bring them, the minimised loss of life and the potential speed of victory.

Ludendorff wanted a catchy name for this new era of warfare. *Quick war? Certain war? Effective war?*

None sounded right but he finally settled on *Sturmkrieg* or storm war, but he wasn't genuinely happy with it. After touring the empire and giving a series of lectures at the staff college he was promoted as promised to serve on Falkenhayn's staff.

He was given as much free rein with the Schlieffen plan as was reasonable, and occupied an office next door to the minister for war. So began Major General Ludendorff's true ascent to power.

In the meantime, Falkenhayn had used his knowledge of the future to discredit von Moltke and bring about his forced retirement, which proved to be an ugly business.

The sixty-four-year-old was a close friend of the Kaiser and Falkenhayn was forced to play some dirty tricks to convince the court that von Moltke was not fit to serve on the general staff, let alone run it. He took every opportunity to trick the proud old general that he was losing his mind, he paid servants to hide part of his uniform and arranged appointments for him that he never showed up for. Falkenhayn dared not publicly denounce him until it was generally considered that his wits had abandoned him.

The same went for the Schlieffen plan. It was dangerous to decry the fabled document, even as Prussian Minister for War, and he walked a tightrope between tradition and progress.

When two men shared a secret, they could either resent the other for knowing it and despise themselves for revealing it, projecting that onto their confidante. Or paranoid, they are brought closer, each seeing the other as their only true ally in a world filled with ignorant would-be usurpers. It was the latter that drove Falkenhayn and Ludendorff to meet regularly after their initial pact, and as their friendship grew, they became extremely close.

The pair strategized together over the downfall of von Moltke and the rise of an even greater German Empire. They often joked about one usurping the Kaiser while the other ran the chancelry, occasionally swapping for the day to amuse themselves. They knew it was treason, but they did not care, they felt like the most powerful men in Europe because they had the power of foresight; a window from the past into the future. But this power made them paranoid, they felt they had not guarded their secrets jealously enough, imagining French and British spies around every corner.

Falkenhayn set up the Sicherheitsbehörde or *security agency*, to conduct counter espionage throughout Germany, they picked up every tourist bearing binoculars or a camera within twenty miles of a military installation. Sailors and fishermen would feel the sun's heat leave them as the ominous shadow of a great Zeppelin loomed overhead and an officious German voice demanded to know their business over loudhailer. The SB were a menace and not only to foreigners, because soon German citizens also came under suspicion.

As the SB grew in number and worked with the civil police to investigate treasonous activity, more and more doors were broken down, more families were destroyed, and countless innocents imprisoned. Falkenhayn was careful to leave friends of the Kaiser and Berliners alone. In fact, to avoid treading on the toes of the Prussian *Geheimpolizei,* the SB was practically unheard of in Berlin.

The final nail in von Moltke's coffin came in early 1914 when Falkenhayn had become desperate; he knew that war was coming, and he knew that von Moltke would fail disastrously during the first battle by being inflexible with the Schlieffen plan. He reluctantly paid a rent boy to tell the SB that he had slept with von Moltke on several occasions, then he framed the young man for treason. A search of his apartment revealed photographs taken in Sassnitz, Kiel, and Rostock, showing naval installations, ships, and water depths.

Von Moltke was implicated, humiliated, and peremptorily dismissed from the General Staff. The Kaiser took pity on his old friend, though, and gave him an honourable retirement at his family estate in Biendorf on the Baltic coast.

The obvious choices of von Bulow and von Hindenburg were dismissed in favour of Falkenhayn, this move being due mainly to the relationship he had worked so hard to form with Kaiser Wilhelm. Falkenhayn could not stand his emperor, and the obsequious nature of the rest of the court turned his stomach. At first, he had resolved to win his favour honourably, but the great man only responded to the toadying, sycophantic yessiry to which he was accustomed.

So Falkenhayn began to cut away pieces of his soul to be sacrificed upon the altar of the ego of Wilhelm II of the house of Hohenzollern. He urged Ludendorff to ingratiate himself in an equally degrading manner, and much to his consternation he refused, saying he would win his favour his way and the stalwart succeeded.

Ludendorff now had the Friendship *and* respect of the Kaiser, who had looked forward to watching the demonstrations his battalion gave and congratulated Falkenhayn on his judgement when he brought the promising General onto his staff. With Ludendorff in Berlin the three of them met even more regularly, strengthening Falkenhayn's chances of succeeding von Moltke. They also used these meetings to show the bloodthirsty Kaiser plans for a super-weapon, a weapon capable of flattening an entire city. Sceptical at first, Wilhelm slowly became more interested and began asking enough questions for Falkenhayn to reasonably begin development.

Falkenhayn brought Ludendorff with him from the War Ministry to the Great German General Staff and finally, the reworking of the Schlieffen plan could begin in earnest. The first change was to reduce the number of troops sent west to France, reroute them around Belgium and prepare them for the siege of the Meuse Valley. The slow-moving Big Bertha Krupp guns were mobilised without delay to Alsace and Lorraine ahead of the war they knew would come. They were sceptical that this was all that was required to change the course of the war, but in copies of newspaper articles depicting 'The Rape of Belgium' German soldiers were accused of numerous atrocities, including the murder of civilian men, women, and children, and even the eating of babies. One article described a superfluity of nuns ordered to strip because troops suspected that Belgian guerrillas might be disguised in their habits.

This behaviour, along with the breach of neutrality, would eventually bring a further four million enemy troops to bear on the western front, initially by way of the British Expeditionary Force and later a conscript army that would wear the Germans down over the next four years until the entire nation was chewing their belt leather for nourishment.

If this could be avoided, they decided, it certainly should be. They utilised Zeppelins as troop transport and for reconnaissance, setting up regular commercial passenger flights between German cities and the Iberian Peninsula in order to make repeated passes over the fortified border region with France and build up a detailed picture of the ground, to complement the fortress plans received through the time telegraph.

"We do not have to use this weapon, Your Highness. If we were to test it once in a remote location, we would instantly earn the respect of other nations, and the British would finally see us as their rivals and no longer look down upon us."

Ludendorff had arranged this private meeting with Kaiser Wilhelm, knowing that the emperor longed to be in the field with his armies. Ludendorff had shown his monarch that he was a fine officer time and again during the endless manoeuvres and demonstrations. Ludendorff knew that the way to this man's heart was through his delusional notions of being some kind of warrior king like his distinguished ancestor Frederick the Great. He nurtured this narrative and complimented the Kaiser on his riding and other obvious military abilities.

The emperor had been born with Erb's Palsy, leaving his left arm withered and a hand's length shorter than his right. One reason he liked military dress was the opportunity to rest his hand on the hilt of his sword, disguising his deformity quite well. He was a vain man and the General found it easy to manipulate him.

Kaiser and general sat, enjoying the midsummer sun in an open-sided tent, drinking coffee and Schnaps with a commanding view of a division at exercise on the plane below.

"It seems unsporting," Wilhelm complained. "Almost cowardly to flatten a city like that."

"Yes, Your Imperial Highness, we would never *use* the weapon, but it would free us of the encirclement of these lesser European states, and then we could simply take what was ours, for the fear of reprisal would be too great."

"I suppose you are in the right of it. Very well, proceed to the next stage of development," the Kaiser said nonchalantly. Then in the same breath, his eyes lit up. "I should like to see this bomb, arrange for a visit to the site for me."

"I will, Your Imperial Majesty, but there was another matter…" Ludendorff said awkwardly. "It is rather delicate."

"Out with it, man."

"It concerns Falkenhayn, Your Highness." Ludendorff paused as they both turned to watch a cavalry charge in the middle distance. Dozens of lance wielding Uhlans thundered in a geometric formation towards a modern artillery position as the gunners rapidly fired blanks into the air to demonstrate the redundancy of mounted troops against modern rates of fire.

"I say! That is very impressive," the Kaiser stood and slapped his thigh by way of applause. "I said it before, Ludendorff, it is the soldier and the army that have welded the German Empire together. I put my trust in the army." He turned to Ludendorff.

"What was that about Falkenhayn?"

"It is his gambling. It is becoming a problem…"

"I will stop you there, Ludendorff," he waved a hand in Ludendorff's direction. "I know how ambitious you are, and I know that you and I agree on almost everything of importance, and you *will* be in charge one day, but not like this. Now, we will forget this conversation and enjoy this display of German military might," he gestured towards the vast plane and the thousands of troops exercising there for his own entertainment.

"Ja Eure Hoheit," Ludendorff said and stared at a distant column of foot guards marching over the horizon.

That same day, the twenty-eighth of June 1914, members of the Serbian terrorist group, The Black Hand, attempted to assassinate the heir to the Austro-Hungarian throne, Archduke Franz Ferdinand.

The attempt failed. In fact, it was a farce, with one assassin mistiming his bomb throw, swallowing old, ineffective cyanide, and jumping into the ankle-deep water of the Miljacka River in an attempt to escape. The motorcade then sped off leaving several assassins unable to act.

Gavrilo Princip was one of these men, at a loss and with adrenaline coursing through his veins, he'd wandered off, still armed with a Belgian FN Pistol. After about an hour he had stopped for lunch at a delicatessen near the Latin Bridge. By sheer coincidence, the Archduke's driver took a wrong turn onto the side street where Schiller's Delicatessen sat. The Archduke's head of security shouted for him to turn around, flustering the driver, who then stalled the open-topped car right in front of the shop where Princip happened to be eating his lunch.

Princip sprang into action, drawing his pistol and stepping onto the running board where he fired one round into the Archduke and a second into his wife, Princess Sophie. Princip tried to shoot himself next, but he was seized before he had the opportunity. Both his victims died, and the Archduke's final words echoed between the buildings and down through the ages.

"Sophie, Sophie! Don't die! Live for our children!"

Die Mauer – Berlin, 1961

The Wall. 13 August 1961, the German Democratic Republic fortifies the border between east and west.

For most academics the summer was a time to rest, plan lectures and catch up on some reading. The summer of 1961 was unbearably hot, and sticky Berliners flocked to the city's lakes and parks in search of relief and cold beer. Despite rising tension between the White House and the Kremlin, for the first time since 1949 Rudi felt something like optimism. Rudi and Torsten had made significant progress and they spent the long summer days in his cool, dark basement, toiling endlessly on their *Zeitmaschine* until they felt painfully close to a breakthrough.

She'd appeared at just the right time for Rudi. She had dragged him from his depression in the winter and over the spring and summer, romance blossomed.

A mysterious PhD student with a passion for quantum physics that rivalled Rudi's. Her insights and theories were wildly advanced and when Rudi encouraged her to elaborate on Bell's theorem or what exactly a quark was, she would often just smile and draw him in for a kiss so passionate that he would forget all about his misgivings and get on with proving the theory. They had met in the staff room back in February, and after a week of Rudi looking like he was going to come over and say something without actually doing it, she marched over and invited him to a party.

"It's a church thing," she had said in her strange aristocratic accent, "not too religious. The pastor plays Western music and there's dancing," she said, smiling to reveal a mouth containing slightly too many teeth.

"I would love to," Rudi finally blurted out. "Shall I pick you up?"

"Seven o'clock." She scrawled her address on a scrap of paper and pushed it into the top pocket of his lab coat, then walked away without another word.

He pulled out the scrap and read her name back to himself. It felt somehow familiar, like he'd said it thousands of times before "Olga."

The building was a utilitarian affair typical of most protestant churches in Berlin, and inside, the congregation was mostly teenagers. Olga explained that this was the only place she could dance to Western music without walking to the West, and the police always bothered girls on their way back home.

She said it was worse when you took a guy west with you, as the police knew he had no choice but to stand there while they got all creepy, which only made them worse.

The pastor led a brief service before he showed the fifteen or so young people into a back room. He was much younger than Rudi had imagined, closer to his own twenty-eight years, with a dark complexion, shoulder-length, black, curly hair, and a kind, weather-beaten face. After some folk music and a few communist party-approved games, they broke off into smaller groups and helped themselves to Vita Cola.

The pastor worked his way around the room, speaking to everyone for a few minutes. Olga said that this was to make sure everyone was on the level before he broke out the good stuff. He introduced himself to Rudi as Lorenzo, and after a few minutes, Rudi learned that Lorenzo was a Waldensian, an Italian sect of the protestant church. He was the son of an Italian *Gastarbeiter* who, with a million others, had come to Berlin in 1915 to work. His father Mario had fought in the Great War and he, like Rudi, had been one of the many uniformed children fighting in the battle of Berlin. Lorenzo finally took out some illicit Western pop music. The first song was *Shop Around* by The Miracles, and everybody danced, most of them doing the twist, while some did the chicken walk. There were only a few records, so they had breaks in between each song, which gave Rudi and Olga a chance to talk.

"What do you want to do with your life, Rudi?" Olga asked, with no preamble. Rudi was taken aback by the directness of her question; although he knew the answer, he was not sure if he could trust Olga with his secret yet. She would run a mile from the madman, or worse, report him to the Stasi.

"Well, I'm a quantum physicist, you know that," he said feebly.

"I know that, and I think you are brilliant, but what do you want to do with that amazing brain?" she asked, smiling and tapping her finger on his forehead.

"I want to serve the people and further the cause of communism," he said miserably in a mechanical tone, while staring at the ground.

"It's okay, we only just met, and you don't trust me yet, so let's just dance instead." She led him by the hand, and they danced to Del Shannon's *Runaway*.

Rudi desperately wanted to tell this enchanting woman everything, but he had to be sure he could trust her. For now, he would just have to make do with getting to know her. He watched her dance and when she caught him looking, she flashed that wide, beaming smile that showed her uneven, impossibly white teeth, drawing attention to her high cheekbones and broad nose. Rudi thought she was the most beautiful woman he had ever seen. Her skin glowed in the way that skin did not in the GDR, with nourishment and optimism, not one good meal but a lifetime of fresh vegetables and sufficient calories. That night as they danced, talked, laughed, and teased, he fell hard for the mysterious physicist from Lübeck.

She told him that she dreamed of running west once her PhD was finished. As she told him that she wanted to continue her research into quantum mechanics, Rudi began to see how much she would love to be involved in the ZeitZeug, and how much she could contribute. She had an impressive mind and he found that just as attractive as the thick band of freckles that ran across her nose and way her light cotton dress hugged her figure. At the end of the evening, they danced slowly to *Where the Boys Are* by Connie Francis, and Rudi felt something like optimism for the first time in nearly twenty years.

They walked home in a haze of romance, humming the tune they had just danced to. Olga let her hand brush Rudi's and he took it gently in his own, feeling an electricity at her touch as they strolled casually despite the frozen February night.

"I'm glad I'm not your doctoral advisor," Rudi blurted out, and Olga laughed.

"Is that your way of saying that it's okay for us to kiss because it would not be frowned upon by the university?" She grinned and stopped walking, causing his hand to catch as he turned to see her in the yellow pool of light from a streetlamp.

She was so beautiful, so intelligent and funny, full of the care-free exuberance of youth but at the same time with a wisdom that seemed well beyond her twenty-four years. It was as if she had lived many lives and knew all the rules to all the games, but she had such contempt for them and that was what made her so incredible.

Rudi felt himself being pulled towards her, and they kissed. His head swam and he felt like he was home, that he had found the one person in the universe that he belonged with. It was like this had happened before though, many times in many ways, over many decades the only constants being Olga and Rudi.

So began the longest love affair of all time, filled with snatched moments outside Lorenzo's church or tacit assignations at the university, until finally, Olga agreed to move in with Rudi. They still went to the church for music and dancing but not as often, because Olga's presence in their lab meant Torsten and Rudi could not hide their work from her any longer. When they sat her down to explain it, she was enthralled, but better than that, she *understood* it. She got it, she got the theory, she got the motivation behind it, and she wanted to help make this time machine a reality.

Olga's obvious, yet unspoken desire to move to the West made her unpopular with Torsten and he resented the place she had taken in Rudi's life. He had discretely run a background check on her, and she seemed to have simply appeared one day in early 1961, and although all her records were in order, no one could remember her from before then.

Olga never said anything seditious in front of Torsten or any of his hard-line friends at the university, but he knew something was not right and he was determined to get to the bottom of it. He found that on the rare occasions he did sleep, she haunted his dreams, he would see her in crowds and hear her voice on the wind. It became an obsession that was damaging his friendship with Rudi.

"Are you even serious about this time machine anymore, Rudi?" Torsten asked on one of the sweltering August days they spent hiding in Rudi's basement apartment.

"Whoa, man, where did that come from?"

"Man? *Man*? This is what I mean, when did you start speaking this way? It's that girl!" Torsten said petulantly.

"Don't be like this, Torsten. I love her, and you are my best friend, so why can't you just be happy for me?" Rudi pleaded.

"Love? You barely know her, have you met her parents or any friends she's had for more than a year? Do you even know who she is, Rudi?"

Rudi looked up from the papers he was arranging, Torsten was busy at the chalkboard working on the entanglement calculations. All Rudi could see was the back of his head, he stared at it, unseeing, ruminating and grasping at something just beyond his cognitive reach. Have you been checking up on her, Torsten?" he said as things began to make sense.

"Of course not! As you say, I'm your best friend and I only wish for you to be happy, but don't come crying to me when she breaks your heart okay, Rudi. Because I don't want to know about it," Torsten said, as the chalk he was writing with snapped under the pressure he was unconsciously applying.

"I think that's enough for today, don't you Torsten?"

"Ja, Bis Morgen," Torsten mumbled as he hurried from the basement, embarrassed by his outburst.

On a rare impulsive decision, Rudi and Olga decided to spend the day at the Müggelsee, a picturesque lake on the outskirts of East Berlin. Olga said that she would invite a friend if Torsten cared to join them, but he declined, opting instead for the cool basement and a blackboard of calculations.

The whole of East Berlin appeared to have picked the same day for a trip to the Müggelsee, and uniformed lines of *Strandkörbe* adorned the golden sand, every last one of the wicker beach baskets that served as a sunshade, seat, and storage was occupied by those seeking the sunshine.

Instead, they queued for a boat and rowed it out across the shimmering water with a picnic and some beers to find a quiet spot. There they spent a blissful day luxuriating in the heat of the sun and each other's company. They made love and talking seditiously about running west and the lives they would lead there. After a perfect day, they made the short journey back to Aldershof in as near to euphoria as an Ossie could be in 1961.

They found Torsten in a comparable mood when he greeted them with uncharacteristic good humour and took a cold beer when offered. Rudi and Olga were feeling the effects of a day spent drinking in the sun, and they all sat in the apartment with a sense of ease that the three of them had not found before.

"While you were out," Torsten said, standing and draining his beer. "I think I figured out the quantum entanglement calculation!"

"What?" Rudi's wits sharpened immediately. "Show me, please!" He gestured towards the blackboard, where Torsten began to write equations furiously. When he'd finally finished, he underlined the solution three times and turned to observe Rudi's reaction.

"That is astounding...that is *it!*" He stayed quiet as he ran his eyes over the equation to check for the error that must be there. This couldn't be it, they had finally, after years of work, proved that teleportation was possible. What was more, Torsten's equation suggested that they would be able to build a simple prototype in a few weeks.

"We should make a list of parts and start collecting them immediately," Rudi suggested.

"That will mean a trip to the West," Torsten said with trepidation.

"Just think! When we have built this, we can simply cross into the West from here," Olga said, pointing to the ground and making a vanishing noise with her lips and teeth.

"I would like to recruit an ally at the free university, a physicist or a historian, perhaps both?" Rudi mused.

"Is that…" Torsten hesitated, "wise?"

"Possibly not, but we need better access to up to date western research and western history books are far more reliable."

Torsten frowned.

"What do you mean by that, comrade? How can you trust that capitalist imperialist propaganda over the literature produced by the workers' state?"

Olga laughed loudly.

"Is something funny, Olga?" Torsten sneered.

"Nothing, it's fine," she said suppressing a laugh.

"No, you clearly have something to say," he snapped pedantically, "so out with it, girl!" He became angry and the atmosphere grew cold and dangerous.

"My dear friend, your 'Uncle Joe' has been killing 'dissidents' by the million in his gulags for years. Open a state-approved history book and look for that, or the purges in the thirties, or the Holodomor, or any of the other atrocities perpetrated in the name of the proletariat!"

She knew she should hold her tongue, but she'd had enough of this overgrown child and his ridiculous fantasies about Soviet Communism.

"You are upset, mein colleague," Torsten said coolly. "You cannot believe what you say and that is why I will forget that you ever said it, and I shall not trouble to respond to your vile accusations."

"Listen to yourself, you pompous little shit. Joe Stalin was worse than Hitler," Olga stood up and threw her arms about in frustration. "And Nikita Khrushchev is so encumbered by the relics in the presidium that he will never make any traction with his reforms! Ulbricht is another foolish old man with his head up his arse!" She was out of breath now, her face crimson with anger.

Rudi closed his eyes and pinched the bridge of his nose. He could see the crowd of Red Army soldiers clearly again, jeering and watching as their comrades raped his family in the street. He forced himself to calm down, because Torsten would happily report him to the Stasi, such was the extent of his brainwashing. He backtracked; he needed this man, he needed him to save Germany, ironically for his intellect.

"I apologise, comrade, please forgive her outburst." He did his best to look contrite. "She has... had too much to drink, and it has clouded her judgement," he added, aiming a warning look at Olga who either failed to comprehend it, or simply did not care.

"I don't need you to speak for me Rudi, I'm not drunk, I'm very much awake... It's you who needs to fucking wake up! The East is not a socialist utopia, it's a totalitarian nightmare."

She paced the room, gesticulating and pointing at Torsten as she spoke angrily.

Torsten decided in that moment that he would have to report this to his contact in Normannenstraße, and he even warmed to the idea, beginning to imagine that he could present their research to the party as his own and they might recruit him to work at the All-Russian Scientific Research Institute of Experimental Physics in Snezhinsk and, like all good communists, he would use what they had discovered to destroy capitalism.

He could not alert them to his intentions, or they might decide to run, so he had to play it cool. He sat down and asked for another beer, watching as Olga stormed from the room in disgust. He smiled to himself at the thought of what would happen later, after his chat with the Stasi. There were rooms in the basement of Normannenstraße, rooms filled with instruments designed to inflict pain and garner secrets. Torsten imagined Olga tied to a chair, naked and drenched in sweat, her face bloody and bruised as she begged for clemency. The sound of her screaming as faceless men slowly extracted her fingernails or attached electrodes to her exposed flesh.

He found that he had become aroused and wondered what that meant, what it said about Torsten Schweighöfer. Perhaps he would stroll down to the canal on his way to inform on his friends and find a prostitute? Perhaps there were places that he could pay to do those things to a woman that looked like Olga?

Torsten shot a furtive glance at his partner, before staring guiltily at the bulge in his lap. Both men sat awkwardly and sipped their beer.

"I think we can just forget this ever happened," he said, breaking the silence. With that he stood, drained his beer, and left the apartment.

As soon as he heard the lobby doors slam shut, Rudi scribbled down Torsten's calculations and wiped the blackboard clean. He placed the sheet with the rest of his papers in the floor, covered it again, and joined Olga in bed.

They came in the night. Olga tried to fight, but there were too many of them. It only took one blow to Olga's perfect face to quell Rudi's urge to resist, and he kept telling himself they would explain the situation and be home in the morning.

Olga continued to struggle, to kick and scream, and she landed some nasty blows so that it took four large men to restrain her. Rudi pleaded with them to allow her to dress, but the policemen seemed to be enjoying the fact that she was naked. Rudi finally snapped as he watched a fat old man grope Olga's bare breast. She bit her captor's hand, drawing blood and Rudi, who the security men had taken to be no trouble, twisted free and set about the bleeding man. He straddled his chest, blindly hurling his fists into the man's face with more fury than skill, inflicting some serious damage before his victim's colleagues finally pulled him away and beat him viciously with clubs. The Stasi officers dragged Olga and Rudi still fighting out into the street. The neighbours looked on helplessly as another household was shoved into the back of a Barkas B 1000 and driven away for good.

Ausgelesen – Grunewald, 2035

The choice

Olga did not let the austere environment below stairs or her depressing room in the attic dampen her mood, she felt she had made a genuine friend in Frieda, and she was rattling away in German like a Prussian royal. She danced along the wide corridor to the playroom singing a German nursery rhyme Frieda had taught her:

"Ah, bay, say, die Katze lief im Schnee, O jemine! O jemine! die Katze lief im Schnee," she twirled and glided along the plush carpet as she sang.

"Hello, my dear," Altstötter said gently from the end of the hall, standing still in the darker wood-panelled main stairwell. Olga gave a start, feeling foolish and immature to be dancing to a nursery rhyme. Altstötter was wearing slippers made from boiled wool with a linen suit, although he had removed the jacket to reveal a pastel shirt and brown braces, and at his neck instead of a tie he wore a silk scarf.

"I'm sorry, I did not mean to scare you, I see that your German is already improving." Altstötter spoke in flawless English and Olga replied admirably in German.

"Thank you, Herr Altstötter, Frieda is an excellent teacher."

"Where is that daughter of mine?"

"She is bringing us coffee and cake in the playroom."

"She is bringing coffee and cake *to* the playroom for us." Altstötter corrected, then smiled fondly. "Well, enjoy your tea," he said, casting his eyes about the hall for a moment. "Olga, I would like you to come and see me after tea on Friday in my study. Freida knows where it is." He smiled again. It was a warm, reassuring smile that Olga could not help but return.

"Of course, Herr Altstötter."

"Goodbye," he called as he padded down the stairs

Olga felt a modicum of anxiety about being summoned to Altstötter's study, but mostly she was excited because she felt sure this was the first step to getting out of her cell in the attic and on the same corridor as Freida. She had five days to get this right. She also felt sure that, despite her caution, Freida genuinely liked her and that they would become even closer friends over the coming weeks.

Olga considered these things as she sat in the playroom with Freida, eating her *Appfelkuchen* with lashings of cream. Freida had patiently named all of the items on the tray and waited for Olga to repeat them back to her.

"Your father has asked to see me on Friday," Olga said through a mouthful of cake.

"I see," Freida said, fighting back her disgust at this lack of basic manners.

Even an English officer is not going to marry this culturally bankrupt peasant, she mused.

"He said you could show me the way to his study?"

"Of course."

Why does he have to involve me? I wish I knew nothing about it. Isn't seven enough? Frieda thought as she stood and started pacing the room to mask her feelings.

They spent the rest of the week avoiding the family and speaking German. While Freida learned the innermost desires of Olga's soul, Olga learnt how to speak German like a lady of the imperial court. They took walks and sang German songs. Freida was merciless, making Olga practise all day from seven in the morning until she had to change for supper with her parents at six. Olga would eat alone in the servants' hall and then spend the evening mutely practising what she had learnt that day.

At night she would dream; there were the old dreams, the ones she had always dreamed, a handsome blond scientist and a brave priest, a world on fire and drowning at the same time, protesters, and brutal police clashes. Then there were the new dreams, the dreams of acceptance from the Altstötters, her new life in London society, trips to the opera on the arm of a handsome officer, Herr Altstötter's study. Every night she awoke to the sound of Freida's warning of trouble - *die Schwierigkeiten*, the near-full moon would place a square of light on her rough wooden door, and she would stare at the shadows cast there until sleep reclaimed her.

On Friday they walked to the stables and Freida had her student name everything in the tack room, then she found a German servant and had him tell Olga his life's story. Freida made notes and grilled Olga on every detail over tea that afternoon.

"We can go now if you like, to my father's study."

"Okay," Olga said through her final mouthful of cake.

Frieda shuddered inwardly at this and then again as her charge slurped the dregs of her tea. *She may speak like an aristocrat, but she can never be one of us. The child is delusional.*

"Come," Freida beckoned from the door, and Olga naively floated over to her as if on the wings of her innocence and followed.

When they reached the door to Altstötter's study, Freida knocked loudly.

"Enter," came the familiar voice from within. Olga looked to Freida for permission to enter but she was halfway up the hall in a brisk walk. Olga turned the ornate brass handle and pushed the heavy oak door.

The study was stereotypical of such rooms. The wood panelling, hunting scenes by Herring, two wingback armchairs angled towards the fireplace above which hung a set of elephant guns. The enormous leather-topped desk faced the door, so that the natural light from the tall windows fell on the work of the occupant. Floor-to-ceiling bookshelves lined the wall opposite the fireplace, a fixed ladder on a linear rail providing access to the uppermost tomes, and there was even an old-fashioned globe drinks cabinet.

Olga took in the scene before her. To her it was not clichéd, but refined. It was elegant; a demonstration of both power and intellect, of culture, and taste, and she wanted to live in a house that contained a room such as this one day.

"You like my study?" Altstötter said in German.

"Naturally. It is very handsome. Very tasteful."

Her German was impressing even her now, and she felt confident when she spoke it in the cultured accent of her hosts. She felt the power of the Reich, of Valkyries, of her German speaking queen and of the understated elegance of girls like Freida, who was four years her junior yet seemed so much more mature. She wanted to be seen as mature, capable, womanly, not a silly girl but a real woman. A Germanic wife. This was it. Now, when she had gained acceptance into this family, the world would be open to her, and she would belong to the class of people that ruled the civilised world.

"How beautifully you speak and in such a short time. Please, sit down." This was the first time he had spoken to her in German. Altstötter gestured towards an elbow chair in front of his desk, the pattern of ostrich plumes on deep red, lit by a dagger of sunlight penetrating the branches of the ancient oak outside.

"Thank you, Herr Altstötter. Freida is an excellent instructor."

"I admire your modesty, Fräulein. Would you like a drink?"

"I would love one, Herr Altstötter, you can choose for me."

She felt so confident, it was as if speaking this language, the language of power, the language every major decision for the last one hundred and twenty years had been made with, gave her all that power too.

"Champagne it is, my dear." He made a barely perceptible movement under his desk which must have summoned a servant, because less than one minute later, a bottle of Krug 1985 came in with glasses and an ice bucket. The maid removed the cork and poured two glasses mutely before leaving. Altstötter passed a glass to Olga.

"Prosit," he said with unwavering eye contact as their glasses connected, and Olga after returning the toast and seeing that Altstötter had drunk his all in one go, proceeded to do the same with the first alcohol she had ever consumed. The dry acidic taste combined with bubbles was an unpleasant surprise and it took all of her composure to hide her reaction.

Altstötter filled their glasses again and walked across the room to a record player, where he found a record and played Mendelssohn's *Lieder ohne Wörter, Songs without Words*.

Altstötter asked Olga about her family and her home, he asked about her ambitions and fears, and she poured out her soul in German until a second bottle came, and they toasted the Kaiser. Then Altstötter's mood changed, and he began pacing the room as he spoke and his eye contact became sporadic.

"Olga…we have helped several young women like you here at Grunewald," he said, pausing to sip his champagne. "You have a rare opportunity before you, with your father's commission and your extraordinary beauty. With the right patronage, you could marry far above your social station, and never will you have to perform the menial tasks you were shown in the maidens' school. You can forget that ever happened… the years of domestic toil your mother endured only to be publicly humiliated like that."

He changed the record, Chopin this time, then walked over to where Olga sat.

"I know you feel the power you could wield. I can see that you have acquired a taste for it, and it suits you, my dear." His tongue darted from his thin-lipped mouth to wet his lips,

"Now, we can give you all of this, your future would be nearly as promising as young Freida's. We will introduce your father to the right people and find you a minor aristocrat to marry. Your children will have titles, Olga. *Titles*." He was leaning forward now, staring at her.

"Would you like that?"

"Yes, Herr Altstötter." She could feel the bubbles in her stomach and a lightness in her head. She felt amazing. The world was literally at her feet, she could be a *Freifrau* or a *Gräfin* or at least at least a *Frau* in the noble sense of the word.

"Well, you must first do something for us."

"Tell me, Herr Altstötter, tell me what I must do to have this most valuable gift of your patronage?" she implored in flawless, German.

"You must do what all good German women must do for their emperor." He was completely at ease now, sitting in his brown leather office chair, leaning all the way back and looking down his nose at Olga.

"Yes, Herr Altstötter, but how can I do that before you find me my prince charming?"

Altstötter smiled at her in amusement. It made her feel vulnerable, childish, and she saw through his manners to recognise how much he looked down on her.

Then it dawned on her: Freda's warning, her remark about seven not being enough. There were seven beautiful blonde girls and a newly decorated nursery. Ava had not had seven children. These past weeks had been a test of intelligence, of endurance, of commitment, and now she had reached the final hurdle. She would have to give herself to Altstötter, older than her own father and not at all handsome. She appraised him while he strode across the room to play another record, *the Lohengrin* by Wagner.

He was tall but skinny, he did not smell bad, but he was so old. *How much do I want this? What would they do to my family if I refuse?*

They could certainly ruin her father and brothers' careers; reduced to the ranks with no prospects of promotion, they would lose the house, her home, her mother would be humiliated again.

Could she do that to her family? Was she being selfish? She knew what would happen if she agreed; she would lie there and he would huff and puff for a while and roll over, then, nine months later she would have a baby and move on to her amazing new life. What if she could not part with her baby? What if they reneged? She would be disgraced, a fallen woman, damaged goods with a baby in tow.

"I want to know where the other women are now, the mothers of your seven children. Show me that you kept your word." She felt so confident still, but she suspected it was the champagne now instead of the might of the Reich.

"Clever girl," he said, waggling a finger at her. "I wondered what you were mulling over all that time." He handed her Piano Concerto number one in G minor. "Put this on and I will get their SB records."

He tossed six dossiers onto the desk. Each had a passport photograph of a beautiful blonde-haired woman paperclipped to the outside cover. She picked up the first, but the name was redacted. From the age of the woman, Olga guessed this must have been Freida's mother, and a second look at the picture confirmed it. She was a *Gräfin* now, a countess, with three children of her own and an estate worth two million Goldmarks a year. No information on the husband was given, but the report tracked her rise from warrant officer's daughter to countess, including one year's domestic service at Grunewald. She looked through the other five; some had fared better and some worse, but all were wealthy and titled with children of their own.

"Where is number seven?"

"You *are* a quick one. Alas, she died during childbirth. Here is a file on those she left behind. You'll see we did some very fine things for her siblings and her parents. I have agents looking out for all our surrogates and their families, they are better protected than the Chancellor or even the Kaiser."

"I don't think I need to ask what will happen if I refuse?" Olga shot Altstötter a meaningful look, but his own expression dropped in mock surprise.

"No, it would not be like that at all. You would agree to keep silent, and if you did, then your father and brothers would have unexceptional careers and you would marry a man with few prospects. I would not have anyone harm you or your family. You are not stupid, you know the damage I could inflict, I could have all five of you disappear one day and no one would even look for you, but I am not inclined towards petty vengeance."

"So, I need to lie with you or resign myself to a life of mediocrity?"

Altstötter shrugged and showed Olga his open palms.

"My dear Olga, you were already resigned to such an existence, you just did not see it that way before."

Olga was drunk by now and unable to think as clearly as she would have liked, but she also thought that she did not really have a choice. She felt selfish every time she considered not having sex with this fifty-year-old man. She was eighteen, legally allowed to marry, and typically girls did this domestic service until they were eighteen and then married fairly soon after that. She could get it over with tonight, have the baby, and stay here for another three months to recover.

"What if I am barren?"

"You are not barren." He looked away as the sun set over the Sussex downs, the clouds outside their south-facing window beautiful pastel shades of pink and grey.

"How can you…" Olga stopped herself from asking, no good can come from questions like this.

"When you're one of us, my dear, I will tell you everything."

"Please clarify that for me. Is that after I lie with you, after I conceive, or after the baby is born?"

"Now dear, there is no need for that, our records show that you could be ovulating now. I could press a button for more champagne, say one word to the maid and when we are done, you would go to your new room in the guest wing. I have allocated you our Gardenia suite if that suits you. That was the name the previous owner gave it. He was in Intelligence too, only for the British, not SB. I'm rambling, so, what is it to be? More champagne, or do you need another night living in squalor to think on it?"

Olga's heart rate increased because for the first time this was real, not some abstract proposal.

She looked at him again. Was he that bad? She kept thinking about how he didn't smell offensive. She stared at him; he was old, and he was not handsome, but he was not fat, and he was tall, he was nice to her, and he had promised her the world, or more than she could ever hope to have of it, anyway.

He had shown her evidence that he was true to his word. This was so hard for her, and she just kept staring at him and tried to force herself to find him attractive, but it was the power and the money and the position that aroused her. Not only the thought of these things for herself, but these things in him.

She thought of the beautiful Ava, she was alluring, confident and powerful. She had slept with this man, perhaps for the same reasons. She realised that she knew she would go through with it but decided to go through the pretence a little longer.

"Would it be in here?"

"There is a connecting room, it is comfortable and you can take the servants' corridor from there afterwards if you want to, or we can sit and talk in here again, or play some more music."

He said the words awkwardly, and she realised that he felt just as uncomfortable as she did in this moment. She was in no doubt that he wanted the sex and the resulting baby, but right now, this was his least favourite part.

"Olga, you do not have to…"

"No! No… call for the champagne, please."

She fell back into an armchair and sighed heavily, deciding that she could simply think of her family, and it would make the whole thing bearable.

The champagne came and the word was given. The servant's eyes glanced over to Olga, but Olga could not read the expression, and whether it was pity or disgust, she told herself that she didn't care because she would have twenty women like that working for her after tonight.

The servant opened the third bottle of champagne and left to prepare Olga's new rooms. Altstötter opened a concealed door into a large anteroom with a couch and a shower, towels, and pillows. It was a room for sex. If Olga had ever imagined one, this was it.

Altstötter poured two glasses and followed her in as he dimmed the light and toasted her a third time.

"To populating the Reich."

Olga drank it in one go and walked to the bed, her pulse quickening as panic set in. What was she doing? Was she a whore? Was she going to go to hell for this? Was it a trick?

It didn't matter, because what she knew for sure was that he would ruin her and her family's lives if she did not do this now, or soon at least, so she might as well just get it done. His assurances to the contrary held no weight in her dizzy mind, and in that moment, Olga could hear her father's words on the train platform. *Don't doing anything regrettable.* She felt sure that she would regret this for the rest of her life, but she also knew that the alternative would bring unimaginable hardship upon her and her family.

Altstötter was undressing now, folding everything carefully on the back of a chair. Olga wore the same simple brown dress of the Germanic girls league, two buttons, the work of two fingers left her wearing only the slip she beneath it. She wriggled from it and the two garments lay at her feet. Her breasts reacted to the cold, and she felt only fear and shame. He came to her and drew her into him. He was warm but she did not feel comforted as he lay her down onto the couch and kissed her forehead.

She began to shiver, and he tried to sooth her with shushing which made her want to scream. He lay on top of her, supporting himself on his knees and elbows, and as she began to weep, he kissed her tears and pawed at her breasts. He began to try to enter her, and she sobbed loudly which only seemed to encourage him, so he redoubled his efforts.

She tensed, pushing him back off her as he pressed his weight down and tried to force her legs apart. Olga drew in breath to scream, but a noise made her freeze.

It was barely audible, but she definitely heard something, the distinctive noise of metal on wood, the near silent rustle of well-fitted clothing, the sound a sling makes on the stock of a Micro-Galil. *How do I even know those words? This makes no sense?*

The sound Olga heard was a flashbang grenade hitting the floor next to the couch where she lay about to be raped.

Welt Krieg – The Ost Front, 1914

World War.

Feldwebel Otto Kessler loathed Russia. He loathed the bitter weather, the surly locals, and most of all he loathed the taste of vodka.

The war had been brutal. They marched hard, fought relentlessly, and slept rough. With every step eastward he'd felt colder and further from home until he could not recall what true warmth felt like. But the dynamic nature of the advance, and his position at the very tip of the spear, meant that the odours of shit and putrefaction, the morale-sapping nature of trench occupation and the squalor that came with it were distant memories.

He thought about the march west at the start of the war. Their place at the rear of the order of battle meant they had met little resistance until Verdun, where the German right flank had feinted an attack on Belgium and turned south. The army group centre had withdrawn from Alsace at the first sign of French resistance, luring the main force of the French army into a trap, with the Alps to the south and the wall of the imperial army to the north and east.

The French, dressed in blue tunics and red trousers suited more to the parade ground than the modern battlefield, appeared ridiculous when faced with the *feldgrau* or field-grey of the *Deutsches Heer*. The French, who desperately wanted the regions of Alsace and Lorraine back after the Franco Prussian war of 1871, fought bravely for their ground, but the superior numbers, discipline, and weaponry of the German army ground them down.

Until finally, the French were forced to beat a bloody retreat. Harried by German cavalry until the guns of the French fortified line came into range. Otto's unit arrived later, occupied hastily dug trenches and waited in the filth and squalor, while the devastation brought about by Krupp's Big Bertha Howitzers reduced Fort Douaumont to rubble.

He watched as the might of German technology did all the fighting for them. By the time Otto's unit climbed out of their trench there was no fighting to be done, and they gingerly picked their way through the carcases of French border towns. Most notably the City of Nancy, where the magnificent baroque cathedral lay in ruins, the beautiful stained-glass windows now mere fragments and the only colour in a grey, dust-filled vista.

Otto felt cheated. He felt that his opportunity to show his mettle had been snatched away and he cursed the French for the cowards they so obviously were. This scene was repeated throughout France. Otto Kessler marched on and on all the way to Paris without discharging a single round.

He jostled for position in the crowd on the Place de la Concorde, stealing glimpses of French Commander-in-Chief Marshall Joffre. He stood stock still in full ceremonial uniform, moustaches bristling against the cool November air and fixing Ludendorff will cool, vengeful eyes.

"What can I say Joffre," Ludendorff said in heavily accented French, "the Germanic people will always triumph over the Franks. We are superior in every way."

"My sword, Herr General," Joffre smartly drew the artillery sabre he'd carried since the last great humiliation at the hands of their German neighbours in 1871. The ornate knuckle guard bore two crossed ten pounder guns surmounted by a flaming grenade. With a flourish the sword was offered to Ludendorff.

"Merci beaucoup," he said, taking the proffered symbol of France's surrender and glanced at it briefly before passing the sword to an aide. The crowd gasped, murmurs rose from the assembled commanders and politicians and all eyes fell upon Joseph Joffre. It was normal for a defeated commander to offer his sword, but for the victor to *keep* it demonstrated a profound disrespect.

"Your servant, Herr General," Joffre said stiffly, with a deep bow. Otto could not have seen it from his place in the crowd, but the great general's bottom lip quivered ever so slightly at the insult. Ludendorff smiled and made his own perfunctory bow.

"Citizens of the French Third Republic," Ludendorff boomed, turning away from Joffre and towards the crowd. "Once again you are defeated, once again the Germanic people reign victorious. But this time, you will not be allowed to run amok, paying a few meagre reparations before returning to your old ways. This time there will be no commune, no rearmament and no alliances with Russia. The Franks will become citizens of the Reich, subjects of the Kaiser and productive members of a new era of governance." Ludendorff allowed that to sink in for a moment, enjoying the looks of horror on the faces of those closest to him in the crowd. "Liberté? Non. Égalité? Non. Fraternité?" At this last word Ludendorff simply shrugged. The crowd erupted, surging forward, and clawing at the space in front of them as if trying to gouge out the tyrant's eyes.

This was when Joffre understood the sword, for if he had been holding in that moment, he would gladly have cleaved Ludendorff's head from his body. Instead, he lurched forward, grabbing him in an attempt to throw the man into the crowd who by now were only metres away. That was that last act of Joseph Joffre; a bright young hauptmann of the West Prussian Cuirassiers discharged his pistol into the Frenchman's temple.

The shot rang out above the noise of the crowd and for a brief moment the surge waned, but at the sight of their dead general, the civilians redoubled their effort and broke through the line of soldiers.

Otto found himself swept along and, fearing for his life he effectively swam for a side street, lest he be recognised as a member of the occupying force. With a suitable hiding place in sight, he felt the crowd turning and realised that they had indeed changed direction. Otto turned to see a squadron of Uhlan's were formed up and from their elevated position in the saddle they raised their carbines and began to fire over the heads of the crowd. Otto was used to gunfire, but he had yet to be shot at and this was as close as he'd come. He ran for the alleyway and turned to witness a second deadly volley from the horsemen. Men, women and children were cut down in the street with impunity and the air filled with screams and the smell of powder. As they reloaded and smoke eddied about the heads of the crowd, they took up a cry.

"Liberté?" called a handful of men.

"Oui!" roared the reply of the rest.

"Égalité?" they asked.

"Oui!" they crowed demanded.

"Fraternité?" came the cry.

"Toujours!" *forever* screamed the crowd as the remainder of the Uhlan regiment thundered into sight and bore down upon the unarmed sons and daughters of the republic. Sabres drawn they slashed and hacked as hooves bludgeoned and ground flesh and bone into the old Parisian cobbles. As the crowed surged for the Pont de la Concorde, the bottle neck forced some into the Seine while others were crushed against the walls and lampposts of the bridge. Acts of resistance like this one were repeated in Toulouse, Cahors, Orleans and Lyon. They too were met with unyielding brutality. Other cities, those that had heard the story of the massacre at the Place de la Concorde chose to comply, chose to become citizens of the Reich, subjects of the Kaiser.

All Otto could think to do was to thank *Gott* that he was part of the crowd and not forced to kill those Parisians himself. He re-joined his unit and headed for Bordeaux.

With France secured, the German Chancellor, Bethmann-Hollweg, set in motion his plan for the reorganisation of Western Europe, otherwise known as the September Programme.

The entire northern coast was declared German, and the terrified occupants driven inland. Experts from the SB were brought in to quell resistance and prisoners of war remained in camps to prevent an uprising.

The Germans now held all major French Channel and North Atlantic ports, plus a twenty-kilometre strip inland. As soon as these areas were secure, Ludendorff ordered all the German artillery that could not be moved by train to support fighting in the east, to be emplaced strategically overlooking the channel ports of Dunkirk, Cherbourg, and Le Havre, as well as the Atlantic ports of Brest and Toulon.

Admiral Tirpitz instructed forty U-boats of The High Seas Fleet to begin unrestricted submarine warfare against all ships of the Royal Navy and British Coast Guard. A series of simultaneous attacks were planned on key North Sea and Channel naval installations. The effect was devastating, the promises of neutrality from Bethmann-Hollweg had deceived Britain, and they'd failed to place industries on a true war-footing.

The direction given was to target ships that felt safe in harbour, so that these were sunk out of hand and the ships on patrol were avoided. The most atrocious of these attacks occurred at Scapa Flow in northern Scotland while sailors celebrated Christmas day ashore, leaving only skeleton crews on harbour watch. A squadron of U-boats slipped though the patrols, the mines, and the blockships to enter the harbour undetected.

Of the fourteen battleships of the squadron waiting in harbour, only three remained afloat. Similar scenes unfolded at Moray Firth, the Firth of Forth, Humber, Yarmouth, Harwich, Sheerness, and Dover.

When Britain declared war on Germany on Boxing Day 1914, The High Seas Fleet moved out of Heligoland and made for the Channel. Tirpitz had sacrificed nearly two thirds of his submarines to significantly even the odds against what had been a vastly superior force. Tirpitz' desire was to draw the Royal

Navy out into an action, confident that they would send a limited force, not wishing to risk too much of their greatest Imperial asset.

Vice Admiral Reinhard Scheer on the flagship SMS *Friedrich der Grosse* led a fleet of over one hundred ships with a combined broadside weight of sixty tonnes. They steamed along the Dutch coast, a formidable sight in uniformed straight lines. Several battlecruisers peeled off into The River Scheldt to secure the key Belgian port of Antwerp as ground troops approached from further inland, finally breaking Belgian neutrality.

The losses suffered by The Royal Navy during the Christmas attacks included the crack ships *Agamemnon, Agincourt, Indefatigable* and *Bellerophon*, among many others. This left an available broadside weight of seventy tonnes. The British sailors had taken a heavy blow and were thirsty for battle and a chance for revenge. Radio communications from The German High Seas Fleet were intercepted by the Naval cryptanalysts at Room Forty, and the various squadrons of The British Grand Fleet were mustered.

Scheer's Fleet was in the Dover Strait by the time Admiral Beaty's squadron came into range. The Dreadnoughts of the Royal Navy boasted a heavier armament and longer effective range, but the squadron could not take on an entire fleet, so their only option was to harry the afterguard while they waited for greater numbers.

As the fleet passed the French port of Dunkirk, more ships peeled of and sheltered under the newly emplaced guns. Before a force of any useful size could be mustered, the German High

Seas fleet was safe in the newly captured French and Belgian ports. With the loss of only a few ships at the rear. Germany now had control of the northwest coast of Europe and was ideally positioned to defend trade routes in the English Channel, and the risk of Britain landing troops in France was negligible.

Their eye well and truly wiped, the greatest naval power in the world had been bested in less than twenty-four hours. The British Expeditionary Force was chomping at the bit to have a go at the Hun, but crossing the Channel was now a risky business, and with only a few hundred thousand men and no allies, the German army would surely crush them.

Asquith appealed to Woodrow Wilson for help, but the American president had his own problems at home. Ludendorff had sent his ambassador, Heinrich von Eckhardt a coded telegram in 1913, instructing him to woo President Victoriano Huerta with the offer of weapons and support in the event of renewed Mexican hostilities at the American border. Eckhardt was instructed to promise ongoing assistance with a campaign of reclamation in the former Mexican territories as far north as San Francisco.

A shipment arrived in 1914 with Machiavellian diplomat Wilhelm von Mirbach, who with Eckhardt's help, united the warring factions in Mexico against a common enemy. The tiny standing army operated by the USA was scattered throughout the world, and it made up one only third of the combined strength of the battle-hardened Mexican forces. Now Wilson was looking at a map that showed the states of California, New

Mexico, Texas, and Arizona all back under Mexican rule, and he could not assist Asquith even if he wanted to.

In Britain, the recruiting that should have been going on for months began in earnest, with propaganda campaigns warning of a German invasion urging Britons to do their bit. Production of munitions and uniforms began, weapon plans captured by British spies were adapted and developed for production. Ship building was accelerated, and the Royal Navy began the tiresome duty of blockading the French ports, much as they had done during the Napoleonic wars.

Colonial soldiers were recruited and brought up the Mediterranean to Gibraltar and a shaky alliance was formed with Spain. Spain would help to feed and house British troops and allow them to move unhindered to the Southern border of France, then Spanish troops would guide the army through the Pyrenees in order to stage an invasion. The plan was put in place in January of 1915, expecting preparations to take six months or more.

~

After marching the breadth of France, witnessing the horrors of the Massacre de la Concorde and boarding another troop train, young Gefreiter Kessler enjoyed twenty-four hours' rest in Bordeaux. He saw the Atlantic Ocean for the first time and lost his virginity to a girl named Valerie. They met on Boulevard Deganne and ate ice cream as they watched the ships in Arcachon bay. She and Otto walked along the seafront smoking cigarettes and laughing at one another, although she spoke no German and he spoke no French. They sat on the dunes and watched the sunset, and in the magical twilight he touched her face with a trembling hand. Valerie blushed and looked at the ground. He saw her eyelashes and longed to tell her how beautiful she was in words she might comprehend, while she thought that she loved him and wished that he would just hurry up and kiss her.

He kissed her and it made his head swim, she kissed him back and *knew* that she loved him. They fell back onto the sand and held each other, kissing desperately, tugging at buttons and buckles, exploring, and feeling. Finally, he was on top of her, desperate and desperately out of his depth, until she helped, and it was happening. She smiled and he blushed in ecstasy and then fatigue. They lay there for hours wrapped in his greatcoat, exploring each other, and they made love several more times until finally, in the very early hours they fell asleep. They washed in the sea and ate breakfast at a café, they paid for a photograph, he wrote his address on a packet of Heer und Flotte cigarettes and promised to write.

Neither did, and later, on the day he married his wife, he burned the photograph of Valerie Ledoyen.

Troop trains arrived full of reservists and old men to man the new frontier of the German Empire. Newly promoted Gefreiter Kessler, along with one million other young men boarded the now empty trains, this time bound for East Prussia. The train carriages were little better than cattle cars with windows. Along the way, Otto's rowdier comrades would open the large sliding door, hanging out of it to jeer at the forlorn looking French, now citizens of the German empire. When the train entered Germany proper, the soldiers enjoyed waving to cheering civilians, exultant in victory and proud to be German.

Der Mauerfall – Berlin, 1990

The fall of the Berlin Wall.

He was fifty-six, but his reflection in a storefront showed him the face of a man closer to seventy-six, but twenty-eight years of hard labour would do that to any man.

He turned the corner onto Hackenbergstraße and took in his surroundings, finding it even more run down than he remembered. He didn't know who lived there now and whether or not they would let him in, but he would have to try. He rubbed his hands together against the cold and felt the stubs of the three fingers he had lost to frostbite, and as he moved on his limp reminded him of the one remaining toe on his left foot.

Sometimes it felt like they were all still there, and he would wiggle them and look down, almost surprised when he saw that they were gone. The first years of his ordeal had been spent laying railway track, year-round, in a lignite mine, and it was during that first winter that he had lost the fingers and toes to frostbite.

He was tired all the time these days and fell asleep frequently in awkward places. The colourful synthetic clothes given to him at the refugee centre hung from his emaciated figure, and he would have appeared ridiculous if he didn't look so miserable. A kind woman had trimmed his hair and shaved his straggly beard before he saw the doctor, who ended up running a lot of tests.

Hohenschönhausen had killed stronger men than Doktor Rudolph Kessler, but he'd had something – someone – to keep him going. He had clung to the memories of Olga and the time they had spent together in the summer of 1961. He had no idea if Olga was dead or alive, but he knew that if what he was looking for on Hackenbergstraße was still there, everything would be alright. He would make it right.

The biggest shock to Rudi was not the number of cars, nor the herds of colourful angular punks, but the 37-kilometre scar through his beautiful city. The Berlin Wall, or anti-fascist protection barrier, was a pair of three-point-six-meter-high concrete walls, as far apart as one hundred and forty-six metres, sandwiching all kinds of horrors. This nether zone was known as the death strip or *Todesstreifen,* and contained mazes of barbed wire covered by machine guns and spotlights to stop any escapees that managed to climb the first wall.

Rudi shuffled into his old building and made for the basement, finding the door open. The air was damp and foetid, and it choked him, causing him to cough; a loud, baying agony in his chest that he could not stop for some time.

He woke on the floor minutes or hours later, cold and confused. He took in his surroundings, seeing that his old laboratory had become some kind of squat, with signs of drug use and a layer of grime on every surface. His heart leapt when he saw the ruined, rotten remnants of a rug, made filthy by half a century of spillage and other depredation in the dim light of the street-level windows. The rug had become stuck to the floor after years of neglect and Rudi had to use a fire-blackened knife he had found to prise one edge up. The rug peeled back to reveal a square of plywood that sat flush with the floor. Rudi used the knife a second time to pry the board up and, with tears running down his face, he saw his life's work untouched for nearly thirty years.

He picked the papers up with his broken hands and smiled a near toothless smile, his eyes screwed up, causing the tears to blur his vision. These pages represented over thirty years of hope. They represented a life unlived, a love unloved, and a world unmade. He thought of her as the world around him went dark again.

~

He woke on the floor to the sound of voices, and he was on his feet with the speed of a much younger man, protectively clutching his papers to his chest. The voices came from a youth with unnaturally bright red hair, long on top and shaved on the sides. It looked deflated, like it had at one time been a tall mohawk but had not been washed for some weeks.

With him was an emaciated girl who could not have been more than twenty-one, though she had the lined face of a thirty-year-old and black dirt under each of her fingernails. These were, apart from the fashionable clothes and hair, the kind of malnourished, ghost-like souls that Rudi had spent the last twenty-eight years with. Despite the GDR's claim to be a 'land without drugs,' heroin and AIDS were as much a part of Hohenschönhausen as any other prison in Europe.

He decided to let them get high, make sure they were okay, watch them pass out and then continue with his work. Drug addicts were easily controlled, so long as their addiction was satisfied, and he might need some compliant helpers. He was, after all, trying to save the world.

"Good evening," Rudi said. "This is my place, but if you need somewhere safe to get high, then you can go through there." He pointed towards the bedroom and smiled his gummy smile.

"Cool," the youth said smiling and giving Rudi a thumbs up before pushing past him. The girl smiled and followed nervously.

"Junger Mann?" Rudi stopped the boy.

"Ja."

"Don't fucking die in my house."

"Ja, ja." The punk made a dismissive gesture with his hand.

Rudi made to say something else to the punk, but he began coughing again. It was not quite as bad as before, but it alarmed his guests and they backed away cautiously. He recovered, but the coughing fits were exhausting.

He sat down and began to sort through his research until eventually he found Torsten's quantum entanglement calculations. The paper had aged, damp had crept in at the corners and its smell mingled with the foetid air of the basement.

These were the key to teleportation and the moment Rudi had copied them down was the point in time he must reach. He knew that he was not capable of this kind of work, time travel would not be possible without that traitorous Marxist swine. Rudi had come prepared, and now produced a folder from his day-glow bag to protect this precious document and several others that were vital to the project.

101

The couple in the bedroom had completed their preparation and were now applying makeshift torniquets. Rudi had watched this time and again and paid little notice, carrying on with sorting through his trove.

He took some blank pages and carefully wrote out the gravity calculations he had memorised over fifteen years ago during a forced march. The guards were shooting stragglers and the pain in his extremities on that bitter day in January 1974 had become unbearable. He had forced himself into a meditative state and it was then that the pieces had finally fallen into place.

By the time he had finished both kids were out cold, so he checked their pulses and covered them with a soiled blanket against the chill. Taking one last look around, he left the basement on Hackenbergstraße for what he hoped would be the last time.

Rudi turned onto Dörpfeldstraße and headed west until he reached a tram stop. He used the handful of Ostmarks given to him upon his release to buy a ticket. Turning to a blonde-haired boy of about twelve wearing a red Number One FC Union Berlin shirt, he said:

"Junger, if I fall asleep, please wake me at the University," and as he said this, he placed a grotesque hand on the boy's shoulder. The boy recoiled in fear, made worse by Rudi's toothless smile, and he promptly moved to another part of the tram and stared at the floor.

"I'll wake you up, old man."

Rudi looked around for the source of the words and saw another punk, a young man in a black leather motorcycle jacket.

He had bright blue hair shaved in strips either side of a mohawk. Was this city populated entirely by punks now?

"Danke, Junger Mann," Rudi replied as he dozed off.

No matter the length of his repose – from a cat nap to a full night's sleep – Rudi's subconscious would transport him back to those first days in the prison at Hohenschönhausen. He went there now.

~

He was roughly shaken awake to have his senses assaulted by the stench of piss and shit.

The guard dragged him to his feet and slapped his face, another guard threw water over him, and the pair retired into the corridor.

He had quickly learned not to react or resist, because the first time they had beaten him badly, and the second time they had given him a week in the dark room – a cell lined with black padding – and the only light he saw came from the sporadic opening of the serving hatch when thin gruel or some water appeared.

Once, in his desperation to eat, he had knocked over his bowl, spilling the grey watery meal onto the filthy cell floor, and he'd had no choice but to suck the foul substance from the fabric into his mouth.

The next time he upset the guards, Rudi was taken to a cell filled with water, where he stood for nearly three days. Several times he collapsed with exhaustion and hypothermia to wake up drowning. That drowning sensation, that hideous, terrifying jolt of primal fear, was how he felt every time he woke up now, such was the depth of his trauma.

~

"Man, hey man?" The punk gently shook him awake. "We are at the university."

Rudi woke with a start and recoiled against the window of the tram into the foetal position. He was mortified when he realised where he was, "Entschuldigung… Danke, Junger Mann," Rudi answered groggily.

Rudi disembarked the tram and looked up at his alma mater; it was almost as neglected as his apartment with cracked masonry, sunken eves and boarded-up windows. The pavement was fractured and the stone steps leading up to the main doors were worn to a curve.

This is good, thought Rudi, *I am a broken old man, and this is a broken old institute, so they are more likely to hear me out.*

Rudi wandered through the halls looking for his old lab, he thought of his former partner, although he knew that he would not find Torsten. When he had informed on his friends, the Stasi had taken him too for good measure. He had been unable to convince them of his innocence, so he had tried to tell them about the time machine. Assuming he had lost his mind, they took pity on him, and he died in the Daldorf mental asylum at Pankow after years of electric shock therapy. Rudi felt an abstract pity for the man who had once been his best friend, but little else.

"Hey, you," came an authoritative voice from inside a lab. "You! What are you doing in here?"

"Please, I am Doctor Rudolph Kessler, I used to work here before..." He paused and sighed a deep, sorrowful sigh, "... before the Stasi took me away."

"Rudi Kessler, it that you? It's Max, Max Klein." He was a large man in his late forties. "I hardly recognised you."

"*Kleine*," Rudi beamed, and made to embrace the ironically named giant.

"What happened to you? To Olga and Torsten? Some said you'd escaped to the West just before die Mauer, others say that you were all killed in an experiment."

"Torsten told the Stasi that Olga and I were dissidents helping others to escape, and they took us in the night to Normannenstraße, then to Hohenschönhausen. I saw Olga..." he trailed off, "...Torsten died in the Dalldorf a few years ago."

Max could tell that Rudi had said all he wanted to on the matter, so he did not press further.

"Come to my office, my friend, sit down and drink coffee with me." Max showed Rudi through his lab to a connected office. When they had drunk about half a cup, Rudi produced Torsten's calculations on quantum entanglement and placed them silently on Max's desk, and the sight of his frost-bitten fingers made Max winced involuntarily.

He took the proffered sheets without speaking. By the time he looked up from his reading the coffee was cold, and Rudi had fallen asleep in his high-backed armchair. Max smiled at his old friend and looked around his office at the reminders of a life spent in academia, by no means comfortable according to Western standards but one of relative ease compared with his fellow East Germans. He looked back to his friend; a brilliant man destroyed by communism.

Max looked over the other documents in Rudi's folder, it took him several hours and by the time he had digested all the material, the streetlights on Rudower Chaussee were casting shadows on the wall of his office. As he finished what he was reading, he stood excitedly and strode off to the engineering department.

Rudi woke in the dark to a loud thump and the sound of Max cursing. He was instantly alert and wearily peered into the lab. Max had gathered all kinds of *zeug* in his lab. Rudi loved the word, which usually brought a smile to his face. *Zeug* – "stuff" – could be added to practically any word. *Werkzeug* would be tool, *Spielzeug* would be toy, *Schlagzeug* would be drumkit, and so on.

Rudi could also see a microwave oven, something he was aware existed but had not seen before. Of course, he understood how they worked and the theory behind the rotation of polar molecules, but he wouldn't know what to put inside it or how long for. Max had stripped this particular model down to its component parts and appeared to be making some sort of electronic weighing scale. In fact, what he had built did resemble a weighing scale with a digital display and a stainless-steel top, and the scale itself was connected to a desktop computer.

Max had dropped an unrelated item and was annoyed that he had to stop what he was doing in order clean it up. He had been about to input the last line of the formula to attempt a teleportation.

"Is this what I think it is?" Rudi asked with tears in his eyes. "Mein, mein *Zeitmaschine*, my life's work?"

"Ja," Max said, sheepishly. "I was so excited by the entanglement stuff, I read everything else you had in that little folder. I didn't want to wake you, though. I hope that's okay?"

"Ja, never mind about that," Rudi replied, waving his arm impatiently, "talk me through all of this."

"Like I said, I got so excited by all your research that I went straight to engineering and grabbed a trolley full of anything that works on a particle level and started bolting stuff together."

"What should we send?"

Max cast about the lab feverishly for a suitable object.

"We need something with a simple structure."

"Aside from gases like hydrogen and argon?" Rudi rubbed his stubbled chin. "Copper!" he said, raising one of his good fingers in the air.

"Natürlich, I'll strip a piece of electrical wire." Max rummaged in a draw for pliers.

"Ja, genau," agreed Rudi, and he took the stripped wire from Max and folded it into the shape of the symbol for the Greek god Chronos, then placed it onto the stainless-steel top of the weighing scale.

"Now, we input the data into the computer." Max typed hesitantly on the keyboard of a VEB Kombinat Robotron, a GDR manufactured computer that left much to be desired.

"I'll set the coordinates to the other side of this lab, but in theory it doesn't matter where we want to send it, as long as we can provide a vector." He pressed enter as he quoted Goethe: "*Doubt can only be removed by action.*"

The Robotron clicked and whirred as it listed the tasks it was performing on the monitor. It had to store a molecular copy of the copper and download that to the new location. For a more complicated molecular structure, more processing power and memory would be required, but this experiment would give them the raw data needed to calculate what exactly would be possible.

Rudi stood by the lab bench that Max had chosen for a destination. He watched the spot marked with a square of masking tape, waiting for something to happen. Three seconds after Max had hit the enter key, smoke started rising from the scales, there was a loud click, and the computer screen showed a message.

"*Zeitmaschine* disconnected, connect again?"

"*Disappointments are to the soul what a thunderstorm is to the air,*" Max said with a sigh, quoting yet another great German.

"Never mind," Rudi said, "we can keep trying. Got anymore micro—" another coughing fit racked him, this time so bad that Max called an ambulance and Rudi spent the night in hospital.

The next morning, "We Didn't Start the Fire" By Billy Joel played on the radio as Max took Rudi home in his mark I Golf. Driving down Müggelheimer towards the Lange Bridge, Rudi was speaking animatedly about the time machine and their research when Max cut him off.

"Don't you think you should rest, Rudi, take it easy for a while?" he said, one hand on the wheel and the other glued to the gearstick.

"What for, Max?"

"To get better, Rudi, to make sure you don't end up back in the *krankenhaus*?"

Rudi looked at his old friend with the watery eyes of a very old man.

"I'm dying, Max. The next time I go in an ambulance, it'll probably be taking me to the morgue."

"Rudi, I'm so sorry."

"Don't be sorry, Max, just help me finish this time machine. Help me finish what I set out to do nearly forty years ago!"

"What is it you want to do with it, Rudi?"

"I wanted to stop all this suffering," he gestured vaguely around him at Berlin and perhaps Germany too, "but I'm too near to death for that, so instead, I want to use it to prevent mine and Olga's imprisonment." Rudi raised a gnarled hand to quieten Max's protests.

"I simply mean to warn myself of Torsten's betrayal, giving Olga and me a chance to run west."

Max was silent for a long time before he spoke softly.

"*Keep true to the dreams of thy youth.*"

He looked at the broken man his friend had become, at the life he had led, at the decades of suffering etched upon his face, and he could not bring himself to say no.

Rudi turned up the radio and listened for a short time.

"He's right Max, the world *is* on fire…"

~

At Max's place Rudi showered in private for maybe the second time in thirty years, and they stayed up talking about the old days until Rudi fell asleep on the sofa. The next day Max had his assistant take anything useful into an empty room in the basement. Rudi toiled away down there with Max's assistant Bobby; a young woman who had earned a place on the PhD program through a scholarship at the University of Namibia. Amazonian in stature, she had tested her strength more than once catching Rudi as he fell into another coughing fit.

For days on end the pair laboured, Bobby was an astute physicist and had brought herself up to speed quickly. Only Rudi's intermittent sleeping slowed their progress, and Max spent every moment he could snatch with them.

One month and ten microwaves later, they were ready for attempt one hundred and forty-seven. Bobby placed the copper wire on the scales and nodded to Max, who typed hesitantly on the keyboard of the Robotron.

"Now, the data is already in the computer, so I'll set the co-ordinates again."

The Robotron clicked and whirred as it listed the tasks, while Rudi and Bobby watched the spot marked with a square of masking tape. Three seconds after Max had hit the enter key, the copper wire appeared. Rudi picked it up in amazement and bit it with a couple of his remaining molars.

"It's real!" he exclaimed, and he looked at the clock on the wall. "At four thirty AM on thirteenth February 1990 we became the first men to teleport matter." Tears filled his eyes and he looked at his friend.

"But not for long," he added.

"Just think what we could do with Western technology?" Max was pouring Schnaps for them.

"I bet the Amie's have computers that could transport a Cadillac," Rudi joked. "Prost!"

"Well done, Herr Doktor, you are a bona fide genius."

They stopped to eat breakfast then carried on all day, spurred on by their success. By March they had a data set that could be used to work out the requirements for most inanimate objects. They always used the box on the lab bench as a control and didn't worry about other destinations. By Sunday lunchtime they were ready to send a sentient being, so Max left the room and returned with a small white rat.

"This is Helmut, he will be the first rat to travel from one point to another without traversing the physical space between." Max paused, looking at the rat fondly. "He's our little pioneer."

They held their breath. Max had to type a lot of information into the computer for this test, and he spent a long time checking and rechecking his calculations. Finally, when he was satisfied, he placed Helmut onto the scale and used the delicate scaffold to stop him from running away.

"Viel Glück, Helmut."

Max hit the return key, and Rudi rushed over to the drop box, as they had begun to call it. It took longer still to upload Helmut's molecular details, then he seemed to appear like white noise, flickering in and out of existence, until eventually the whole of the rat was visible.

Helmut looked around, confused for two or three seconds before he let out a blood curdling squeak, writhing in pain on the bench as cerebral fluid ran from his ears.

Nine rats later, Max and Rudi concluded that it was nomologically impossible to teleport sentient life without it dying shortly after. Rudi had a horrific vision of a giant version of his machine being used by the Nazis to racially purify the Third Reich. He shuddered and remembered his purpose, the task he had begun nearly forty years before, and it would ensure those atrocities never happened in the first place.

"I think we've hit a wall, Rudi. How about we try some time travel tests?"

"*You see, my son, time turns here into space,*" Rudi said, quoting Parsifal.

"Wagner? I had you down as more of a Mendelssohn kind of guy."

Max had built the *Zeitgerät* after studying both the quantum entanglement calculations and Rudi's latest time evolution equations for density states in the presence of closed time-like curves. The requirements for this were built into his first iteration. Max had also calculated that, with Western technological advances, this machine, or a simpler, more limited version, could have been built as early as 1962.

It became a case of repeating the most data-rich experiments of the last few months with time as a variable. Rudi placed the copper Chronos on the scale and they began their tests by sending the Chronos to the drop box, then observing any changes in their memory, until soon it became necessary to change the location to Rudi's desk in the next room. Shortly after sending the Chronos back a few days, a sudden nausea overcame them all.

"What happened?" Rudi asked, taking in his surroundings. Passing out and coming around hours later had become par for the course recently, but this was different, nor was he used to seeing his companions sleeping beside him.

"I'm not sure," Bobby said, massaging her temples.

"We should take it easy for the next hour while we try to figure out what has happened." Max. Suggested

They discussed the implications of what they were doing, deciding to attempt to change something arbitrary, like the outcome of a minor sports competition. First, they would have to figure how they might affect something like that by dropping a small object blindly in spacetime.

"What if we just stop play mid-way through a match?"

"How?"

"We could make a fake bomb and place it under the stand the morning before the match, then the bomb would be found, and the match would be called off, then we go and buy a paper and read about it."

"What if the discovery of the bomb causes mass panic and a stampede, killing hundreds of people?" Bobby Said.

"Okay," conceded Rudi, "that was a bad one." He scratched his stubbled chin with the stump of his thumb and forefinger. "We could write you a cryptic letter asking you to wear a brightly coloured tie or something on Friday morning?"

"Then I'd still be wearing it," Max said, sniffing his armpit. It was the early hours of Monday morning, and he was beginning to smell ripe.

Max typed the letter so as not to freak himself out too much and Rudi worked out the coordinates of Max's apartment. Shortly after they hit send, Max's dull brown necktie dissolved, and a red spotted bowtie appeared, slowly replacing it.

Again, nausea descended, and they were forced to rest. They could all sense the gravity of the moment and decided to drink another Schnaps, though unsure whether it was celebratory, or medicinal.

"We need to change something more material than your neckwear, Max."

"Carl is due to begin his first day in a few hours." Max looked at his wristwatch. His latest PhD student would just be making his morning coffee.

"What if we wait for him to arrive, then place a letter on his doormat instructing him to come in late?" suggested Bobby.

"So, while Carl is standing with us in the room, we prevent him being there in the first place?" Rudi rubbed his chin. "That could be very conclusive, but it does carry risk."

They were all so tired at this stage that their judgement was clouded, and they agreed to the test.

Carl arrived and took in the sight of his doctoral supervisor, asleep over his desk, with what appeared to be a homeless man snoring loudly in a chair. The room stank of unwashed men, which he attributed solely to the unshaven septuagenarian snoring loudly in the corner.

"You must be Carl," Bobby's deep voice caused him to jump and as he turned to see a weary African woman towering over him and proffering coffee.

The two old friends woke to the smell of a fresh brew and the sight of very a confused Carl standing awkwardly in Bobby's shadow.

After introductions were made and explanations given, Carl was invited to sit down in a comfortable chair while Max programmed the time machine and Rudi typed a note telling Carl to come in two hours later and placed it on the scales.

"We should all take a seat in a comfortable chair," Bobby said as she pushed an armchair through the lab for Max to sit in and arranged two more close by. All four scientists were now arranged in a semicircle around the *Zeitmaschine*. This was the moment that Rudi had been building up to for the past thirty-five years. He nodded to Max, then he leant forward to hit enter on the keyboard.

"*Who dares nothing need hope for nothing?*" Max said, as they passed out cold.

They awoke to the smell of coffee and the sight of a confused Carl standing awkwardly at the door of Max's office. They were sitting in the same positions Carl had found them in earlier. Although as far as they were concerned, this was the first time Carl had walked through that door.

"You must be Carl," Bobby said, offering him a coffee.

"You're two hours late," Max said, checking his watch, "that's not a great start to your first day, is it?"

"Herr Doktor, please excuse me, there was a note sent to my apartment—"

"A note?"

"From you Herr Doktor."

It occurred to Rudi that if for some reason Carl had not made it to work this morning, they would not be aware that anything had changed or that they had even tested the theory. If Carl were not aware that he was delayed by a letter from Max or chose not to mention it, could they have lived the same two hours for eternity?

"I guess we'd better send this stuff to myself in 1961 before we really mess things up in 1990," Rudi said when they had finally convinced Carl to leave.

"I was thinking, there are other things that we can do to help you in the past, Rudi. I could write letters from one prominent physicist to another. Who was the director of Max Planck in the sixties?"

"Werner Heisenberg, the fucking Nazi bomb maker," Bobby Spat.

Rudi reached a gnarled hand out towards his friend and grabbed at thin air, his face contorted, and he plummeted to the floor. Max carefully turned him onto his back and propped him up, holding his head with one hand and his grotesque hand with the other.

"Rudi?" he whispered, "I'm here."

"Max," he said hoarsely, "you are a brilliant physicist and a dear, dear friend." With two strong fingers he pulled Max closer by his tie and croaked, "save... Olga."

And then he was gone.

Befreien – Grunewald, 2035

Rescue

Altstötter cried out in agony and fear as the flashbang detonated. His body protected Olga's vision, although her hearing was rendered useless for now. A blanket was thrown over her and she was bundled out of the room through the house and out of the main doors. She felt the gravel on her bare feet and then her shin struck something, bringing excruciating pain. It was the rear bumper of the van she now found herself in, speeding along dark country lanes at breakneck speeds as she ventured to look at her captors.

Looking back at her, shaking out their beautiful dark hair were two fierce looking olive-skinned women. They smiled at Olga, and one reached out to reassure her in some way, but she recoiled, not used to people who looked like this. Or the concept of women with guns. She wasn't ready to process it, so she scrambled further into the corner of the van.

"I'm Yael, and this is Ruth."

Olga did not recognise the accent, hearing something European with an American twang. Overwhelmed by the noise of the van and being bumped around in it, she was also in shock from the ordeal she'd just escaped and desperate to wash herself. She began to cry loud, heavy sobs, snot and tears covering her face and hands.

"Here." Yael tossed her a towel and ventured closer to Olga, and now her words were tender. "Shayna Punim, everything is going to be fine, *alts vet zeyn fayn*," she murmured as she took Olga's hand softly.

"Are…are you German? That sounded like German?" Olga was scared. She snatched her hand away and looked into Yael's big brown eyes, her thoughts serving to confuse her.

But a German wouldn't hurt Herr Altstötter, no matter how much he deserved it.

"No, that was Yiddish, it's something the women in my family have always said to sooth and comfort." Yael shuffled closer to Olga. "We are Israeli."

"You are Jews!" Olga was now even more confused because Jews were rat-like caricatures of humans, with hooked noses and stooping postures, they were cowardly and remained hidden among the Arabs and the Blacks in Africa.

"But… you are so beautiful." Olga knew how ridiculous she sounded and reflected that she had never actually met a Jew. She was simply repeating the words of her parents and teachers, who had likely never met Jews either.

The generations of indoctrination inflicted on the people of the Reich had slowly become less fervent as the threat of Jews seemed more distant.

"I am sorry, I have… I have never met a Jew. I am sure you know what they teach us at school?" A little less sure now of her understanding of this, Olga voiced her apology making it sound more like a question to the new strangers.

"I'm sure I can guess," Yael smiled at Olga.

Olga attempted a smile, but she could not quite bring herself to achieve it.

"I want to wash… and I'm thirsty." She was aware she sounded like a petulant child, even though she had not meant to and now she felt the tears come back. Yael handed her a canteen, and she took a long drink.

"You can wash soon. Did he…" Yael stumbled, "…were we in time, before?"

"Before I had sex with him?" Olga spat the words with venom.

"Before he raped you, honey." Yael looked at her with compassion and something else, perhaps understanding.

"What is rape?" Olga demanded. "Is it a Jewish word?"

"No, Mami, it is an English word, it means sex against your will."

"Then it wasn't rape." Olga turned from Yael in shame and tried to hide under the blanket.

"Oh, honey," Yael said as she searched for the right words, "it also means when you're made to feel like you didn't have a choice. Maybe he said he would hurt you?"

"He wasn't going to hurt me; he was going to make me a Gräfin. Now I'm a whore and I will know only shame for the rest of my days." Olga burst into tears again, and although those words were the words of her schoolteacher, in that moment she truly believed them.

"What did he say would happen if you didn't let him rape you?"

"He said that my family would live lives of mediocrity, nothing worse."

"And did you truly believe that?"

"Not really, I know how powerful he is… did you kill him?"

"It was safest, we needed to think about your family, and you can bet that if he were alive then they would be on their way to colonial Africa by the end of the week."

"What will happen to them now?" Olga's absence would surely implicate them through her.

"We have left a corpse to be mistaken for yours when they search through the ashes of the house."

"What about the rest of the Altstötters?"

"They should escape unharmed. The fire was set in that weird sex room with the hidden door. Although without a man's protection, in your society…" she trailed off. "Listen, I need you to understand that what that man was about to do to you was rape. You knew he would hurt you or your family if you refused, he promised you the other things to make it easier for you to say yes and to make you feel just as you do now. You shouldn't feel that way at all, you are the victim, and he was the rapist."

"Where are we going?"

"Bristol, and there we board a boat to Israel."

"I don't know anything about Israel," Olga said in a horrified tone, realising that she had just resigned herself to her fate. She had been rescued, kidnapped by these fierce, beautiful, women who came from a land of equality and freedom, and she had never imagined anything more than the life of obedience planned for her by the Reich. Of making a home and bearing children.

"Well, put these on and I'll tell you." Yael handed Olga a bag of dark, practical clothing. "About one hundred years ago, the

European and Russian Jews were coming under ever-increasing persecution, and many had emigrated to America, but when the Great War began it wasn't safe to cross the ocean. The Zionists – the Jews that campaigned for Jewish autonomy – petitioned the Kaiser for a land of their own. The Kaiser, who had many Jewish friends, indulged their request, and promised the land of Israel to any Jew who wanted it."

Olga continued to dress, covering her body as best she could as the words tumbled through her mind.

"Many, feeling the situation was too volatile in Russia, fled south and made the epic journey thorough Arabia to the Holy Land. After the war, anti-Semitism became a major problem for Jews in the continental Reich, so Chancellor Ludendorff's government decided to purge all Jews from the Urals to the Atlantic. He said this."

Yael did not sound sad. This was the story of the birth of her nation, and it had happened so very long ago, but Olga was confused and frightened.

"They sent the same soldiers they had used to drive the Slavs east through Russia, to remove the seven hundred thousand Muslims from Palestine. It was brutal, but far easier and cheaper than what we discovered years later was the other solution."

"What was it?" Olga was enraptured, for she knew nothing of global history other than what the state had told her through her teachers, and the talk of Arabs and epic journeys excited her and distracted her from the harsh reality of her own situation.

"Ludendorff and his cronies wanted to round up every single Jew in Europe and Russia, put them into labour camps and work them to death. There is evidence to suggest worse than that..."

Olga gasped at this because Ludendorff was a hero of the Reich. There was even a statue of him in Parliament Square.

"They were persuaded by bureaucrats that this brutalism over the Arabs would have far less political impact, cost less and take a fraction of the time. For this assistance they imposed sanctions upon us before we were even a sovereign state."

Yael looked at Olga, who was following every word with fascinated horror.

"Still to this day, Germany does not allow us to operate a navy and our army must be a defence force only, restricted to half a million soldiers. Thankfully, they thought an air force beyond our reach, and we have developed some of the finest aircraft in the world, and of course you know that we put the first astronaut on the moon back in 1973. Her name was Yael Rom." She said with a smile that suggested she might be the equal of her namesake.

"Man just landed on the moon for the first time this year, and it was German astronaut Johannes Baumgartner," Olga said indignantly.

"The Reich has so much control over information, over the media, that it effectively controls history," Yael said with scorn.

"We're at the docks," Ruth said, speaking for the first time. She checked her rifle and opened the door of the van a crack, peering out before exiting fully, then Yael ushered Olga out and followed her in a tactical stance, weapon up and eyes darting in every direction.

Olga had imagined a great ship, like those she had seen in this port upon her arrival, but they weren't in Bristol. The sign welcomed her to Portishead Marina, although she had no idea where that was, and guessed they'd said Bristol for that reason.

The boat Yael had mentioned was a fifty-foot catamaran, black hulled with black sails. It was the darkest black she had ever seen, almost invisible against the night sky. The wind blew through the rigging of countless boats, producing an orchestral braying of steel ropes on aluminium masts. Ruth led the way to the jetty followed by the driver, then Olga, with Yael in the rear.

"Where are the crew?" Olga asked as they stepped aboard.

"We are the crew, we left our skipper Daniel on board as a harbour watch, but Ruth, Chaim and I, we sailed it here and we just know you are going love helping us sail it back to the Mediterranean and to Israel." As she said this, the mooring warps were rigged to slip, and the skipper made his final checks. The jib was unfurled, and the boat pulled away from the jetty.

"We've just caught the ebb, guys, perfect timing," Daniel turned to Olga. "You must be Olga, I'm so glad we got you out and to have you aboard the *Herev*, you have the forward cabin in the starboard hull." Olga blinked and stared blankly at him the dim light from the binnacle, he had kind eyes and she felt like she could trust him.

"Come on, I'll show you." Yael led her into a spacious saloon with a curved seating area around a tessellating table. There was storage everywhere, and the kitchen, or galley, was generous and well equipped.

They descended a companionway into the starboard hull and turned left down a short, narrow passage, at the end of which was a cabin. It was simple but comfortable with a queen bed occupying most of the space and lockers on every available wall.

A small window gave a view of the Bristol Channel by moon-light.

"I'm going to let you get some rest. There are clothes in the lockers for you and the head is next door. You share with me as I'm in the aft cabin," and she jerked her thumb behind her at the rear of the boat.

"Can you stay with me?" Olga felt ridiculous, but she was terrified because this had been the most traumatic thing that had happened in her short life, and she did not want to be alone.

"You get yourself a shower and I'll come back. Try to be sparing with the water, we can't put in for more until North Africa," she said as her head disappeared around the door.

On deck, the mainsail was set and the *Herev* was flying along at twenty knots. She was an exceptionally fast boat, by and large, with a tolerable weather helm and beautiful lines, a fine blue water sailor with provision enough for three months on full rations. The immense battery bank powered everything, from the electric prop to motors for the furling main and the desalination system used for rendering seawater drinkable.

Ruth was derigging their kit and making the weapons safe while Daniel and Chaim – the pair could have been brothers with their thick curly hair and caramel skin, although the notion was dispelled when Chaim brushed a stray lock from Daniel's face a kissed him gently on the lips – set the course plotters and consulted the charts for the treacherous sandbanks of the channel. They had to be clear of the land before first light or they would be sunk out of hand by the shore batteries. Yael joined

Ruth in the last few tasks as they transitioned from deadly Mossad operatives to seasoned yacht crew.

"She's shaken up quite badly," Yael said, speaking in hushed tones.

"Wouldn't you be?"

"Of course, but she asked me to stay with her tonight."

"Sure, that's why I've kept my distance. I can be the tough one if she needs it later on, because this voyage will be hard for her, but right now she needs someone to be there," Ruth said.

"I'll see you in the morning, then," Yael said, affectionately punching Ruth's shoulder.

She found Olga weeping in her cabin as she quietly climbed in beside her and Olga snuggled down. Yael's arms were like rock, Olga's father and brothers were strong and toned but their hugs were never like this. She felt safe and right now, that was all she needed.

By four in the morning the *Herev* was rounding Bull Point, tearing along at thirty knots, close hauled on a port tack. Water was creaming along the hulls and soon they would be able to change course for the open sea and an even faster point of sail.

Daniel had stayed up through Chaim's watch and now he sat at the navigation table while Ruth carried out her rigging checks for the start of her four-hour shift at the helm. This would bring them into daylight and the relative safety of the open sea and international waters. All the tactical gear and weapons had been stowed in a secret compartment, now they were Chilean pleasure sailors headed down to the Med via the Gibraltar Strait.

They passed the puffin-covered Lundy Island at half past four, and the crew knew this would be their last landfall for many hundreds of miles. At six degrees of longitude, they put the boat about and set a southerly course on a beam reach, making forty knots with ease.

Daniel decided that if the sun came out, he would put the motors on too, gaining a further ten knots of speed. He wanted to be out of British waters and well into the Atlantic by noon.

Olga emerged bleary eyed at six, closely followed by Yael. The sun was hanging low on the eastern horizon by now, a deep orange ball turning the sky around it into a pastel inferno.

"Good morning, Olga, Yael," Chaim nodded at the port cabins. "Daniel is still sleeping, but Olga, I would like you to speak with Ruth and after breakfast, we will go over some basics to keep you safe. Then we'll see about teaching you to sail, and if you're a quick learner, we may have you on your own watch by the end of the voyage. That means we will all get a little more rest. What do you think?"

"Err," Olga looked to Yael for guidance. She did not know why because it was a simple question, but she felt helpless. She was surrounded by strangers from a foreign land, a people she had been taught to hate and distrust, even though they had saved her from being raped and protected her family from the fallout of Altstötter's death. On the other hand, they had also kidnapped her, and they were taking her thousands of miles away.

"What for? Why did you rescue me? Why are you taking me to Israel? And what were you doing here in the first place? It's a long way to come for just one girl."

126

The group looked at one another, then back to Olga, then everyone looked at Yael who rolled her eyes and sighed.

"We were here looking for you. You are Olga Felsen, and we need you. Humanity needs you. But you have to trust us four, just know that the world needs you and because of that, we will keep you safe, Olga. Israel is the safest place for you and after last night, it's the *only* place for you." Yael took a deep breath and watched for Olga's reaction.

"How can you know that? I can barely read and write! My maths is only enough to bake cakes and organise parties." The admission made her feel worthless, the acknowledgment of these shortcomings contrasting to these highly trained soldiers.

"I don't know anything. In the train station at Bristol, there were all of these beautiful machines and I don't have the first idea of how they might work. I am for making babies and cooking meals, and I…" she broke down in tears; the loud cathartic sobbing that comes from epiphany.

She knew how ridiculous it all was. Now that she had seen these strong, capable women empowered to lead and to fight, to navigate seas and to storm buildings. The men had waited in safety and let these two women face the danger, make the decisions, and did what was necessary. Women of the Reich had certainly shown strength. Her mother was a strong woman, but this was not about individual strength, this was about the combined strength of a nation empowered, emancipated from patriarchal constructs and the power that this gave these women was something Olga had never imagined.

She wanted it, she needed it. The power she'd felt when she harnessed the language and behaviour of the ruling classes was nothing by comparison, that was the power of fear, of perceived superiority. This was a new kind of power, power from within which could only come from without, shared for the common good. If this was what they were offering, she wanted it, wanted to be part of it, she wanted rock hard muscles and freedom, freedom to choose her vocation, freedom to choose her lover, her clothes, her life, what books she read and how to wear her bloody hair.

"What do I have to do?" she asked.

Yael could see that she was sold and there was no need to win her over. The Germans had eased up on the indoctrination over the last couple of generations, and it showed. If this had been 1970, Olga would have tried to kill Yael in her sleep and swum for the shores of the Reich and back into her gilded cage.

"Ever heard of time travel?" Ruth asked as the others looked at her meaningfully. "What? This is going to take ages, she's just had her world torn down around her, and now is the time for the big one."

"Time travel? They don't teach girls any science in the Reich, so I have no idea if it's possible or not and if the government had it, they wouldn't tell me about it, would they?"

"This is going to be easier than we thought. So, we have the ability to travel through time, and you don't want an explanation?"

I want a basic education, can you give me one of those? she thought. "That doesn't mean anything to me." She shouted, standing and throwing her arms up in frustration, "I'm fucking stupid alright. I don't understand. You throw all these fancy words at me and expect me to be shocked or whatever, but I don't know what is and isn't possible! I thought going to the moon was a big deal, until she tells me you lot went there sixty years ago!" Olga fell back onto the settee, panting and hot with exasperation, "why don't you teach me something simple and we can start from there," she said, not expecting an answer.

"How about start with the rudiments of sailing and navigation," replied Daniel tolerantly, the wind whipped his hair about his face, and he turned his head trying to clear it from his eyes.

"What for? What does sailing have to do with time travel?" Olga asked impatiently.

"We don't have passengers on the *Herev,* only crew," Chaim said. "If you're not willing to learn to keep a watch, then we'll stow you in the bilge with the rest of the ballast."

"Ballast? Olga Asked.

"Dead weight," Ruth said slowly.

"Fine, I'll learn to sail. But why me? Of the thousands of people in the world, why Olga Felsen?"

"We've used you before," Yael said, " according to the files, you've always been one of our best time agents, but you are not always in the same place so it usually takes until your late teens to find you. But it's always worth it and there are billions of people in the world, not thousands honey."

"I don't... I can't..." she stood just as a heavy lurch threw her to the deck, she scrambled up and ran for the safety and isolation of her cabin. As she lay in her berth, the boat pitching a rolling on the ocean, Olga reflected on the gravity of what these people were saying. Her narrow-minded outlook on the world had been blown wide open over the last twenty-four hours.

All her life she'd believed her purpose was to be a good wife, to cook and clean and try to have babies for the Reich. So much so that she was willing to allow that man to rape her and to carry his child in order to better fulfil her ideological purpose. She would be eternally grateful to Yael and Ruth for saving her, and she saw now how restricted her horizons had been. She wanted this life of adventure, she felt that maybe she had always wanted it.

Could she be this woman? This time warrior? Like all Germanic League girls, she took her exercise seriously and she was reasonably fit; nothing like her new crewmates, but she had a solid base. She prodded her stomach to feel her abs and clenched her buttocks. She felt strong and fit and capable of anything.

Ost Front, 1915

Eastern Front

At the battle of Bolimów, the eager Otto Kessler, fresh off the train from France, finally got his wish. The storm tactics wouldn't work with the Russians because they didn't dig in, they simply marched forward until the Germans engaged, then retreated behind machine guns and artillery, and with six million troops on one front, who needed tactics?

The first round that flew past Otto's head was a wakeup call. The first shell screamed and whined. It shook the earth so hard he could hear nothing, and made him shit in his trousers.

Screams of agony came from men beyond help with jagged slashes to their guts and charred stumps where healthy young limbs had been minutes earlier. He had trained with these men and toured the breadth of Europe with them and now he looked on helplessly, as without moving the scene seemed to grow further away, the sound became muffled, and he began to shiver.

The experience paralysed him with fear, and it was something that he would relive many more times when he lay awake in the dark hours before dawn. Otto was finally brought back to reality as the contents of a comrade's skull sprayed across face. He ran to one man he'd known since training, a farmer's son from Hess, and as he tried in vain to put back the bloody pile of meat that used to be his bowels. The boy cried for his mother and Otto gave up, holding him tight until his heart finally gave up.

"Mutti," he whispered into Otto's ear as he faded away.

The Russian machine-gun fire was devastating, and hiding behind a substantial tree, Otto focused his mind and gathered his frayed nerves. He felt the sticky blood and viscera on his hands and the smell brought up his breakfast. As he stared at the ground on his hands and knees, he knew he should move, should point his rifle at the Russians and be a man, but the screaming of his comrades was almost as loud as the fire.

Why am I still here? What if someone sees me? I could be shot for cowardice... but I am not a coward! Get up then, Otto!

Eighteen-year-old Gefreiter Kessler finally manged overcome his fear and when he did, he moved about the battlefield searching for the scattered remnants of his squad, a calmness descended, the fear was still there, but subdued from paralysing emotion to a tame reminder to be careful.

The first able man he found was the platoon commander. He lay in a shell hole sobbing, staring up at the sky.

"Herr Leutnant!" he called, "Herr Leutnant, we must do something about that Russian machine gun." But the man, perhaps two years older than Otto, just screwed up his eyes and sobbed harder. Chunks of potato and sausage covered his uniform tunic and shook from his moustache as his face contorted. Otto joined him in the hole and offered a hand to get the man on his feet. He recoiled, bringing his Luger to bear, and screaming at Otto. The subaltern looked Otto in eye, set his jaw and raised the pistol to his temple.

"I'm sorry. I have failed you."

The shot rang out before Otto could prevent him and the officer became yet another in a litany of the dead that would haunt Otto's dreams.

He moved on, collecting frightened boys and terrified men from every conceivable hiding spot on the battlefield.

Eventually, they found themselves in cover in a mud-filled shell hole. Otto stared around him at the dirty, bloody faces of the men he had rallied to him, and although they were no doubt brave and capable, with no leadership they would die here today.

Otto was one of the youngest here, but no one stepped up, so he steeled himself and asked for some covering fire as he carefully peered over the rim.

Everything seemed oddly peaceful. He could hear the sporadic fire of his own men further down the line, but the Russians seemed to have stopped. He was just about to tell the others that the Russians must have gone when the dirt next to him exploded as the Russian machine-gun team finally managed to get their gun going again. He could see the muzzle flash and identified a route using cover to a point that he could launch an assault from. He called for more covering fire and grabbed the fastest of them, a wiry youth from Spreewald named Axel Weber.

"When I tap you on the helmet, run for that clump of trees," he screamed into Axel's ear.

Axel ran full pelt with his comrades covering him and made it to the safety of the cover. Otto went next, and watched as all but one of them manged to run the gauntlet unscathed. Poor Rolf Krüger, a corpulent drayman from Munich, was too slow and died where he fell in that Polish field.

Otto led a charge to successfully take the Russian machine-gun nest, which turned out to be a key objective. When reinforcements arrived and word of Kessler's calm and confident conduct under fire reached his company commander, he became Obergefreiter Kessler and took command of a squad of riflemen.

He suited command and over the weeks and months his men came to love and respect him, and as the German army advanced further east the fighting grew more intense, causing the butcher's bill to grow ever longer.

Otto's unit boarded another troop train, this time north to the Masurian Lakes, where his unit was re-subordinated and found itself under the command of Hauptmann Fedor von Bock, the nephew of General von Falkenhayn.

He proved to be an unyielding aristocratic Prussian with little regard for his men or their lives. Von Bock disagreed with the recent tactical changes and preferred to throw wave after wave of men uselessly at the enemy, eventually taking the objective and citing his heavy casualties as proof of his men's valour.

"Feldwebel Kessler?"

"Ja, Herr Hauptmann," Otto replied, springing to attention.

"You are new," von Bock said, looking Otto up and down.

"Ja, Herr Hauptmann."

"Where is your platoon commander?"

"Dead Herr Hauptmann."

"You and your men are a disgrace."

"Herr Hauptmann?"

"Your uniforms are filthy, and you haven't shaved."

"These are the uniforms we were issued at the depot, before France, Herr Hauptmann and we have spent the last three weeks on a troop train with insufficient water to wash and shave."

"So you haven't washed either?" sneered von Bock. "Do you know how lucky you are to be here? Do you know what it means to have the opportunity to die for the Fatherland?"

"Ja, Herr Hauptmann," Otto said, confused; he wasn't here to die.

"*Dulce et decorum est pro patria mori*, Feldwebel, do you know what that means?" Von bock refused to make eye contact with Otto.

"It is sweet and fitting to die for the homeland, Herr Hauptmann?" Otto replied, unsure where he had heard this and regretting it already.

"Do you think you are clever Kessler? do you presume to mock me? I am set over you for many reasons but the most important is breeding. I am inherently better than you, I was born better, and I will die better. I hope you remember that and my words on death tomorrow when you and your platoon lead the assault. This is a kindness, Kessler, I am giving you the honour to be my *Vergebliche Hoffnung,* my forlorn hope and the opportunity to cover yourself in glory, to die for the Fatherland." Von Bock turned on his heel and strode away.

The dawn came, Otto had not lost sleep, he was at home with his mortality and he had led more than a few attacks before this one. When he and his men formed up in the half light, the moon still visible in the grey, cloying sky, they were nervous, *Vergebliche Hoffnung* filled most men with dread. At the line of departure, they fidgeted and waited for the preparatory barrage. Otto sat and ate dry bread with last night's stew and encouraged the men to do the same, always aware that soon the great guns would strike up their dirge, fraying the nerves of some and awakening the beast in all.

"Attack," came the call and it was echoed up and down the line.

"Why is there no barrage?" Otto cried, dashing away his food and throwing on his equipment. Before him lay an open field, devoid of cover, with obvious Russian machine gun positions at the far end. He had no choice, he advanced —slowly. Every step brought him closer to death and he dreaded that familiar staccato rattle, the screams that inevitably followed and more pointless bloodshed. He had no plan, but far to the north was ragged tree line hardly what he'd call cover, but it ran all the way to the likely Russian positions and it was all they had. He gave the order and they made for the trees. The men of Otto's platoon used the cover to come within accurate rifle shot of a Russian gun. Suessmann was a fine shot and lead man in the first squad for that reason.

"Take out the trigger man first, I know the loader is a larger target, but you may not have the chance to hit him if we're spotted," Otto whispered. The sun hung low in the east now casting long morning shadows and causing the dew to glisten on the grass between Otto and the Russian line. He listened to Suessmann's controlled breathing and watched it mist in the cool air as the machine gunners head flew back at the very same instant he heard the shot. Suessmann reloaded and rather than move his sights he waited for the loader to take up the trigger position and made the same shot again and again the man's head flew back.

As they did this the second squad were moving fast and low through the trees, unobserved by the enemy who were taken up by their snipper problem. Suessmann had killed five would-be machine gunners by the time second squad were posting their grenade and wreaking havoc behind the poorly manned Russian line. Otto gave the order and the rest of the platoon joined them, turning the Russian gun through ninety degrees and decimating the line with impunity.

"Kessler and his men fought bravely, but they fought intelligently, with tactical awareness and well-practised skill. They took the nest with minimal casualties and sent a runner to report their success." Von Bock's aide gushed at the professionalism of the soldiers, giving a blow-by-blow account of the textbook operation. But it was Ludendorff's textbook. Ludendorff who had betrayed his uncle Erich, taking Falkenhayn's place as chief of the general staff from him and removing von Bock's most influential patron.

And he would be damned if the jumped-up son of a Junker would tell him how to fight a war.

"Bring me Feldwebel Kessler!" von Bock roared at two military policemen "I want that man in irons and brought before me."

The two *Feldgendarmerie*, with highly polished gorgets hanging on chains from their necks, sprang to attention.

"Ja Herr Hauptmann, with what is Feldwebel Kessler charged?" the older of the two asked, a Bavarian with an easy, respectful, yet informal manner that suggested he had been a civilian policeman before the war.

"He disobeyed orders," von Bock said, regaining his composure.

"Ja, Herr Hauptmann," the elder man said with patience. "I have to write down the charge and the exact order that has been disobeyed in my notebook before I can make a lawful arrest."

"Listen to me, you officious little shit," von Bock said calmly through gritted teeth. "Write whatever you want in your *verdammt* book, but I want that man in front of me in irons and I want him here now."

The *Feldgendarmerie Wachtmeister* looked von Bock in the eye. He was only notionally subordinate to this man with his tailored uniform and his imported cigarettes, and he knew that von Bock was used to his well-connected status and all the perquisites that brought.

But Falkenhayn was disgraced, Ludendorff *had* betrayed him, he *had* got his job and now von Bock was embarrassing himself over the apparent bravery of an insignificant Feldwebel. "Herr Hauptmann," he said with almost sarcastic deference now. "In order to arrest this man for disobedience, I must have the facts," he said calmly, his breath misting in the frigid air.

Von Bock exploded once more, bawling out the older, larger man while *he* stood looking indifferent, waiting for him to finish.

"What is all this shouting, von Bock?" The ancient regimental colonel appeared at the door of his tent, moustaches bristling and trouble in his grey eyes.

Von Bock sprang to attention. "Herr Oberst," he said with surprise as he clicked his heels together and straightened his back.

"Well, man? I asked you a question." The colonel was a supporter of Ludendorff and despised this privileged and, until recently, influential man-child.

"This policeman," the word dripped with disdain, "will not arrest one of my men."

"Is this correct, Wachtmeister?" the colonel asked in a conversational tone, so different to the condescension he practised upon von Bock.

"The Herr Hauptmann will not tell me the order that the Feldwebel disobeyed, Herr Oberst," he replied, glancing at his notebook out of habit.

"What order did Feldwebel..." he glanced at the Wachtmeister's notebook placing a hand on his arm to lower it and read the name. "*Kessler* disobey?"

Von Bock blustered, casting about for help or inspiration.

"Show me Kessler's written orders," the colonel sighed and held out a hand while von Bock and his aide searched for the written orders.

"Hauptmann von Bock, you will report to me with the written orders and a statement describing how Feldwebel Kessler has directly disobeyed them."

He turned to the older man who still stood with his open notebook.

"You may stand down, Wachtmeister."

Colonel Esser had one of his aides dig out Otto Kessler's war record. He was impressed and pitied the man for ending up on von Bock's bad side. Then a broad, satisfied smile spread across

139

his often stern and unyielding countenance. He called for a runner.

"Bring me von Bock's aide de camp and send my clerk in with him."

The aide hurried in some thirty minutes later.

"Would you like to be posted, Leutnant?"

"Ja, Herr Oberst," the young subaltern said hesitantly.

"Perhaps to another part of the front? Maybe to a command? The chance for glory and perhaps promotion?" The colonel fixed him with cold grey eyes. "Indeed, maybe you would go anywhere to be away from..." the old man waved his hand in a vague circular gesture as he trailed off.

"Ja, Herr Oberst," the leutnant's expression altered perceptibly.

"Give me an account of Feldwebel Kessler's actions today, and please bear in mind," another pointed stare, "that I am of a mind to promote him."

The officer gushed with professional admiration for Kessler, he went as far as an officer might when speaking of an NCO.

"...So, you see, Herr Oberst, as I said to Hauptmann von Bock, it was textbook. Textbook."

"Did you get all that, Fischer?" Esser asked his clerk. "Good. Now, leutnant, I have decided that I can probably recommend you for promotion to oberleutnant, but first we have some work to do."

The two officers spent the next three months constructing a case against von Bock. The leutnant would visit Esser once a week and report any infractions, incompetence, or indecision on the part of von Bock, and the clerk would write it down and the colonel would smile.

They ruined him, he was sent in disgrace to the punishment battalion, which was little more than a deferred death sentence. He was used in the worst of the fighting against the most professional and well-equipped Russian units, commanding a company of men who were also expendable.

As fat became muscle and pomp became purpose, von Bock grew from a petulant boy in the uniform of a captain to a hardened killing machine. Those of his men who survived feared him more than anything the Russians might throw at them.

He became bitter and resentful, and where he'd already been callous and unfeeling, now he was focused and driven. For the long six months he spent fighting relentlessly through the harsh Russian winter and into the bleak spring, von Bock became fixated on the catalyst for his suffering. If it had not been for the insolence of Otto Kessler, a man promoted for his insubordination no less, he would probably be Major von Bock by now, a man who had leave and a comfortable bed, with aides and fresh rations. Not the coarse, sinewy, bringer of death that he had become.

In no doubt that he was a better officer for the experience, he resolved to excel. He would win his promotion to major and while he was at it, he would find and ruin Otto Kessler.

~

To the frustration of General Bolimov, as soon as the Russians got a sniff of defeat they would retreat east. At first this tactic, used successfully against Napoleon to stretch his supply lines and draw the *Grand Armée* ever deeper into Russia, was working, but when the sailors of Deutsches Flotte took the port city of Riga with a company of naval infantry from the first *Seebataillon*, the tactic began to fail.

Supplies came by barge down the Daugava River and found the line in a timely fashion. The Deutsches Flotte continued to use naval convoys and cities on estuaries to supply the German army in this way.

That was until the battle of Petrograd, a city defended by a series of fortresses in the Gulf of Finland. The German navy suffered devastating losses and was forced to retreat to Helsinki in neutral Finland for refit. Luddendorf, now the Chief of the Great German General Staff had identified Petrograd as the key to supplying his armies in Western Russia. The Imperial Army held Riga in the north, and the cities of Minsk and Kiev, while the Austro-Hungarian Army held Kharkov and Sevastopol in the south. Having Sevastopol meant that, with their alliance to the Ottoman Empire, and with the Royal Navy crippled and outnumbered, supply lines could now come from the Mediterranean via Constantinople.

But this would take months to establish, and Luddendorf knew that he must have Petrograd in time for the summer offensive.

Meanwhile, Hauptfeldwebel Kessler had been fighting through Lithuania, Latvia, and Estonia with von Bülow's Second Army or *Armeeoberkommando Zwei*. His Battalion was moving through the rich farmland of the Pskovsky District in order to take the City of Pskov on the banks of the river Velikaya.

Otto worked closely with his company commander. Oberleutnant Hauptmann, was a diminutive man with a strong Silesian accent and a shiny, bald head. Kessler liked the man and respected his leadership abilities; unlike several of his leutnant's, he was not of the aristocratic class and did not affect a superiority that could often be despised by the lower ranks. The commander of 3 Pommersches refused to promote his best company commander on the grounds that Hauptmann Hauptmann was a ridiculous name for an officer of the Imperial Army. He had secretly filed the paperwork months ago and would, when circumstances allowed, recommend the unwitting captain for promotion to major.

Otto Kessler's main task as Sergeant Major was to maintain discipline in the company. He was proud of his rank but hated the role of martinet, and he felt that these brave young men could do with a break when the fighting eased off. He thought they should be concentrating on clean weapons and full bellies, not the kind of in-barracks nonsense that peacetime armies employed as busy work.

When some of the young leutnant's of the Prussian Officer Corps had spoken to him about the appearance of the men and the state of their uniforms, he had politely explained that while supply lines *were* effective, it would not do to replace perfectly good uniforms just because they had a little Russian blood on them. This was received with varying measures of indifference from the young officers he addressed, but he was sure that on some level they hoped, too, to get a little Russian blood on their own pristine uniforms.

Otto knew they had not yet seen the true horrors of war. Their heads were filled with *Dulce et decorum est pro patria mori*. Whereas Otto's was filled with the screaming of young men, the smell of churned earth and the way it feels to run into the teeth of the enemy guns while the shit in your pants dislodges and starts to run down your leg.

As fourth division closed in on Pskov, the fighting became fierce and the Pommersches took heavy casualties. Hauptmann was killed almost instantly by the shockwave of an artillery shell as it vapourised his viscera and stopped his heart. When none of the fresh new platoon commanders took the initiative, Hauptfeldwebel Kessler stepped up and began to control his company. He cycled his platoons through attack, suppression, and reserve to ensure they all got some rest before assaulting another position, cleverly briefing the platoon sergeants and not the officers, thus avoiding their embarrassment and any second guessing of orders.

He formed a plan to take the objective, an industrial area with a commanding view of the battlefield, and he executed it with few casualties. He decided to use Ludendorff's new doctrine of storm war and had the men leave all their equipment with a rear guard, fighting with only a bag of stick grenades and their MP40 submachine guns – Hugo Schmeisser's miracle weapon – decades ahead of the once class-leading Russian Fedorov.

They moved quickly under covering fire from the suppression platoon, taking enemy positions with lightning efficiency.

He instructed the platoon commanders to lead from the front because the men respected this, and soldiers would go that extra mile for a man they respected.

When the young officers saw the results, they were grateful too.

Not for the respect of the men, as might be imagined, but for the glory of victory and the approval of their superiors. These young subalterns, products of the cadet schools and barely seventeen, had been indoctrinated to treat these brave men as little more than counters in a game. They had spent the last five or sometimes ten years on a course designed to dehumanise and harden the future of the Prussian Officer Corps.

Soon the high ground was theirs and the rear guard followed up with the equipment, and with them came a summons for the company commander. Kessler reported to Battalion HQ to speak with his colonel about what had happened, and to request a new company commander.

"Hauptfeldwebel, where is Oberleutnant Hauptmann?" demanded the regimental commander, a wizened old man with a faded duelling scar on his cheek.

"Dead, Herr Oberst. Blown up, just beyond the line of departure."

"Who led the company?"

"I led the company, Herr Oberst." Kessler said the words deadpan, trying to hide the note of pride in his voice.

"Where were your other officers, man?"

"They… they preferred to remain with their platoons, Herr Oberst."

He almost winced as he heard the words come from his mouth. He went on to give an account of the day's fighting, trying his utmost to convey the bravery of the teenagers that felt unable to command an entire company of infantry.

"I see," the colonel responded, his wrinkled face taking on a knowing look that transformed his majestic moustaches. He eyed the twenty-one-year-old carefully for a moment, fingering the ribbon in the second buttonhole on his tunic that marked him as a recipient of the Iron Cross second class. The colonel's eye fell upon the ring Otto wore on the middle finger of his left hand, a barely perceptible movement in the old man's face showed his surprise, though he remained stock still.

"That ring, show it to me."

"It was my Opa's, Herr Oberst." Otto removed the iron ring and placed it in the waiting hand of the colonel.

"Your Grandfather's, are you sure?"

"Ja, Herr Oberst."

"*Gold gab ich für Eisen.*" He turned the ring in his fingers and read the inscription.

"Gold I gave for iron?" Otto was lost now because he had hoped for a pat on the back, maybe a few weeks commanding the company until a replacement could be found, but instead he was having his heirloom scrutinised by a geriatric Prussian colonel.

"As far as I am concerned, this ring means that while you and your family are not necessarily noble, you are certainly loyal Germans, and once again here they are, heeding the call when their Kaiser needs them. Do you know what this ring is?"

"No, Herr Oberst. Both my father and my grandfather died before I was born, and I was raised by distant relatives in Gutersloh."

"It means that during the war of 1870, your grandfather gave gold for the Kaiser's war chest, so you are a devoted German with a loyal bloodline. You have distinguished yourself many times since we left Prussia, and today you commanded a company of infantry with the kind of mettle I need from an officer in my Battalion. Of course, that will mean leaving your men to command a platoon in one of my other companies."

The old man's lips moved ever so slightly in what Otto could only assume was a beaming smile the most emotion the old man had shown since the day his daughter was married.

Sippenhaft – The *Herev*, 2035

Collective punishment

Olga lay awake, staring out of her cabin window, unseeing. She tried to process the enormous amount of information, the sheer gravity of it and what it meant to *her*. Many times she heard the words of Yael and Ruth echoed in her mind – *billions of people, time agent, we always use you* – it was too much for this sheltered girl from the bubble of the Reich. She broke it down in an attempt to understand her situation.

Time travel exists. I had never considered it, it never occurred to me that it was or was not possible, the only reason it shocks and frightens me is that I will actually travel to the past. I'm some sort of agent, specially equipped for this kind of work. A time agent.

The words rung like a bell in her head, *time agent*, something fell into place for her, the words felt correct, proper somehow. This only confused her more, the unlocking of some, until now, dormant part of her brain. She continued to mouth the words that the Israeli sailors had said and every time she said them, they felt more appropriate, more comfortable, like well-worn shoes.

Soon it felt right, she felt right, like this was what was supposed to be happening and her old life, the life she'd always hoped for in the Reich the military wedding, the idyllic home and the children. A life that now seemed to be one of servitude, restrictive, oppressive even. Now a new life stretched out before her, one of adventure, one that would see her realise a potential that she had never considered. Certainly there would be danger, but instead of apprehension, she found an excitement building and as this excitement raised her pulse, she sensed a change in herself, one that she knew was irreversible. The knowledge hit her like a train, it overwhelmed her, muscles twitched and synapses erupted with information, so much so that sleep claimed her. That night, as her prostrate form rocked with the pitch and roll of the sea, Olga dreamed, she dreamed of Berlin, of tall blond man whom she loved, of dark-haired man with a drooping eye and the word *Zeitkreig*.

Olga woke to the sound of winches rattling and sails flapping as the boat lurched and settled on a new tack.

She washed her face in the communal head and made her way upstairs to find all four of her new companions settling down for a breakfast of eggs and coffee.

"What do you mean, you always find me? How many times?" Olga demanded without preamble.

"We don't know, you usually leave a debrief for us to find, with what you did in the past and how it affected the timeline. There are never any clues as to how many times you've tried to get it right, but how would you even know?" Yael shrugged and forked eggs into her mouth.

"Why me specifically?"

"We have sent many agents through time, but most die seconds after landing, and as far as we know, you are the only person who can survive it," Ruth said.

"What if I don't this time?"

"Then we will warn ourselves of that and prevent you from jumping," offered Daniel.

"What do I do, where do I go?"

"Again, we only know what you did last time around," Ruth said exasperatedly. "But your last brief spoke of a physicist named Rudi Kessler and his time machine." She looked at the girl sitting opposite her and drew in a deep breath, before exhaling appreciatively. "You seduced him, helped him develop a time machine and smuggled him out of the Reich."

Olga felt a jolt of recognition at the mention of Rudi's name, instinctively hiding the reaction from her companions, and she suddenly felt very old. Not physically, but she felt the knowledge of years weigh down on her like a heavy winter coat. She tried desperately to recall more from the depths of her consciousness, but she felt the eyes of the group on her and realised that she had been silent for a suspiciously long time, so she resolved to play along with them for as long as she felt safe.

"When is it I go to?"

"Last time you said you were in Berlin in 1961, and that is the furthest you *can* go, seventy-five years." Only Ruth spoke now, the others seemed to be deferring to her. "We did some digging on this Kessler character."

She handed Olga a file, attached to which was a photograph of a bespectacled man in his thirties with thin, blonde hair and a prominent jaw.

It was everything Olga could do not to react as she felt memories come flowing back to her, unlocked after a lifetime of unconscious repression. Any scepticism she harboured was gone, and she believed fully in what these people were telling her.

150

That did not mean, however, that she trusted them, but she suddenly felt a lot more capable of dealing with that if the need arose.

The document described Rudi's upbringing in Berlin during the thirties and forties, his membership of the German Boys League and his education at Humboldt University of Berlin. It went on to describe his time at the Max Planck Institute and a horrific lab accident in his thirties that left him horribly disfigured and missing several fingers and toes.

After a period of recovery, he tried to return to work but he could no longer conform to the strict protocols demanded by the Reich. Zealous colleagues informed on him, and he was brought before a tribunal where every minor infraction and dissentious comment was hyperbolised and dissected. This was how the Reich operated, and it would go on and on until even *he* believed he was guilty. The truth was, that a hideously deformed physicist with mental health issues could not be allowed to walk the hallowed halls of the institute and the board wanted him swept away.

His defamation was swift and absolute, no doubt remained in the mind of even his closest friends, that Doktor Kessler was a dangerous and seditious traitor that had to be, for the good of the Reich, dealt with in the most severe manner the law would allow. The execution was scheduled, and Rudi was, according to protocol for the politically condemned, weighed and then sedated until his sentence could be carried out to prevent him from subverting other prisoners while he awaited his fate.

Berlin, 1965.

Rudi awoke to find his tongue had been crudely removed. He tried to scream, he did scream, but the pain was unbearable. The bastards had inexpertly cauterised the wound and every so often he would be forced to expel the puss that had gathered in his throat. Guards came for him early on the day of his execution, he was dragged into the snow-covered courtyard of the prison, blindfolded, and shoved against a wall. He heard the men loading their rifles and the orders to fire. Rudi soiled himself as tears ran down his face and he braced for the inevitable pain, hoping for a headshot.

The gunshots echoed, followed by the heavy flapping of wings as frightened ravens fled their nests in the eves. Rudi's heart sang as he realised he had not been killed.

Was this a reprieve? Had the guards refused to kill him? His blindfold was removed. Had he led a different kind of life, Rudi might have noticed that the empty cases on the ground at the guards' feet were misshapen from crimping; these had been blank rounds, a fake execution just, a psychological prelude to the main act.

He sobbed quietly as men dragged him onto a flatbed truck and lashed his arms to a vertical post. The truck drove slowly through the crowded streets of Berlin where thousands of men, women and children of the Reich had taken the day off to watch the spectacle as Rudi continued to cry and spit out the yellow puss that threatened to choke him. The people jeered and threw vegetables and rocks at him. One cut him above the eye causing him to cry out, which was even more painful than the blow from the rock.

As the truck rounded the corner into the open square of the Gendarmenmarkt, Rudi's reaction to what he saw was to vomit. He had not eaten for at least twenty-four hours and the acidic bile he brought up burned the tender flesh of his tongue, but he was beyond caring. He watched through tear-blurred vision as his mother, sister and brother-in-law were led up the steps of a scaffold. *Sippenhaft*, the principle that the family shared the responsibility, was rarely observed, and in the few instances that it was, it usually involved the patriarch of the family being forced to pull the lever for the trapdoor on a hanging scaffold.

But this was something else entirely. A spectacle as cruel as it would be entertaining to the baying, bloodthirsty onlookers.

Two scaffolds had been erected facing one another; on the left was Rudi's family, who were having nooses fitted, while on the right stood a barrel. Suspended above the two platforms was a series of ropes and pulleys, with three stout ropes hanging in front of each of Rudi's family members.

Rudi was untied and led straight off the truck bed onto the platform with the barrel. As they tied a loop of rope around his torso, an official read out his crimes in a whiny, nasal voice.

"The vile traitor will now be suspended above the barrel of redemption. The barrel contains hydrofluoric acid." He paused, allowing the crowd time to make the obligatory gasp. "This acid will consume the wicked flesh and, we pray, leave the soul redeemed and welcome by Saint Peter."

"In the spirit of *Sippenhaft*, the family will lower the traitor with these ropes.," the German word *Verräter* dripped with hatred as he spoke.

The official smiled widely, enjoying himself as he gestured to the three ropes in front of Emma, Carla and Lothar.

"If they can control themselves and lower him slowly enough to achieve redemption in the eyes of God, then the carefully engineered floor will not break, and they will not be dragged upward by the weight of the falling barrel and hanged to death." He let that sink in as Lothar's swollen, and bruised face registered something like hope.

"Begin!"

Carla and Emma wailed with despair. They had spent the last three days in a house somewhere near Oranienburg, enduring a cycle of kindness, then beating and eventually rape repeatedly for three days, while Lothar had been made to watch his elderly mother-in-law and his wife suffer this ordeal.

On the one occasion he protested, before things had become really bad, a soldier simply slapped him, seized his face in one iron hand and pointed to the corner, where a squeaking bucket of rats lay next to a blow torch. Lothar slowly comprehended and began to sob as he truly submitted to the wretchedness of his situation. He knew that the bucket would be placed upsidedown on his horizontal stomach with the rats inside. The bucket would be heated, and the terrified rats would burrow furiously into his flesh to escape the heat, and he would die with the filthy animals writhing around in the tattered remains of his viscera.

Lothar grabbed his rope first and began to heave, but he was a bureaucrat used to lifting pen and paper, not six-foot-tall men. He was weak and the crowd laughed at his pathetic attempt. Rudi felt the rope gather up under his armpit and tighten painfully, eventually lifting him off the platform after the guards forced his mother and sister to join in. The crowd cheered as he moved through the air and the executioner positioned him over the barrel. Rudi could hear the acid fizzing. He had seen the effect it could have on a chicken leg and as he recalled this image, he soiled himself a second time.

The trapdoor on which the barrel stood was designed to give way if anything more than the combined weight of the barrel, the acid and Rudi were placed upon it. Rudi's family would have to lower him very slowly in order to save their own lives, lest the barrel fall and hang them too.

This ensured prolonged torture for Rudi, as he knew that Lothar would do anything to save his own skin. The rubber soles of Rudi's shoes entered the solution, and the reaction was instant. The acid foamed around his feet and turned the leather and rubber first into a goop, then dissolved it altogether. Rudi was thankful in that moment for the horrific accident that had taken so many of his toes and most of the feeling from his feet, but only seconds later he was screaming in agony despite the pain it caused in his mutilated mouth.

The barrel was shallow and broad-rimmed, which meant that his feet would touch the bottom before his knees were fully submerged. Now was the time his family would need to start being very careful.

If they happened to raise Rudi back up at this point, the crowd would see only bone left from the knee down. Carla, Emma, and Lothar kept lowering as slowly as they could, sobbing and wailing, while Rudi's screams filled the square and the crowed bayed for more suffering.

As she watched her son writhing in agony only metres away, Emma's will to survive departed and she finally broke. Up to now she had been fighting for the lives of her daughter and her son-in-law, but she could not inflict this torture on her son any longer, so she let go of the rope and saw the tension snatch it from the hands of the others. Rudi dropped into the barrel fully submerged, his weight breaking the bolt on the trapdoor, pulling all three up by the neck so that they began to dance in mid-air.

Just before the light left Carla's eyes, she managed to convey a look to her mother, which told Emma she had done the right thing.

Rudi was on the cobbles of the square now as he continued to thrash about in pain, but the acid now drained away, leaving him appallingly disfigured and blinded, a pink and red sinewy abomination clinging to life by a thread. The official nodded to a guard and pulling his luger, he walked across to Rudi and finished him with two shots to the head.

Thick, salty tears flowed down Olga's cheeks as she read the egregious account of the life of a man she had loved, albeit in another reality.

"It's disgusting, right?" offered Ruth.

"That's an understatement," Olga said, staring into Ruth's eyes through the tears of deep, unexpected pain. "How do we stop this from happening?"

"You'll need training. We have three or four months to get you to a standard most agents spend years working towards, not to mention the thousands that fail." Ruth sighed.

"First," Daniel said, his chirpy attitude contrasting so violently with how Olga felt, "we get you sailing, and when you can be an effective part of our crew, we will be able to train you in almost anything else."

"I'll teach you to fight on the trampoline," Yael nodded towards the rectangle of netting at the front of the boat. The others offered to teach Olga things like world history not tainted by propaganda, trauma first aid, the art of lying and, how to tell when others lie to you. When they arrived in Tel Aviv, Olga would learn to drive and to shoot.

"I have a few more questions. Why don't we just send an agent all the way to the Great War to stop that?" Olga sniffed.

"That's over seventy-five years ago. Hell, it's over a hundred and we can't make a jump that far," Ruth Said.

"Okay," Olga sighed. She picked up a rope that lay at her feet and asked, "What's this do?"

"That's the spirit. I'll give you a tour of the deck and explain what everything does as we go," Daniel said leading her to the bow to begin her training.

Faulheit – The Ost Front, 1915

Idleness

Leutnant Otto Kessler found command to be a lonely place. His brother officers looked down upon him and made him feel unwelcome in their company. His soldiers, who loved him to a man, kept a respectful distance and even his company sergeant major, HauptFeldwebel Max August, maintained a purely professional relationship preferring to spend the long hours of waiting with the other senior NCOs.

Since his battlefield commission, Otto had taken command of a platoon in another company of the battalion. Barges carried them north up Lake Peipus to Nava, a port city already taken by the Sea Battalions.

The eerily silent airships cast disconcerting shadows over the land as they glided from west to east, leaving a trail of death and destruction in their wake. Throughout the one-hundred-and-fifty-mile voyage to Nava he watched, numb to the horror of the Zeppelin raids that did his job for him and spared the lives of his men, as they destroyed the towns and cities to the south of Petrograd.

There were no civilians left in Nava, and when asked, a sailor simply said that they had been moved on. He didn't press the matter because asking questions could earn an interview with the SB, and such uncomfortable encounters rarely ended well. The city was reduced to rubble by the naval bombardment and represented a key strategic foothold in the campaign. It was to be the staging ground for the last push to Petrograd.

Otto trained his men hard. Weeks had now passed since they had last seen action and they were growing soft. The empty city allowed them spacious civilian accommodation and large brothels were opened for each mess, the girls bused in from somewhere, emaciated and glad to be away from wherever they had been.

~

"These communists will cost us the war!" Ludendorff roared, thumping his fist on the table in a now characteristic gesture.

"My dear cousin and his family are in that city. We must take it with ground troops to ensure their safety!" the Kaiser demanded petulantly.

"How many German lives is your *dear* cousin worth? Because we have already thrown one hundred thousand young German boys away trying to take it." Ludendorff was still animated but he had lowered his voice slightly in deference to the Kaiser.

"On this point I am immovable." The emperor folded his arms and turned away from his General Staff.

Major General von Ludendorff's rise to power had been swift. Falkenhayn had been true to his word and given him the Western Front. Ludendorff smashed the French at Verdun, Nancy, Toul, and over the Marne to Paris where he received Frances' surrender in the form of Marshall Joffre's sword.

Ludendorff's armies swept through behind the Stormtroopers, or *Sturmtruppen,* who, behind a perfectly controlled creeping barrage of artillery, would crush the enemy at previously scouted weak points to destroy headquarters and other key strategic objectives.

A second wave with machine guns and flamethrowers followed, slower than the first wave but still focusing on key objectives such as artillery sighting posts and communications exchanges, and all through easily exploitable terrain, avoiding insurmountable strong points which had now become islands in the battlefield as opposed to part of a line. Afterwards, the regular infantry marched through, mopping up. The key to this kind of fighting was momentum, and soldiers could only run into the teeth of enemy guns for so long. Supply lines were imperative, and Ludendorff understood that, which was what set him apart from the other would-be supremos in Berlin.

Victory in France earned Ludendorff ennoblement and he became Major General Erich *von* Ludendorff. Conversely, Falkenhayn performed poorly in the east. Initial gains were quickly pushed back, and some Prussian aristocratic estates were overrun by the Russians. These families put pressure on the Kaiser to replace von Falkenhayn with von Ludendorff, and the Kaiser acquiesced happily, giving his friend the top job.

The poorly organised, ill-equipped Russians did not stand a chance against Ludendorff's storm war. Using his zeppelins, he scouted positions and called in artillery. The Russian peasants that made up most of Brusilov's army were terrified of the eery behemoths silently combing the skies above, and they nicked named them *Zvey* after the flying beast of Slavic folklore. When they connected their appearance with an inevitable, devastatingly accurate bombardment, they ran. Mass retreating along the line resulted in the execution of thousands of Brusilov's own men as they ran into the teeth of Russian machine guns. As the psychological effect of these tactics began to take their toll, men like Otto Kessler found their war became less of a struggle. While his opposite number in the Tsar's uniform began to lose heart and mutiny broke out up and down the Russian line.

Finally accepting that his men would run anyway Brusilov turned it to his favour, drawing the enemy into more easily winnable battles as Kutuzov had done when Napoleon had invaded one hundred years earlier. This worked once or twice, then the flying beasts saw what was going on and punished them for it. Ludendorff's southern armies combined with the Austro-Hungarian forces and mercilessly drove the Russians further and further east, resulting in a last stand on the banks of the river Don.

It became a callous slaughter as the Russians fought a standing battle with no means of retreat. Eventually, on a battle line nearly one thousand miles in length, when charge after charge into the maw of the German guns failed, the remaining men attempted to swim the two-hundred-metre-wide river. Afterwards, the German engineers used bulldozers to push over two million bodies into the Don, which eventually washed up in the estuary at Rostov, bloated and faceless, but undeniably Russian.

"Hey, Kessler?" asked Heinrich Thurn, a tall slender youth of about nineteen. He had been with the company since Poland and was a good officer; it was just a shame that he had to be such a terrible human.

"Ja?"

"Come and have some Schnaps with us?"

Otto was on his way to company headquarters to check for new orders and mail and if he did not have any, he would go to the brothel because there was nothing else to do. His NCOs ran his platoon because he had trained them well and they liked him, but he still felt alone and as he wandered through the ruins of Nava, he had been glad to spot some familiar faces.

"Natürlich," Otto strode over to the other leutnants in his company. "Why the change of heart?"

"Engelmann said you will be our hauptmann one day and we should not be so stuck up," Horner, another subaltern said.

"Ja, hey, you are a decent fellow, you know what you are doing, and we should not be so pretentious. It is bred into us, from twelve years old, we are told that we…" Thurn made a circular motion with his bottle of Schnaps, "…are better than you." He slurred the last few words and handed the bottle to Otto.

"To being better than everyone else," he said, the sarcasm lost on his peers.

"Better than everyone else!" they cheered.

"Sit down, sit down," another young platoon commander gestured towards an empty chair. They had taken some beautifully upholstered dining chairs from a looted house, and they now sat in the road in front of it around a small table, drinking Schnapps.

"Did you hear the news?"

"No, what news?"

"Army group south has driven the Russians' Eighth, Seventh, Eleventh and Ninth armies into the Don, literally *into* the Don. My brother Armin is down in Rostov with the engineers, he's had his men in boats on the estuary trying to unclog the water course. It's clogged with dead Russians." He waved a grubby scrap of paper, apparently the letter from his brother with army group south.

"So, we are celebrating!" Thomas Horner said, a diminutive boy of seventeen who had arrived recently and had yet to see action. He raised a glass to the Kaiser and General von Luden-dorff and the rest of the group joined him.

Otto wanted to grab the boy by his shoulders and shake him, ask him if he had any idea what the slaughter of four Russian armies would look like, smell like, sound like. But he was so desperately lonely, he needed this, so he simply smiled and toasted his monarch and his General.

"I heard a rumour that a big push is coming," Thurn said, looking around the group. "A big push on Petrograd!"

"I long for a taste of action," lamented Horner.

Otto checked himself again because he had been like this less than two years ago, but he could not imagine his first taste of action with the additional responsibility of a platoon to lead. He felt bad for the boy and decided that he would try to help him where he could.

"That's nothing for Kessler," Thurn said. "He led a company attack in Pskov, which is how you got your step, isn't it?" He sneered. "By showing up all the platoon commanders, then running to Engelmann and taking all the credit?"

"My company commander had to die first, Thurn, try to remember that." He gave Thurn an intense look of warning. "My officers wanted to stay with their platoons rather than hunting glory and promotion, so it was left to me. I did not ask for any of this." His tone remained calm but decidedly firm.

"Okay, Kessler, try not to get upset, I was only baiting you. It is what fellow officers do." He poured Otto another Schnaps.

"Look, both of you," Otto said, pointing with his empty glass before filling it himself this time, "if what you're saying is true about Petrograd, I want you to know that regardless of my personal feelings, I will look out for you, and I will help you in any way I can." He raised his glass again and forced a smile. "To my brother officers!"

"Brothers!" they both exclaimed.

Otto helped them finish the bottle and they rose to walk back to the mess.

"Hold on, the night does not have to be over yet," Thurn slurred. "This could be the last time we can get away with sleeping late before the big push," he said, making perverse hip thrusting motions. "Let us look in at the brothel?"

Horner looked down at the ground and kept quiet

"What's the matter, Thomas, afraid you might mess your shorts?"

165

Otto was about to tell Thurn to be quiet, when he looked at the nervous seventeen-year-old and thought that he would hate for him to die a virgin.

"Come on, Junge, I'll keep the biters away."

"Wunderbar," Thurn cried as he threw his arms above his head.

Otto gave Horner a playful shove and the three of them walked through the decimated city towards the officers' brothel.

The onion domes of the brothel stood defiantly in the moon-light, the only building left standing on either side of a long, wide avenue, like a solitary tooth in an otherwise empty mouth. The first German officers to enter Nava had found this old hotel and claimed it as a mess, but when divisional HQ set up on the other side of town it became the officers' *militarbordelle*.

As they approached Otto and his friends could hear the sound of tightly wound young men letting go after months of hard fighting. An overweight major sat in a chair in the portico, his uniform tunic unbuttoned at the collar. He had clearly had far too much to drink and was trying to compose himself before heading back to his mess. The three of them nodded to the jowly old soldier as they walked up the steps into the majestic old pile.

Inside, Otto found a beautifully appointed hotel in the tra-ditional style, with wood-panelled walls to match the bar, elbow chairs and upholstered benches arranged for entertaining.

A large civilian man wearing a German pistol played Chopin on a mahogany grand piano. The girls, and that is what some of them were, looked only superficially happy.

"Kessler," Thurn had sat down with three of the prostitutes and Horner had a girl of about his own age on his lap who was looking relieved not to have an aging Prussian pawing at her for once. "Come, there's a good fellow, we're keeping this one warm for you."

He winked at Otto and patted her behind. Otto felt uncomfortable, but he was also drunk and possessed the recklessness that young men who have been forced to accept their mortality time and again often did.

He approached Horner from behind and, placing a hand on either shoulder, he discreetly made sure that he was okay. The girl on Horner's lap placed a hand on Otto's cheek and stroked it downwards to his chin, then tapped him on the nose with her forefinger playfully.

Otto could feel months of pent-up sexual desire coursing through him, and he resolved to stay and enjoy himself. Moral fortitude was for men who would live to be grandfathers. She was beautiful, but she was also drunk and heavily made up, with the haggard look of someone who had not slept well for some time. He smiled at her and took his seat. The girl Thurn had allocated to Otto had gone for drinks, and now she returned with a bottle of dark brown liquor.

"Vana Tallinn," she said in a thick accent, "only left." She was slightly older, maybe twenty, with porcelain skin and thick dark hair. She poured six small glasses and raised one, "terviseks!"

"Terviseks!" the other two girls said.

Thurn looked at his companions and shrugged, "Terviseks."

"Terviseks," Otto and Horner chorused.

After they had drunk three more, the girl with the Vana Tallinn sat on his lap and turned to Otto, "Kalevala," she said, pointing at herself.

"Kalevala," he repeated, smiling nervously. She poked him gently in the chest and turned her head to one side, inquisitively.

"Otto," he used his thumb to point to himself. She shifted her weight on his knee and clasped his chin with her thumb.

"Otto," she smiled lasciviously then kissed him hard on the mouth. They had both stretched their respective linguistic skills to the limit, so Otto kissed her back, feeling a heady rush. When he opened his eyes, his companions had left, presumably with their new friends.

Otto looked into her icy, blue eyes and breathed in her musk as he kissed her again before scooping her up and carrying her off to a room. After what felt like a long time, Otto left the new love of his life in bed to find his friends. Wandering drunkenly though the opulently decorated corridors of the hotel, his postcoital bliss was interrupted.

At first the shouting did not register, then he could make out the German voice and a distinctly female whimper. He could see it now, at the end of the long corridor. An open door, a German Officer raising his arm and a pale girl cowed in front of the bed. Without thinking, Otto strode across the threshold and spun the Officer around.

"Hey, that is not…" Otto broke off. He was staring into the face of an incredibly drunk major of Hussars. A man who could ruin him, break him back to the ranks or worse, and Otto had him in a vice-like grip on each arm. He released him, recoiling as though he was contagious.

Rudi's action seemed to have been too much for the man and he fell to the floor in a drunken stupor. Otto looked about for witnesses, he had put his hands on a superior officer, one who now lay at his feet barely conscious. He caught something at the edge of his peripheral vison, but before he could turn Otto was grabbed from behind by two men. Fighting to look around, he saw that they were Horner and Thurn.

"What is this?" he demanded angrily.

Otto turned back to see a third man standing over the prostrate major, the man looked up at him, it was Hauptmann Fedor von Bock. He raised an immaculately polished hessian boot and brought it down hard onto the major's face.

"Kessler," he said with immense pleasure. "I have you now."

He did have him, a sick feeling of realisation that began in Otto's guts rose like bile. He had put his hands on a superior officer and now von Bock would make sure everyone believed he had beaten the man in a drunken rage, proving that the orphaned son of a cobbler was not fit to serve in the elite Prussian Officer Corps.

Von Bock, he realised, would have him court marshalled. He would face death, or at the least imprisonment. He thought to himself with perfect clarity now that he had done nothing wrong, but he would certainly be punished. So he let himself go, he gave over to the hatred he harboured for this man, the anger over the lives he had thrown away so carelessly. He struggled free of the young officers and flew at von Bock.

Otto laid into him, something von Bock had not planned for, and he found himself on the ground with Otto's weight crushing his chest. Blow after blow rained down on his face and head until he passed out next to the major. Otto was pulled off by Thurn and Horner who both received similar treatment until the armed locals running the brothel appeared, clearly shocked at the carnage and expecting a very different scene.

Otto was thrown on to the street and staggered back to his mess with blood dripping from his knuckles and a sick anxiety churning in his stomach. He knew it was over for him, his only chance was that this major remembered what von Bock had done to him.

Republikflucht – Berlin, 1961

Republic flight, the GDR term for leaving the eastern sector of either Germany or of Berlin.

"That is astounding! That is *it!*" Rudi exclaimed. He was quiet as he ran his eyes over the equation to check for the error that must be there. The night once again took a turn as tempers ran high, and Olga and Rudi said the words that would ruin both their lives.

Torsten slithered out of the basement to betray them and destroy his own future in the process. Olga washed up the picnic things while Rudi took a last look around for anything that should be hidden in the floor. When he checked the work bench, he found a sheaf of papers he did not recognise, the cover sheet of which read: *"Time travel using gravity manipulation and quantum entanglement,"*.

He frowned at it. The title was in his handwriting, but he had no recollection of writing it. Rudi took a furtive glance around the room and read on, his pulse quickening as he read the typed script.

Rudi, we did it! You do it, time travel is possible, but you must take your research and go to the West. DO NOT TRUST TORSTEN! He has gone this very minute to betray you to the Stasi. This is the earliest we could send this to you because you needed Torsten's entanglement calculations. You must trust that your mother and sister will be taken care of and GET OUT.

Take Olga and run West, TONIGHT!

All the information you need to build a working Zeitgerät is either in these pages or under your old rug. So far, we can only move objects, not sentient beings, but we hope that, by sending you this, we can further our research and give ourselves more time. Go to the Max Plank Institute in Munich, I have told them you are coming. Good luck!

Rudi leafed through the pages in amazement. His mind raced as he thought of leaving, glancing at schematics and scanning pages of calculations. He was torn because he was obviously elated as his dreams were made reality on the pages in front of him, but he had sworn he would not leave his sister and mother to the mercy of the Stasi who, when they discovered his defection, would make his family pay.

He reread the words, "leave TONIGHT."

He figured that future Rudi – or an expert forger – must know more than he did about what was going to happen that evening. He felt sure that this was a message from the future, and he decided to pay heed to it.

"Olga!" Rudi panted as he burst through their bedroom door. "Pack a small bag – a *small* one – we have to leave now. Tonight!" He fixed her gazed to emphasise his words, handing her the cover sheet and waiting as she read it.

Olga's reaction was almost as surprising as the message he'd just received from his future self. A tacit nod and immediate compliance. No questions, no protest, no disbelief... she simply reached under the bed and produced a duffle bag.

"We should say that we are working in the west and off to a split double shift," Olga said as she checked the contents of the bag, adding a few toiletries before zipping it up. "there's no need," she said when Rudi began packing his own bag, "I have all we need," she frowned at his confusion, "let's go!"

"If we are suspected of trying to flee, then we will be arrested for *Republikflucht*," Rudi said, clearly distressed at the harsh reality of what he had proposed.

"Deserting the republic? How could they prove it?" Olga scoffed.

"It's the middle of the night. This is a suspicious time to be crossing into the West...if we wait a few hours, we might be more convincing for factory workers."

"If we leave it too late, Torsten's betrayal might have already happened and the Stasi would be looking for us anyway," Olga said coolly.

That Torsten would betray him was more disappointing than surprising. Deep down though, Rudi knew Torsten was a brainwashed zealot who would sell out his own Opa and Oma if he thought they threatened the socialist millennium. Rudi decided to risk it, and he turned to Olga and took her in his arms.

"It's going to be alright," he said, more for himself than Olga. He was shaking, but she was oddly calm.

"We should go to Lorenzo," she said, pulling away from him.

"The rock and roll pastor?"

"Rudi," she said impatiently, "he is an anti-communist ally, and we are on the run!"

"Would he hide us?"

"There's a crypt under the church, he's hidden people there before."

"I don't have any other suggestions, and we can't stay here," he conceded.

As they crossed Hackenbergstraße, Olga dragged Rudi into a side street, covering his mouth as she pressed them deep into the shadows.

Who is this woman? He thought.

The alley was briefly flooded with light as a Barkas B 1000 screeched around the corner and braked hard in front of Rudi's building. Two more arrived on the scene and en force, they stormed the apartment block. The street level windows lit up and the silhouettes of their would-be assailants filled the tiny space as muffled shouts spilled onto the street.

"Come on," Olga whispered, dragging Rudi deeper into the night.

They had to force themselves to walk casually through the empty streets so as not to attract attention. It was a thirty-minute walk to Lorenzo's tiny apartment behind the church in Köpenick, and when they reached it, their nerves frayed to breaking point, the pastor answered the door quickly enough to suggest that they had not woken him.

"Olga, Rudi, is everything in order?"

Olga nearly knocked the cleric over to be off the street and into the safety of his kitchen, still cajoling Rudi along like an errant child.

"That snake Torsten sold us down the river," Olga said, her words dripping with hate.

"Come in." Lorenzo said sarcastically, taking a furtive look around in the street before closing the door.

"We need to get to the West," Rudi pleaded. "Tonight!"

"You guys have the worst luck." Lorenzo nodded at the battered radio on the kitchen counter. "Remember that wall Ulbricht said he wasn't going to build? Well, it sounds like it's going up tonight. Taxis stopped taking fares around midnight and people have reported barbed wire work parties up and down the border."

"*Sheiße*!" Olga exploded. Rudi had not heard Olga swear before tonight, and he was shocked not only by the outburst but by her entire demeanour.

"I can hide you guys in the crypt and wait for my contacts to establish routes across, but that could take some time, and Torsten may have told the Stasi about this place... or…"

"Or *what*?" Olga demanded; her tone sharper than she intended.

"Or I have a boat."

"A boat?" Rudi said.

"Ja, a boat. It's a small rowing boat, big enough for three. I could row you guys up the Spree while it's still dark and drop you off on the West bank?"

"You would do that?" asked Rudi.

"Natürlich, you are my friends, and you need my help, and God, I guess?" Said Lorenzo remembering his cover as a man of the cloth.

175

"Let's go," Olga said impatiently. She seemed to have changed since Rudi had shown her the letter, as though reading it had activated some hidden purpose, and he had no choice but to comply. This was their only chance of salvation.

Lorenzo produced some black clothing from somewhere and handed it to them. He remained in his black ecclesiastics and produced three balaclavas and a sturdy duffle from a concealed panel in the wall.

"What's in there?" Rudi asked.

"Insurance," he said flatly, clearly annoyed by the question.

The church was one block away from the Spree River, which meant they needed to carry the boat through the streets. It was cumbersome and neither Lorenzo nor Rudi was accustomed to manual labour of any kind, so, with Olga carrying the oars and keeping watch, the going was slow.

They shuffled loudly through the deserted streets, banging the boat on lampposts and road signs. Finally, at two in the morning, they launched the little skiff, and as large as it had felt while they were carrying it, now it seemed to shrink as the three of them climbed in.

"I'll row there, you save your energy for the return journey," Rudi said as he placed the oars in their rowlocks.

They made their way slowly south down the river Spree, from Köpenick where it widened to become the Dahme before heading west along the Teltowkanal. They followed this for about an hour when Olga silently gestured for Rudi to stop rowing.

Rudi craned his neck to see what they were both looking at. It was a brightly lit building site in full production at half past three in the morning. There were workmen and soldiers on both sides of the canal, and they could see they would be dangerously exposed. The shape of the works, including guard posts, created a horseshoe along the south bank, over the Wrede bridge and back along the north bank.

"It's suicide," Rudi hissed.

"We can say we're lost and ask for directions back to the Müggelsee. Better swap here." Lorenzo slid into the rowing thwart and Rudi Joined Olga in the stern.

"It's suicide," Rudi repeated. Olga produced a pistol from somewhere and began to check it with the deft movements of a woman accustomed to such things.

"Who are you?" Rudi whispered. Olga just smiled, kissed him hard on the mouth and placed it in his hand. She rummaged in Lorenzo's duffle and produced yet another surprise for Rudi.

"The safety catch is off, just point and shoot," she said, as she checked the readiness of some kind of machine gun and placed it in Lorenzo's lap. She had another for herself and when she finished with that, she placed a balaclava on Lorenzo's head while he rowed, and handed one to Rudi, winking as she pulled her own down over her face with a wicked grin.

"Not a sound from now on." She gave Rudi's knee a reassuring squeeze and sunk low in the boat, indicating that he should do the same, "And welcome to the *zeitkreig*."

Welcome to the time war? Rudi thought, his brow furrowed in consternation, he looked down at the pistol in his hand and the girl who had handed it to him, a girl he loved, a girl he thought he knew.

The noise made by the construction teams drowned out the gentle lapping sound of Lorenzo's rowing as they inched closer and closer, until they were past the point of no return. Rudi could feel his heart pounding in his chest. He was terrified, not so much of getting shot, but of capture.

Somehow, he felt like he knew how bad it would be, less like a premonition, more like a memory.

Extreme fatigue. Freezing water and the unshakable feeling of failure. A pang of loss as he realised that if captured, he would likely never see this incredible woman again.

He looked at Lorenzo, valiantly rowing on, unable to cower in comparative safety like he was. The steadfast clergyman was sitting upright, defiant and brave. Every so often, Olga would silently give him a direction or warning as he rowed back-first into the jaws of the communist security machine.

Periodically, a guard would shout to his comrade across the bank and Lorenzo would flinch, Rudi would shriek inwardly, and Olga would tighten her grip on the stock of the submachine gun in her lap.

"This is the Wredebrücke, once we pass underneath it, we will be in Rudow and the free West," Olga whispered in Rudi's ear.

The Teltowkanal was forty-five metres wide, and at this point the borderline changed direction, going from north to south along Rudower Chaussee and ninety degrees to the left over the Wrede Bridge and ninety degrees to the left again. Just before the bridge, Rudi's university sat on the north bank and just after that, in the West sector, were the imposing towers and chimneys of an asbestos plant.

Although he knew they were there, it was too dark to see anything except for the lights from the construction site and the silhouetted towers of the factory. All they had to do was travel a further seventy metres undetected and they would be free. Rudi felt a pang of regret for Lorenzo, who had to make the perilous trip back to Köpenick, for they owed everything to this brave man. As the lights grew closer, he could make out the mass of coiled barbed wire and neat stacks of large, square concrete blocks. Workmen moved through the area laying out the wire and stacking the blocks, and a watchtower was being erected on the southern bank.

What are they doing to my beautiful city? Rudi thought, desperate to voice his outrage, to shout at these bastards that would separate mother from daughter, brother from sister and father from son.

The silhouettes of soldiers, all armed with rifles, were visible, and they had commanding views of the canal and the site. Although the wall was only being built tonight, the shoot-to-kill order or *Schießbefehl* had been in force for over a year. Sometimes escapees would get a warning shot, it all depended on the kind day the *Grenztruppen* were having and how charitable they felt.

The GDR soon realised that Berliners were not going to shoot one another, so they brought conscripts in from elsewhere in East Germany with fewer scruples. The bridge passed overhead, and they were plunged into darkness. They had made it; the southern bank and freedom were only a few dozen metres away.

Just as Rudi dared to relax, to believe that the hard part was over, night turned into day as a flare illuminated the canal and the surrounding area. The boat was still in the shadow of the bridge, but due to works on either side, Lorenzo had stuck to the centre of the waterway and now they were sitting ducks. Rudi dared not breath as he lay still in the boat waiting for the firing to begin. He could hear boots and voices coming down the towpath. Lorenzo passed him an oar and used the other to scull silently to the southern bank. Another flare, the footsteps grew louder as the shore came into view, they could now see that the entire area underneath the bridge was covered with barbed wire, and they would have to move further West.

Olga had her submachine gun at the ready and was straining her eyes for the first sign of the soldiers as they reached the shore. Rudi joined the paddling effort and they moved quickly along the bank, but it was still another twenty metres to a useable section of shore.

"Don't be the first to shoot," Lorenzo hissed. "They might be conscripts, fresh off the farm and happy to let us—"

The first shots came from beyond the barbed wire. The muzzle flash gave Olga a target and she returned fire in bursts. Both men paddled hard now, no longer concerned with making noise. As they left the shadow of the bridge, the water around the boat erupted with splashes as guards fired from the roadway above. Olga lay on her back and fired rhythmically to keep their assailants' heads down. With Rudi paddling hard, Lorenzo took up arms and began to fire upon the bridge as well. Rudi's heart pumped hard in his chest as he leant over the side of the boat and pulled for all he was worth. It struck him that only twelve hours earlier, he had been rowing a similar boat in the sunshine on the dreamlike water of the Müggelsee. But now his feet felt wet, and he called out to tell the others that he thought the boat might be hulled.

Olga's gun ran dry with a click, and she reached over to grab Rudi's pistol to start firing aimed shots.

The shoreline was coming up and Rudi just kept pulling, his shoes filled with water by now. The boat hit the concrete embankment with a bump as rounds hit the wall by Rudi's head and sent dust and debris flying.

"Go," shouted Lorenzo, "GO!" his machine gun opened up and he fired on the bridge to give Olga and Rudi some cover as they climbed the wall onto the tow path. First went the all-important document case. Rudi struggled but Olga flew up it and was lying flat pulling him up when Lorenzo cried out. Rudi caught his weapon and passed it to Olga, then grabbed Lorenzo, who was surprisingly light. He held him under the shoulders and pushed him bodily onto the bank. Then he found some strength from somewhere and hauled himself up. Now that they were out of the water the firing ceased, the guards under strict orders not to cause an international incident by firing into the West. They dragged Lorenzo off the towpath and onto the grass, where he lay still, breathing quiet shallow breaths.

He put his hand on the back of Rudi's head and pulled him close.

"It all depends on you from here, Rudolph Kessler! Beware der Englander! And welcome to the *zeitkreig*." He gasped the words, staring into Rudi's eyes with a burning intensity. Rudi

181

didn't know what to say, but even if he had the words, it was too late.

Lorenzo was gone, another victim of the regime. Rudi and Olga embraced, and Rudi realised that it was not water in his shoe but blood. As the adrenaline wore off, the pain came, and he would later discover that he had lost all but the big toe on that foot.

A GDR patrol boat arrived at the same time as the West Berlin police and ambulance. Olga had discretely disposed of the firearms as soon as the shooting stopped.

"What happened here?" a weary police sergeant asked. "Another case of psycho communists shooting their own citizens?"

"*Natürlich.*" Olga nodded, before looking to Rudi, indicating the conversation was over.

"*Genau,*" Rudi agreed, the Stasi in the patrol boat pretended not to hear but Rudi managed a triumphant smile before collapsing.

In the ambulance, Olga gave a brief statement while a paramedic dressed Rudi's foot.

Olga slept in the room that night, refusing to leave his bedside. When Rudi was discharged, they were directed to Marienfelde refugee transit camp, where they were both given West German passports.

The next day they boarded a train for Munich, and while Rudi stared out of the window at the rolling countryside, Olga snored loudly in the seat next to him. He felt so much hope and excitement for the future, but he felt regret too, because he had abandoned his mother and sister. His best friend had betrayed him, and the brave Lorenzo had died in his arms on the canal side.

It all depends on you, Lorenzo had said.

What did that mean? And who was der Englander? What is the time war?

Rudi awoke to the smell of coffee to find that Olga was no longer next to him, but he assumed she was at the bar or in the toilet and drifted back off. When he awoke a second time to find her gone, alarm bells started to ring. Neither of them had bags, just the document case and that was still under his seat. With nothing else to do, he checked the contents; everything was as it should be and he felt bad for checking, like he was somehow accusing Olga of something. Tears came an hour later when it finally hit home that she was gone. Some part of him felt as though they had known one another for many years and that meeting for the first time in February was more like a reunion. He had imagined they would grow old together, he had pictured their children and their home, and he began to sob, until it drew the attention of other passengers. So he went to the toilet and then to the bar, where he sat with his briefcase and drank.

He drank as he mourned all of his recent losses and toasted the future, or perhaps a new past.

Malta, 2035

By the time the *Herev* rounded the Rock of Gibraltar Olga was keeping her own watch.

She could hand, reef and steer in all weathers and she was beginning to grasp the rudiments of celestial navigation. When there was halyard to fix, she lay aloft like a monkey, flying up the rigging without fear.

Sailing was not all she had learned, but it felt like it, with the other new skills she seemed to be discovering old friends; forgotten talents and muscle memories that simply could not exist. When she sparred with Yael, handling herself like she had been fighting her whole life, she could not explain it. Ruth's weapons felt familiar in weight and her fingers knew just where to find catches and levers. Sixteen hundred miles of sailing had transformed her, shown her – *reminded* her – who she could be, and under the careful stewardship of her crewmates, it had armed her with some of the skills she would need to travel back in time and save the world from the evil of the Reich.

Yael and Olga became friends, although it was much harder for her to trust anyone since Frieda had betrayed her. She dreamed of Altstötter often. Dark, vivid dreams that left her lying in her berth sweating and terrified, until Yael would come in, lie down next to her and hold her while she found sleep again.

Olga started to open up to Yael soon after setting sail, confiding in her. She spoke openly about her dreams since she had read the distressing report on Rudi and his family. She told her that she felt shame over the joy her newly discovered memories brought her. Of the dreams that she had of Rudi and her time in East Berlin, some were about working on the time machine and others about their escape. The idea that she could handle herself like that excited her.

"I can't explain it, I... I think I *love* him," Olga bit her lip, ready to be scalded for her foolishness, only to find that Yael was smiling patiently and nodding gentle encouragement. "I feel like I would do anything for him, I know it sounds stu—"

"Let me stop you there, Mami, love is never stupid! Love is the strongest thing you will *ever* know. Love conquers armies and topples empires." Yael looked away briefly as if she were somewhere else, with someone else. But she turned back to Olga and smiled wickedly, "What else do you remember?"

Some dreams were sexual, and she giggled with embarrassment when she told Yael about the day they had spent making love at the Müggelsee or the way even the memory of Rudi's touch made the hairs on her skin stand on end.

"Don't be ashamed Olga, that day is a beautiful, precious memory and you should treasure it and never let it go." She took Olga's hand and looked her in the eye. "I will do everything I can to get you back to him."

Yael told Olga about growing up in Israel, about the war with Syria and the attacks on her parents' farm, about the orphanage and national service. She told her that the first time she had felt at home again was with the IDF, and when her time was up and she did not want to leave. She had volunteered for new, more dangerous assignments, before eventually, Mossad picked her up and gave her the opportunity to avenge her parents' death.

Olga was beginning to understand the psychology behind human behaviour, which was difficult for her because she was learning how the world she'd grown up in was so obviously messed up; the simple tricks the propagandists used to keep them happy in their ignorant bubble, worshipping the patriarchy and the three Ks. The gaping chasms in her education left her woefully inadequate in some areas. The mathematics required for basic navigation was a foreign language to her, and the calculations required for celestial fixes seemed beyond anything she could hope to grasp.

The *Herev* was well over halfway to Israel now and running low on essential supplies.

Still notionally a British protectorate, Malta was a dangerous place to be, but the other options lay north to continental Reich, which would be suicide, or far south to the barely inhabited wastes of the North Afrikan Reich. The rocky island was something of a safe haven, much like Casablanca had been in another reality. Misfits from all over Europe and North Afrika seemed to end up on this tiny island in the Mediterranean Sea.

Daniel prepared to put in at the smaller island of Gozo, where friends of Israel had arranged to meet him with enough supplies to make it the last twelve hundred miles. Before they made landfall, he ordered that the mast be struck to reduce their profile and they proceeded under the twin electric motors. Silence was maintained and as night fell, the *Herev* ghosted into the tiny inlet at Wied il-Għasri.

The steep walled cove was just wide enough for the catamaran, which only added to the tension, because the threat of capture, interrogation, and torture was all-too real. The barely audible hum of an electric outboard motor drew the crew's meercat-like attention and Daniel signalled with his torch. The boat returned the coded signal and approached.

"We're going in cold, no weapons." Announced Ruth in a muted yet firm order.

"Damn it Ruth, not even side arms?" The look Chaim received at this comment was withering at best, at worst it reminded Chaim of his lowly position in the pecking order of this crew.

The boat was friendly and carried the requested supplies, plus a few treats. The exchange was like lightning, and before Olga knew it, the boatman was away again with nothing more than a whispered shalom. Daniel put out to sea immediately while the others stowed the food and water. A crate of Arak, the liquorice-flavoured Israeli spirit, sat in the saloon looking both inviting and mischievous.

The *Herev* motored south for a few hours well into the dawn before Daniel had the crew step the mast and re-rig the sails. With the visibility so good, the batteries were dangerously low by the time it was safe to set sail and finally turn off the motors. No sooner had the sails been unfurled than wind failed them, and with the batteries depleted, they were forced to wait for the sun to charge them. They bobbed around hundreds of miles from any land, pitching and rolling on the swell, an experience made far worse without the forward motion of the boat to absorb it.

Olga experienced seasickness for the first time while the others drank Arak and talked about their days in the IDF. This was the *Herev's* first opportunity to relax since leaving Israel three months before. After lying in her bed feeling sorry for herself for the rest of the day, Olga woke that evening to find her crewmates three bottles into the crate and having a little party.

The sea was much calmer now, so she risked a drink. Soon she was up and dancing with the others and genuinely enjoying herself. She danced with everyone and drank some more. This was amazing to her, she had never felt so uninhibited, she no longer cared what the others thought or what they were doing, she was flying, dancing, spinning, falling.

After a while the party calmed down into sitting and talking, and she saw a more human side to her rescuers, especially Ruth, who told her about her childhood and the war with Syria, of her wife and her death at the hands of the Reich. Ruth carried a lot of scars and most of them came with a thrilling tale, but Olga was too dizzy by now to pay attention, so she made her excuses and went to lie down on the trampoline and stare at the night sky.

She was rewarded with a shower of Leonids which she watched as the tiny lights moved through the sky. For a while she felt small, but then she realised that she was not small, she was enormous.

So much rested on her shoulders; the lives, deaths and suffering of billions of people, and for the first time she felt the true weight of her calling and she embraced it. She bathed in it, she was going to get it right this time and the world would be the way it should be, the world would not even realise that she had saved it or that it had needed saving, but she would know and that was enough.

The voice came from the north. It was harsh and loud, and it promised violence.

"*Unbekanntes Schiff, hier ist das deutsche Flotte schiff SMS Travemünde. Bereiten Sie sich auf die Inspektion vor. Wenn Sie versuchen auszuweichen, werden Sie beschossen.*"

"Unknown vessel, this is the German Navy ship SMS Travemünde. Prepare to be boarded for inspection. If you attempt to evade, you will be fired upon." Olga's brain translated the words in real time, but her shock and fear were paralysing.

Yael appeared and placed her finger gently to Olga's lips, beckoning her to follow. They moved carefully to her cabin where she proceeded to throw off her mattress and retrieve two large, black, dry bags from the locker beneath. Ruth came to the door with two pistols and two Micro Galil's. She said nothing, simply smiled and nodded.

"Put this on," she said, handing her a wetsuit with gloves and a hood as both began to strip.

Olga turned to see Chaim filling her cabin with spare sails and other stores.

"They have to make it look like there are only three," Yael said as she reached behind her back for her zip.

They donned hard-soled neoprene boots and quickly stowed their weapons in the prepacked emergency bags.

"Listen to me, Olga," Yael whispered, "we are going to slide gently into the water and wait under the boat until they have gone. Use the bag for buoyancy, we may be in the water for some time."

"Good evening. Are you the master of the vessel?" a voice called loudly from the German ship. It was enough to quicken Olga's pulse as adrenaline coursed through her veins.

Yael opened an escape hatch and helped Olga through, and she came out in between the two hulls under the trampoline. Yael passed out the bags, hers much larger and heavier than Olga's, then finally she slid silently into the water and led the way to their hiding place, slowly inflating the bags to full size.

They could hear the German sailors onboard now, asking questions and searching the boat. They could hear their heavy boots through the thin hull, tossing the beds and tearing out the contents of lockers, pots and pans crashing, and mattresses being slashed open.

Olga had not realised until that moment how much she had come to think of this boat as home, and now these bastards were wrecking it. They searched for nearly two hours, all the while Olga bobbed silently in the dark water and tried not to shiver, until they concluded that there was nothing to find.

After inspecting their Chilean passports and chatting about the yacht and how lovely she must be to sail, the German mariner asked where they were heading.

"The Ionian," said Daniel.

"Ah, it is beautiful there," he said with a friendly smile, "not the time of year I would have chosen to go, but you can't have

190

it all." And as he turned to leave, he gestured around him at the once opulent yacht, now torn to shreds by his dogs.

"Kill them and scupper the boat," he said, emotionless and without missing a beat as he stepped across to the red-sided ship's ladder.

Yael clamped a wet hand over Olga's mouth before she could cry out. The sailors all carried carbines, which they now swung round from where they had been slung.

"Get over to the bow," one said, motioning with his gun at his hip.

As one, as if acting on a silent signal, the three Mossad agents attacked.

Carbine barrels were swatted aside. Gun stocks were twisted. Bodies moved with a speed and ferocity that the German sailors had no way to resist.

Not a single shot was fired, but as the three agents all acted as if controlled by a single purpose, the three Germans slumped to the deck. Each felled with a single blow, and none were brought down by brute strength. Instead, receiving vicious impacts to the neck, throat, or temple.

Shouts rang out – cries of alarm in German – as the three broken bodies were tipped over the rail into the water.

Yael, pre-empting this, was waiting below the water, knife in hand to finish them off. She and Olga used the ensuing turmoil to swim away to the south.

Boots Hammered on the deck as gunfire broke out, and Olga flinched, squeezed her eyes shut trying to make herself as small as possible.

Olga flinched again, screaming involuntarily as huge chunks of the light hull were blown apart to shower them and splash more water over her head.

The German sailors weren't prepared for such savagery, such a well-trained and disciplined resistance, and the accuracy of the *Herev's* crew took a devastating toll on the second wave of boarders.

Seconds became minutes as Olga's lungs threatened to explode in her chest. She dared not looked back, focussing only on the dark shape of Yael just ahead. The only sound, the gentle waves and the splashing of their feet as they swam. Then came a noise, a noise Olga knew, not from this life, not from her sheltered existence in the Reich, but from deep in the recesses of her psyche. The rhythmic thwomp of a heavy calibre weapon that stretched across the decades to bring other memories flooding back to her.

The first 25mm round from the M242 Bushmaster was aimed at the white canister containing the *Herev's* life raft, the second and third low in each hull, and after that the remote operator in the bridge did his best to cut the boat in half lengthways. They didn't stand a chance; the three brave agents were dead before they hit the water and by the time the captain called it off, only the mast of the *Herev* remained above the waterline.

They were too far away to see the destruction, but the sound of the Bushmaster had been harrowing. When Olga turned to look, all she could make out was the muzzle flash and the navigation lights of the sinking *Herev* and much higher, the lights of the German ship. When Yael felt sure that they were out of sight and out of range of any optical equipment the Germans might have, she allowed them to rest.

The sea had picked up by now and there was a light swell and an increasing northerly wind. She told Olga to let go of her bag and tread water, then resting her bag on top of Olga's, she opened it and produced a large roll of rubberised fabric. Instructing Olga to seal and reinflate her bag, she swam away a metre or so and pulled a cord on the fabric, and as it inflated it took the shape of a small, square, covered boat, greyish-blue in colour, presumably to avoid detection. Olga's heart leaped because she had been afraid to ask before, in case the answer was: yes, we *are* swimming all the way to North Afrika.

Erlösung – Russia, 1915

Redemption

Despite the amount he had drunk, Otto did not sleep at all that night. He lay awake imagining all the things that could happen to him and what he might have done differently.

It was still dark when the Feldgendarmerie came to take him away.

"You have been accused of striking a superior officer, Leutnant Kessler. It's a death penalty offence, did you know that?" The policeman's tone was consolatory, as if to put him at ease.

Outwardly, Otto *was* at ease. He stood stock still and stared straight ahead as they read from their notebooks. Inwardly, the knot in his stomach that had been there all night grew to the size of a football.

"You will come with us now, Leutnant Kessler." They did not place him in irons or put their hands on him, they simply walked at his side with solemn faces.

Colonel Engels, the man who had raised him from the ranks and found his ring so fascinating, did his best to protect Otto. He gave a shining account of Otto's devotion to his men, his exemplary service, bravery, and loyalty. It was pointed out that von Bock was recently back from punishment and aspersions were cast on his integrity and judgement.

Von Bock, however, had obtained eyewitness statements from three commissioned officers as well as his own sworn statement. Thurn and Horner had betrayed Otto, lured him to that place and paid that beautiful girl to take him to the right room so that he could happen upon the major like that. Von Bock had a deep purple bruise on his left eye, which was bloodshot and half closed from swelling. Conveniently, the major was too ill to attend the court martial or even to provide a statement at this time. Things may have been different if he had, but Otto would never know.

Otto had tried desperately to reach Colonel Esser to beg his assistance, but he was home on leave and unreachable for some days, by which time it would be too late.

It was hard for a man of honour and integrity to stand silently by while he is mendaciously defamed so publicly by men who misled and betrayed him. Thurn gave his statement with pride, enjoying every minute of it, believing he was shoving Otto one step closer to the firing squad with every word. Horner had the decency to look shamefaced as he gave his account, lying a man into his grave.

The worst part was von Bock's testimony. He stood there, scarred and brilliant in his perfectly tailored uniform, with an Iron Cross first class on his breast pocket, the only blemish being his horrific injury; an eye swollen to the size of an apple and the same colour, fluid oozed from the slit where once a keen blue eye had darted about intelligently.

The officers of the court were visibly offended that the splendour of this German hero – his sins conveniently forgotten –

was so besmirched by the actions of this peasant with pretensions of command, with his Iron Cross second class, bandaged hands, and his dirty, crumpled, and ill-fitting uniform.

Engels did turn the tide back in Otto's favour, but only enough to save his life, so that he was to suffer the same fate as von Bock. The presiding officer returned to the folding table that was his makeshift judiciary bench and nodded curtly at his fellows before fixing a cold, disdainful gaze on the defendant.

"Death." The word hung like smoke in the air as Otto's heart began to pound against his ribcage. "Death," he said again, "would be the usual punishment in a case like this and I have no doubt that in time, death will come for you, Leutnant Kessler."

Otto's spirits dared to lift ever so slightly from the pit of his stomach as he hung on the word of this trussed up peacock.

"As a platoon commander in the punishment battalion, I image that six months should be long enough to be rid of you." He let that sink in, expecting this to be a blow to Otto's morale. These units were fodder for the Russian guns, used on suicide missions and little else. But Otto Kessler was a survivor, he was a skilled soldier, with a singular talent for keeping himself and his men alive.

"You will, I am pained to say, retain this commission you have somehow obtained and perhaps that way, the Reich might get some use out of you." Otto dared not show his relief, though he felt it in every inch of his being.

Otto had been a capable officer, hardened somewhat by the fighting over the last year, but still compassionate and empathetic, amiable, even, but that was all about to change.

The *Strafbataillon* transformed him beyond recognition; he never lost his fighting spirit, but almost everything else about him became twisted or broken. He no longer cared for his own life and found it difficult to care about the lives of the men under his command.

They were misfits. Some were victims of malicious officers, while others had deserved their punishment and had to be watched constantly. They would help themselves to extra of the meagre rations, sleep late or wander off when they were on patrol, looking for something else to do.

His unit received the worst of everything, being given near rotten food that would otherwise have been discarded. They were given inappropriate or damaged clothing, old equipment, accommodation unfit for the lowest of dogs, and positions in the line that were little more than a unit-wide death sentence. The uniforms were the old style with the spiked *Pickelhaube* helmet, now outdated and ridiculous in both appearance and function. They were issued with the Gewehr 88, a rifle designed in 1888, and a stark contrast to the modern semi-automatic Walther issued to other troops. The bottom line was that they were expendable, and therefore not worth wasting good equipment on.

The fighting was hard, periods of rest scarce, and morale came from the darkest of places. After just six weeks in the unit the men were ghouls with dead, sunken eyes, unfeeling, uncaring; eat, sleep, fight. Otto learned at first to ignore physical and emotional feelings, then after a short while he simply stopped feeling altogether.

He stopped feeling pain, feeling guilt, or feeling fear. The only things he experienced now were hunger, fatigue, and rage. Sometimes he would get that old rush of adrenaline back during an assault, but as soon as it was over, he would just feel hollow again.

Bewährungstruppe eighty-four, his new battalion, was rare. Other penal companies were under the direct supervision of the *Feldgendarmerie* and commanded by officers and NCOs of good standing which was a punishment assignment all the same. In the eighty-fourth, the officers and NCOs retained their rank and commanded the company themselves, often doing the work of a rank above or spanning two jobs.

They only saw the military police during the infrequent rest periods when soldiers might decide to run or when the fighting was expected to be particularly fierce. But if they happened to look behind them for long enough, one might spot a *Feldgendarmerie* car, rider or even a machine-gun position lurking in the tree line, waiting to execute them for cowardice.

Otto had regular meetings with his commanding officer and although he might have given Otto a certain amount of autonomy, it was clear that the man thought he was here to be punished and if he died, then, that was just too bad.

Once Otto's soul was sufficiently depleted, he took to terrorising his men and regularly used corporal punishment, often making the man's closest comrade inflict the brutal penalty. He dreamt of von Bock, that smile when their eyes had met that night in the brothel, his testimony, the testimony of Thurn and Horner, and it fuelled his cruelty. He began to fantasise about killing them, about torturing them. He would call his least favourite men after them and taunt them, using the name von Bock as an insult.

"Who's going to be von Bock today?" he would shout as they marched. "Who is going to piss me off?" Otto would single one out. "You, are you von Bock?" he would pull someone from the line for a minor infraction such as talking or falling out of step, then shove them to the ground.

"Get up, von Bock!" he would shout. "Get up, you snivelling little Thurn," he would grunt as he pushed the sole of his mud-caked boot into the man's backside while he tried to stand. "Fall back in and don't let me catch you being a von Bock again!"

This was part of the daily routine for his company and soon the men were using the names pejoratively too. He would hear them bickering and calling each other Horner or von Bock. Despite all this tyranny, the men remained disciplined and loyal because they had resigned themselves to their mortality, and they inexplicably loved this despotic ex Feldwebel-turned-Leutnant who punished brutally and never gave praise beyond the odd approving grunt.

They believed that beyond all that was a genuine desire to see them survive this ordeal and return home with their limbs intact, so they trusted him to keep them alive.

Otto was four months into his punishment when the line reached the outskirts of Petrograd. They were given a rare opportunity to rest, fresh rations were issued, and the mobile bathing unit was brought to their part of the line for the first time in over a month.

As Otto and his platoon dug into a hearty beef stew, a pair of canvas-covered trucks pulled up. A diminutive man in the ill-fitting uniform of an artillery major climbed down, he removed his wire-rimmed spectacles and began to polish them with a cloth. He was joined by a taller man with a slight droop to his left eyelid who also bore the badges and piping of an artillery major. This man's uniform was tailored, and he carried himself like an actual officer, the contrast between the two men almost comical.

"Sinners," called the taller man in an ecclesiastical voice, "you are here to atone." He paused and surveyed the bedraggled men with their ludicrous spiked helmets and outdated equipment.

"Redemption comes in many forms," he paused again, "and today I come bearing just that." Another pause, suggesting the man must have received some kind of public speaking training, but it was clear that he was merely following the instructions given without grasping the concept. It sounded wooden and rehearsed, almost as if German might not have been his first language.

"Those of you who choose, because this is a purely voluntary mission, those of you who choose to come with me today will receive seventy-two hours' rest, a clean uniform and, once the mission is complete," he paused again until an anonymous voice from the congregation told him to spit it out, "a full pardon with the option to return to regular service or to go home to your beloved families!"

Excited chatter began amongst the ranks, and Otto, without turning, simply raised a hand, receiving instantaneous silence.

"Herr Major," Otto said as he got to his feet and fixed the man with his cold, soulless eyes, "what's the catch?" He said this with a barely perceptible jerk of the head.

"Ah, now that is it, is it not? The catch indeed?" He looked at the assembled troops again. "This mission has the potential to be dangerous because there is an experimental weapon that could make you very sick. We think it is unlikely, but the chance is there."

"What kind of weapon, Herr Major?"

"A bomb," said the smaller man. "A prototype bomb. We will drop it in…" he looked at his watch, "we will drop it soon, so if you want that seventy-two hours' rest, then hurry up and get in the truck to my left, which will take you to a hot bath, a hot meal and a warm woman. If you do not wish to volunteer, get in the truck to my right, which will take you straight back to the line." He turned on his heel and climbed back in the front of the truck.

All of Otto's company lined up at the left-hand truck, and realising this, the taller major moved the right-hand truck to be level with the left and encouraged the soldiers to climb aboard. Otto tried to climb into the front with the driver, only to be stopped.

"No! You travel in the back with the rest of the inmates, *Herr Leutnant,*" the man laughed, his words loaded with facetiousness.

The trucks drove west for an hour, finally coming to a halt outside a large country house. The residents were long gone, and the signs of neglect were starting to show; long grass and weeds, water marks on the windows and ivy that had once climbed the wall politely was now very much an integral part of the structure. The taller man climbed down from his truck and called into the back of both vehicles.

"Leave on the truck your weapons and helmets and any clothing you no longer want. New uniforms and equipment will be issued before we leave this location in three days' time."

The soldiers and officers of the eighty-fourth parole company dismounted and fell into three ranks without prompting, as the shorter man addressed them.

"This place was being used for officers' err, rejuvenation, until recently, but it is too far away now that headquarters has moved further east, and the girls are..." he smiled sickeningly, "past their best, but they are still here somewhere."

He cleaned his glasses as he spoke. "We have stocked the kitchens and told the cooks to give you as much you want. A detachment of *Feldgendarmerie* will be here in a few hours with some barrels of beer and some wine. Enjoy the next seventy-two hours."

With that, he climbed back into his truck and drove away, followed by the taller man.

Instantly, chatter and even some laughter could be heard, while Otto stood motionless, trying to process this sudden twist of fate. For the last four months they had been the lowest of the low, treated like dirt and given the worst of everything. Now he stood and stared appreciatively at the country house, with no heavy mud-encrusted equipment to bear, no embarrassing spiked helmet, and the house was full of fresh rations and only half worn-out whores.

The weather was fair, and he could not imagine there being room for an entire company inside, so he arranged for the men to set up tables on the lawn and had the cooks bring a cold lunch out so the men could eat right away. He took his three platoon commanders to one side.

"Let's go and find these women before the men get the same idea. I don't want old Smidt's leavings."

The three men, two young officers and an old Feldwebel-Leutnant, nodded in agreement.

The rank of Feldwebel-Leutnant was created to exploit the experience of senior NCOs with having to welcome these ill-mannered slobs into the officer's mess. They could lead a supply platoon or carry out administrative duties normally designated to a Leutnant, for less pay and without tying up the young sub-alterns that were chomping at the bit for action. It was extremely rare to find such a man leading a frontline infantry platoon. In the Parole battalion however, officers were rarer, and paradoxically, NCOs often found themselves promoted as part of their punishment.

By the time they returned most of the men were sleeping off their lunch or smoking and playing cards in the sunshine.

203

"Sergeant Major," Otto called to his company HauptFeld-webel. "Sergeant Major, there are fifteen women upstairs. I want you to take your senior NCOs up there, and when you have finished making your assessment, I want you to write out tickets for the rest of the men. Let's make this orderly, then when every man has taken his turn, I want the upstairs off limits for the rest of the night. We want the fun to last the whole three days."

Otto caught his reflection in a window. What had he become? He stared for a moment at a man he did not recognise, a bully with cold, dead eyes who was calmly arranging for the orderly rape of fifteen women by his company of one hundred and fifty men. He shook his head.

"Fucking von Bock!" he said quietly to himself. Although he wasn't sure if he was cursing the man who had done this to him or himself for succumbing to the depravity of it.

His plan worked and by the time the MPs arrived with beer, wine and tobacco, every man in the company had waited his turn and visited the upstairs of the house.

The house was declared out of bounds to all but the four officers, who had taken some rooms out of the way with the four girls who weren't part of the fifteen he had allocated to the Sergeant Major.

He spent the rest of the night in this enclave with the three men he had become closest to over the last four months, and they finally told their stories.

"...and the worst part is," Otto slurred, wine in one hand and a girl in the other, "I wasn't even there when they fucked him over, it all happened after I was gone."

"You want a story of injustice?" said the old Feldwebel-Leutnant, a Bavarian called Meyer, a scarred and wizened veteran of the Herero wars in South Africa. "Listen to me, then," said the giant as he lifted a huge stein of beer to his mouth and drew from it thirstily, and followed up with a belch not dissimilar to the roar of a lion.

"My unit, Landwehr Infantry Regiment Number seventy-five, was also at the battle of the Masurian Lakes," he said, nodding to Otto. "The fighting was hard, and casualties were mounting up." He pointed at the ceiling with a finger like a bratwurst. "I was Company Sergeant Major, and my Company Commander was also a potato head." Again, he nodded to Otto. "He threw men's lives away like they were nothing, wave after wave of full-frontal attacks decimated our company and soon nearly half of our men were replacements."

He looked pensive and stared out of the window at the darkness for some moments and no one spoke.

They had too much respect for the old soldier. A man they had seen more than once run into a hail of Russian bullets to scoop up an injured man and carry him to safety. "Anyway," he said eventually. "As I stood one evening in the Hauptmann's command tent, watching him casually giving the same orders to take the same hill that we had failed to take that morning, with no change in strategy whatsoever, I snapped," he clicked his fingers as he said this.

"I slammed my hand down on the planning table," this he did on the coffee table now, scaring the girls and shaking the bottles and glasses with the force. "No! I said, how many more boys need to die before you understand that this is not how we

205

fight anymore? The officers all stood there watching me, like I was the mad one," he chuckled, shaking his head at the stupidity of the story he recounted.

"This made me so angry, I lost control and grabbed my Hauptmann by the lapels of his greatcoat and lifted him so that our eyes were level. Me!" He jerked a thumb at his chest, "A *zwölfender* with over twenty years' service, I lifted my Hauptmann up and shouted in his face. I couldn't remember later what I shouted, but they read it out at the court-martial. I said something about him being a heartless butcher and a *Dummkopf*, until eventually I was restrained and the chained dogs," he tapped two fingers high on his chest, referring to the metal gorgets that hung from the neck of all military policemen, "took me away to wait for my punishment. And the worst part?" He smiled wryly at Otto. "The attack went ahead the next day and we lost so many men that the company had to be disbanded and the Hauptmann was reassigned to a staff position in a *Gemütlichkeit* headquarters somewhere. He didn't even stay long enough to speak at my trial."

The giant man stood with some effort, drained his tankard, belched again, and silently led his female companion by the hand to a bedroom.

München, 1961

The Bavarian city of Munich

Werner Heisenberg walked over to the calendar he kept on the wall of his large, comfortable office at the Max Planck Institute for Physics and Astrophysics. It showed him that five days ago a scientist from the East should have arrived with some very exciting research. He knew this because one year ago, shortly after the institute had relocated here from Göttingen, while Heisenberg was visiting a colleague down the hall, a file appeared on his desk.

His secretary had not seen anyone enter the office, nor had she seen the document before. The covering letter instructed him to keep the contents of the file to himself and to expect a brilliant young physicist from East Berlin. This mysterious physicist would have research that proved time travel was possible, and the letter asked the director to assemble a small team of trusted physicists, engineers, and historians ready to begin a project in August of next year.

Werner, sceptical at best, found the rest of the document to contain an array of verifiable evidence that the sender was, in fact, from the future. The first were photocopies of the front-page of tomorrow's *Abendzeitung* and a few other days over the next week or so.

There was a headline from an American paper announcing JFK's victory over Nixon in November of that year. Heisenberg

207

later checked the voting figures published after the election with those on his copy, and they were indeed accurate. There were various sporting results and other trivial news. He was encouraged to use this information to discreetly raise funds for the project through gambling. What had been deliberately omitted was anything that might affect events in Germany, should Heisenberg choose to act on any of the information.

By January 1961, after watching Kennedy's inauguration on the colour television in the staff room, Werner made up his mind to prepare for the arrival of this physicist in August. He discreetly assembled an intimate team to assist in the building of a time machine. They were told it was part of an experiment, that their task would be to assume time travel was possible and decide, if anything, what to change in the past fifty years, discussing the ramifications of changes and potential obstacles. A lab was prepared, and materials sourced. The funding–necessary to bridge the financial gap between his winnings and what was needed– was pushed through under a false pretence that would surely come back to haunt him.

Now the damn fellow was five days late and it looked like he would have to face the great minds he'd assembled to tell them the project was a no-go. Procrastinating, he decided to head to the staff room for Kaffee und Kuchen. There he found the room was buzzing with excitement.

"Herr Direktor, have you seen the Berlin papers?" asked a colleague through a mouthful of *Quarkkuchen*. He took the proffered Berliner Zeitung, and it seemed that in the confusion of the wall going up so abruptly and the closing of the historic

Brandenburg Gate the following day, the story of a daring escape by a Pastor and a pair of physicists using a rowing boat had been missed by the journalists. Sadly, the pastor had been shot dead by *Grentztruppen*, but the scientists survived, minus a few toes.

Werner Heisenberg decided to wait for Rudolph Kessler, for he now knew his name, and his partner Olga Felsen there at the institute because it seemed likely that they would arrive soon. After some discrete enquiries, he discovered that Rudi had been discharged from hospital two days ago, meaning he should be on his way to Munich already.

On the seventh day, Doctor Rudolph Kessler limped up the long entrance ramp and through the doors of the ultra-modern Max Planck Institute for Physics and Astrophysics. The receptionist, seeing his condition, directed him to a seat and sent for the director. A man appeared of average height with thinning grey hair and a kind face grown soft with age, and he greeted Rudi enthusiastically. They walked slowly together to a meeting room where *Kaffee und Kuchen* were set out for them.

"So, my mysterious traveller, where is your partner?"

Rudi grew pensive, staring into his coffee for far too long, until he realised the director was waiting for an answer from him.

"Torsten? He betrayed me, he's probably in the basement of Normanenstraße trying to explain how we managed to escape," said Rudi, misunderstanding the question.

"Forgive me, I meant Fräulein Felsen, will she be joining us?" Werner understood something of what Rudi had been through and conveyed that empathy in his kindly tone.

"She disappeared…" he paused and looked out of the window, "we were on the train from Berlin, I woke up and she was gone." His eyes grew glassy, and he added, "I thought she was in the bar."

"Have you informed the police?" asked Heisenberg, genuinely concerned.

"She… she knew things. Things that she should not know. She knew about machine guns and quarks and Bell pairs," he blurted out, unable to articulate the thoughts racing around his fuddled mind.

"I'm not sure I follow you." Werner was concerned now, and although he felt for this man, his own reputation was on the line.

"I fell in love with a physicist, then she turned out to be some kind of… some kind of soldier," Rudi threw his arms in the air in frustration. "I'm sorry, Herr Direktor Heisenberg, it has been a very difficult few days."

"I imagine your whole life has been difficult, Herr Doktor. If you don't feel up to meeting your team, we can reconvene tomorrow?"

"My team? I thought that I was here to convince you to take me seriously?"

"I was convinced that you were serious some time ago, so now we're all ready for you to hit the ground…" Werner trailed off, glancing uncomfortably at Rudi's freshly mutilated foot. "This way, Doktor Kessler," he continued, grimacing and gesturing like an air hostess in an attempt to cover his faux pas.

Using his considerable influence, Werner had secured a spacious laboratory filled with state-of-the-art equipment as per his enigmatic instructions from the future. Rudi looked around in amazement at the standard of the scientific apparatus and felt something like hope. He could not feel joy as he would were Olga by his side, or if Lorenzo had not died in his arms only days earlier. He did his best to look grateful and thanked Direktor Heisenberg for the opportunity and all the work that had clearly gone into this excellent facility.

Rudi imagined that this lab was the origin of the letter he had received, and undertook at that moment to add to the letter a warning to himself about Olga's disappearance on the train.

Rudi was ushered into an anteroom, lavish compared to the drab, grey utilitarianism of his faculty in the east. Sitting around a large oval table, were four men and one woman, aged between thirty and fifty. Rudi, who at the age of twenty-eight was the youngest, found himself directed to the head of the table. He sat patiently and added the occasional greeting as Werner introduced each of the scholars in turn.

It was clear to Rudi that Werner was pleased with the team he had assembled and had looked forward to this moment for some time. Rudi hoped that Werner would not become overly involved in the project and try to usurp his control, however innocently.

Nearest to Rudi on his left was Professor Mirabelle Kaufmann, an anthropologist on secondment from Frankfurt. He found out that she was a preeminent authority on early twentieth century European history and the author of several books about the German empire and its eventual collapse.

Next to Kaufmann sat Doctor Winfried Schroeder, an engineering scholar from Hamburg who had worked with Werner on government projects during the war and came highly recommended. Schroeder smiled broadly at Rudi, revealing perfect white teeth, a sight that in 1960s Germany was rare for a man in his twenties, let alone in the fifty-year-old sitting before him.

Werner went on to introduce Erik Boelek, a physicist who spoke German with a slight American accent. It transpired that he had spent the last fifteen years in America working with Hugh Everett, and Werner was keen to draw particular attention to their work on game theory and how that might be employed to explore the many variables when meddling with time.

A broad-shouldered, swarthy man in his mid-forties with prominent facial features looked churlishly at Rudi as he stubbed out a cigarette. Embarrassed, Werner introduced Hubert Krause, a weapons engineer and former Wehrmacht officer. Hubert was the first of his team not to speak in greeting, he merely made eye contact with Rudi and grunted with a slight bow of the head.

Werner moved quickly to the last member of the group, a fussily dressed, corpulent Bavarian with a grey goatee and a shining bald pate. Doctor Tobias Eder, a military and political historian and, professor emeritus of Göttingen University, stood and formally greeted Rudi, expressing his excitement most vehemently.

Now came the moment Rudi had been dreading. He had to address this group of academic titans, not as their intellectual equal, but as their leader – the man with knowledge from the future.

"Good morning," he said formally, making eye contact with the friendlier members, "thank you for coming." Rudi's internal monologue was already reproaching him.

You sound like an idiot, say something important you kartofflekopf.

"Herr Direktor Heisenberg informs me that you all know why you are here and what we hope to achieve." He was looking around again for signs of acknowledgement, when his gaze fell on Krause as he stood, revealing his true height. Krause wore a collared shirt with the sleeves rolled halfway up his forearm, showing tanned, muscular arms covered with thick hair.

"All I know is that Direktor Heisenberg," he gestured towards Werner with one of his ape-like arms, "is convinced that you know how to build a time machine?" Krause had hurled this challengingly at Rudi in his strong Rhineland accent and now stood silently lighting another cigarette.

Rudi refused to be intimidated.

"What you must understand, Herr Krause, is that while I have the plans, and much of the research is mine, this time machine was built by a future version of myself that cannot exist now." As silence descended on the room, Rudi continued.

"The efficacy of this device has been proved to me by the existence of these papers." He held the sheaf aloft to emphasise his point. "And it has also been proved to Direktor Heisenberg several times over the last year." He let that sink in and could see Werner nodding in his peripheral vision.

"We are here because Germany is broken, we are the sick man of Europe, everybody hates us, including a lot of Germans. We are here to change this; we are here to put right the injustices

213

that lead to national socialism, we are here to prevent our fore-fathers from losing the first World War!" he said climactically.

"Ja, like you said, Werner has already told us," Mirabel said through the side of her mouth that did not contain a cigarette. Rudi was thrown completely by the way this clearly intelligent woman had just dismissed him so casually.

"Ja, but Krause said…" Rudi trailed off and shook his head and began again with renewed vigour. "We must address two main problems. The first is practical; we need to build this ground-breaking machine and test it. The second is the more theoretical; what will we send back in time and how will it affect the present?" Rudi felt pleased with this and received some congenial looks from his audience.

"I would like us to split into two subgroups in order to achieve this. Mirabel and Tobias, I would like you to work together to produce some stratagem that could lead to a swift German victory. Once we have these, then Erik can war game them for us. In the meantime, Erik, I will need you to work with Winifred and me on the device. Krause, you helped to design and build the MP40?"

"*Genau.*" He nodded.

"Please go over the design and, where necessary, alter it so that it might be mass produced in 1913."

"Natürlich," Krause smiled, evidently pleased with his assignment, while Mirabel looked at Eder and back to Rudi, clearly feeling he had jumped the gun, rushing forward without first discussing the implication of this venture.

"Okay colleagues, you have your assignments, let's get to it," Werner said with an awkward fist shake and a slight American accent. Rudi frowned; this was exactly what he didn't need from Heisenberg right now, when his leadership was at its weakest.

Rudi had arrived in Munich deflated. He was finally in the west, but freedom was ashes in his mouth. Werner had found him a spacious apartment overlooking the clear waters of the *Schwabinger Bach*. Western luxuries like butter, coffee and fresh meat were in comparative abundance and his kitchen had been well stocked. While he still drank the much-needed coffee without relish, Rudi had no appetite for anything more than the black bread and root vegetables of his youth. The love of his life had deserted him, and he had abandoned his mother and sister in the East. During his darkest moments, usually in the small hours, he would lie awake imagining the worst; poor, fragile Carla in Hoheneck Women's Prison, a forced labour prison with grey walls, grey uniforms, and grey-faced inmates with broken souls. It was said that the regime there was so oppressive that a prisoner's menstruation would mysteriously stop shortly after incarceration. Rudi couldn't imagine a place so horrifying that it would deny nature.

What if Olga had been taken from the train while it travelled through East Germany en route to Munich?

Thoughts of her haunted him most early mornings, until he resolved to simply get up and go to work on the *Zeitmaschine*.

He could not, however, do anything to stop the nightmares. While sometimes he dreamt of 1945 and his cold-blooded, violent revenge on that depraved Russian conscript, he also dreamt of Lorenzo and his ominous last words. Most nights, however, he dreamt of the horrific conditions in the GDR's prisons.

These dreams were vivid and were impossibly, disturbingly, about his own confinement, and so he felt inexplicably guilty. Even though it was on a subconscious level, he dreamed more about something that had not happened to him than something that probably was happening to his sister and to Olga. He would dream of unbearable cold, of back-breaking labour, ruthless guards, and cruel mind games.

Every nightmare ended the same way. He would be staring at his own reflection, looking down at broken hands with missing fingers. When he looked up, the man peering back would look like him, only older and sadder, with barely any teeth, and the man would start to shout at him. It was mostly incoherent babble, but sometimes he received obscure warnings of *der Engel*, although why an angel would feature in that Godless pit of suffering was beyond Rudi's comprehension. It sounded like a warning, but he invariably woke lying in a pool of sweat.

The word remained, however. *Der Engel.*

Rudi spent most of his time assisting the practical team with building the device. Erik's role in America had been 'the computer guy', and he concentrated on both the interface that would control the time machine and the war-gaming program.

Every Friday Rudi would sit with Mirabel and Tobias and discuss early Twentieth Century history. He relished these weekly delights, as both scholars were a joy to converse with, never pedantic or condescending, and they explained each problem patiently and suggested solutions for polite debate.

One Friday, however, the firebrand in Mirabel bubbled to the surface during a discussion of the role of women and women's suffrage, but ultimately, it was generally agreed that while the war had eased some restrictions on women and allowed them to demonstrate that they were just as capable and intelligent as men, a delay on the vote by a few years would be worth avoiding the abomination of national socialism.

The main discussion however, revolved around one key question: prevent World War One or engineer a way for Germany win it convincingly? On the face of it, the former was the most desirable. Both scholars put forward the argument that since the Kaiser was hell bent on war, he would have one by any means.

"Assassinate the Kaiser?" Rudi suggested one Friday.

"Ja, Eder argued this for a while, but you see, the Machiavellian shitheads in the corridors of power at the time would use that to cause untold political instability. Berlin, not Saint Petersburg could wind up being the birthplace of communism." She became animated when she felt strongly about a point she was making, and Rudi found it admirable.

"Not to mention the heir to the throne will grow up to be a verdammt Nazi!" She added.

"What about preventing communism?" Rudi asked.

"How can we deny those wretched people their revolution? The Russian nobility were despicable, their attitude to those humans, their countrymen…" she sighed, "…they got what they deserved." She turned to face Rudi. "Alone, you're not going to be able to control anything beyond the initial info drop, Rudi. You have to accept that this is humanity and people will continue to behave so, however many of tomorrow's newspapers or drawings of guns we send them."

She smiled and leaned back to face both men.

"And as for communism, we will just have to rely on the judgement of the rest of Europe to either follow in moderation and adopt a form of social democracy or reject it altogether in favour of capitalism." She was calm now, matter of fact, almost aloof.

"Okay, so if we ensure that Germany wins World War One, what do you expect Bethmann-Hollweg to do?" Rudi asked.

"That's an easy one," Eder said, putting down his apple cake and brushing the crumbs from his embroidered waistcoat. "Bethmann-Hollweg produced a document called the September Program, outlining exactly this. Essentially, he would cripple France financially by ordering war reparations of at least ten billion francs and take the Pas-de-Calais into either German or more likely Belgian control, naturally pushing the Franco-German border a little further west." He spread his arms to suggest that this was reasonable enough.

"Belgium and Luxembourg would be either absorbed into Germany or become puppet states. In the east we expect that Germany would want the Baltic states under their control as well as Poland, Belarus, and the Ukraine, with the strategically vital port of Sevastopol. Naturally, the colonial territories of these nations would fall under German Imperial rule too.

"It may sound harsh, but if it prevents the further slaughter of prolonged trench warfare and the atrocities of the Third Reich, then it's worth it?" Rudi said this as a semi-rhetorical question, inviting some correction from the experts, and when none came, he continued.

"So if we've decided what we're going to do, then I'll let you guys figure out how we do that."

"We have some ideas, actually," Mirabel said, producing a separate notebook. "We've covered the inadequacy of the Schlieffen plan already, and outlined what changes we would make in that regard. We also know that von Moltke is the key to changing this because he has the ear of the Kaiser as well as being the man in charge of the armed forces. There is the additional bonus of his dying in 1916, at which point the war should be over and Bethmann-Hollweg, with his desire to work with Great Britain and establish a stable peace in Europe, can step in to calm the marshal fervour."

She looked at her colleagues for assent and continued when she received nods.

"Now, another key factor was the British naval blockade. If we were to avoid entering Belgium until after France was defeated, we could keep them out of the war. But we need them to prepare for British aggression and have the navy ready, so perhaps we can include detailed information on the British fleet and shore-based naval installations. I will, of course, defer to Herr Eder in these matters, but it seems to me that with Britain's standing army being so small, a decisive victory early in the war could keep them peaceable, or force them to surrender, whichever is most expedient." Rudi noticed in Mirabel a level of contempt for the British that exceeded the general mixture of apathy and irritation most citizens of 1960s Germany showed for their one-time liberators.

On the subject of the National Socialist German Workers' Party, both Tobias and Mirabel agreed that Hitler was merely a 'Betriebsunfall' – an unfortunate accident – of history and could not possibly have gained any traction in a victorious Germany.

Rudi asked if it were not good practice to 'deal' with him just in case?

To this they were adamant, it was immoral to punish a man for something that he *might* do.

"Surely he will still live through the war on both fronts and emerge the same twisted man, bent on revenge and racial purity?" The words still made Rudi uneasy, it wasn't so long ago that he'd been singing the egregiously vivid songs of the Hitler Youth and harbouring genuine hatred for those considered *Untermensch* by the Reich.

"Irrelevant!" Mirabel exclaimed, "the NSDAP was a product of the treaty of Versailles and the humiliation inflicted on Germany by the Entente. Hyperinflation, demilitarisation, and French control of the Rhine." She counted each point of on her fingers while Eder nodded in agreement.

"It could also be argued that a victorious Reich would have kept *Gefreiter* Hitler too busy for all of those beerhall meetings and rallies," Eder added.

"Surely his wartime experiences had something to do with it?" Rudi persisted. "All that death and the relentless shelling? I was in Berlin in 1945 and…" He trailed off unable still, after all this time, to verbalise his trauma.

"How many millions of men do you think came back messed up from the war?" Mirabel asked, softening her tone slightly. "And how many of those men became tyrannical mass-murderers?"

"Well…" Rudi said, ready to reel off a list of Nazi war criminals.

"Let me rephrase that. How many went on the lead a grass-roots movement that became a despotic regime capable of some of the greatest atrocities ever perpetrated by humankind?"

Rudi was not the right kind of scholar to debate this with any efficacy, so he reluctantly dropped the matter. Though he gave it some thought.

"Fine. Without you two onboard, I don't have the knowledge to dispose of an obscure Austrian painter anyway, not remotely from 1961.

Libya, 2035

The rising of the sun was welcome respite as Olga shivered in Yael's arms, and there was no such thing as dry in a raft like this. Shortly after climbing up and into the high-sided floating tent, a bitterly cold Tramontana – the frigid north wind common in the Mediterranean – and a westerly swell cut the sea up drastically.

Both women were sick, filling the tiny space with vomit and eventually their other bodily fluids. They had rations and water, but they saw no point in eating or drinking if they could not keep it down. They had watertight survival suits that they longed to climb into, but again with a hooley like that outside, normal human requirements were impossible to manage inside a suit like that.

So, they lay shivering in their own mess, unable to do anything but wait. At first the sun warmed the dark canvas of the raft, giving comfort after a long night of suffering. As the sea calmed and the wind became no more than a gentle breeze, they were able to bale sea water in and back out again until the raft was clean. They ate, and drank the chlorinated water, but as the sun rose in the late morning, it baked the darkly coloured raft and they suffered once more, taking it in turns ineffectually throwing sea water on to the roof to cool it down. Olga, in her desperation to be free of the sun's oppressive heat, donned her survival suit and lowered herself over the side, sighing in delight at the relief she found in the cool water.

Yael joined her and they spent the middle part of the day treading water in the tiny shadow created by the raft.

"Should we try to push the raft towards land?" Olga asked as they drifted.

"There would be not point Mami, we can't hope to navigate without the proper equipment, and we don't have the rations to waste calories paddling in the wrong direction." Yael said, she'd hooked one foot through a loop on the side of the raft and was floating on her back, her arms spread wide while her neoprene clad chest rose and fell with her steady breathing.

As the sun moved across the sky and its power waned, they climbed back in and took turns sleeping, while the other kept watch. They had two spare inflation canisters for the raft, meaning that if they spotted a vessel in time, they could deflate and become almost invisible from any kind of distance. Yael thought that small oxygen breathers would have made a handy addition to the kit, allowing full submersion in an emergency and wondered if she would ever have another mission like this or any other for that matter.

As boredom became delirium and thirst became dehydration, their bodies began to consume muscle in order to function. The seas picked up and the wind blew powerfully, but the little raft never failed them. One advantage of this heavy weather was the deluge of fresh water collected in bladders from the roof of the raft and stored for dryer days. Yael forced Olga to eat and drink as much as possible during the calm, but when the weather came around again, so did the vomiting and the purging of vital nutrients. Eventually, after twenty days of this ordeal, the mistral blew itself out and calm dominated the rest of their voyage.

As the wind pushed them gently south while the currents dragged them eastwards four hundred miles into the Gulf of Sidra, they ate their rations and caught Luna, Groper, Hake, and Sea bass. They took turns swimming in order to rebuild their fitness and on one very special occasion and a pod of dolphins joined them. The creatures chattered and played for hours with the women, but they never returned.

From the raft they could see the acres of shining solar panels that powered the desalination plants, the Reich's latest attempt at getting some use out of the constantly expanding desert that seemed to be consuming Africa.

They found themselves off the coast of Brega, where the sea finally washed them ashore after thirty-eight days adrift.

There were no panels here, just the remnants of the once busy town fed and clothed by crude oil, now a ghost town on the edge of a desert. Many places in the Middle East looked like this now, Yael told Olga. Since fossil fuels were obsolete there was no industry to keep people here, they simply left and abandoned the town to decay.

Olga and Yael buried the raft on the beach before first light and Yael produced sturdy boots and some locally acceptable clothes from her huge bag, covering Olga's blonde hair and still comparatively pale complexion. The waterproof bags turned inside out to become backpacks, they repacked what they needed and buried the rest with the raft, keeping their weapons out of sight.

The town was a series of rusting pipes and chimneys leading to a harbour that housed only one decaying hulk of a cargo ship. The houses all seemed deserted, and the cars were long dead, with flat, perished tires and opaque glazing. Further inland they found even more signs of abandonment. Windowless shop fronts displaying evidence of looting from years before, a pharmacy with a trail of medicines, the labels browned and curling in the sun; dented tin cans in the smashed window of a grocery store, overturned shopping trolleys inverted and wheelless like dead cockroaches in the heat.

Yael guided them through the town in search of a vehicle for the two-thousand-kilometre drive across the desert to Israel. They still had combustion engines here, fed on the dregs from the refineries or an overturned tanker, cooking oil or in some cases biodiesel, the production of which carried a death sentence in the Reich.

The two of them had been searching for over three hours when they heard an engine, something Olga had never experienced and Yael barely remembered from her parents' farm; agriculture had been the last industry to electrify, especially on smaller family-run farms. The noise grew louder, and Yael pulled Olga off the street and into what had once been a music shop, drawing the pistol from her bag.

"There must be oil or fuel left here somewhere," Yael whispered, risking a peek at the increasing engine noise.

The engine note changed as it slowed to turn onto their street, and they moved silently behind the counter, ducking down as it grew louder until it eventually passed them. Yael watched through a reflection on the rear wall of the shop. It was perfect. An open cab, military style Landcruiser with large tyres and a covered back, and best of all, it was driven by a boy no older than twelve.

She flew over the counter, gun in hand to dart out of the shop and startled Olga.

She ran down the side of the building, cutting in front of the truck as it looped around the block to come back at her. Olga followed her, seeing how the tough woman radiated confidence as she took a stance and aimed her weapon at the driver shielded only by a flimsy pane of glass.

The engine note wavered, then roared with a dark of black smoke erupting behind it, but Yael raised the barrel a fraction and fired a single shot. She blocked the road, forcing the driver to either run her down or stop. As if Yael knew the outcome before the driver did, the shot glanced off the metal beside the windscreen and the engine note hesitated before the truck slowed and stopped.

Olga moved. Her feet and legs pumped the ground as though they knew what to do, even if her mind felt that it didn't. She ran, launching herself at the truck to rip open the door and drag the boy from behind the wheel with startling ease.

The gun was in her hand, her arms braced to accommodate any recoil if she was forced to pull the trigger, and her voice was so firm, so full of authority that she scarcely recognised it.

"Don't move!" she yelled, only the words weren't spoken in English, nor were they German. She spoke in Arabic, frightening herself that she had a whole other language stored deep inside her mind.

The boy, who turned out to be a little older than they'd first guessed, was distracted by the beautiful girl screaming at him in Arabic and pointing a gun like she knew exactly what she was doing. Yael crept around his blindside and spun him over onto his front to search him with quick, practised movements.

"Are there others?" Yael demanded in perfect Arabic, the words translating in Olga's mind unbidden.

He burst into tears.

"Please, it is not my truck, most honoured lady, I must return it."

"Return it to who?"

"The Sheik, he will punish me if I return without it."

"He just lets you drive around in his truck?" Yael snapped.

"He was..." he hesitated, "... he let me drive because he made me sad."

"Where is this Sheik?"

"He has a compound about twenty miles east of here," the boy said placatingly.

"Are there more trucks like this?"

"Why?" He stopped crying, his facial expression slowly transforming from that of a pained child into a conspiratorial grin.

"Because we need a truck!" Yael said impatiently. The boy's eyes fell upon the high-quality firearm in Yael's hand and his expression changed from abject terror to hope, greed even.

"You know, this is the truck he would miss the least. Perhaps if you do something for me, then maybe I could leave a gate unlocked?"

"What do you want?" Yael asked suspiciously.

"Come on now, if we are going to be friends, we need to be polite to one another."

"What is it that you would like, most *honoured* gentleman?" Yael said, her words dripping with contempt.

"Is that a Jericho Desert Eagle Magnum that you have there?" he asked raising his eyebrows emphatically.

"What if it is?" she retorted, playing his stupid game now.

"If you gave it to me, I would make sure that you could enter the compound and leave with a fully fuelled truck, hours before anyone would notice it was missing."

"If you were to do that for us, I would certainly give you this gun," Yael agreed readily.

"First the gun, then the truck," he bargained.

"Listen kid, I hold all the cards here. I've already got the gun and the truck, what's to stop us just leaving you here?"

"Okay, okay," he conceded. "Maybe we can leave the gun somewhere together and after you have the truck, I will go and find it."

"That could work," Yael negotiated, wiggling the gun in his face

"Works for me, can I hold it?"

"Can I drive?" she asked as she dropped the magazine into her palm before ejecting the last round and making sure that Olga was watching him.

"Awesome," he immediately held it sideways and pointed it at Yael, "Freez…"

Before he could draw breath, he was on the floor again, winded and minus his new toy.

"Never!" Yael snapped, shoving hard on the boy's arm locked tight behind his back. "*Ever*, point a weapon at anything you don't want to kill. Do you understand me?"

He wailed that he understood, that he was sorry, that he didn't mean it, and as suddenly as Yael had attacked him she stood and let him go. She held the gun out to him, offering a clear opportunity to do it again, and do it right.

He climbed to his feet and dusted himself off sullenly, taking the pistol carefully and checking it for any signs of damage.

Yael walked to the music shop and retrieved their bags.

"Olga, get in the front, it's time for a driving lesson."

She was nervous when she climbed into the Landcruiser. She sat behind the wheel and looked at the unfamiliar knobs and dials, jiggled some of the levers and gripped the steering wheel, all while Yael watched her expectantly.

It gradually fell into place, and she reached down only to stop in hesitation.

"Where is the on switch?" she asked, prompting a laugh from Yael before the woman composed herself and pointed at a key. Olga looked at it, then back at Yael who was miming turning it.

Olga grasped the key between finger and thumb. As soon as she heard the engine roar to life and felt the vibration through the steering wheel, she knew. She knew that she could drive this thing, and drive it well. All she had to do was *remember*.

She jammed it down in gear and punched the gas pedal. Everyone was thrown back in their seat, the rear end kicking out slightly, creating a cloud of dust as they turned the first corner. It was slow going on the unmaintained roads and twenty miles was not a quick trip. Yael noticed during the drive that the vehicle was knocking and grinding when it should not, that the brakes were purely ornamental, and the smell of hot, old oil was pungent.

"You," she said to the boy, watching him recoil into the far corner of the back seat, "what is your name?"

"Ibrahim," he replied with a nervous smile.

"Ibrahim, we are not going to hurt you, so long as you don't point any more guns at us," she said with a compassion in her voice that had not been there before.

Ibrahim looked shamefaced, but he was so used to dodging blows and cowering, that evasive manoeuvres were second nature.

"So, Ibrahim, you said this was not the best of the Sheik's vehicles?"

"Yes," he said hesitantly.

"Well, we don't want this one, this one is shit. We'll be lucky if we'll get to the end of the street with it."

"Okay, there is one other that I could get you, it is better and more reliable, but…" he trailed off.

"What?"

"I want bullets for the gun."

"Nine *rounds*."

"Two clips!"

"One *magazine*."

"Okay, but you t—" He paused and looked at the two beautiful women in his car. "Take me with you," he said, sensing his way out of the existence he hated.

"No."

"Please?"

"No."

"Please, I'll do anything you ask, I can be your driver and your guide and carry your bags and find fuel for you! Please take me, where are you going?"

"East, and the answer is still no."

"I'll take that as a maybe."

Olga leaned towards Yael, shooting a suspicious glance at the boy who grinned at her nervously.

"You know he isn't going to give us a shit vehicle if he thinks that he'll be stuck in the desert with us when it breaks down," Olga said, relishing the way it felt to say the word *shit* with the joy of a first offender.

"Oh, fuck. Fine!" Yael conceded, punching the seat.

"Will you teach me to fight?" Ibrahim asked excitedly, clearly unaware how far he had already pushed his luck.

"If you shut up right now, I'll think about it." She thought for a moment. "Will this truck get us to the Red Sea, Ibrahim?" He shrugged.

"The person who predicts the future is lying, even when he is right."

"What the fuck does that mean, I'm asking if you think that this truck is reliable!" Yael snapped, annoyed at his evasion.

"Oh, I still don't know," he said, beaming a smile not dampened by potential failure.

They sat in silence for a while, bumping and grinding in the heat along the cracked road, azure sea to the north and foreboding desert in every other direction, and the signs of the now obsolete oil industry everywhere. Tankers were abandoned jackknifed at the roadside, haze rising from the hot metal, filling stations with weather-beaten signs reading: "Fuel for food" or "Allah has forsaken us!"

Yael had seen all of this happening as she grew up.

Countries like Israel, with a diverse range of exports managed and even gained from the temporary period of low fuel prices before total electrification known as the Arab Winter.

The once oil-rich states had collapsed, first into civil war, then when international borders broke down and the fighting spread, refugees in their millions wandered the desert in desperate search of food and water. The havens of the rich and powerful fell apart, plunging those regions into war and misery in a perverse reversal of fate.

Some had boarded boats for Europe, but the Reich simply sunk them without mercy. Isolationist America did not want to know, and rumours emerged that they were sinking ships too and blaming it on the Germans. The death toll rose and there were few who cared enough to help. The citizens of the Reich in its propaganda bubble knew nothing of it, deeming it dangerous or irrelevant, so the newspapers did not print it.

The truck crested a hill and Olga gasped when she saw a verdant oasis lying in the distance. Rows of greenhouses, solar mirrors, and photovoltaic panels alternated with rows of green hedges. These backed onto hundreds of acres of saplings. Kilometres of irrigation ditches ran throughout the site which appeared to be fed by a large bore pipe stretching out to the north. Olga followed the pipe with her eyes to see that it led to directly to the shore. The enormous farm was surrounded by watchtowers which formed a perimeter, and at the very centre of the site, beautiful walled gardens within which stood modest looking dwellings.

"Pull over here," Yael instructed.

Olga stopped the truck behind a long-abandoned compound.

"Is that where you live, Ibrahim?" Yael asked.

"No," he said, laughing. "That is paradise. If I go near there, I will be shot."

"Who lives there?"

"*Ajanib*. The white settlers. They have mirrors that turn sea water into river water, they use it to grow trees in the barren soil," he said, in awe of the technology.

"Where then?"

"There," he said pointing at a tiny patch of green next to a compound about five Kilometres further down the same road, "we buy water from paradise."

"What happens," she said, fighting to remain patient, "if we drive past those watch towers?"

"Ah."

"Ah?" Yael barked, "What is *ah*?"

"Well," Ibrahim started, then he looked away, searching for the right way to phrase it, "if they see you, they will likely kill me and take you for," he blushed, "for pleasure."

"And you didn't feel that this was relevant before? Were you even going to stop us?" Olga said angrily.

"Is there another route? A way we can avoid making any new friends?"

233

"Yes."

"Anything else? Or just *yes*?" Yael asked, her eyes closed to keep her calm.

"The coastal road."

"Any surprises on that road we should know about? Pirates? Bedouin bandits? sea monsters?"

"There are always Bedouin bandits, they are the only people who knew how to survive after the oil stopped. But they do not come this far because of the guns of paradise." He pointed at the watch towers in the distance as if they weren't obvious.

"Is there fuel at your father's compound?" Yael asked after a pause.

"My father is dead. I live with the Sheik. He... he looks after all of the orphans," he trailed off and turned to look out of the window.

"Is that why you want to come with us? Because you don't like living with the Sheik?" Olga asked in a kindly tone.

"He is most generous, but sometimes he is wicked." Tears threatened in the boy's eyes, and he climbed down from the truck and began to pace around, kicking the Calotropis plants and swinging his gangly arms at his side. Olga joined him, placing her arm around him, and turning him towards her; they were a similar height, both about five foot eight.

"Listen, Ibrahim, I once had a master that wanted to do things to me."

She spoke in Arabic, marvelling that such a skill came to her so easily as though she was beginning to unlock the true potential of her mind.

234

Is this memory? she asked herself *Have learned this in another time? Another... life?*

"How did you get away?" Ibrahim asked in a small voice, prompting her back to the present.

"Yael and her friends saved me, and we want to save you, but we must get far away to keep you safe. Will you help us get a better vehicle and some food and fuel and, most importantly, water?"

He was crying now. Tears rolled silently down his dust-covered cheeks running rivulets along his smooth skin. He cuffed at his running nose with a hand.

"I want to, but I am scared that we will be caught. They will sell you to the Sheik of paradise and beat me or even cut off my hand."

"Yael is a super soldier and I... well, I can do things too. We won't get caught!" She winked at him and dried his eyes gently with her thumbs.

As they shared the last of the water, Yael gave them her plan, which was simple enough. Ibrahim would return as expected, while she and Olga waited nearby until nightfall. Ibrahim would discreetly load a reliable vehicle with supplies and fuel. When the coast was clear, he would open the gates and meet the women on the road outside, and if there was any trouble, Yael promised that she and Olga would deal with it. Ibrahim assured them that he could manage it, and Olga held her tongue. She was concerned about the risk which was all the boy's to take.

Ibrahim drove them along the coastal path and the women stayed out of site in the rear, until he set them down at yet another abandoned petrol station.

"Ibrahim?"

"Yes, Olga?"

"Don't take any unnecessary risks, there is always tomorrow." She winked at him and smiled weakly.

"You can say that Olga," Yael said, tapping the last drop from an upturned bottle onto her tongue, "but it doesn't make it true. See you later kid and don't fuck it up."

"I won't let you down" Ibrahim called over the engine as he sped away.

Yael spent the rest of the day showing Olga the basics of weapon handling with her Micro Galil and the Jericho. The weapons felt familiar, and Olga felt again like she had always known how to do these things. They practised moving tactically and how to find and use cover effectively. Yael made Olga carry out drills until they were second nature and then sent her to sleep in the stockroom until dark. Again, it felt to Olga as if she was being reminded of something she already understood more than being taught something new.

At twilight the pair moved into position near the road outside the compound and lay in a culvert listening to the cicadas as they waited for Ibrahim. Olga had fallen asleep by the time Yael heard the gate creak, and a pool of light grew on the road as it opened.

"Wake up," she whispered to Olga, giving her an abrupt shove.

Headlights shone for the briefest of moments before they were snuffed out. An engine started and a truck emerged, slowly at first, then picked up speed. Thirty metres along the road Yael signalled with a small light. Ibrahim approached in the truck with doors open and a healthy purr coming from the engine. The two women moved back from their hiding place into fire positions. When they were sure it was Ibrahim and not an ambush, they climbed in. Ibrahim stamped on the accelerator pedal, and they sped off into the darkness.

They drove for long enough to believe that they had got away without detection, when a shout startled Olga.

"Shit! They are following us, stop the truck! Stop!" Yael's words were angry more than frightened, and her tone set Olga's resolve as she flowed from her open door to spread out and aim her own weapon towards the following threat.

Yael knelt in the road, closing an eye to protect her night vision. Carefully, she aimed her weapon at the grill of the vehicle following and fired three rounds. Steam enveloped the front vehicle as it ground to a halt, but two more sets of headlights appeared either side and sped around the stricken truck. She fired on them too, as did Olga, with equal success.

"Did you get the fuel, water and food?" she called into the truck.

"I have fuel for five hundred miles in the tank and six hundred in cans, I got water for ten days and food for eight," he called back.

She could live with the food and water, but fuel was so rare and there was some right there.

"Do the other trucks have fuel cans?" Yael barked at Ibrahim.

"Yes, but they may not be full."

She moved round to the front of the truck and reached into the engine bay, ripping out the lighting relay to kill the tail and the reverse as well as the headlights.

"Olga, with me. Ibrahim, wait for my signal, then reverse down the road towards us. Do not leave the truck and do not press the brake pedal."

Olga and Yael moved back the way they had come, using the darkness at the side of the road as cover, until Yael told Olga to stop and go to ground.

"Wait until I fire," she whispered. "Once they see our muzzle flash, they'll have us and you will need to move again every three rounds."

The Sheik's men ran down the middle of the road, clustered together and shouting. Olga saw their outlines, feeling scorn for their lack of tactical awareness, then realising with a smile that she hadn't known what those words even meant until she had remembered them.

"Ibrahim, where did you get a gun, little boy?" a mocking voice called out. "When we find you, we are going to take it from you and kill you with it."

As the rearmost Sheik's man entered Yael's killing field she opened up in three-round bursts, closely followed by Olga. Four of them were down before they knew what was happening, and by the time the other two had brought their weapons to bear, they too lay gurgling their own blood on the dusty ground. Yael signalled with her flashlight again, and they heard the wine of the reverse gear as they rushed over to the trucks and began searching for fuel.

"Take them all, even if they are empty," Yael said.

They found three full cans and four empty ones. Walking back with their loot, they saw Ibrahim in the road, kicking one of the dead men, and shouting through tears of anger.

"You bastard," he wailed. "You *bastard*."

Olga tried to lead him gently away but Ibrahim shoved her and ran back to the truck sobbing loudly. Yael shone her light over the pile of bodies. She took any jewellery and compatible ammunition, rifling the corpses without emotion. One man had a Russian-made PKM machine gun with belts of linked ammunition, which Yael snapped up and hauled to their truck where she found everything else loaded. Olga was behind the wheel waiting to go and Ibrahim was sobbing softly in the back seat, suddenly the young boy he was and not the piratical entrepreneur he pretended to be.

Yael's head snapped back as Olga pulled off in silence. "Two thousand miles to go." Yael said under her breath.

"What?"

"You did well back there, both of you, I'm glad to have you on my side," Yael's words may have been platitudes, but they meant everything to both of them.

Zeppelin – The Ost Front, 1915

A technician filled a small balloon with gas and tied it off, then after a nod from the engineer, he released it. The engineer observed the flight of the balloon through his theodolite and noted down his findings before both men jogged off to their station in the engine nacelle. Dozens of ground crew hauled upon guy ropes, carefully leading the LZ 120 Zeppelin *Bodensee* on tracks from the gigantic storage shed in Silesia. The four Maybach engines roared into life, the captain waved from the window of the control gondola and the guy ropes were released simultaneously. The behemoth took flight, lurching up and forward into the spring sunshine.

"All yours, Leutnant Stindt," the captain said as he stepped back from the con. "You have the course, and you have my orders."

Kapitänleutnant Gunter Neumann of the Imperial Naval Airship *Bodensee* retired to his spacious cabin, the largest private space on the airship, sat down in the comfortable chair and dragged his hand down slowly over his face. His eyes fell upon the suitcase and the knot in his stomach tightened as he thought back to his briefing that morning.

"Kapitänleutnant, thank you for volunteering for this mission. Are all of your officers and men aware that this mission is purely voluntary?" His commanding officer was flanked by two officers with the badges and piping of artillery majors.

"Thank you, Admiral, we can take it from here," said the taller of the two majors, who looked around the room distractedly as the admiral got up and left his own office. The other man stood dwarfed by his colleague, apparently uninterested and polishing the lenses of his wire-rimmed spectacles. Now that he thought about it, Neumann could not place the Major's accent, the smaller man; Geiger, was clearly Bavarian. But the taller man, Felsen, it was too perfect, too crisp. It unsettled Neumann who thought of himself a something of an aficionado when it came to German accents.

Kapitänleutnant Neumann was a bachelor, formerly a capable sea officer, whose skill in navigation had earned him a recommendation for the Naval Airship division in 1913. He'd spent the early part of the war surveying the French line, making detailed maps of their defences, and spotting for artillery.

Later, when the war with Britain started, he moved to bombing raids, which involved long, cold missions over the North Sea waiting for dark before embarking on nerve-wracking sorties over the naval bases along the East coast of England and Scotland, or a bombing raid on the heavily defended capital of London, if they were unlucky. When his captain suffered a heart attack during one such raid over the Humber estuary, Neumann assumed command and, after the payload was dropped, brought the crew and vessel home safely.

Neumann was promoted for his actions that night and, most unusually, remained with the same crew. After the battle of the channel Neumann's unit headed to the Eastern Front where instead of naval targets, they bombed cities full of civilians. They were told by their commanders that this was different, that the Slavs were different from them, that the Germanic people needed this land for their *Lebensraum*.

This did not sit right with Neumann, but orders were orders and he had seen what happened to imperial officers with a vocal conscience. He had a reputation as a lucky captain, because during his whole time with the division, the only man to die on one of his Zeps was his own captain. Men called him *Glücklicher* Gunter when they thought he could not hear them.

It was with this crew that he flew now, and he thought about them as he sat staring at the briefcase. All they knew was that this was an incredibly dangerous mission and possibly a one-way flight but, if successful, this raid had the potential to end the war and stop the meat grinder on the Ost front.

Not one man had hesitated and at the time and he'd felt immense pride over that, but now he was assailed by doubt. His crew knew nothing of the target or anything about the abnormal payload. Nimitz, the *Bodensee's* bombardier, was taken sick at the last minute and replaced with a civilian no one knew, and it was this man alone who oversaw the shipping of the payload during the night.

"Kapitänleutnant, these are your orders," the small major handed him a sealed package. "Do not read them until you reach twenty-one degrees of longitude, and please heed the advice of your new bombardier, Herr Müller. He is also a volunteer, and he understands the device as well as anyone can." He used the German word *Gerät*, meaning gadget.

As he crossed the Vistula River, Neumann opened and read his orders.

Duetches Flotte Special Projects Division

Air ship Bodensee-Kapitänleutnant G. A. Neumann, Imperial Germany Navy

You are hereby required and directed to repair forthwith on board his Imperial Majesty's Air ship Bodensee and proceed with the upmost despatch to 59° 55' N, 30° 17' E, at which time you will defer to Herr Müller for further instructions.

Herr Müller is to be kept abreast of course and distance from target every two hours.

Hereof nor you, nor any of you may fail as you will answer the Contrary at your peril. And for so doing this shall be your Warrant.

Unsigned – Deniable.

Neumann had spent a gruelling two hours pacing the keel corridor from the engine nacelle and back to the control gondola, counting seventy-five turns as he waited. Checking the chart obsessively and waiting some more until he could read those orders, he was annoyed because had told him next to nothing. He had already worked out from provision of fuel and their initial course that they were headed to Petrograd, as had the navigation officer, engineering officer and the steersman.

"Bauer, pipe the crew, I have an announcement," Neumann said wearily. Bauer dutifully pulled a cork bung from the speaking tube and stooped to bring his mouth level.

"D'you hear there? D'you hear there? An announcement from the captain will follow," Bauer called, stepping back to make room for his captain.

"*Meine guten Männer*, we have just passed over Warsaw, meaning I can now tell you our final destination," he pinched the bridge of his nose and rubbed his jaw before continuing. "Some of you may have guessed that we are on a heading for Petrograd. You may also have noticed that we have shipped a different bombardier for this mission. Herr Müller is a guest and vital to the success of the mission, so please show him the same courtesy you would have shown to Nimitz. We ought to be over target in roughly eight hours, the time is 1600. Carry on."

He felt wretched, and he could not shake the portentous feeling that this mission was going to be their last. The weight of that responsibility threatened to crush him.

It was at this point that he met Herr Müller for the first time as the man climbed down into the windy control gondola, wearing civilian flying clothes; hessian boots not unlike those issued to the crew, with insulated trousers tucked into them, a leather jacket lined with sheepskin and a padded leather flying cap. He was a small wiry man with a large nose, a good six inches shorter than Neumann, and he spoke with a high-pitched nasal accent.

"Herr Kapitän," he said respectfully as he took Neuman's hand is his, limp and clammy from the thick gloves, "thank you for having me aboard and for volunteering for this mission."

He shook hands with the rest of the gondola, except for the steersman and the elevator man, who could not be distracted. The control gondola was not a spacious place, crammed with instruments and equipment. Mounted next to the wheel was in a sort of bowl called a gimble was the all-important azimuth compass. The rest of the gondola was littered with all kinds of switches, gauges, and wheel valves to monitor the ship and alter the way it sailed through the air.

"May we speak in your cabin Kapitän Neumann?" asked Müller in a conversational tone.

"Certainly, but my quarters are very cramped. Perhaps we might sit in the gun room?" Neumann lied.

The plans sent through time by Rudi Kessler and his companions were for the LZ 120 Zeppelin, far larger than the H class Zeppelins that would have been built in the first iteration World War One. These airships had been built for commercial charters, accommodating twenty-six passengers in addition to the crew of twelve. The passenger compartment was now the bomb bay, but the airship had the relative luxury of a gunroom, a spacious area with soft furnishings and a constant supply of hot coffee to warm the crew on these bitterly cold flights.

Neumann invited Müller to sit, and he did the same.

"Herr Kapitän, this is the single most important mission of the war," he said without preamble.

"I see."

"Yes, do you know what I have back there in the bomb bay?"

"Some big bombs?" Neumann answered, spreading his arms wide in a gesture that suggested he either did not know or that he did not care.

"Not some big bombs, Herr Kapitän, a single bomb capable of flattening an entire city. A true destroyer of worlds." He used the German word *Weltenzerstörer,* as he fixed his gaze on Neumann who resisted the urge to tug at the high collar of his uniform tunic.

"We are going to flatten Petrograd," Müller said staring out of the window into the dark night, "with one bomb?" he made a fist a let it fall into his open palm.

"One bomb?" Neumann asked, incredulity sharpening his question.

"Yes, Herr Kapitän," he said impatiently, "now, it is a fairly simple device, but it has a lot of safeguards in place to prevent early detonation. These take time to remove, so I will need to be kept informed of our position regularly once we cross Lake Peipus."

"My orders are clear," Neumann responded coldly. "I am to defer to you in all matters relating to the bomb."

"*All* matters? Herr Kapitän, from now, there is only the bomb." He paused to stare again at the captain. "We will not return from this mission, it is a," another pause, and this time he smiled morbidly and used the English phrase "a one-way ticket."

"I had surmised as much myself. There isn't nearly enough fuel for a return trip." It was Neumann's turn to make eye contact.

"Tell me, Herr Müller. What will become of us?"

"We will likely be vaporised somewhere over Petrograd," he replied matter of factly.

"I see, what will happen if we are shot down by antiaircraft guns before we can drop the bomb?"

"It will be primed well before we come within range of the guns and there are two triggers. One is a simple timer and the other works on altitude, so in the event of a crash, as long as I have completed the priming sequence, the bomb will detonate."

"Indeed, is there anything else, Herr Müller?"

"Yes, Herr Captain, may I have the briefcase containing the charges and breech plugs please?"

"They are in my cabin. I will have them brought to you."

"Is there somewhere I could take a nap for a few hours?" Neumann thought of this nasty little man sleeping in Nimitz's bunk near the bomb bay and decided that here was probably best.

"Make yourself at home," he said flatly, standing to leave and wondering how a man about to destroy an entire city could think of sleep.

Neumann decided to spend some time talking to each member of his crew, and he could not remember the last time he had walked all the way to the stern and climbed the ladder to the rear gun position.

"Pipe the gun positions, Bauer, let them know that I will be coming to see them over the next hour or so." He did not want to catch them huddling down out of the wind to keep warm, it would sour the *gemütlich* atmosphere he wanted for this most final of missions. He was a taut officer, demanding strict discipline, but he also knew that slight and unofficial relaxation of certain rules could have a significant impact on morale. If ever there was a time to bend those rules, he knew, this was it. He looked at Stindt, tall and slender with an aquiline nose reminiscent of Wellington. He watched as he and Freiburg poured over the charts, occasionally making notes in the log.

Neumann climbed up the short ladder from the control gondola into the keel corridor – a creaking aluminium gangway that ran along the bottom of the airship inside the envelope – and made his way aft.

In Stindt he had a first Leutnant that he could trust in all matters, enabling him to do things that other captains would not entertain, like climb the ladder to the gun at the top of the Zeppelin. He did this now, eighteen metres of narrow metal rungs, thousands of feet in the air. The gunner and loader were expecting him, and he found them dutifully manning their gun.

"Dreyfus, Wable, how are you?"

"Herr Kapitän," they said in unison as they sprang to attention. Neumann did not insist on saluting during flights, and he waved dismissively, uncomfortable about their deference.

"I just came to see how you were doing and to thank you for volunteering for this mission." He never spoke like this to his men, but a certain sentimentality had come over him. He felt emotional, and he wanted to try to do something – anything – to make it up to them.

"Ja, Herr Kapitän." They eyed one another nervously, unsure of what to say to their captain, whom they both admired and respected, but that was as far as it went. They did not know the man, because they spent every mission sequestered in their gun position, messed separately on the ground and only spoke on official naval matters if they spoke at all.

"Indeed, well, I wanted you to know that I am proud to have served with you." He was horrified to find that he was becoming emotional. "You... you are aware of the nature of this mission?"

"Ja, Herr Kapitän."

"Well," he cast about for inspiration, desperate to convey the fact that they would not return, without saying the words outright, "that um, those letters you gave me for your families, I have left them with the adjutant."

248

"Ja, Herr Kapitän." A shadow crossed the face of Dreyfus, then a few seconds later it crossed Wable's, and they looked even more uncomfortable than before.

He longed to offer them some sort of respite, for them to be allowed to take their ease for an hour in the gunroom, but the Imperial Russian Air Service was effective and ruthless; ramming Zeppelins with devastating effect if permitted to get close enough.

He resolved to organise a relief for them, despairing at the thought of their last hours of life spent bitterly cold and frightened, staring out into a moonless sky over a foreign land and reflected that the four-hour watch system employed on surface ships was far more humane.

"Listen, chaps, I may try to send Bauer up to load for you, Dreyfus, then Wable may come and rest for an hour and then Wable, if you feel confident to gun, he shall load for you while Dreyfus rests." While this sort of kindness was not unknown in the Imperial Navy, it was rare, and a beat of discomfort hung in the air before Neumann received a response.

"Vielen Dank, Herr Kapitän." Again, they were unnerved by this strange behaviour but unwilling to look a gift horse in the mouth.

Neuman descended the long ladder and looked into the engine nacelle, where he had an equally uncomfortable conversation with the engineer and his mates. At least they were warm and occupied with their engines, he reflected, although he did not know how they could stand that noise for hours on end.

He left them for the sailmakers' workshop; a cavernous space inside the envelope filled with rolls of canvas and a sewing machine for bag repairs. Again, he tried to convey the gravity of the situation, but naval discipline prevented the men from relaxing and from speaking candidly with their captain. Neumann walked dejectedly back to the main gondola where he knew he could speak more easily with the men in there. He sent Bauer, the radio operator, to rest in the warmth before relieving Dreyfus. He would need his regular men back on their posts before the threat of Russian aircraft was realised.

Bauer was a quiet man, competent at his duty but no more. As he sat in the gunroom listening to the strange civilian snore loudly, he contemplated the words of his captain and began to piece together an image of Petrograd 'flattened'.

The revolution would be crushed before it had even begun. Bauer was a socialist and an admirer of Marx and Lenin, he had read with excitement the story of Lenin and the small group of his supporters being smuggled into Petrograd last winter and organising an uprising in the city when they had taken control of the Duma and were holding the Tsar and his family hostage.

Kaiser Wilhelm was publicly outraged at this affront to his family and demanded their release. Ludendorff and Bethmann-Hollweg, however, urged their emperor to see this as a weakening of his enemies. In fact, they had between them organised for Lenin to be in Petrograd to assist with the revolution, Bethmann-Hollweg because he saw it as a strategy to end the war and Ludendorff because he wanted the Russians to kill their Tsar and motivate the Kaiser to use the bomb he had been developing for the last three years.

It was not public knowledge, but German agents acting from within the revolution had led the storming of the Winter Palace and had made sure the entire royal family were killed, three years earlier than Rudi Kessler's history books told.

Bauer walked slowly to the rear of the Zeppelin, racked with anxiety and waiting to drop the most powerful weapon ever made onto the birthplace of the Russian revolution. He tried to prepare himself for the bitter cold of the gun position as he trudged up the ladder.

Absicht – Munich, 1962

Intention

Munich is known throughout the world for its *Bierhallen* and *Bierkeller*, and it was in a dark, foetid corner of the least frequented of these beer cellars that Henry Clive now sat chain-smoking and nursing a stein of pilsner.

Henry Clive was an employee of the British government who had come down from Oxford in 1941, bright eyed and ready to join one of those new intelligence outfits with an abbreviation instead of a name. His fluent Latin and Greek were of no interest to the Special Operations Executive, but his fluent German and French were. After a year spent in training at Arisaig House in the northernmost reaches of mainland Scotland, Clive had found himself alone on a beach in Brittany.

From the moment they dropped him there to well after VE day, he had been perpetually terrified, on edge and filthy. He snatched sleep where he could and ate what others could spare, washing in rivers and streams. Three years in borrowed clothes, unable to trust anyone he met and none trusting him destroyed a man's nerves, leaving him broken; an unfeeling, soulless husk that not even victory could recover. The invisible scars of a secret war. The only sign being a slight ptosis of the left eye, a reminder every time he looked in the mirror of his low deeds and the ghosts that followed. There had been no great homecoming for the Baker Street Irregulars, no parades and no VE day. Clive had

252

simply moved from Hamburg to Berlin and continued the darker form of ungentlemanly warfare.

His dark, tailored Saville row suit hung about him like a sack. His handmade brogues were scuffed, and his Baliol tie was askew. He looked every inch the archetypal English public-school boy.

Unkempt hair and sunken, red eyes were evidence of Clive's inability to sleep. He used to enjoy a whisky before bed to ensure a sound night, but twenty years of toying with the lives of others, of manipulating and lying, had taken its toll. Now it was the better part of a bottle. Any bottle.

He needed a clear head tonight however, so he stuck with pilsner. He lit another Gauloise from the silver monogramed case his father had given him after *finally* graduating from Oxford. The old man had acted like the war was some sort of indulgent sabbatical. The worst part was that he knew the visceral truth of it. He knew because he had been there too, commanding a company of Buffs in the Great War.

He *knew,* but they had never spoken of the horrors of war, and he doubted they ever would. The closest they had come was a brief conversation about his father's physical injuries and Henry's miraculous lack of them, his only visible scar from his decades at the sharp end being the slight droop to his left eyelid; that conversation had ended abruptly when Sir Gerald Clive had referred to his son's 'sneaking and lurking' as 'not real war fighting, not honest, not gentlemanly straightforward battle'.

"You're late," Clive spat in German.

253

"I had to make sure I wasn't being followed." The man sounded nervous, his lyrical Saxon accent betraying all emotion.

"Do you have it?" Clive meant a precis of the time travel project so far.

"In the bag by your feet."

Clive felt the black leather attaché case brush against his leg and pushed a similar one across to his interlocutor before speaking.

"These are the plans we discussed. You are to send them to the coordinates written on the cover note and insert the small instruction sheet into the main consignment."

Clive made eye contact with his agent to ensure that they understood.

"And remember, we want the same thing, you and I, and my masters for that matter. Get this right and you'll wake up with your land and title restored. Communism would have died in the cradle forty-five years ago." Clive smiled, revealing two rows of uneven, nicotine-stained teeth, but his eyes conveyed no emotion.

"There's a few marks in there to tide you over until you get your uranium mines back."

He chuckled mirthlessly, standing to leave and tossing a few *pfennigs* onto the table for his beer and walking out with his new attaché case.

At another table in another dark corner of another Munich *Bierkellar* sat Rudi and Mirabel. They were the only two left standing from a night of drinks and relaxation for the team after an intensive year building the time machine.

"Why do you want this so bad, Rudi? What drove you to these lengths, to do what no man has ever done before?" asked Mirabel, drunk but composed.

"Doesn't every German want this?" he said with a shrug and upturned palms.

"Bullshit!"

"No, listen I'm…"

"Bullshit!" She punched him in the shoulder playfully. "We all have a *real* reason why we are doing this. Eder cannot live with his role as a block warden in the Anschluss. He feels responsible for the disappearances of many of his neighbours. Krause wasn't Wehrmacht, he was in one of those special police battalions, rounding up partisans behind the Ost front."

"They told you that?" he said incredulously.

"People talk to me," she said with a shrug.

"How about Schroeder?" he asked.

"He's too damn cagey, never really speaks to me anyway." Rudi was disappointed, and he felt shocked at how much of a gossip he was being.

"What about Boelek?" he asked, taking a long drink.

"You heard of Operation Paperclip?"

"He was on *that* list. I mean, he knows his stuff, but some of those scientists were way out of his league. I don't get it, a golden ticket to America and immunity from war crimes, why is he tanking it?"

"We've all got our reasons, Rudi." She said, needlessly adjusting her blouse again.

It felt like she was flirting but Rudi was no expert and even a year on, he wasn't over Olga. He didn't think he ever would be, but could he resign himself to a life of abstinence in case she showed up one day? He didn't know, but he did know that Mirabel was giving him some sort of signal and he was so damn lonely.

"Oh yeah, what's yours?"

"I'll tell you mine if you tell me yours?" she said, holding his gaze just too long.

Shit, this was going to be a turn-off. Rudi had never spoken about those final days in 1945 with anyone, especially not his mother or sister, though it was ever present when they spent time together. The memory of it was like an unwelcome family member.

"You first," he said obstinately.

"Alright, alright, there's not much to tell. We, my family I mean, we were unlucky enough to live near Dachau and my father, who was a bank clerk, was eventually conscripted. But he was too old for the army, and he tried for the Luftwaffe" She paused to take another drink and leaned back.

"But his eyesight was too poor, so they forced him to be a guard at Dachau." She breathed a deep breath. "We had this house right in the centre of town and when he tried to refuse, I was listening at the door. They came with this order, they said to him, I remember it word for word.

"Herr Kaufmann, they said, you must report to the camp to-day, or" her voice cracked with emotion as she attempted an officious tone, "or tomorrow you can report with your whole family".

"Oh, mien Gott, that is awful." Rudi consoled. She dropped the affectation and gave Rudi a wan smile.

"I don't need to tell *you* that he went."

Rudi blew air through his lips silently. His father had been a soldier, but he did not know how he would have felt if he'd known for sure that he had taken part in the kind of atrocities perpetrated at places like Dachau.

"I know, but at the time, us kids, we didn't know what that meant." Mirabel said tiredly. "We saw the camps and our teachers... well, you know what shit they fed us about undesirables and communists and Jewish people, but my sister, Ursula, she was older than you, Rudi, and in 1945 they got her too. She went into the *Volkssturm* and they made her a guard at the women's camp. She came home after her first day and she and my father had this huge argument. I remember her shouting at him, "how could you, daddy?" beating on his chest and screaming that he was a monster." Her voice cracked again and as tears began to fall from her eyes in large drops onto the table, Rudi squeezed her upper arm and pushed a stray hair from her eye.

"My sister, she hung herself from her bedroom window that night. They didn't find her until the morning." She tilted her head back in a vein effort to stem the flow of tears. "When they found her in the morning..." she fixed him with her red puffy eyes and took his hand, "when they found her in the morning,

257

they saw that she had left a message… *Du sollst nicht töten*! She wrote it with her own blood on her uniform tunic."

"Thou shalt not kill," Rudi intoned.

"That's not all. They beat my father in the street, they wouldn't let us take her down until they had finished beating him. But you have to remember that he had Mutti and Claudia and Ernst and me to think about, he knew that we would all wind up there, if he didn't… When they finished beating him, my father that is, they came inside to cut her down and they let her body fall onto my father as he lay there, bleeding in the street. Then they turned her room upside down, destroying nearly everything she had owned, and they stole this necklace. It was this bumble bee." She rested her forehead on the table, but when Rudi made to come around to comfort her, she raised a hand, "I'm fine, it's just that necklace, I remember when she got it and she always wore it on special occasions. Now bumble bees make me so sad. Then my father, when the Amis —do you call them that?"

"Amerikaner? Sure, we call them Amis."

"When the Amis came, he was free from the Nazis and from that awful job, where every day he had to choose between the suffering of his two little girls, of his wife and his baby boy, between their suffering and the suffering of tens of thousands of other human beings. The Amis, they threw open the gates and they shot a load of the guards. I mean fair enough, but that's when he realised that it wasn't over for him, that it would never be over, so he made his own sign, *Vergib mir, Vater, denn ich habe gesündigt*!"

"Forgive me father for I have sinned," Rudi lamented.

She sniffed and closed her eyes briefly.

"He shot himself the day they liberated Dachau, and that is why this can never happen again. If you'll excuse me," she said as she stood, Rudi stood with her, and they embraced. When they separated, Rudi's shoulder was damp with Mirabel's tears. She came back and Rudi was ready to tell his story.

"Well," he said, "you know that I grew up in Berlin?"

"Ja."

"And you can guess from my age that I was in the Hitler Youth. Well, by the end, most of us were drafted into the *Volkssturm*. I had a safe enough job was assigned to a task in Böckler Park, loading ten-centimetre Howitzers." He smiled, his eyes staring at nothing. "The old men who had manned those same guns in the Great War used to let us play in the playground sometimes."

"Jesus Christ, that's all you should have been doing, you were a child." She squeezed his arm and gave him a look that made him really want to open up to her.

"One day I found it, the emplacement I mean. Well, it was destroyed, a direct hit from a Russian 203. I didn't know what to do, but I was terrified of being accused of desertion." She took both of his trembling hands and held his eyes with hers, which were soft and green and kind. He was finally telling someone, and the feeling of catharsis was dizzying, "So, I went looking for something else to do," he bit his bottom lip and sighed as tears filled eyes, snot ran down from his nose, and she gave him a tissue. He used it and screwed it up tightly in his trembling fingers, "I was cycling through this… this square, and there were these three soldiers, one was an officer, and they were friendly at first," he stifled a sob, and looked away in shame.

"It's okay," she said, "it's good to say these things out loud. Once you say it, it will have less power over you."

"They had this old man..." Rudi was crying properly now, screwing his eyes up and sniffing loudly.

"I shot him," he blurted out, his voice becoming high pitched so that people were looking, and his neck muscles strained as he fought down the tears. "I... I murdered him, and they laughed."

She moved closer and put her arm around his shoulders.

"His name was Rolf Schilling," he buried his face in Mirabel's shoulder and cried. He cried the tears of seventeen years of repressed emotions, for the loss of Olga, for the death of Lorenzo and for his mother and sister.

~

"After months of deliberation," Mirabel said firmly, "it has been decided that the contents of the package must necessarily be divided into three categories: proof, technology, and information. Proof - enough to convince our lucky victim to act on what they have received. Technology - just enough to give our boys the edge without causing unwanted repercussions, and information - battle plans, doctrine, plans of the fortresses at places like Vaux and Douaumont."

The presentation represented months of research and debate, careful consideration, and planning.

"The following list is open to discussion," Eder said, "but please remember that we have spent months weighing the pros and cons to come up with these. Krause, please advise us when relevant topics come up."

Krause, brooding in a chair near the back of the room, nodded.

"A copy of the treaty of Versailles," Eder went on, "with pictures of the signatories. Photocopies of headlines showing Germany losing the war, British propaganda about the invasion of Belgium and the Americans entering the war after the sinking of the Lusitania, and the Zimmermann telegraph."

He looked up from the list, seeing impassive faces looking back at him.

"The stormtrooper tactics that nearly won them the war in 1918, Wehrmacht doctrinal literature from the 1940s and a copy of the Manstein plan. Plans of fortresses at Verdun and other Franco German border towns."

Gott, Rudi thought, this man gives lectures.

"And lastly, blueprints for weapons from the Third Reich such as the MP40. Modern automotive engine plans. Information on medical advances, penicillin etc. and lastly, research to accelerate airship development."

Eder took his seat, deferring to Mirabel for the remainder.

"Who will receive this miraculous package?" she said, standing and eyeing the room. "The Chief of the Prussian General Staff and Great General Staff Helmuth von Moltke the younger. Now there are many excellent reasons for choosing this particular man; first of all, he's already in charge, so it's his job to win the war for Germany. The Schlieffen plan is his to change and he has the unique power to act on this information with impu-

261

nity. Incidentally, he dies in 1916 so there might be less collateral damage, because his secrets will die with him." Mirabel was getting into her stride now and enjoying the limelight. "He is easily our best choice. Second in line is the Prussian minister for war, Erich von Falkenhayn, but he will not be in power until 1913 and that is not a lot of time to act, and he would need to convince von Moltke anyway."

"What about Ludendorff?" asked Schroeder.

"Top of our list of people we do *not* want to get this is Erich Ludendorff, because he was a supporter of national socialism for some years, then his political views eventually went too far for even Hitler, and they parted ways. We do *not* want this man to get that kind of power!"

"Hitler promoted him to field marshal on his birthday and organised his state funeral," Schroeder said indignantly.

"You want us to pick him because Adolf Hitler liked him?" Mirabel asked incredulously.

"No, it's just that you said they fell out and…" he trailed off.

"Okay, so von Moltke," Rudi said, moving to the front of the room. "Does anyone have anything to say about the list?" He waved a hand at the list on the wall that he had helped to come up with.

"Why Zeppelins, why not aeroplanes?" queried Boelek in his American accented German.

"We discussed it at length, and we decided that given the devastation wrought by bombers in the last war, we cannot give them that kind of power," Eder said. Boelek nodded in tacit approval.

"I have redesigned the MP40 so that it can be mass produced as early as 1910," Krause said. "And since the research into metallurgy and production techniques was much the same, I have done the same thing for several other weapons, and the Mercedes OM 654 engine. I can, if you would like, take a look at the LB 3000 truck that takes this engine?"

"Fantastic work, Hubert, thank you. I think the truck plans are an excellent idea," and turning to Mirabel and Tobias, Rudi said reproachfully, "I cannot imagine how the Manstein would be carried out with no trucks."

"What about tanks?" Schroeder asked. "The Manstein plan had tanks, didn't it?"

"We have to draw the line somewhere and I think that tanks and long-range bombers are it. Didn't the French suffer enough from the first invasion?" Rudi asked. "Now, I understand that the device is ready for testing?"

~

Henry Clive had been tempted to get drunk.

Violence had always been easy in his twenties and on into his thirties, but over the last few years as it had become less necessary, it had also become harder. He had a reputation among the British intelligence community as a man who was not scared to get involved in the rough stuff. It was a well-deserved reputation, but violence was easy for a man of six-feet-four who knew that getting hit in the face only hurt.

But he had grown cautious and inflicting violence had become distasteful to him. Nevertheless, he was a professional, so he psyched himself up and waited for his prey.

He reached out from his hiding place in a poorly lit alley and grabbed at the shoulders of his unsuspecting victim from behind. He dragged the man back into the shadows, pushed him up against the wall like a rag doll with his left forearm on the man's back and his flat palm on his left ear, forcing Winifred Schroeder's face into the rough surface of the concrete wall.

"What the bloody hell are you playing at, old chap?" Clive hissed through gritted teeth. "That spiel material you gave us, was that your idea of a joke?"

"I need more time!" Schroeder pleaded.

Clive applied pressure to Schroeder's eyeball using his thumb, prompting a strangled yelp of pain and fear.

"How much time do you need, Winny, old boy?" Clive asked affably. "Not that it matters. It's too bloody late. We want you, the contraption, and the plans.

Clive's demeanour changed then, switching from violent alleyway thug to gentleman. He straightened, smoothed down his clothing, and politely gestured for Schroeder to exit the foetid darkness with a slight inclination of his head. When back on the street he clamped a warning hand on the scientist's shoulder and steered him towards a waiting BMW 502. Clive wasn't the kind of guy who covered your head so that you didn't bang it on the door frame.

"Take us to Max Plank, Bernie," Clive told the driver after shoving Schroeder into the back seat and joining him.

As the car sped off and shadows played on his face from the streetlamps flying by outside, Clive turned on the interior light and tossed a photograph at Schroeder.

"I do sincerely hope that showing you this is enough, and I don't actually need to threaten your family?"

Schroeder looked at the photograph in horror but made no move to pick it up.

"You are a cold-blooded bastard, Clive. How do you sleep at night?"

"Whisky. Now, tell me you're going to comply, tell me that you know where this bloody machine is and that you know how to work it."

"I have an idea, but... but Erik is the one who knows how to set it all up. It could take weeks to figure it out without him." Schroeder sounded desperate now, and it was clear to Clive that he was telling the truth.

"Erik Boelek? The bloody naturalised American *citizen*!"

He was furious, the CIA would not put up with his taking of an American.

"Change of plan, Bernie. Take us to safehouse Watermill," he said to the driver before turning back to Schroeder. "We're going to get you nice and safe, old chap, get you cleaned up and talk all about this time machine, eh? Then tomorrow morning, you're going to ask to test the bloody thing and keep a close eye on what your man Erik does on that computer of his, aren't you?"

"We need to bring the launch forward to today, Rudi," Schroeder said, trying to keep the pleading tone from his voice. Rudi looked hard at his colleague.

"Are you okay, Winifred?"

He knew that look; he had seen it all too often in the east. He was carrying a great weight, as if someone was pressing his buttons or twisting his arm.

Rudi was right in that assumption. Schroeder was desperate now, having spent the entire night with that monster Clive. He was too smart to harm him noticeably, but there were other ways to torture a man and Schroeder was hanging by a thread, ready to snap, with tears forming at the corners of his red-rimmed eyes. He had one chance to save Germany and to save his family.

"They are threatening my family, Rudi, we must do it today, not the test but the real deal. Its ready, the papers are ready, I prepared the special mono-particular ink and paper." He looked into Rudi's eyes; he was really crying now. "If I do not help them steal it tonight, they will hurt my wife and my daughters. They are dangerous people, we both know what these people can be like, Rudi." The desperation in his voice was tangible, Clive had made him rehearse it all night.

"It is nine o'clock," Rudi said, looking at his watch, "we have all day to prepare, then we will do it at sixteen-thirty." Rudi smiled at Schroeder, he did know and had a feeling that no matter the outcome of today's operation, he always would.

"Unforeseen circumstances have forced us to carry out the operation today. Tobias, Mirabel and Krause you have seven hours to ensure your documents are in perfect order. Winifred, Erik, we begin testing now." Rudi looked at his watch again as they left the room and said, "Erik, how did you get on with your war game program?"

"It's not quite ready. I mean, we could try running some scenarios through and see what pops out?" he said with an exaggerated shrug.

"We'll see if we have time."

They spent all day testing the machine. They knew the limitations from the plans Rudi had brought from Berlin, so they tested for accuracy more than anything else. They had acquired detailed plans of the Bendlerblock and photographs of von Moltke's office in the years preceding the Great War, in order to estimate the exact location of his desk. The last thing they wanted for the plans was for them to land in a wall cavity or roof space.

When Krause had finished his own work he offered his assistance with any engineering matters, and by lunch time they were satisfied that they could send sufficient ink-covered paper through both space and time. It occurred to Rudi that if he needed it, he could send himself a note warning him of Schroeder's betrayal that could buy him more time, but everything seemed to be going so well.

During lunch, Schroeder slipped away from the engineering team, moving swiftly through the lab to Krause's office, where on the desk he found the blueprints that Krause had been working on for months. Krause, that grumpy ape of a former soldier should have been his patsy, but Clive decided to do it this way and he was in no position to argue.

Schroeder looked at the blueprints for Little Boy, with explanatory notes and the instructions for gaseous diffusion that Clive had provided him with, as well as the location of uranium on his family estate. He placed them carefully in amongst other documents in the pile. This was not the agreed plan. He was supposed to send them somewhere else, with only a note for von Moltke in the main pack telling him where to find them.

He had to hand it to Clive and his masters in Whitehall: they had truly done their homework. Clive had prattled on about dead drops and secret hiding spaces, the implications if these plans fell into the wrong hands. But Clive was not here, and Schroeder figured that if von Moltke did not find the plans for whatever reason, then they would sit there, in their hiding place. *What if they remained hidden for decades? What if the Nazi's found them? Imagine the Irony if a young Werner Heisenberg found them?*

The von Schroeder family's Saxony estate *had* been rich with uranium, until the Soviets had confiscated it and told them that their land belonged to the workers now. He hated the Russians, and he hated communism. The von Schroeders had been struggling financially even before the Great War, but like most prominent Germans, they had thrived under the Nazis, and he'd jumped at the chance to reset his fortunes. It wasn't until Mirabel had pointed out that their changes might prevent nuclear weapons from ever being developed that he had started to worry.

The uranium on his land was worthless without the nuclear arms race and subsequent discovery of nuclear power generation. He loathed the Americans, so he approached the British.

It took him months to convince them he was not crazy, and they were not in the business of giving nuclear weapon plans to former Nazi scientists unless presented with conclusive evidence.

He had smuggled a lot of material out of the institute and betrayed his colleagues many times over to get this far, but the British paid well and he'd been comfortable for the last few months. With this final act of treachery, as long as von Moltke received the plans, then his family's wealth and prosperity was secure for generations to come. He hoped they never actually used the weapon, but the message Clive had made him place in the main pack made it pretty clear that if Lenin and Trotsky were left alive and Leningrad – or Petrograd as it was known – was not taken, then the spread of communism would lead to another world war.

"I think we are ready," Rudi said as he consulted a clipboard and looked around at the assembled group of intellectual behemoths. Werner had even appeared, looking excited and nervous. Rudi cleared his throat to make the solemn announcement.

"Begin the ignition sequence."

Rudi had arranged for seven comfortable armchairs to be placed in a semicircle around the time machine. Schroeder and Boelek stood up and walked to the control station, a grey, powder-coated console with a series of switches and dials. Boelek sat down on a swivel chair and re-checked his inputs. He nodded to Schroeder and they both produced keys, inserting one into each of the two locks on the console. Both turned to Rudi who remained, ridiculously, in his armchair with the rest of the group, and he nodded assent so that they both turned their keys.

The lights flickered as power surged into the machine, which produced a steady whirring as the capacitors charged. Mirabel stood from her chair and crossed the room, and with due ceremony, placed the package of documents, onto the platform. It was a much larger version of future Rudi and Doctor Klein's weighing scale. She nodded to Boelek and returned to her seat.

"The frequencies are stable," Schroeder announced in an officious tone.

"Commence countdown," Rudi said. Schroeder and Boelek flipped switches, nodded to one another and to Rudi, then returned to their seats.

"T-minus thirty," came the recorded voice from the console at the same time as the main doors to the lab burst open.

"What the hell is this?" Clive sauntered through the door, pistol in hand and smiling widely. "Schroeder, you little bugger, did you have them bring the launch forward?"

"What is this?" Werner demanded as both he and Rudi stood.

"Sit down, Fritz, you won't be the first German I've killed just for pissing me off." Clive moved to the centre of the room and looked at Rudi. "What happens if I kick these papers onto the floor?"

"No, it's in there! I put it in there!" Schroeder pleaded, his eyes saying far more than he dared to speak aloud. "If you move it now, the consequences will be dire."

"T-minus twenty."

"Sorry, Winny, old chap. I simply don't trust you anymore."

"FÜR DAS VATERLAND!" Krause roared as he came out of nowhere and spear tackled Clive. They wrestled on the ground for control of the gun, both men staring down it's barrel more than once. Krause had the weight advantage and used it to good effect, but Clive was vicious and jabbed relentlessly at any exposed vulnerability on the bigger man's body.

Both men grunted and cursed as they rolled like a pair of rival animals warring for dominance. Krause's superior size and weight turned the tide, allowing him to crush Clive's chest under him as he reared back to strike a savage blow liable to kill the man. Clive's cunning and experience – the result of gaining victory in so many desperate brawls – turned death and defeat into recovery, thrusting upwards with his hips to launch Krause over his head where the two men clawed at one another for control of the gun.

When the pistol finally spun across the floor to Rudi's feet, both men collapsed breathing heavily in a puddle of blood a sweat. Rudi picked it up and, pressing a foot on Clive's forearm, pointed the gun into his face.

"To save all we must risk all," Rudi whispered, quoting Schiller.

The pistol backfired, exploding in Rudi's hand. He let out a blood-curdling scream as he stared in horror at the bloody, blackened stumps where his fingers used to be. The ear-splitting noise of the misfire and the mist of blood in the air silenced everyone.

"T-minus ten."

Clive used the distraction, the horror of Rudi's injury, to elbow Krause hard in the side of his head and scramble to his feet. He staggered slightly, the air driven from his lungs by the savage impact and the subsequent brawl, but he regained his balance and tried to flee for the exit when another blow took his legs out from under him.

Schroeder, his face a mask of pale horror, dropped the heavy chair he had struck Clive with and staggered back from the unconscious man.

"Everyone get back, away from the device," Krause called, dragging a stunned Rudi to his feet before propelling him into a chair.

"T-minus five, four..."

"Schroeder, what did you do? What did you add to the folder?" Rudi called over the countdown, the panic evident in his voice.

"An adapted blueprint for Little boy," Schroeder wailed, his eyes screwed shut and his head lolling about in despair. He knew it was too late. If his machine – for he saw it as his own as he *was* the engineer who built it – if his machine worked, he would no longer exist. At least this version of him would no longer exist. So, what did it matter?

"Two... one..."

Clive moved. He scrambled away, still trying to flee. He tried to stand and fell forward, confused and disorientated from the heavy blow to his head. To their combined horror, he fell directly onto the scale.

It was too late; Rudi knew that all he could do was stare at the scale. He wept for himself, for Olga, for all of the lives he had tried to save and instead condemned to a new hell whose bounds they could never know.

He had sent a dead British spy and an atomic bomb to a Prussian General in a country on the brink of war, a country ruled by a man bent on military superiority, and he wept for the millions they had just sentenced to death.

More of Schiller's words came to Rudi as he faded from existence: *Lose not yourself in a far-off time.*

U-Boot – The *Bodensee*, 1915

As Dreyfus entered the gunroom, frozen to the core and unable to feel his extremities, he disturbed Müller, who woke with a start and a disgusting wet snort.

"Coffee?" asked Dreyfus.

"Coffee. Ja, ja, bitte" he said drowsily. "Danke." He took the proffered cup and eyed Dreyfus suspiciously as he took in his facial features and his dark hair and the star of David visible at the open collar of his flying jacket. Müller asked the obvious question, his words dripping with hatred.

"Are you a Jew?"

Dreyfus stared at the man as he wrestled out of his flying suit, taken aback by this unexpected hostility.

"Ja, mein Herr," he said frowning in confusion. Like almost every German Jew, Aaron Dreyfus was depressingly familiar with anti-Semitism, but never so bold as this, from an apparently sober man in a place of work to a uniformed serviceman in the course of his patriotic duty. Dreyfus was justifiably outraged.

Müller spat out the coffee and threw the cup at the wall, smashing it and spilling the hot liquid.

"How dare you try to give me food handled by a Jew?" He stood up, demonstrating a significant height difference, but having Dreyfus towering over him did not affect the vehemence of his outburst.

This was Dreyfus' precious rest time, personally organised for him by the captain, and he was spending his last moments of peace under attack for his faith.

He was going to die tonight, up there in that unbearably cold gun position, and this horrible little man was stealing the last moments of comfort and warmth that he would ever know. That knowledge of his mortality gave him courage.

"Who are you?" he demanded, his lip curled with disdain.

"Who am I? Who am *I*?" Müller spat. "I am the German hero about to win us the war. How dare you demand to know who I am?"

"You don't look like a hero." Dreyfus looked him up and down, "You look like a shopkeeper."

Dreyfus was amazed at how calm he was able to be, while inside a fire raged, adrenaline pumped around his body, and his muscles grew restless.

"A *shopkeeper*?" It was Müller's turn to be outraged and he showed it by screaming at the top of his voice. "How dare you speak to me like that, you Bolshevik Russian, traitor Jew? I am a close friend of General Erich von Ludendorff, and he has plans for your kind. Your days of stealing from hard working Germans are numbered!"

"We are in a gas-filled bladder, thousands of metres in the air on a suicide mission and General von Ludendorff is a few hundred kilometres that way," Dreyfus shot back, pointing a thumb over his shoulder in the direction of Berlin.

"*Untermensch*," Müller spat, his hatred flowing now. "You are less than human and not worthy of this uniform." Müller prodded Dreyfus in the chest, noticing the medal pinned there.

"Oh, what is this, Jew?" He tugged at the black and grey ribbon on Dreyfus' left breast. "A Pour le Mérite? You must be a very special kind of Jew to have won this, unless…" Müller fixed the young man with a conspiratorial eye, "did you *steal* this, Jew?"

Every person had a breaking point, and Aaron Dreyfus had reached his. The strict naval discipline that had held his tongue and stayed his hand evaporated, and he could feel his self-control slipping through his fingers. The medal, the one this slimy little man was now tugging at, was a reminder of the most horrific day of Dreyfus' life. Originally a submariner, he had taken part in the Christmas Day attacks on the British home fleet.

Christmas, 1914 – Somewhere off the coast of Harwich

After navigating the sandbanks, submarine booms and sunken blockships, the *von Der Goltz* struck.

Firing all eighteen torpedoes, it decimated the squadron at anchor in Harwich, sinking or disabling the light cruisers *Carysfort*, *Cleopatra*, *Conquest*, *Aurora*, and *Undaunted*. The destroyers *Laforey*, *Lysander*, *Miranda* and *Myngs* were similarly ravaged by the ungentlemanly act of a sneak attack.

Shirtless men glistening with sweat worked furiously within the confines of their steel prison, reloading the torpedo tubes, or tuning valves to maintain their depth as each shot reduced the submarine's ballast. As the observation officer at the periscope announced each hit, the crew, forced to be utterly silently for the last twelve hours through fear of detection, now roared with delight as their fear and stress found an outlet. The captain, equally elated, allowed this lapse in discipline as he fought his vessel.

With her torpedoes gone, the von Der Goltz made to run, and within sight of the open sea, caught her propeller on the prow of a sunken blockship causing her to spin wildly and throw the crew violently against the unforgiving interior of the U-boat, injuring many hands in the process. The jagged rusting hulk of another blockship tore into the von Der Goltz's hull, setting pressure gauges to spin, and the submarine listed to port, which made it almost impossible for the crew to stay on their feet. The submariners worked frantically at the numerous valves to right their ship and isolate the many leaks.

The combination of the hull and propellor damaged proved crippling, and the von Der Goltz was forced to surface in order to repressurise. As the conning tower rose with the U-boat limping eastward at five knots, a mere fifth of her top speed, Obermatrose Dreyfus assumed his secondary duty of surface gunner, opening the hatch and clambering into position on one of the two fifteen-centimetre guns.

His clothes had been soaked with sweat for hours so he threw on a heavy woollen pea jacket as he emerged into the wintry night. The gun crews ran on the wet deck, and as the stern team made their way aft the forecastle gun's loader, a young man called Weber whom Dreyfus had taken under his wing a few months ago and who was now a devoted comrade, made his way forward. The two lifted the watertight hatches, revealed the gun and heaved it up into its working position.

The ammunition was passed up and the hatches were sealed behind them, isolating them on the surface of a boat designed to sail below the waves. The gun crews knew that if the captain decided he had to dive to save his command, there would be no time for them to return to safety below decks, and it would mean taking their chance in the lifeboats which would have to be unlashed before the submarine took them down with it.

So began the two-hundred-mile passage to safe waters at a painstaking five knots. After two hours hot food was passed up from a hatch, and they knew that their comrades below would be working fervently to keep the submarine on an even keel and moving in a forward direction. As for relief, there could be none, because the tiny crew would be stretched to breaking point down there, so they savoured their hot stew and kept scanning the horizon.

They heard the attack before they saw it. The HMS *Thunderer*, an Orion class super-dreadnaught of thirty-three guns, in consort with the *Penelope* and the *Galatea*, both Arethusa-class light cruisers of nine guns. The sound bore down on them with terrifying speed, covering six miles to their one. Dreyfus unbunged the speaking tube and called the warning with a description, course, and estimated speed and as he replaced the bung, he heard the captain's order to dive.

"Unlash the boats, Weber!" he demanded no emotion in his voice. "Quickly now, then make fast the painter to your belt. Your belt, do you hear?" He focused himself, shutting out the

278

stinging in his eyes from the relentless spray, his brain working in overdrive to counter the pitch and roll of the sea and the constant corrections made by his mates below deck. He waited for the black shape hurtling towards him to come into range. He fired his first round which landed short, throwing water high into the air and drenching the deck of the dreadnaught. The stern gun scored a deflection and its crew cheered maniacally, making Dreyfus silently reapproached their lack of professionalism.

"Help me reload and then provision the boat!" Dreyfus commanded. They reloaded and Dreyfus waited for the pitch and roll of the sea to be just so, and with bitterly cold fingers he fired. This time the round flew in a satisfying arc through the air to hit one of the *Thunderer's* gun turrets. The enemy gun shook violently before bursting into flames, forcing burning bodies to jump into the sea as their shipmates attempted to douse the fire with hoses. Dreyfus watched the flaming, flailing figures fall into the oil-black sea and realised that this was the first time he had been directly responsible for the death of another human being. Quickly, his sharp mind processed the morality of kill or be killed and he was able to move on beginning another reload.

The *Thunderer's* guns began to fire, as did the *Penelope's* and the *Galatea's*. But a submarine, even when surfaced, is a singularly difficult target. Shells, somehow growing quieter as they flew overhead, sucked the air from Dreyfus' lungs forcing him to fight for concentration. Behind him the sea erupted with the impact of a dozen shells, causing him shake with both fear and cold.

The *von Der Goltz* began its dive and with one last wild, desperate shot, Dreyfus clambered into the boat with his friend. They pulled clear as they watched the stern gun crew, who had not unlashed their boat, struggle desperately with the ropes.

They hesitated only a moment before calling to them and daring to inch closer to the sinking behemoth but just before the stern of the U-boat disappeared beneath the waves to safety, one of *Thunderer's* torpedoes struck her.

Water gushed upwards forty feet into the night sky, and the resulting wave of Icy water soaked the pair and threatened to flounder the tiny boat. Dreyfus could see the shadow of the U-boat beneath the surface like a great steel whale. He dashed his jacket into the boat and dove into the black, icy water without thinking.

He was a strong swimmer and made straight for the main hatch, reaching it quickly. He knew that to open it was to aid in the eventual sinking of the submarine, but he also knew from experience that this U-boat, already limping home, was beyond saving. As these thoughts rushed through his head, the von Der Goltz gave a lurch, then partially resurfaced as the deck rose beneath his feet. Flames shot from the great hole made by the torpedo and the vessel shook violently, Dreyfus winced as hundreds of tonnes of metal twisted and creaked beneath him.

"Now or never," he whispered to himself as he heaved on the hatch wheel. The second the seal was broken, and he was hit by a wave of screams. The acrid stink of smoke, burning oil and fresh blood engulfed him. He called Weber to bring the boat nearer and glanced north to see the searchlights of the three enemy ships scouring the oil-black sea for survivors. The unofficial

German policy was to gun down any survivors, even in merchant ships, and Dreyfus now saw this to be his fate too.

He had no way of knowing that the Royal Navy would prefer to profit from any intelligence gleaned from a live prisoner delirious with hypothermia, rather than kill them out of hand. Dreyfus turned his head into the fresh air, breathed in deep and plunged himself into hell. It was hot, close, and terrifying below deck. He cast about him for ambulatory survivors, his eyes falling on the captain, evidently dead from the jagged shrapnel protruding from his temple. He made his way forward to the torpedo room, but despite the clamour of screams, he found no men mobile enough to be rescued, and there was no way one strong man could push a dead weight above deck in this rough sea. He was ready to give up and go back amidships when he lit upon the unconscious form of the observation officer, a minor royal and a well-liked member of the gunroom.

With no visible injury, he dared to hope, and with a firm slap to the face, he noted the ghost of an eye movement beneath the lids. He shot a cup of cold seawater in the man's face, which brought him round.

"Herr Leutnant." He shook him by the shoulders. "Get up, Herr Leutnant, we must go now!" The man was dazed and therefore eminently biddable, so he guided him up the companionway and onto the deck where he found Weber keeping his station admirably, and the searchlights of the ships closing in. They were moving dead slow now, just enough to maintain steerageway so as not to accidently kill a potential source of intelligence.

Weber and Dreyfus got their charge into the boat and stretched out their oars like mad men to get clear, as the *von Der Goltz* finally sank. They felt the draw she created as she went down and feared they would break an oar as they pulled to the relative safety of the North Sea in winter.

When Dreyfus was sure they were out of sight of the ships, they got their sail up, a neat little lugsail, similar to the boat his father owned back in Rostock. But this wasn't pleasure cruising off Warnemünde in summertime, this was surviving in the icy *Deutsche See* in wartime. Weber had done well provisioning the boat and they had blankets, food, water, charts, and an azimuth compass.

Leutnant Joachim Sigismund snored noisily in the stern sheets as the two sailors reckoned their position and figured out a course for safe waters. As the sun finally rose a few points off the port bow of their little skiff, they ate the cold ships' biscuits from the ration tins and drank the heavily chlorinated water.

The sky turned an evil red. It would have been beautiful to a landsman, but to any seaman worth his salt this was an omen of heavy weather, dirty weather, the kind of seas that a boat such as this could not be expected to handle.

They had been sailing south southeast on a broad reach for about an hour according to the sleeping Leutnant's wristwatch. The boat did not possess a sextant and neither man could have completed the calculations for it anyway. The officer might have, perhaps, but he slept on, refusing to be roused, so dead reckoning was all they had and soon they would reach the treacherous Friesian coast where, if they ventured too close, they could run aground on a sandbank, stranded for hours until hightide. So, they kept a weather eye out and sailed on when a sound like thunder arose from the east.

"How?" Weber cried. "How do they encircle us so?"

"That's not three boats, my friend, that's an entire fleet! We are saved!" Dreyfus stood in the tiny boat and shook his fists aloft.

Weber turned to the sleeping officer and shook him by the shoulders, "Herr Leutnant, Herr Leutnant," and the man started to wake, "we are saved, here is Admiral Scheer and the High Seas fleet.

~

Dreyfus returned from his reverie to find himself face to face with the vile form of Müller, a stark contrast to the memories of that night and his pride after receiving a Blue Max for saving Prince Joachim. He then recalled the rumours of a commission for his actions and the gut-wrenching disappointment he felt when it turned out that they would never commission him because he was Jewish, while the faithful Weber, who felt he owed Dreyfus his life, made it clear that he would not accept any reward for 'merely sitting in a boat.' The emotion of all these things overflowed and Dreyfus finally lost control, clenching his fists as he drew back his arm and squared his feet.

"What is going on?" demanded Neuman.

"This *Jew*..." Müller began.

"This is my roof gunner Matrosenobergefreiter Dreyfus, and his religion is of no consequence to me."

"He is racially infer—"

"Herr Müller, you will confine yourself to the bomb bay for the rest of the flight," Neuman instructed him as he raised his hand for silence. "Here is the briefcase you asked for, now kindly leave my gunner in peace."

Müller raised a finger halfway and, seeing Neumann's face darken, thought better of it. He trudged off in the direction of the Bombay in silence.

"Remarkable display of discipline, that, Dreyfus. I can only apologise that you had to hear it," he looked at his Lange & Söhne marine wristwatch. "You have another forty-five minutes left, sit down and try to enjoy it."

~

"Twenty degrees, fourteen minutes and seven seconds," Leutnant Kurt Freiberg said as he lowered the sextant. Matrosen-Gefreiter Hess handed him the sheet on which he had written Freiburg's observations next to the exact time of the airship's chronometer, along with the words: Arcturus, Altair and Rasalhague. Freiburg studied the almanac for twentieth May 1915 and made note of the declination on the sheet next to each of the three readings.

Each adjusted reading was then subtracted from ninety. He accounted for parallax error, dip, altitude, refraction, and the fact that they were sailing through the sky at one hundred and thirty-five kilometres an hour on a course of zero-four-five degrees. He then took a pencil and protractor and drew three lines on the chart that intersected to make a small triangle. Inside the triangle was a small town on the Daugava River called Jēkabpils.

He knew that his observation was accurate because this town was on the rhumb line that he had drawn to plot the airship's course at the start of the voyage.

"Ah, Herr Kapitän," he said, turning from his calculations, "we are two hundred kilometres to Lake Pihkva and four hundred and fifty to target."

"Thank you, Leutnant Freiburg."

~

Müller paced the Bombay, periodically stopping to look at his bomb. It was *his* bomb now, even if it had not always been. At the beginning he was one of many technicians, running errands and performing calculations for the great men of science assembled by Ludendorff, but now....

Ludendorff had overheard him one day espousing rhetoric about the superiority of the Germanic people and taken him to one side. At first, he thought he would be reprimanded, but Ludendorff agreed with him on many things, and after that, they would talk discreetly every time he visited the facility, even exchanging books and ideas.

Müller began to notice that his superiors gave him more responsibility, his pay grade was increased and after about six months he was given his own team. He was to head up the replication of the detonation system, and this placed him in prime position for the role he now played. With what he knew about this bomb, he could make it go off under almost any circumstances.

What Müller failed to see was that his sick ideology, though similar to Ludendorff's, was not the root of a friendship. It was not the meeting of like minds, but the foundation for the reason he had been groomed for two years. Ludendorff's attention, his increased standing among the other technicians, all of it reinforcing his prejudices – his hatred of Slavs and Jews and Africans – all of it had been calculated to use him as a willing pawn. A fanatic prepared to die for the cause.

Ludendorff was a ruthlessly efficient megalomaniac who, upon hearing the first utterances of Müller's perceived racial superiority, formed a plan. That plan was to make sure that the man detonating his treasured bomb would not get cold feet, that the man in that bomb bay hated the people he was going to vaporise.

Of course, there was no one alive, who had yet lived at least, who knew the devastation that this bomb would inflict. The physicists had made predictions, but no one would know until it was too late to decide that maybe, just maybe, this bomb was a step too far.

When the message came down that they were two hours from the target, Müller opened the briefcase Neumann had given him and began the painstaking arming process.

He circled his bomb like a bull fighter, inspecting every inch of it admiringly. He placed a hand on the fuselage and closed his eyes, letting his hatred drive him, fill him, and consume him.

From a small tool roll he took a screwdriver and began to unscrew the plate at the rear of the bomb. Müller could feel the sweat forming on his brow and his heart pounding in his chest.

The plate removed, he used a specially built spanner to loosen the breech plug. His wet hands shook as the breech plug came away, and he placed it carefully on a rubber pad. He stood up at this point and breathed deeply, then he took a sip of water and dried his hands on a rag. Blowing air through his closed lips, he knelt at the open compartment and began to insert the four silk bag charges.

At times of high stress, Müller would distract himself by reciting something he knew by rote. It wasn't usually related to what he was doing but on this occasion, he decided to recite the firing sequence of the bomb:

"The pull-out plugs count to fifteen, the altimeters engage, the optimum height is reached, the firing switch closes, the primers set off the charge and projectile is launched, the chain reaction begins and... *BOOM*." He laughed maniacally, with all the glee of a madman, before repeating his vile recital, laughing every time.

Müller resumed his work, still muttering the sequence like some kind of macabre poem. He refitted the breech plug and secured it with the spanner. Now was the moment of greatest danger, when he was about to connect the firing line which would make the bomb live. As he had chanted, the pull-out plugs would arm the bomb as it left the Zeppelin, but once he made this connection, the circuit was complete to that point. His hands trembling and sweat running into his eyes, he made the wire fast and installed an armoured plate over the top of the whole assembly, followed by the cover he had removed at the start. When the last screw was secure, he fell back flat onto the floor and let out a deep sigh.

His part in this was nearly complete, he had merely to pull the lever releasing the bomb and in just over an hour, it would all be over, a new age for the Reich would begin, by his hand.

"Who dares nothing, need hope for nothing?" Müller whispered, wholly convinced of the righteousness of his actions.

Egypt, 2035

Yael dozed restlessly in the passenger seat while Olga snored in the back, and Ibrahim drove slowly through the unchanging desert. As mile after dusty mile passed by, he thought of his new life and how happy he was. He owed very little, ate short commons and spent most of his time in a hot truck bumping along through an environment that was ready to kill him for the slightest misstep. He'd never been happier.

Ibrahim's brutal treatment at the hands of the Sheik and his men had driven him to attempt to suicide more than once, but his captors had always found him and prevented it. They were always kind to him for a while afterwards and it became a habitual cycle; the abuse would start, he would spiral and eventually attempt to take his own life, the abusers would show him kindness and make promises. It was after one particularly horrible episode with the Sheik himself that he was allowed to take the truck for a joy ride on the promise that he 'forgive his wicked Sheik.' Ibrahim saw the opportunity for freedom and snatched it, even for a few short hours, freedom was everything.

He looked at Olga in the mirror, and Yael beside him, both dribbling, there heads lolling around with the motion of the truck. In that moment he realised that he loved these women. Of course, they were both beautiful, fierce, and lethal, but it was a platonic love.

They had saved him from a life where the only light at the end of a horrific tunnel was becoming too old to be appealing to his abusers. He feared, however, that as with those before him, he would begin the cycle again. He swore it would not happen, but he had seen it with the older boys who had all sworn that they would never be like those monsters.

But with nowhere to run to, once they crossed over into manhood, they resisted for a time until eventually caving to peer pressure, and it seemed inevitable that he too had been destined to become that which he despised most in the world.

They drove all night and slept in the unyielding heat of the day, usually in abandoned buildings, sometimes caves and once in a long abandoned troglodyte settlement.

True to her word, Yael trained them both in Krav Maga in the mornings and in the evening. Ibrahim did most of the driving while Olga received more in-depth training in spy craft and tactics.

Their journey had taken them north along the coast for a few hours, before turning east for five hundred kilometres and then south into the Sahara Desert. Yael insisted that they cross into German Egypt at a remote location to avoid border controls. As they entered the desert proper and the road became more of a track, safety demanded they drive during the day.

The truck had used up its original tank of fuel and she estimated they would need four more cans to reach the Red Sea. As they approached the national border, Ibrahim gave Yael playful shove. She woke with a start.

"What do you want, fuckstick?" she said when she had taken in her surroundings.

"We will turn east towards the border soon, dildo," he said, grinning.

"You need to work on your banter, buddy. Olga," She reached back and tapped her leg, "Olga, you little shit, stop snoring and focus!"

"What?" Olga said from the depths of a dream.

"The border in thirty clicks," said Ibrahim, satisfied with his use of jargon.

"Fucking clicks? You sound like an idiot," said Yael, prodding at his ribs, causing him to flinch and swerve the truck.

"Easy." Yael warned.

"You go fucking easy," Ibrahim countered. "I nearly killed us."

An hour later the truck crested a rise, and the map told them they should see a series of lakes called the Siwa Oasis. What they saw caused Ibrahim to slam on the brakes and reverse back down out of sight.

"What the fuck was that?" Ibrahim said, turning to look at his companions.

He pulled off the road, and they moved carefully back to the hilltop.

"Looks like some kind of mine," Yael said, playing with the focus of her optics.

Sprawling out across the valley was an enormous mining operation, acres of solar panels and what looked like two camps, one large, densely populated camp and a smaller one apparently with a swimming pool and tennis court. The perimeter comprised a series of watchtowers and a wide ditch, presumably to slow down would-be absconders so the guards could shoot them.

When a horn echoed across the valley, the three of them jumped. They thought they had been spotted, but the thick, black strip at the bottom of the mining face began to disintegrate into what turned out to be thousands of miners shuffling wearily into four separate lines. Overseers appeared on horseback in German military uniforms and began herding the workers into their camps.

"It must be lunchtime, it's early though," Olga said.

"No," Yael spat with disgust, "they will sleep now when the sun is at its hottest and go back to work through the night until this time tomorrow."

"It is inhuman, why are they allowed to do this?" Ibrahim demanded with indignance.

"The same reason we thought of coming this way, nobody comes this deep into the desert," Yael answered him gravely.

"Can we help them to escape?" Olga asked.

Yael was silent for a moment before she responded.

"There are eight watchtowers with two guards each, probably on an eight-hour rotation, so that's forty-eight armed guards without counting the overseers or any other camp staff. We don't stand a chance, Mami." Yael lamented, sad but firm in her decision.

It was obvious that Yael wanted to help too, but she was not about to risk all of humanity for it.

They watched in horror at the number of slaves that went into each of the huts.

"Sakhif aljahim, they must be bunking four high to fit that many in," Ibrahim speculated.

"There must be something we can do. We can't just leave them here to suffer." Olga protested.

"Olga, a word," Yael said through gritted teeth as they moved further down the hill and away from Ibrahim.

"Now you listen to me," Yael had Olga by the shoulders, looking into her eyes, Olga's mouth was already forming her retort so she held up a silencing finger. "It is my job to get you to Tel Aviv in one piece, so that you can jump back to 1961 and help Doctor Kessler to fix this mess. If we die here then this *never* stops, this cannot be the only one like it, and we certainly can't stop them all. But by getting to Israel and jumping, all of it stops. *All* of it, do you see?"

"If we do nothing, then we're as bad as they are!" Olga said, looking away and rubbing her face with her hand.

"Until a few months ago you were one of them!" Yael said, knowing she had gone too far. "Olga, I'm sorry, I didn't…" she called after Olga as she moved around the back of the truck, leaning against the shaded side and folding her arms.

Olga did not feel like she wanted to cry. She no longer felt like the little girl she had been in England. She was frustrated, she knew that nothing could be done to help these people without risking the overall mission, but the knowledge, the acceptance of it all was difficult to bear. She had all these skills now, and she wanted to put them to use, but she knew deep down that this was not her fight; it was suicide and she needed to think of the bigger picture. She walked back up to the others.

"Come on," she said. "We need to figure out how we get around this abomination."

"What changed your mind?" Yael asked.

"Logic, cold heartless logic," Olga replied bleakly. She looked at Ibrahim, but he looked away, pawed his eye's dry and climbed back in the truck.

They looked at the map and found a way to skirt the complex without being seen, but still Olga could not shake the guilt. She wanted a shower and a soft bed, she stank, she was sick of ships' biscuits and she hadn't even begun to process the death of their three companions.

Their only option was to push south, then east through the Great Ubari Sand Sea of the Sahara Desert. They checked their stores, topped off the tank, and pressed on, debilitated by the crushing guilt over the wretched prisoners they were forced to leave to their fate.

All through this work Ibrahim's mood was tangible. He said nothing and refused to make eye contact. The oppressive heat and the disappointment both women felt prevented their speaking up and explaining more to him. Both knew that would be impossible, not without telling all and risking all.

With the hope of shelter unlikely, they opted to drive straight through in eight-hour shifts, resting if and when they found an oasis or suitable shelter. It was slow going on the constantly shifting sands, and more than once the truck became bogged down. Each time they wasted hours and crucially, precious fuel, painstakingly extricating themselves from the latest situation.

On the third day they reached an oasis with luscious palms and crystal blue water, and all three rushed to swim in the inviting pool where they washed, splashed and wallowed, naked in their own private paradise. Olga lay on her back in the water, eyes closed, and arms outstretched, enjoying the coolness against her skin. She began to feel a breeze, she noticed the susurration in the palm fronds and the sound of insects dying away. The air pressure changed markedly, and she could see the others had noticed too. She swam for the edge of the pool as the wind grew stronger and the light began to diminish.

"Don't get dressed, just pick up your things and run for the truck!" Yael shouted over the increasing noise. A *haboob*, a violent sandstorm, whipped up the eighty-degree sand particles from the desert floor and began lashing at the eyes, skin, and throats of the travellers as they dashed for the truck, desperately clinging to their clothes and trying not to breathe.

The high-speed, superheated sand burnt them all. But Olga, who had the palest skin and furthest to run, had the worst of it.

Fortunately, the kit from the *Herev* included lotion for sun burns and after Yael washed the sand from her eyes, she carefully removed the abrasive grains from her skin and tenderly applied the lotion to her battered body.

With the sand blocking out the sun and beating at the sides of the truck, Ibrahim learned something about himself that afternoon, trapped in what might have been a very uncomfortable position. It concerned the sight of one beautiful woman rubbing lotion into the body of another, only feet away while he too was naked. What he learned was that, while he found women to be wonderful creatures that he could admire objectively and enjoy the company of immensely, he did not feel uncomfortable or aroused, he just felt concerned for his friend. He did not know what this meant but he knew that it could not be a bad thing.

Olga fell asleep in Yael's arms while Ibrahim dozed in the front, and when the storm cleared he dusted the truck down, paying particular attention to the air intake and the radiator fins. Chewing on an interminable ships' biscuit, he drove the only true friends he had ever had east towards the Red Sea.

Soon after the oasis they reached the desert autobahn, and now they travelled at night and hid during the day. This was Reich territory, and they could be challenged for no reason at all by any citizen of Germany who suspected undesirable activity. Besides the ever-present threat of arrest, torture and eventual death, the next major obstacle was the river Nile, over six thousand kilometres long and nearly three hundred metres wide. It was all that stood between them and the last four hundred kilometres to the Red Sea. Olga and Yael sat in the back of the truck consulting the map, while Ibrahim drove.

"Show me Israel again?"

"It starts here, in the Sinai Peninsula," she pointed to the eastern banks of the Gulf of Suez, "and then it stretches up, with the Mediterranean on this side and the Jordon River to the east, all the way to the Al Kabir River in the north."

"What is this country here, to the southeast of Israel?" asked Olga, pointing at the map.

"Arabia, and that is Syria to the north. They have been at war on and off since the fall of the Ottoman Empire, and when they are not, they fight amongst themselves or with Israel. Right now,

Israel is at war with both Syria and Arabia." She indicated the borders on the map to illustrate her point. "This has been going on for nearly ten years. The Reich gives the Arabian Skulls just enough money to keep fighting, in the hope that we will all destroy each other, but Syria has a large, diverse income much like Israel. Although a good deal has been wasted on civil wars and fighting with Arabia. I think that when the Arabians finally run out of soldiers, there will be a big war between Israel and Syria, not just the border skirmishes we have at the moment."

"What will happen if there is a big war with Syria?" asked Olga, her face a picture of concern.

"Well, we have more trained soldiers, and our equipment is far more advanced. I mentioned we have a space program, and our infrastructure is not damaged after years of civil war. But Jaysh al-Islam, Syria's President, is desperate to take back the Golan Heights and gain control of Beirut and its port."

"Hey, enough history," said Ibrahim from the driving seat, "how are we crossing the Nile?"

"The way I see it, with the bridges controlled, we have two options: one, we find a boat to cross with, ditch the truck and find a new one on the other side," Olga suggested.

"They will all be electric here in German Egypt, and electric vehicles are very difficult to steal," said Yael.

"Then we must find a ferry or a bridge with no officials manning it," Olga replied.

"In that case, we could drive all the way down to here," said Ibrahim, pointing at Qena on the map, "it is only one hundred and sixty kilometres to Safaga, where we can take a boat across to Israel."

"If we had to, could we walk or even cycle to Safaga?" asked Olga.

"It looks as though there are some hilly areas, so it would be quite hard, but with the correct preparation we could walk it, and cycling should be fine with the right bicycle," said Yael, but when she glanced at Ibrahim, he quickly turned away, feigning interest in something to his left.

"Ibrahim, can you err, ride a bike?" she asked.

He laughed nervously. "Of course I can ride a bike, it is mere child's play, of course I understand the working of an infant's toy."

He looked nervously at the women and hung his head.

"No, I cannot. And I do not think I will ever learn."

"I can teach you, Ibrahim, it's easy, I taught my... my brother Klaus," she said, unexpectedly upset at the memory. He was one of those stubborn children who could not take instruction from their parents, but his beloved older sister 'Ogga' could make him do just about anything. Her parents had been so pleased when they saw him riding home from the park that day, Olga jogging at his side, proud as punch.

"Okay," said Yael, changing the subject as she placed a hand on Olga's arm, "the probability is that we will find neither car nor three working bicycles, so I think that walking by night and hiding to sleep in the day is the most likely course of action. So, drive to Qena, was it?"

"Yeah," said Olga, still feeling low.

"Then, either using a stolen boat or the reversed backpacks, we cross at the narrowest point, check the immediate area for a gift from God and, empty handed, we throw on our packs and get walking. We have thirteen hours of dark this time of year, so we can probably walk it in three nights, taking plenty of breaks," Yael said,

They were practically nocturnal animals by the time they reached Qena, where they parked out of the way, slept all that day, and then drove their beloved Landcruiser right into the river after dark, letting the surprisingly strong current take it away. This encouraged the taking of a boat and after a search, they found one; a dismasted felucca — a sort of traditional Nile boat, similar to a sailing dinghy —it floated listlessly under the sign for a shipwright's workshop.

"This'll get us across," said Ibrahim who, despite growing up by the sea, had never been on a boat in his life.

"It has no means of propulsion," Yael chided him. "But if we can find something to use as oars, we shouldn't drift too far down river before reaching the opposite bank."

"How about these oars?" asked Olga, grinning for what felt like the first time since the *Herev*.

They reversed their backpacks into the waterproof bags. Yael insisted that, given their lack of spare clothing, they stowed their only set in the watertight bags.

"You only tab in wet clothes once," she said with the conviction of someone who had tabbed in wet clothes and suffered the hideous chaffing.

"What is tab?" Ibrahim asked.

"Tactical Advance into Battle, but it has evolved into a general military term for a long, fast march with weight," Yael answered, hefting her pack.

So it was, that as the cicadas chirped at midnight, they embarked, naked, in a dismasted sailing dinghy, to cross the raging river Nile. They paddled hard to counter the strong current and avoid adding unnecessary distance to their long journey.

"Does the Nile have crocodiles?" Olga panted.

"Yes, why?" said Ibrahim, the beginnings of panic in voice.

"No reason," she answered with a giggle.

"You two shut up and paddle!" Yael hissed.

Reaching the far bank having only travelled half a kilometre downstream was an achievement hard won, and after they'd dressed, they lay in the tall grass, listening to the mechanical call of a distant nightjar, the rushing water and Ibrahim's heavy breathing. A few moments rest before beginning the 160 kilometre walk to the Red Sea.

Vergebliche Hoffnung – Russia, 1915

Forlorn Hope

As last hurrahs of one hundred and fifty men condemned men went, this one was reasonably subdued. That was relative, because at least ninety men of the eighty-fourth Parole Company sported at least one black eye by the end of the three days. The military policemen had decided to depart halfway through the second day, leaving the beer unattended, so the girls had to be locked away in the attic for their own safety.

But no one died, no one punched anyone too far up the chain of command for it to be an issue, and a good time was had by all. The beer did last until the third night, but it ran out before anyone was too far gone, so Otto allowed the ticket system of the first night to recommence and the girls came down from the attic.

He moved amongst the men and chatted amiably with them. For some of them, this rest period was one of the joyous memories they would replay in their mind on their death beds. For others, though, it was a shame-filled horror show that they would never speak of again.

The trucks arrived on the morning of the third day and the men received their new clothing and equipment. In addition to the regular issue, the troops got a small black badge to be worn on the back of their helmet, and each squad received a state-of-the-art camera and a Geiger counter, a handheld device that clicked with increasing volume the closer you got to the danger. The men were not told what that danger was. They were not told that it measured radiation, nor were they told what radiation was, or the effects it could have on the human body.

The company filed into the trucks and drove north to Petrograd. They drove themselves, sandwiched between a pair of military police cars each with a mounted machine gun trained on them. The cars towed all the company's ammunition in small trailers, only issuing it at the last possible moment when they barely stopped, simply pulling their lynch pins and speeding south, leaving the trailers behind.

It was night by then, but instead of making camp, when the men had received their ammunition, they remounted and continued to drive north.

"Herr Leutnant?"

"Ja?" Otto sat in the front of the truck with the old Feldwebel-Leutnant driving. They preferred to drive themselves in the heated cab, rather than have a driver listening to everything they said. Otto could tell that the old man was steeling himself to say something, and he had an idea what it might be, so he decided to put him out of his misery.

"I know what you are going to say, Meyer."

"Oh, what is that then?" he asked with a tone of mock surprise. They had worked well together these last months and had developed a certain sense of one another. Meyer could often anticipate orders and be ready to carry them out at no notice and Otto always knew when Meyer disagreed with a plan, without hearing his concerns aloud.

"You want to stop driving north towards this bomb that is going to make us get sick and die. You want to wait it out somewhere and approach afterwards, when it is safer?"

"Natürlich," Meyer shrugged.

"How? We must do it in such a way that we do not get caught," Otto said, serious now, all comedic overtones stripped away because the two men were plotting mutiny.

"Why? We are already condemned men. If we keep going north, we will become very sick or die, if we stop and live but are caught, then we will go back to the front with the parole battalion."

Meyer's logic made sense, but Otto needed more than that, he wanted a plan to keep him and his men from being caught. Maybe, just maybe, could they walk free from this?

"Perhaps we should just stop and double check the map?"

"I can see where you are going with this, Herr Leutnant."

"Please, just call me Otto, I am half your age, and we are about to die."

"Otto," he tried it on for size. "No. I do not like it… So the plan is to continue towards Petrograd until this über bomb is dropped, and we do not know what will happen afterwards, except that it might make us sick."

Otto gave a thoughtful grunt in agreement.

"Maybe we should stop to look at the map and try to find somewhere to wait it out then?" Meyer conceded.

The night was clear and still, and a waning, near full moon illuminated the landscape aiding the men who were surveying it and trying to get their bearings.

"We are heading east on the road from Narva to Petrograd," said Otto as the other two officers, who also rode in the front and drove their truck, joined them.

"What-ho?" said the older of the two.

"We are planning a mutiny, are you in?" said Meyer in a semi-jocular tone, one that could be back peddled easily as 'all a bit of fun' if these two junkers decided to be holier than thou.

"I see, indeed," Greot, the oldest looked at Bethe knowingly. "Did you not fancy dying painfully from a mysterious sickness then?"

"Or worse, watching your men die from it?" Bethe retorted drily.

"Something like that," said Otto distractedly.

"We were having a similar discussion. In fact, we were trying to decide the best way to flag you down to put our ideas to you, old fellow." Greot was the youngest son of a wealthy junker, and as such did not stand to inherit, so it was suggested that he might attend a British public school to broaden his horizons. Three years, and several expensive indiscretions later and Greot had found himself at the cadet school at Lichterfelde. As a legacy from his time at Winchester, Greot had acquired a few very English affectations, including a surprising level of indifference to most things. He was, though, a fine officer, capable and respected by his men.

The unfortunate circumstances that had brought him here to the penal battalion were another topic of discussion for the ranks, of which Greot had promised to tell the story when they reached the line of departure for this mission. The men had taken bets on the nature of the officer's transgression, with the highest odds offered being on the crime involving something sexual in nature, and the lowest odds being for gross insubordination.

"What are your ideas, Greot?" asked Otto patiently.

"Well, may I?" He positioned himself over the map where the others could see him. "As you say, we are heading northeast on the road from Narva to Petrograd, and as you will see, there are check points along this road. We passed through the last one at Cheremykino just before the chained dogs left us. Then we drove for another five miles, which puts us... here," Greot used the tip of his pencil to point at the road just outside a town called Kipen.

"I suggest that we leave the road at this point," he pointed again at another spot on the map, "and make for *this* high ground, where we would be a safe twenty kilometres from the bombing of Petrograd. We dig in and observe, and by the time the main body comes up, we can be anywhere we want to be."

"Sounds good, Erwin," Otto said, "I am in complete agreement. I am also conscious of time. The small Major, the one that cleaned his glasses all the time..."

"Geiger," Bethe interjected.

"That is right, Geiger, he seemed to suggest this bomb would be dropped very soon after our seventy-two hours' rest was over."

"It has been over for at least ten hours," said Meyer, looking at his watch.

"Let us go then. Greot, you lead the way."

"What do you think they will use to drop it?" Otto mused as they bounced along the dark pothole-strewn road, following Bethe and Greot in the exceptionally bright moonlight.

"A Zeppelin, most likely," Meyer looked out of his window at the town Greot had pointed to on the map, desolate now, not a building left untouched. It appeared that the German army had only pulled back from here in the last twenty-four hours or so, and the signs were visible everywhere to those who knew what to look for: ration tins, damaged packing cases and the stench of death.

"What about the anti-aircraft guns?" Otto knew that Ludendorff had thrown wave after wave at Petrograd by land and by sea, but the city still stubbornly held. It had become the subject of many quiet conversations; had the genius field marshal lost sight of the true objective, or more likely, was it something they could not see? There had been Zeppelin raids before, and the airships had been torn to shreds by the planes and the anti-aircraft guns. The behemoth would glide through the air, apparently creeping so slowly in contrast to the fighters buzzing around it like wasps and pouring bullets from their guns.

Some planes even purposely crashed into the side in a suicidal attempt to kill it and stop the devastation wrought by the immense payload of incendiary bombs it carried. The envelope would rip, and the gas inside would catch fire, causing a ghastly chain reaction that illuminated the night like an exploding sun. The heat from that explosion would melt the aluminium frame, leaving next to no evidence that the airship had ever existed.

"What's that?" Otto could hear a faint hum over the truck engine.

"Don't ask me, I'm almost deaf," Meyer said with a shrug.

"Stop the truck, Meyer." Otto jumped out before it came to a complete halt. Meyer flashed his lights at the lead vehicle, and they stopped too. Otto looked up into the night sky and there was a hum, now becoming a drone. From the southeast the entire sky was filled from horizon to horizon with planes. There were Rumpler bombers, Albatross Bombers, Albatross fighters, Fokkers, Junkers and Pfalz. This looked to Otto like every plane available on the whole of the Ost Front, and the sound became deafening.

"Keep moving let's get to that high ground," he shouted in Greot's ear, beckoning Meyer to do the same.

The trucks bounced on, Otto leaning out of his window to watch the blanket of noise draw over the night sky.

Weltenzerstörer, 1915

Destroyer of Worlds

"We are one hundred and fifty miles from the target, Herr Kapitän, but that verdammt, moon will be the death of us,"
Leutnant Freiburg called as he put away the charts and dividers.
"One hour to go." He blew air through closed lips and ran a
trembling hand through his thick brown hair as she stared out
into the endless expanse of night.

"I thought this might lift your spirits," Neumann said as he
climbed into the control gondola holding a bottle of cognac to
a collective gasp from the assembled crew. Neumann was a stick-
ler when it came to drinking on duty, he had broken officers
before now for drinking on watch. The act demonstrated the
desperation of their captain and their circumstances, or perhaps
it encapsulated the fatalistic feeling in the air perfectly. Bauer,
desperately cold from his two hours on the roof gun and eternally grateful that he was a radio operator, handed out tumblers
with numb hands.

"Prosit," the crew said in unison. The entire crew was present, except Müller and the two gunners, Webel and Dreyfus.
The control gondola was crowded, but the packed space lent a
Bierhalle atmosphere and for a few snatched moments the condemned men of the naval airship *Bodensee* felt something like
calm.

Then, like a wave of icy water, the anxiety, pressure, and dread washed over them. The negative emotions fed one another as each man made eye contact and quickly looked away, or worse, attempted a smile, and it spread like plague.

"Let us move to the gunroom and leave the steersmen to their task."

Neumann felt it too and he was desperate to make these men, with whom he had experienced so much and some of them little more than boys, feel something besides fear and hopeless resignation. The crew sat awkwardly, scattered around the spacious room, while Neumann quietly instructed Bauer to pass around the drink and find a record to play.

He checked his watch. In forty-five minutes, Müller would drop the bomb, and shortly after that they would all die.

The young sailmaker's mate sang out in desperation "*Oans, zwoa, drei, Gsuffa!*" meaning 'one, two, three, drink!'. They all drank, the sailmaker cuffed the youth.

Bauer began riffling through the records furiously, and played '*Ein Prosit*,' the song from which the sailmaker's mate had taken his inspiration. Bauer called him over and gave him the bottle, the boy topped everyone off and they slowly started to sing along with the record.

"*Ein Prosit, ein Prosit der Gemütlichkeit,*"

'A toast, a toast, to cheer and good times', and by the second refrain the whole room was singing, then the plucky young Sails stood and gave another, "Oans, zwoa, drei, Gsuffa!" This time everyone stood and drank. The song finished and young Sails, now well into his cups, stood on the table and began to sing the national anthem, "*Heil dir im Siegerkranz*" to the tune of 'God save the Queen.'

Again, the crew joined in, standing dutifully, the officers among them saluting. At the end they drank again.

"Quiet!" Neumann held a hand to silence his crew instantly. "Do you hear that?" He rushed down the companionway to the control gondola, followed by Freiburg and Bauer.

"Look, Herr captain," said the steersman, pointing ahead.

At first, his guts wrenched with horror when he thought he was looking at a sky filled with Russian Imperial fighter planes. He slowly realised that, although the gap between them and the sea of hot metal was closing, they were, in fact, flying away from him, and with his night glass he could just make out the distinctive black cross of the Imperial German Flying Corps.

"Calculate their speed and match it. We don't want to overhaul them before they have cleared the way for us."

"Herr Kapitän?"

"Those are Germans, Freiburg, they are the cavalry!" he said with something like hope in his voice.

Freiburg said, "One hundred kilometres an hour," under his breath, then he called into the speaking tube, "slow to one hundred kilometres an hour." The engine note changed audibly, and the airship stopped gaining on the armada of planes. They watched for another few minutes before the fireworks began. First, the anti-aircraft guns glowed on the ground, then jets of light showered the outskirts of Petrograd like deadly rain. Just a few minutes later, the bombs started to fall. They had little chance of taking out the emplaced guns, but the shock and awe factor had advantages.

310

When the Imperial Russian air service finally scrambled their Sopwith Triplane fighters, the observers in the airship barely noticed, such was the immense firepower of the assembled forces. Brought back from exile in the Arctic Circle, Joseph Stalin looked up at the sky that May night and reflected, right before an incendiary bomb melted the skin from his body, that quantity did indeed have a quality all its own.

Neumann had given himself a gap of about twenty minutes between the arrival of the planes and his airship. This allowed him and his men to watch the destruction an armada of bombers could wreak on a city the size of Petrograd. But they also looked on in horror at devastating vulnerability of the flimsy aircraft as flak tore through the paper-thin metal and even wood of wings and fuselages. The sacrifice was immense, and the twisted logic was not lost on the crew of the *Bodensee,* as they watched hundreds of men die so they would be afforded the opportunity to die in the process of killing thousands more. The window between the initial raid and the Zeppelin's time over target gave time for the terrified citizens of Petrograd to emerge from their basements, cellars, and shelters. To start trying to save their neighbours and dowse the inferno raging in their city in the way that they had done many times before, as air raids had become a part of daily life.

As dawn approached and the eastern sky began to colour, Leutnant Otto Kessler and his entrenched men had witnessed

311

the air raid, seen planes peel off and fly back towards Pskov, and they were beginning to think that it was all over. Otto was ready to send a patrol to reconnoitre the damage when a shadow fell over the men of the eighty-fourth parole company. The scene was eerily silent as night returned to the morning, and the hill that they occupied grew unnervingly dark. The men who had the courage to look skyward saw the airship *Bodensee* moving at one hundred kilometres an hour over the silent landscape like a gigantic grey whale. The darkness was fleeting and the Zeppelin moved doggedly onwards towards the centre of Petrograd.

Otto continued to watch through his field glasses. He did not see the bomb bay doors open, he was too far away for that, but he did see the tiny, black shape of the three-metre-long, five-thousand-kilogram bomb fall from the behemoth

"Gas! Gas! Gas!" Otto's cry was echoed up and down the line until the whole company had fumbled into their unfamiliar equipment, sweating and terrified.

"Will these things even do anything?" Meyer said, fidgeting with the straps, checking and rechecking the seal.

"Gott knows, my friend, we are in unknown territory now..." Otto's words died in his mouth as he watched the bomb tumble through the air from his hilltop fifteen kilometres away. He didn't see the pull-out plugs detach or the charges priming fifteen seconds after that, nor could he have known that when the bomb reached the optimum height of six hundred metres, the altimeter would close the firing switch, igniting the charges and, in turn, launch the hollow uranium projectile down the two-metre gun barrel at a velocity of three hundred metres per second, whereupon it would collide with more uranium and the chain reaction would begin.

This process took less than forty-five seconds and at that very moment the airship *Bodensee* and her crew were vapourised to become little more than a footnote in the history of the Great War.

A fireball as hot as the earth's sun temporarily blinded Otto and his comrades, and the sheer force of the blast destroyed all the buildings in a radius of one kilometre, including the lavishly onion-domed Saviour on the Spilled Blood, the Winter Palace and the luxurious Astoria Hotel.

Every man, woman, and child inside the blast radius became no more than a shadow on the pavement, vapourised by the twenty pound per square inch of pressure exerted by the blast. Anyone unlucky enough to be outdoors within two kilometres of the epicentre was exposed to superheated air that set their clothes on fire and burnt their skin with such speed that the nerve endings were gone before they could feel the pain. Funnelled by the buildings on either side, the slightly diminished blast tore south down Moskovskiy Prospect, hurling trams full of commuters through the air, smashing windows and killing thousands more.

Otto's vision was little more than bright specks on a black background when the same shockwave of superheated air, generated winds of hurricane strength carrying a blizzard of debris including glass, rubble, and anything else lighter than a building from ground zero outwards. The dust enveloped the hillside like a sandstorm, the noise was deafening and the debris cut and bruised men cowed by the blast's monumental force.

After a period of maddening sensory deprivation Otto began to regain his vision, he cleared the thick layer of dust and grime from the rectangular eye piece in his mask. He swallowed down vomit as he watched a huge, black cloud forming in the sky thousands of metres above Petrograd. The upward thrust of this drew fresh air into the centre, feeding the flames and creating a firestorm from the fuel stockpiled in the naval dockyards, the barracks, and the factories. The fire became so hot that the rubble burst into flames.

From his vantage point just outside the city, Otto could see the scale of the destruction this solitary bomb had wreaked. A circle of charred ground covered with fast-spreading fires moved outwards in every direction but west, where the Baltic Sea steamed as it halted the inferno at the edge of Vasilevskiy Island.

Seventy thousand lives were extinguished with seconds of impact, and the same number again died painfully in the days and weeks following the attack.

The eighty-fourth treated their minor casualties and began to move towards the city centre with their cameras rolling and their Geiger counters clicking wildly. The horrors they witnessed that morning in May 1915 brought tears to the eyes of every man in the company. These were hardened veterans of both fronts, criminals deemed beyond redemption, reduced to blubbering wrecks on the side of the road.

Rapists, thieves, cutthroats and blackguards all whimpered to a man at the inhumanity of the spectacle before them. Hideously burnt children wandered the streets, groping for their parents because the heat of the blast had boiled the vitreous fluid in their eyeballs. Naked and hairless, their crimson skin glistened in the midmorning sun. Hundreds of them bleating like lost sheep, unable to cry because their delicate tear ducts had been cauterised. For every living horror, three more lay dead on the ground, and the soldiers had only reached the outer perimeter of the blast zone.

Otto decided that they would go as far as the edge of the two-kilometre circle of flames, then turn back. He felt that if there were any hope for redemption, it lay in the safe return of these men to German soil, because the citizens of Petrograd were beyond any help that he could render.

He pictured the two artillery majors, one tall and imposing in his tailored uniform and the other, short and scruffy, like a sack of potatoes tied at the middle: the architects of this living hell. He wondered how he might reconcile with fighting on the same side as men that could want to do this, to inflict this level of suffering on innocent civilians.

They stood at the precipice of hell with their cameras and Geiger counters, staring at the swirling, roaring flames.

The firestorm was hunger incarnate, and the city was food.

Grey-black, crimson red and deep orange, the flames devoured everything in their path, leaving only scorched earth in their wake. The enormous mushroom loomed overhead, blocking out the sun and now depositing a black rain onto the city. The rain contained radioactive particles, irradiating the few unaffected citizens and the sodden uniforms of Otto's men.

Otto gave the order and the company, now free men, walked the distance back to their trucks, the inferno hot at their backs and the moans and screams from the rubble growing louder the further they walked from the epicentre. After mounting their trucks, they began to realise the true scale of the devastation. While the half-kilometre-wide firestorm was like gazing into the blazing depths of hell, the whole province seemed to be under the shadow of the gargantuan black cloud. Forlorn peasants stared at the black mass above the glowing horizon, inhaling the toxic ash that covered their faces as they cried, while their tears left tracks of white skin on their cheeks.

As the trucks passed, the Russian refugees began to follow. They had no hope of keeping up, but the road only led in two directions and the other seemed to lead to certain death. Soon thousands of survivors formed a wretched procession that stretched for miles like a grotesque tail following the orchestrators of the unfathomable destruction.

Otto and his men had no space on their trucks and no supplies to aid them with, so they left the peasants to walk and soon the road was empty.

When they had travelled about ten kilometres, they found German soldiers maintaining a checkpoint, flanked on either side by machine guns. A staff car was waiting for them on the other side and the passengers who stepped out to meet them were the two majors from the country house; one small and bespectacled, and the tall, gaunt man with the drooping eyelid.

"Kessler!" said the small one, greeting Otto excitedly like an old friend. "Tell me what you saw! How wide was the firestorm?

What happened to the people near ground zero?" He was eager, aroused, almost envious to have missed out on the fun.

"It was hell," Otto croaked, staring fixedly at the small man until he shifted his feet and looked away. "You made hell, Herr Major. *Hell*."

Otto was too disgusted to say more because the deep and seemingly unending guilt he felt for the minor role he had played was crushing him. The resilience he had built up over months in the penal battalion and even before, fighting and losing friends on the front line, could never have prepared him for this. In his mind, each traumatic moment had seemed to add another layer of armour, to the point of feeling invincible. Only now he realised that the invincibility he felt was merely apathy.

It was apathy over death, over seeing his home again, over life itself. Now the weight of his armour was crushing him, each traumatic experience weighing heavily on his young mind, he felt anxious, his guts were in turmoil and he just wanted to weep in anger and disgust.

The taller man could see the emotional wrestling going on behind the glassy eyes of this young subaltern, who days ago had been a steely-eyed infantry officer with a reputation for reckless valour and pitiless discipline, and he understood it.

He knew that his bomb had wrought levels of destruction these men could never have imagined. He remembered the photographs of Hiroshima and of Nagasaki, the bikini Atoll and Christmas Island. He resolved to take control; this was a man on a knife edge, he had a history of violence against superiors, and he wanted as many first-hand accounts of the detonation as possible.

317

"Oberleutnant Kessler," he watched as surprise registered on Ottos face. The major smiled.

"That's right, von Bock was discredited, and the plot to entrap you unravelled shortly after that. You may also be pleased to know that Horner and Thurn were caught in compromising situations. They were cashiered and are now serving as lowly *Gemeine* in the transport division. The brass decided to give you a promotion instead of apologising or admitting that they were wrong." He looked at Otto carefully, and saw the intense desire for revenge satiated, keeping the man's demons at bay for now.

The major's accent was odd, it was too perfect, too precise, like a factory reproduction of a piece of art, and it lacked the organic imperfection that humans were so good at.

"I don't think we've been formally introduced. I am Major Heinrich Felsen."

He offered his hand to Otto, who took it automatically and shook it firmly as their eyes met.

Something occurred between the two men as they touched, a feeling neither understood, but each knew the other had felt it too.

Otto was abruptly and dizzyingly aware of things he had not known before, his surroundings and this man were suddenly familiar to him. He felt tired, not the fatigue he was feeling already, but a weariness that came with age, and he felt the years weigh him down like a heavy winter coat yet comforting and warm.

"Otto, Hans, come, let us get these men back to the camp and begin the debriefings. Otto, would you like to ride with us?" He gestured towards the staff car with its comfortable leather seats and fur blankets. Otto looked back towards his men waiting patiently for him.

"No, I will ride with my men, one last time." He rubbed the back of his neck ruefully; he longed for the comfort of that staff car.

They drove in convoy, following Felsen's staff car for about five kilometres before Otto noticed something on the horizon and he squinted at the black line forming there. The sun began to pick out the shinier elements of the black mass, and it seemed to span Otto's limit of vision from north to south. As they bumped along the road towards it, he could see a dust cloud above it and eventually realised that this was the main invasion force heading to Petrograd.

OPERATION JANUS, 2036

After acquiring some suitable footwear for Ibrahim, the three travellers set out to cover fifty kilometres per night, hiding in the day amongst the rocky foothills that flanked the autobahn from Qena to Safaga. The pace that first night soon increased from five to six kilometres per hour, and they found that they would arrive in Safaga towards the end of the second night, hopefully with time to locate a boat before sunrise.

On the second night, however, Olga and Ibrahim awoke unable to move and their stiff legs took a few hours to ease, the optimism of the previous night gone like the skin from Ibrahim's feet. Yael used the time on the road to continue Olga's training, when they discussed every possible tactical scenario, and after geopolitical and military history, they began elementary physics. Olga's cover had always been a physics PhD student in previous attempts. She wondered at the disparity between a childhood that resulted in a doctorate and the one she had led in the Reich. She had other ideas about her cover story but kept them to herself for now because it was still important for her to understand the basics.

On the second day, they took turns sleeping in a disused mosque.

"I hope the worshippers don't mind," Olga mused as she packed her things away.

"The Reich drove all of the Muslims from Egypt many years ago," said Ibrahim, demonstrating that the transgenerational trauma that all Arab Muslims inherited, practising or not, was still real.

"They do that sort of thing a lot," said Yael dryly.

"Well, I'm going to try and make it right," Olga exclaimed, then looked at the faces of her companions and realised what she had done.

"What do you mean, you will make it right?" Ibrahim demanded, his face twisted in anger and confusion. "Unless you have a time machine, there's nothing you can do." He picked up the pace slightly, causing the blood to squelch in his shoes.

Olga and Yael exchanged a knowing glance

"Ibrahim. Ibrahim, slow down, we need to tell you something," said Yael.

"What now? Are you going to tell me that yes, you do have a time machine and the first thing you will fix is the mass genocide and enslavement of my people?"

"Well, yes, and no," Olga said cautiously.

"What!" he shouted. "The suffering of my people is a joke to you?"

"No, please listen, Ibrahim, we do have a time machine."

"Don't, it isn't funny, it was never funny." He sped up again. A fully laden Yael increased her speed effortlessly to round on Ibrahim.

"Look at me, you little jerk." She held him by the shoulders, "There is a time machine, and we don't understand why yet, but Olga is the only one who can use it. Well… she's the only one who can use it without dying immediately afterwards, and we're going to use it to free the world from the yoke of the Reich."

Ibrahim blinked away tears as he stared in disbelief at the two women. For the first time seeing them for what they were; a pair of filthy, ragged wanderers. The dirt thick on their sunburned skin, black fingernails and jaundiced eyes. Why would they put themselves through all of this for anything less than the fate of the world?

"I, I think believe you," he said after a long pause. "But I have so many questions."

"Do you understand now why we couldn't save all those poor people at the mine?" Olga said.

"I understood then, it would have been suicide, and I assumed you would report to your spy lord or whatever when we got to Israel."

"Spy lord? You are an idiot," said Yael laughing. "Now, let's go, the world isn't going to save itself, is it?"

Ibrahim interrogated both women for the rest of the journey, amazed at the sheer magnitude of Olga's task, of the incredibility of the situation and honoured to have a small part to play in what was probably the coolest thing to happen to any fourteen-year-old ever.

They reached Safaga just after midnight on the third day and Olga stood and stared out at the Red Sea. They had made it to the edge of the Reich, and seventy nautical miles was all that stood between her and the Sinai Peninsula. She felt hope now, hope that she had not known since before Grunewald, and even then, her memories were tarnished by her realisation that the regime was so evil.

322

And now her life experience was that of many Olgas. She was not simply Olga, she was *of Olga*, the product of lifetimes of knowledge, skill, experience, love, and deep lasting pain.

She knew what it felt like to make love to the man whose children you wanted to bear, and she understood how it felt to mean it when she said that she loved someone.

She could remember the agony of the basement in Normanenstraße, the electricity coursing through her body and she realised in that moment, staring out to sea that she would do it all again just to have more time with Rudi. This was all about him now and the world could go to hell.

Walking along a jetty in a tourist area was not going to be as discreet as they first imagined, because the German holidaymakers and soldiers on leave from Cairo and Suez were out in force. Yael decided that instead of a pleasure yacht, perhaps they could find a nice gaff-rigged fishing boat in a more industrial area.

"Look," whispered Ibrahim, pointing at a yacht, and what a yacht; a fifty-seven-foot Ketch at anchor out in the bay. The owners, a couple, were climbing into a sturdy looking tender.

"Perfect," said Yael, placing an arm around Ibrahim's shoulders, "let's make sure that it's you they pay to watch the boat."

They followed the progress of the tender and moved along the sea front with it, then Olga and Yael waited in a side street, watching as Ibrahim sidled over.

"Marhaba, most honoured lady and gentleman, I could watch your boat for you, please?" he played the stereotypical Arab the tourists expected quite well, bowing excessively.

"Ja, natürlich. Charlotte, give this fellow a couple of marks. Take good care of it, boy, it costs more than your house." The impeccably dressed, middle aged, German helped his wife out of the boat and waited while she rummaged through her purse. She found the money and paid Ibrahim, who bowed deeply and bid them a thousand good evenings until they turned away, at which point he twisted his face into a scowl and quietly bid them a thousand nights of torment in Jahannam.

Yael and Olga were about to break cover when two enormous Egyptian men flanking one very skinny man strode towards Ibrahim.

"Hey," said the skinny one, "what the fuck are you doing? This is our patch!"

"Good evening my friend," said Ibrahim, not daring to look in his friend's direction

"Shit," said Olga.

Yael moved quickly and Olga followed.

"Fuck you," said Ibrahim emboldened by his approaching saviours and desperate to give them the element of surprise "what are you going to do about it?"

"Fuck me?" said Skinny. "Fuck you!" and he turned to find out why Ibrahim wasn't bleeding already but his heavies were just a heap on the ground. His eye's darted up to see Olga and Yael dusting themselves off. He made to run but Yael grabbed his wrist as he passed, spinning and turning him into her body where she wrapped one arm tight around the man's neck and clamped the other onto his skull. He issued one choking, gargling sound before his face seemed to swell with the effort of trying to stay conscious and his eyes bulged unnaturally. Sinking to the ground, Yael released him, letting his unconscious body flop to concrete wharf.

They dashed back to the alley to fetch the bags and turned to see local police questioning Ibrahim about the pile of men at his feet. His eyes met Olga's and he smiled a sad smile, mouthed the word 'go,' and placed his hands atop one another over his heart, then ran as fast as he could in the opposite direction with the two police officers hot on his heels. Olga gasped as she realised what he had done for her, but Yael, hoping not to waste his gift, dragged her to the quayside and into the boat.

"Brave idiot," Yael said as she spun the throttle in her hand and the silent motor catapulted them across the marina and out to the anchorage.

The *Veritas* was magnificent in every way. German built; steel framed with a sweeping deck in rich teak and accented with polished bronze fittings. Yael disabled the navigation lights and tied off the tender.

"Right, Mami, let's get this beauty underway," she said to Olga, her voice cracking as she chocked down a tear.

"Okay, I'll do the anchor chain if you start motoring?" Olga had failed to hold back the tears and they flowed freely as she ran forward to the bow.

"Shit," Yael hissed.

"What?"

"No keys."

"Shit!"

Yael forced herself to think straight for a moment. There was a stiff land breeze coming from the west, her lee shore was over a mile away and she had a competent sailor in Olga.

"Weigh the anchor, we'll sail from standing," she called.

Olga headed forward to begin hand winching the anchor chain. She turned the handle, moving the yacht forward and over the top of where the anchor dug into the seabed, while Yael began hoisting the mainsail. She would rather have waited to set any sails until they were further from the land, but the chance of that specific couple looking out to sea in the five minutes it would take them to disappear behind the headland was worth the risk.

Yael wrapped the halyard around the winch and began pulling the slack, making the winch mechanism whirr until the sail was almost at full tension. Meanwhile, Olga was winching for all she was worth at the bow, slowly bringing up the anchor.

In the cockpit Yael inserted her handle and wound it the last few inches, by which time Olga had the tiller and was keeping the yacht into the wind. When Yael cleated off, Olga pushed the tiller away from her body and the yacht turned, picking up speed and cutting a healthy white froth at her bow. They raised the jib and the mizen as Olga made for the open water and for freedom.

The same key used to start the electric motor also unlocked the companionway. Yael hit the lock off with a winch handle and threw their bags down. She then proceeded to strip and clean her Jericho.

"Did you want to talk about what just happened?" Olga asked, placing a hand on Yael's shoulder. Yael shrugged and took the pieces of her handgun below to continue her task.

"Okay, I'll just be here then, sailing the boat," Olga called after her.

They continued in silence for some time, the only sound being Yael's fervent cleaning and the sea running along the hull. Yael finally emerged with filthy hands, smiling weakly at Olga and sitting beside her in the cockpit in silence for a while.

"Ready about," called Olga. "Hey." She nudged Yael with her foot to get her attention.

"Oh, sorry," she said, preparing the sheets for a tack.

"Lee Ho!" Olga said as she put the tiller over. The yacht turned through the wind onto the opposite tack and as it did, the sails moved from starboard to port and Yael deftly re-tensioned the sheets.

They yacht sailed onwards around the headland and out of sight of the harbour of Safaga. As they entered the open waters of the Red Sea Olga knew that somewhere out there to the east were the shores of Israel.

"Yael?" Olga dragged Yael from whatever daydream she'd disappeared into.

"Yeah?"

"What's up with you?" asked Olga

Yael sighed and moved next to Olga.

"I realised that when I get you across this sea, it will only be a few days until I lose you for good, Mami." She pushed a stray hair from Olga's face and with sad eyes, she smiled, "I'm really going to miss you."

"You know Yael," Olga said, looking about her at the shipping, the trim of the sails and island growing ever closer to port. "You've been like a sister to me these last months. You've saved my life at least twice and I owe you so much."

"I'd do it all again, and not just because it's my job, you too are like a sister to me." Yael looked away, shifting her position and pretending to check the mainsail sheet.

"I don't think you understand how much my life has changed since you rescued me from Altstötter."

"Of course I know, don't you think I remember? Don't you think my memories, my time echoes come back too?" Yael had abandoned her earlier modesty and now the tears ran freely down her face too. "I don't know how many times I have done this mission, trained you or met…" she sniffed, "…or met Ibrahim, but I'd say that a fuck load would be pretty close."

"Why didn't you say?" Olga cried, torn between her friend and the demanding task of navigating the shipping lane.

"There are notes, instructions on how to deal with you and your memories. We are supposed to let them, come organically, to train you and let you realise on your own that you knew this stuff already."

"Who the hell is writing these instructions?"

"You are, Olga. You are." Yael said, standing a walking forward into Olga's eyeline. "Every time you fail, you debrief yourself seventy-five years in the future."

"Why…"

"We're not allowed to show you, and my telling you is a serious breach of protocol." Yael looked up at the sails and made some adjustments, giving the boat an extra knot or two of speed.

Olga stepped forward, one hand on the helm and hugged her friend, her sister, the woman whose life had been all about saving her own.

328

Yael hugged her back for a long time and then mumbled something about the charts, because if it were left up to Olga, they would probably run aground or something, but she could not hide the crack in her voice as she spoke.

Olga had come to love Yael and cared about her deeply, but the pervading thought as she sailed this magnificent yacht through the wine dark sea with the wind whipping through her hair, was Rudi.

She longed for him, she ached for him, for his touch, his smell, his very being. He had become the only thing that mattered to her, and she would do whatever it took to get back to him.

At eleven knots it only took six hours to make the crossing to the Sinai Peninsula. Yael radioed ahead to the Israeli coastguard, who checked with the local Mossad station chief who checked with Tel Aviv, who authorised the Veritas and her crew to land at the Israeli port of Shalem on the southern tip of the peninsular.

Yael prepared mooring lines and fenders, while with Olga at the helm, the *Veritas* came in under foresail alone, the mainsail neatly stowed. Just before the bow met the jetty, Olga threw the helm over and put the boat upwind, checking their way and gently kissing wooden siding and causing rubber fenders to creak. The sail flapped in the wind as Olga hauled on the furling line to wrap it neatly around the forestay, while Yael tied the boat off and unloaded their bags.

Olga stepped across to the shore and stood for a moment, admiring the beautiful yacht and the crystal waters of the bay, as a flood of emotion washed over her. This was it. She was in Israel, she had truly defected now, and the terrifying concept of time travel was about to become very real.

Yael explained to the coastguard commander, Lieutenant Cohen, that after a hot shower and a fresh meal, she had planned to sail straight up the gulf to Eilat.

"Things have changed while you were away, ma'am. It is not safe in the gulf right now. Syria and the battered Skulls…"

"What are the Battered Skulls?" Olga asked.

"A Skull is tribe of warriors on the Arabian Peninsula," Yael said impatiently.

"Syria and the *defeated* Skulls have formed a new state called The United Arab Republic, and they have taken control of the entire Arabian Peninsula and absorbed what was left of their armies into the new UAR army. Israel is now under attack all along the new UAR border from Homs in the north to Aqaba in the south. We lost the Golan Heights last week and their Navy was bombarding Tel Aviv and Beirut, until our planes sank a few of their ships and they ran away. The second-best air force in the world and the only one to have fully electric supersonic fighters." He was clearly proud of his nation's achievements, and he smiled at the new arrivals welcomingly.

"We need to get to Tel Aviv as soon as possible," Yael demanded.

"The station chief has scrambled a helo, it'll be here in," he checked his watch, "figures ten. We had better go."

"We'll need clean clothes and tac vests."

"There isn't time to go to the stores, ma'am."

330

Yael looked at the at the coastguards in their inferior uniforms and body armour and bit the inside of her cheek. *Fuck it!*

"Strip!" she said, raising her eyebrows for the briefest of moments. "That is an order, Lieutenant, you and your sidekick here."

"You must be..."

"Do it now, or you'll find yourself patrolling the local swimming pool." They reluctantly capitulated, dropped their vests and handed over their blueberries, the term for blue camo. Yael eyed it with contempt, but it was this or the rags that were her clothes three thousand kilometres ago.

"And the watch."

"But it was a gift..."

"I'm joking. Now, fuck off. Neither of us has any underwear."

The sailors smirked until they caught Yael trying to melt them with her laser vision and decided to leave.

Olga and Yael, attired in ill-fitting fatigues and poorly adjusted body armour, ran across the tarmac with the weapons they had brought with them all the way from the *Herev* and waited to meet their all-electric chopper. Yael looked back at the building to see Lieutenant Cohen watching through the glass in his vest and boxers and she began to laugh, a chuckle at first, but the feeling overwhelmed her and soon she was buckled over with it. Olga joined in and she realised that this was it, in a few days they would be ready to jump, and it would all be over. She felt the tears coming now but she fought them back, trying to remain professional and composed.

The chopper came in hard and before they knew it, they were in the air as the Red Sea and the Cascade mountains receded beneath them. Yael produced a laptop from her pack and logged into her government email. She opened one marked urgent and scanned the text with widening eyes.

"So, tell me, what's so goddamn important about a couple of Coasties?" The pilot's voice crackled through the headset in an American accent.

Yael turned her head to look at the pilot in the uniform of an IAF *Seren*, or captain. It was quite common for Jewish-Americans to serve Israel in this way. His eyes were black rimmed under his aviator sunglasses, a day's growth of beard covered his square jaw, and he looked exhausted.

"Do you really think a couple of Coasties would have the sway to pull you from the front line for a taxi mission to Tel Aviv?"

"I guess not."

"Are you familiar with Operation Janus?"

"Err, no ma'am."

"Good, you shouldn't be," she nodded at the laptop and said, "but I need to tell you now that our destination is not Tel Aviv."

"You have got to be fucking kidding me, lady!" The pilot took his eye from the instruments and sky for the first time to look at Yael. "This isn't your mom's minivan, you can't just change your mind, this a highly sophisticated piece of precision engineering, and on top of that, there are flight plans and clearances and fuel calculations…"

"Are you done?"

"Err, yeah."

"Good, now if you check your flight plan, you'll find it has been updated and the waypoints corrected, and the distance to Tel Aviv is near as damn it the same as our new destination."

"Which is?"

"A secret military installation in the Judaean Mountains."

"HLS?"

"No, I'm directing you to a mountain range complex with no helipad." Yael rolled her eyes and turned to find Olga fast asleep, her head lolling about with the pitch and yaw of the chopper. She looked at the landscape below and thought about her homeland and the last few months and how she might just retire to a kibbutz and live the simple life.

"What's that?" Yael pointed north to what looked alarmingly like a full-scale tank battle raging on the northern bank of the Dead Sea.

"Holy fucking shit, it's happening," the pilot shouted.

Squadrons of Israeli Merkava VI Main Battle Tanks moved and fired in perfect formation through the battlefield, while regiments of Chinese-built Type 96 Aleppos, no match for the Merkava on even terms, hurled tank upon tank at their foe.

"We're outnumbered ten to one," Yael lamented.

The first two waves failed to even dent the seventy-fourth *Tempest* battalion of the Israeli Defence Force. They fought with skill and grace, maintaining discipline, and destroying Type 96s wholesale. But the sheer volume of iron thrown at them was too much and soon they were encircled; it became a bloodbath.

Yael looked on helplessly as her countrymen were burned alive in iron coffins. Some escaped their steel tomb, only to be gunned down mercilessly as they screamed for help that was never going to come.

The Judean Mountain range overlooked the Dead Sea, and as the chopper banked on their final waypoint, they saw up close the true horror of armoured combat. She could see the blackened faces of the men who had crawled from their burning machines, now lying forlorn and dying on the bloodstained ground. The infantry dug in along the border were using anti-tank weapons effectively in a futile effort to reduce the amount of armour now rolling out of the Jordan Valley.

Fast air arrived in the form of six squadrons of IAI BARAK all-electric super-fighters. They destroyed dozens more Type 96s, but it was still not enough. Yael watched as tanks and armoured personnel carriers bypassed the town of Jericho, winding their way up the mountain passes and heading in the direction of the Operation Janus HQ.

"We need to go faster," she screamed at the pilot, "that girl is the key to stopping all of this!"

"We can't beat this, just look at their numbers, we're fucked, lady," he said, banking the chopper away towards Tel Aviv.

"We are done when I tell you we are done," she shouted, loud enough to be heard without the intercom and waking Olga. Yael took hold of the co-pilot's yoke banked the helicopter violently, forcing the pilot to slam into his door.

"What the fuck was that, you crazy bitch?" he spat. "You could have killed me!"

Yael produced her Jericho and, resting it in her lap, she pointed it at the pilot's belly.

"Have you ever been gut shot, Captain?" she asked coolly.

The pilot's eyes darted over to the pistol and up to Yael's cold gaze. "You can't be serious?" He laughed.

"It's a slow, painful death," she continued, "you'll have plenty of time to land this thing before you lose control and I can help you there." She caressed the co-pilot's yoke again.

"Listen, Miss…"

"Colonel," she interrupted.

"Ma'am, just put the gun away and I won't have to mention this to my superiors, or anyone else for that matter."

"That depends on you, Captain, change course and get back on your flight plan or feel my hot lead burrowing through your vital organs and out the other side, know the fear that comes of a torso filling with blood while your heart pumps desperately to maintain the supply of oxygen to your brain. Feel the coldness as your blood pressure drops and your organs shut down one by one, desperately trying to keep your brain alive. You look like a fit man, Captain, you could last a few hours before your heart finally gives out. Or who knows, maybe I'll hit your spine and you won't feel a thing." Yael gave the yoke a nudge causing the helicopter to twitch, driving her point home.

"Okay, ma'am," he said as sweat poured from the rim of his helmet, "just make that thing safe and stow it, you're making me nervous." He banked the chopper back onto the original course and stole another glance.

"Good," she said, without moving a muscle.

Olga remained silent in her seat, terrified at this new, even more ruthless side to her companion.

Noticing Olga's distress, Yael turned to her and smiled. "Listen Mami, I'm sorry to spring this on you, but the jump, it has to be today."

~

The headquarters of Operation Janus was carved into the side of a mountain, invisible from the air and impervious to attack. It could either be accessed by road or by the retractable helipad. He set them on the raised helipad that commanded a view of the Jordon Valley. Olga watched the armoured column snake through the foothills and closer to her position.

"Are they here for us?" worried Olga, looking east.

"I have no idea how they would know this is here, and they couldn't get in with twice that number." Yael said sounding more confident than she felt. "This way."

"If you knew I had to jump today at the latest, why did you only pick me up four months ago?"

"The scientists of this timeline must rely upon the scientists of the last iteration of time to hide the research where they might find it, so that they can rebuild the time machine. This time was particularly disastrous," Yael said as she looked into a retinal scanner. The thick steel door built into the rock opened and a breathless man in a lab coat burst through it.

"I'm doctor Katz, come on, we're running out of time," he panted as he led them to an elevator. The polished concrete floor reflected the tiny lights embedded in the excavated walls and ceiling.

"What happened this time?" asked Olga, refusing to let Yael off the hook as the doors sealed them inside.

"The information about time travel and your significance to it was lost when the Reich drove out the Palestinians from the Holy Land. It was only discovered in 2022. I think it's about striking a balance between making sure Israel finds it and ensuring it does not fall into the wrong hands."

"It took you thirteen years to come and get me?" she said incredulously.

"Well, I imagine they didn't just say, 'Hey, this old bit of paper says time travel is real, better do whatever it says'. There was research and tests and government decisions."

"And that took thirteen years?"

"The Reich is difficult to penetrate, it was not simply a case of looking for girls named Olga in the births, deaths, and marriages section of *Der Spiegel*. It took analysts years to place you, and one does not simply walk into the Reich and abduct a soldier's daughter. The operation, agent selection and extraction took years to plan and implement."

"Fine, but..."

Olga was cut off when the elevator door opened onto a cavernous space in the heart of the mountain. The shiny concrete floor was back but that was the only resemblance it bore to the tiny corridor above; the size was such that it required some of the less spritely scientists to use buggies to move from one side to the other.

Olga and Yael strode across the floor, forcing Katz to jog in order to keep up. Towards the centre of the space there were several rows of control consoles, each making up one quadrant of a circle, the circles decreasing in size until reaching the centre.

"This it," said Yael, jerking her head towards a raised platform at the centre of the consoles.

"Is it going to weigh me?"

"We will take every piece of information about you and feed it into the computer, Olga. That's how we transport you through both space and time," said Katz.

"Shall I stand there now?"

"Yes, yes," he said waving his arms impatiently.

"Can you hear that?" said Yael, holding up a hand for silence as dust fell from the ceiling.

A thunderous noise shook the cavern, causing more debris to fall.

"*Oy Gevalt!* We're under attack! Quickly, we have to start the upload. Use the screen and change into the sixties clothing on the trolley there, and make sure you have that shoulder bag." Olga did as she was told, opting not to use the screen.

"I thought this place was impervious to attack?" said Yael.

"Who told you that?" scoffed Katz without looking up from the computer.

Yael rolled her eyes "I'm going to find security and check out th…" another explosion cut her off, "…that," she said.

Olga dressed and Katz bashed away at the keys.

"Doctor Katz, why don't you just send me back with a small time machine?" she asked him.

"Because the computer that we would need to store that kind of data would fill this cavern…Okay, keep still."

A laser scanned Olga from head to toe, and Katz typed some more code as more dust fell onto his keyboard from another explosion that shook the mountain.

Yael jogged over, holding an assault rifle with a rocket launcher slung at her back.

"Okay, so there are like, fifty tanks and a whole bunch of UAR soldiers outside and the head of security reckons we have fifteen minutes until they breach."

"Shit," Katz muttered, still typing furiously.

"Yeah, how long do you need?" asked Olga.

"Fourteen minutes. Look," he pointed to the monitor which read, "currently uploading Olga-dot-hum time to completion 13 minutes 40 seconds."

"It keeps changing, one moment it says ten, then it jumps up to forty-five, then back to ten. I didn't want Windows, I said Linux, but they wouldn't listen to me! No, I'm just the man who built the time machine."

"Try not to watch, it'll take longer," Olga wryly advised as more dust followed, another explosion, daylight could be seen at the far end of the cavern and small-arms fire began to echo around the walls.

"Oh, fuck!" said Yael.

"Indeed," Katz concurred.

"I'll hold them off, don't fucking move," she said and made to leave, until something stopped her. She grabbed hold of Olga in a huge, bear-like hug, "I love you Mami."

"I love you, too."

Both women were crying when Yael jogged off towards the danger, stopping every so often to fire her rifle.

"Nine minutes," said Katz.

The rifle fire grew louder, and Yael came running towards them. She stopped a few metres from the consoles, fell to one knee and fired the rocket as a squad of soldiers came into sight.

"One minute," said Katz.

Yael moved into cover behind a console and began to fire her Galil at the oncoming soldiers.

"Thirty seconds," said Katz.

"Get down," yelled Yael, as she ran towards the centre, changing fire position. The concrete floor around the time machine began to explode with tiny clouds of dust as the enemy fire became more accurate.

"Ten seconds," said Katz as the time machine began to hum loudly.

Yael stood and fired her underslung grenade launcher, but just as the round left the barrel, something hit her, throwing her back to land at Olga's feet. Olga knelt over Yael and gripped her hand as they looked into each other's eyes. Yael tried to speak but only coughed up blood as the time machine activated and both flickered in and out of existence momentarily before they were gone.

Epilogue

As the mountain laboratory disappeared, Olga found herself in a crater, a hole in the ground where a house used to be.

The smell hit her first, one of raw sewerage, decay and smoke. The steady drumbeat of rifle fire seemed close and the explosions, like echoes from the future she had just left thundered all around her. She vomited and failed to stand on the first few attempts, staring around her waiting for the nausea to pass.

Olga still held Yael's hand, limp and lifeless, her eyes glassy and cold. Blood and another clearer liquid ran from her ears, but she was still beautiful, still strong, still Yael and she knew that Yael would not want her to risk her life to bury her.

With a furtive glance around, she took in the enormity of her situation, witnessing a city in flames and a neighbourhood in ruins.

A world at war.

This was not 1961. Was it even Berlin? She had not been taught about a war in Berlin, certainly not on this scale and not in the last seventy-five years. It was not hot enough to be Africa or the Middle East, or Asia for that matter, but she decided that she was certainly in Europe from the style of the surviving buildings, and she could figure out the when and exactly where later.

She picked up her small bag, dragged Yael into cover and stripping her of her futuristic, question-raising equipment, she swallowed hard on her emotions, this was it now, she was alone

341

in the past with the future of the world in her hands. Training was over and she had to act like a professional, no mistakes, no tears, no weakness. If someone found Yael like this, in these clothes, it would cause Olga trouble. She cast about for options and saw that the cellar of the house next door was partially intact. If she left her in there, she would not be discovered for a long time, and perhaps there were even clothes in there.

She looked at Yael's Galil and Desert Eagle and she decided that although the rifle was too conspicuous, the pistol would fit in her shoulder bag with the pages of calculations, and the ammunition was common throughout the world as far back as 1904.

Months of eating survival rations had left her emaciated and comparatively weak, and as she pondered this, she noticed Yael's skin and wondered if her own skin would stand out here in this bleak, grey city, it had taken on a similar hue from months the burning desert sun.

Another reason to stand out. During times of war people didn't take sunbathing holidays. She thought of her dress, a simple floral pattern, modest and selected for 1960s Berlin. What about here and now, though? She spotted a heavy overcoat with an astrakhan collar and threw it on, realising it would conceal both the weapons and Yael's body armour. She decided to risk it, slinging the rifle to the rear and wearing the vest.

Olga looked at Yael's lifeless form. She had prepared herself to say goodbye, but not for this. Not for her actual death. An abstract death perhaps, but not this tangible deathbed farewell. This was grotesque, Yael lying in a foreign cellar, blood pouring from every orifice, staring up at the grey sky, unseeing, unknowing, unliving.

Olga wept silently as she prepared to leave and reflected on the person she had become and the immense role Yael had played in making her who she was now, who she probably would always be. She thought of Ibrahim and his selflessness in the face of great personal danger and she resolved to make the best of whatever this situation was. She would find out and she would complete her mission, however unlikely that turned out to be.

As she reached this resolution dust began to fall around her and it seemed as though now might be a good time to leave, so with tac vest and weapons concealed under her heavy luxurious coat, she stepped out of the cellar and into the crater once more. As she climbed the side to the surface and picked her way down the rubble-strewn road, the building collapsed onto Yael's body, burying her and filling the air around Olga with thick, grey dust.

As she moved through the war-torn streets, signs and notices told her she was in a German-speaking country, but the red flags and strange cross-like symbols were alien to her. The most prominent signage was for the Jewish community and appeared to be banning them from almost everywhere and everything. Eventually, she found a sign that read 'German Red Cross' with one of the cross things and an imperial eagle, so now she *knew* she was in Germany. She crossed the Spree and wandered through a patch of open ground that could have once been a park. The desolate space was filled with statues and naked trees, craters punctuated the muddy, remains of a lawn and the stumps of larger trees protruded from the mire.

When she saw the Brandenburg Gate, she knew she was in Berlin, and this hit her hard because the landmark and the city had always been symbols of stability in her life. Of course, recently they had come to mean a lot more; hate, oppression, slavery, genocide, and fear, but she could not undo years of indoctrination in a few short months.

She walked east along the wide boulevard of Unter den Linden and realised how out of place she appeared. Everyone was wearing a uniform, yes, but it was not her clothing that marked her out. Everywhere she was met with stares from sunken, sometimes jaundiced eyes, gaunt faces and emaciated bodies. The population of this Berlin, whenever it was, was tired, hungry, and unwashed. By contrast, she was tanned and although skinny by modern standards after her months in the desert, her she looked positively healthy. Fortunately, they were all too busy to bother with her and seemed to be either moving east as fast as possible or trudging west in a fatigue-induced daydream. Tank traps and barbed wire littered the streets, uniformed children cycled by clutching envelopes and demanding passage with the authority of generals, while the thunder of distant shelling and the rattle of small arms were a constant feature.

A church noticeboard told Olga that the celebration of easter 1945 would begin next week, but how could this be? One of the few things she thought she knew about time travel was that seventy-five years was the maximum journey length, so how could she be reading a newly posted note about easter 1945? She scanned the board for other information, a clue to the exact date.

She knew it was springtime, but it could be anywhere between the start of March and the end of April, and when nothing gave her any indication, she moved on. She had studied maps of 1960s Berlin and knew where Rudi lived in that time and how to get there from her dropbox in Moabit. She understood the layout of the central neighbourhoods and she carried papers that would pass Stasi inspection. Only time could tell how relevant or useful this would now be.

Olga decided to keep off the main streets and avoid human contact, but people were everywhere and eventually she would meet someone who wanted to see her papers. Yael had been very clear on the need for I.D. in Berlin from Olga's own notes. She mentioned something vague in Rudi's original motivations now that she considered it, something about a war and Germany's disgrace. She had dismissed it as too similar to her own timeline to think too hard about it, but now she wished she had. Did this mean that Olga had somehow travelled back to a different 1945, the 1945 of another timeline, perhaps before Rudi had managed to alter history?

She watched in horror as a shell landed two streets away, and rushed to help without thinking. The road was empty, dust swirled in the half-light of the dying day and then she saw her. A girl of about Olga's age lying in the street, apparently dead. All thoughts of selfless rescue were replaced with those of survival as she eyed the girl. Her hair was light enough and her features were not dissimilar. She wore no uniform and her clothes were homespun and well worn. All these factors meant she would not be missed, and anyone pretending to be her might, with luck, go about their business unhindered. She searched for papers and found a folded white card with the words 'Deutsches Reich' above an imperial eagle, but this eagle clutched an oak wreath surrounding the strange Norse cross from earlier and below this was the word 'Kenkarte'.

Inside, next to a set of fingerprints and staring back at her, was a photo of a girl who could, in bad light be mistaken for Olga. The name given was Annelise Schneider, she was twenty years old. Olga reached out and with two fingers closed Annelise's green eyes for her, promising to honour the sacrifice she had made by making the most of the freedom it could give her. She found several other identity documents, including a red one with the same eagle, only the head faced the opposite direction to the Kenkarte. This red document was called an 'Ahenpass' and it listed Annelise's ancestry, using unfamiliar words like Aryan and Mischling. She put the lot in her bag, dumping her own documents into the nearest storm drain.

Olga found that the dust on her face and coat from the explosions helped her to blend in and she began to feel like she was receiving fewer looks from the beleaguered Berliners. She crossed the Landwehr Kanal and made her way south along Baerwaldstraße and towards the Am Urban hospital, where she saw something that would remain with her for many years. The overcrowded hospital had spilt over onto the lawns and into the street, equal numbers of dead and wounded men, women, and boys in blood-stained Feld grey uniforms lay waiting, waiting for the gravediggers or waiting for death. All of the nurses and doctors were inside, each one like Sisyphus, their toil an unceasing, thankless hell. Olga looked through eyes blurred with tears as teenage boys and old men loaded bodies onto carts to an orchestral moaning from hundreds of forlorn souls in the last terrifying throws of a lonely death.

She hurried on to the only place she could think to go. Aldershof; but Rudi would be a boy, and surely he did not grow up in the apartment he lived in as an adult? It was dark now and she decided to find an abandoned house and to try to get some sleep. She wrapped herself tightly in her huge coat and settled down on a once fine chaise longue. While she lay there, she thought for some time and as the thoughts swirled around unable to order themselves, she drifted off into a deep, restful sleep. While she slept the images began to make sense, she dreamed of her past lives and of Rudi, of 1960s Berlin and of her epic journey through the Great Sand Sea. An abiding image was one of a highspeed intercity train, the signs in German and Rudi with her. He was sleeping and his foot was bandaged but she felt the distance between them growing, and as she watched he disappeared from sight, her arm outstretched, reaching for him, unable to move.

The artillery and small arms continued throughout the night, but it seemed to get louder as dawn approached. This crescendo caused Olga to stir and eventually wake, unsure of where she was. She looked around for Yael and Ibrahim and when she remembered that she would never see them again, she began to cry. She shivered and rubbed her arms to keep warm, her breath condensing on the cold air. Her stomach growled angrily as she realised that she had not eaten since the helicopter ride from Shalem and now she felt the familiar pang of hunger. Olga stood, allowing the coat to fall from her shoulders as she stretched, looking for somewhere to relieve herself.

Olga wandered eastwards through Kreuzberg, searching for a soup kitchen or another Red Cross station. Surely there were

347

thousands like her, homeless and starving with no idea what to do with themselves? All she could think of was Rudi and food and how the man she had longed for, ached for, dreamt of and lusted after for so long would be a little boy. The thought made her angry more than anything else, she was enraged at the injustice of it all, but the strength of her emotion gave her the energy she so desperately needed to trudge on.

Canvas topped trucks rumbled past, the men in the back looking haggard and apprehensive. Olga's thoughts ran away with her as she watched it go by.

They are just boys. Maybe Rudi's in there? Maybe I've done something already that's changed the course of history and will lead to Rudi's violent death in this awful war where there are no men, only boys and grandfathers and emaciated women.

She heard more rifle fire, a ragged clatter of only three or four rounds, very close this time and as she rounded a corner she froze when she saw men in uniforms talking with a boy in a similar uniform with a bicycle. She peered around the corner at the scene, hearing words that chilled her very soul.

"Where are you going, little Rottenführer?"

End of Book 1
Continue the zeitkreig in Altered State 2: *The London Reaction*

348

J. G. Jenkinson is a father, engineer, history nerd and a sailor. He emerged from the burning wreckage of his scholastic career unscathed, but with very little to show for it. This led him to the recruiter's office and over a decade with the British Army. As promised, he saw the world, just not the bits of it that gap year students daydream about. The army taught him to sail and paid for a summer touring the Baltic aboard Herman Goering's old yacht. After a couple of trips to Helmand, the novelty wore off and he sought a living on the Canadian Prairies as an agricultural mechanic. He wrestled steers, drove a pickup, and fished for walleye pike on frozen rivers. After an interesting year running a farm, he returned to England and took up surveying to fund his writing habit. Now he splits his time between windfarm engineering on the North Sea and his home in Worcestershire that he shares with his wife and daughters.